DOGFISH PROJECT

By

Tom Haynie

TOM HAYNIE

With great appreciation to my wife, Sue, who applied her talents as an English and Journalism teacher in a tireless effort to edit the contents of this work.

Cover design by Christopher Mann:Graphic Design. See website at chrismanndesign.com.

Chapter 1
Hangzhou Bay, Northeastern China

Commander Tom O'Donnell stood on the observation deck of a small nuclear submarine. It floated quietly on the cold, dark water of the Hangzhou Bay in Northeastern China. The stars were bright points of light that flickered in the January night sky.

A wind came from the East China Sea and O'Donnell pulled the collar of his Navy parka around his neck. The tips of his ears stung and he shivered as a gust of air slipped past his collar. His nostrils flared to the faint smell of kerosene burning in huts lining the shore.

In the distance, the flickering red and green lights of marker buoys outlined a ship channel. The mournful clanging of their bells and the lapping of small waves against the hull broke the silence. An occasional plaintive cry of a dog barking on the shore punctured the stillness.

Standing with Tom in the sail were Captain Al Hunslinger, the sub's commander, and two elite Navy specialists, Lieutenants Robin Buckner and Pete Wilson. They were dressed in the same dark blue parkas with collars edged in rabbit fur.

The sub had surfaced near the entrance to the largest enemy military installation in the world. They searched the surrounding water through night vision binoculars. No fishing boats were in sight; only an occasional patrol boat appeared.

"There," Tom pointed to two faint red and green lights about two miles away. They didn't move like the rest. "At the entrance to the harbor. Those lights mark the ends of the submarine gates."

Binoculars swung quickly toward the lights, as if to see something other than two lights separated by a thousand yards of dark water.

"Looks innocent enough," observed Lt. Buckner. "Who'd guess twenty feet below the surface lies fifty thousand tons of movable steel and concrete?"

Silence fell over the group once again. O'Donnell turned his attention from the lights on the water to the lights in the sky. He checked his watch and then squinted intensely at the horizon. He focused on each star as if he could make it move by simply looking at it. Shortly he saw what he was looking for.

"Here it comes."

Immediately, the electronic buzzing of the dive alarm sounded menacingly in their headsets. In unison they turned and hurried toward the

3

hatch. The alarm meant the sensors had picked up the invisible probe of an enemy satellite breaking above the horizon. They had a few seconds before the electronic eye detected their intrusion into these dangerous waters.

The sub's radar shields had kept them hidden from the installation's Low Frequency Wide Area Radar, LOFWAR. However, the satellite's electronic eye could pierce the most powerful shields. In a sub-recurrent orbit 1,000 miles above the earth the satellite could detect an object half the size of a man. The system named High Orbiting Reconnaissance System, or HORS, had a weakness. It couldn't see through water.

Now, with HORS above the horizon, the sub had to slip beneath the protective curtain of the water's surface.

Tom waited until the last person dove through the hatch. Then he threw his six foot two inch frame feet first down the hole. The last thing he saw was the seawater rolling over the smooth skin of the translucent hull as the sub's nose dipped beneath the waves. He reached up and pulled the hatch cover shut behind him. A few gallons of water splashed through, drenching him, before the seal was tight.

It was the middle of January in the year 2056, and the water was cold. Tom looked at the monitors and shivered. Water dripped from his nose and chin. His eyes burned from the sting of salt water. His parka and brown Navy shirt were soaked. He removed the parka and the wet shirt clung to his muscled chest like a second skin. The gold dolphins on his collar identified him as a submarine warfare officer.

"Did we make it?" he asked the seaman seated at the radar console.

"Aye, Sir. We made it."

The sensors indicated the sub had disappeared beneath the watery buffer before HORS discovered them.

"Good. Looks like we'll have to stay submerged for the next three hours until the satellite drops below the horizon again." Tom turned to Captain Hunslinger. "I'll be in my wardroom. Call me if anything changes."

Hangzhou Base is the largest of the New World Order's (NWO's) military bases. It lies on China's northeastern coast near the city of Hangzhou at the mouth of the Fuchun River. The river opens to form a protected harbor five miles wide and fourteen miles long.

Within three days, the NWO will launch thirteen more satellites. HORS-II, the second generation of electronic warfare satellites not only will see under water, but will have the power to pinpoint, select and disrupt any electronic system. O'Donnell's mission is to penetrate Hangzhou Base and destroy HORS-II.

The submarine that brought them to these treacherous waters is a Nuclear Ultra Morphic Submersible (NUMSUB) operated by a crew of seventeen. It has capacity for up to eight passengers. NUMSUB was developed for research and converted to combat. The technology in its advanced systems was only a dream ten years ago.

NUMSUB settled silently on the ocean floor while HORS moved slowly across the night sky.

Tom returned to his stateroom in the officers' quarters. The room was small, barely seven by ten feet. There was a fold-up bunk along one wall and a small desk in a corner. It was functional with few comforts. He took off his wet clothes and dried off with a towel. Then he settled back on the bed and began to slip into half-consciousness.

His focus was frequently interrupted by the personal struggles that haunted him from time to time. He dreaded these periods of inactivity that were a matter of course during subversive operations. His thoughts drifted to his father, who had died in the war between the Southwest Pacific Nuclear Coalition and the Middle-Asian Nuclear Treaty Alliance.

These alliances grew after India and Pakistan elbowed their way into the Nuclear Club just before the turn of the century. Feeble attempts to secure peace failed, and neither country would back away from its newfound offensive capability.

Both recruited allies. There was no lack of third world governments eager to develop a nuclear threat. The proliferation of nuclear arms spread quickly through Southeast Asia and the Middle East. Several Arab nations aligned with Pakistan. They adopted the name Middle-Asian Nuclear Treaty Alliance or MANTRA. India made a pact with some of its southwest Asian neighbors and called themselves the Southwest Pacific Nuclear Coalition or SOWPANC.

The new alliances chose to use their new power against each other and anyone who stood in their way. Though neither had the capability to launch a warhead against the U.S., nine cities in Europe, Asia, and Australia were annihilated. Within four hours, the cities of New Delhi, Baghdad, Istanbul, Sydney, Beijing, Hong Kong, Athens, Jerusalem and Cairo were vaporized or severely damaged. The loss of life was estimated at 27 million.

The loss of his father was devastating. Tom committed himself to follow in his footsteps. An appointment to the Naval Academy meant he was on his way to fulfilling that commitment.

He had pushed himself into the top three of his graduating class at the Yard sixteen years ago. He chose espionage for his Navy career, requiring three years of additional intensive training in counterintelligence. His submarine schooling began at the Nuclear Power School in Orlando, Florida and ended with an exhaustive assignment at the Naval Submarine School in Groton, Connecticut.

In the conn, Captain Hunslinger familiarized himself with the activity on the military base and the harbor. At six feet tall and 180 pounds, there wasn't an ounce of fat on his muscular frame. He stayed conditioned in the sub's small workout room. He wore his dark hair in a short, military crew cut. His uniforms were flawless. You could cut your finger on the crease in his pants.

"Are you getting any radio traffic from the installation?" he asked his radioman.

"Nothing more than the usual chatter you would expect as the base closes down for the night. The patrol boat we were watching headed out to the mouth of the bay. It's unlikely he'll be returning soon."

Hunslinger turned to the sonar technician. "What about that signal from LOFWAR a while ago?"

"I don't think we need to worry, Sir. LOFWAR bounced a signal off the hull but the computer picked it up immediately and changed the resonance pattern of the shields. It took no more than a second or two."

"The NWO must have upgraded their system. Fortunately ours stays a jump ahead. Any other surface activity?"

"I haven't seen any other vessels on the radar and sonar doesn't show any activity on or below the surface either."

"Let's hope it's this quiet in two days when we pass through the gates and penetrate the harbor's defenses."

The sonarman suddenly focused on his monitor. "I'm detecting activity coming from the dock area. Looks like a small craft heading this direction at a bearing of two-eight-zero, speed thirty-five knots. He's kicked it into high gear and making a beeline for us. Do you suppose they suspect anything?"

Looking over the sonarman's shoulder, Al studied the monitor for a minute. "I don't know. It looks like a dinghy with an outboard motor. If they were serious they'd send something more substantial. Still we need to be careful."

All eyes watched the instrument.

"If they keep coming toward us, what's their ETA?"

"At the speed they're traveling, about twelve minutes."

"Keep an eye on them. Let me know what they do."

"Aye, aye, sir."

Several minutes later the sonarman gave an update. "Sir, it looks like the craft stopped about six hundred yards to port. It came to rest for about a minute and is now heading back toward the base"

"Did you detect any electronic surveillance?"

"None, sir. He just stopped, then turned around and headed back."

"Something's up. Watch and see if he returns to the docks. Stay alert in case he dropped anything in the water."

Chapter 2
Something in the Bay

Deep inside Hangzhou Base, an officer of high rank sat at the radar console next to an enlisted technician. The officer's salt and pepper gray hair was clipped short as was his mustache. Though not tall, his barrel chest gave him a dominant appearance. His brown uniform, open at the neck after a long day, had three stars prominently displayed on the shoulder boards. His shoes were highly polished. His shoulders were slightly hunched forward, belying the years of tremendous responsibility he had carried.

He was in the electronic surveillance center. The room was large, approximately one hundred feet wide by one hundred-fifty feet long. Surrounding the officer were banks of computer stations, monitors and equipment. At each station, a soldier in dark gray fatigues hunched over his or her monitor, eyes glued to the dancing lines and blips as though entranced by some mystical spell.

Each station faced a high wall dominated by two large screens surrounded by a number of smaller ones. One large screen displayed a map of the base and the different military sectors. The other showed the harbor and activity under and on the water. The underwater submarine gates bordered one end of the harbor. The mouth of the Fuchun River defined the other.

The lighting in the room was dim, provided mostly by the illumination from the screens. The low whir of the HVAC system drowned out the hubbub from hushed conversations. Dark cloth covered the walls of the room to deaden sound.

General Ackmed Battarian's face was drawn into a contemplative expression. He rubbed his chin and carefully studied the monitor of the defensive radar system, LOFWAR. Scientists employed by the High Command had been working on improvements to the system to counteract advances in the Allied West Federation's (AWF's) vessel shielding electronics.

He spoke in a hushed voice. "It's a game of cat and mouse. Every time the AWF develops a technology superior to ours, the High Command frantically gropes for more research to counter." His tone betrayed an obvious disdain for the High Command.

"Yes, Sir," responded the enlisted man carefully, not wanting to take sides. "We received the latest upgrade to LOFWAR's software just a few days ago."

"It's supposed to penetrate the anti-radar shields installed on all AWF naval vessels," sneered Battarian. "It has been untested outside of the laboratory."

The new software still had skeptics and, fortunately for NUMSUB, bugs.

"What do you make of the blip, General?" asked the technician anxiously, changing the subject. The screen on his console had indicated a brief blip that came and went in little more than a second.

"I'm not sure. HORS has not detected any intrusion into our waters. Just the same . . ." General Battarian was trying to decide if there could be something real lurking in the waters outside of the harbor. This could be just a minor malfunction in the program indicating a false reading. It seemed that the more sophisticated the technology and the greater the rush to implementation, the more frequently malfunctions occurred.

Finally, he made his decision. "Ashok!" he barked. His voice boomed across the room. Heads raised and eyes were averted from their mystical trances then returned again to the intrigue of the dancing lines.

Captain Ashok Kumodan commanded the underwater defense platoon. Unlike the General, Captain Kumodan was a slender man, six feet three inches tall. He wore his dark hair slicked back and had a goatee. He had high cheekbones and a large hooked nose. There was a noticeable slant to his dark eyes, evidence of the Mongolian ancestry of his mother.

Kumodan did not like the General, a feeling he attempted to hide with little success. The High Command assigned Kumodan to Hangzhou Base after a mole within the General's staff questioned his loyalty. Kumodan was a plant. He would like nothing better than to see his commanding officer brought to his knees.

Battarian was no fool in the matter. Throughout his long career he had experienced many attempts to undermine him. It was a fact of life for senior military officers in the NWO. Trust would have been foreign to him.

To cover the real purpose of his transfer, Captain Kumodan was given command of an elite platoon of frogman. A team of frogmen, highly skilled in underwater combat, was assigned to each of the three main NWO military installations.

Summoned from his quarters, Kumodan quickly approached the General.

"Yes, General? What's the matter?" Kumodan refused to address his superior officer as "Sir." He may have to work under the General's command, but his loyalty lay far distant.

Battarian ignored the obvious conflict. More pressing concerns were on his mind.

"I'm not certain. A blip appeared on LOFWAR. It came and went quickly. It could be nothing but an error in the system created by those incompetents at the High Command's research center." Battarian was well aware of Kumodan's fidelity to the High Command. He frequently enjoyed taunting him with obviously insubordinate comments.

"Or, it could be something. HORS detected nothing unusual. Nevertheless, you will investigate it."

He continued, "You will send a team to the third quadrant, about three or four kilometers outside the harbor entrance. The corporal will give you the coordinates."

Kumodan's eyes flared wide. "Of course, General. I'll have two men in the water in five minutes." *Incompetents at High Command? Your day of incompetence will come, General,* thought Kumodan.

Kumodan was used to these drills. He never knew if there was real danger or if this was just another one of the General's frequent tests. The security systems in the Bay were nearly impenetrable and on the rare occasion they found something it usually turned out to be an errant fisherman. Still, responding as though every drill was real was good training for his crew.

His men could stay underwater for six hours if necessary with the scuba gear that recycled the air they breathed. The lungs use only a fraction of the oxygen inhaled with each breath. The exhaled air is still rich in oxygen with a relatively small amount of carbon dioxide. Older versions of scuba equipment expelled all of the exhaled air into the water creating noisy bubbles that wasted oxygen.

The new equipment recycled exhaled gases through a system that separated the oxygen from the carbon dioxide. It returned the oxygen to the tanks. The carbon dioxide was diverted through a catalytic chamber that broke down each molecule into carbon and oxygen. The oxygen was recovered and the carbon was trapped in a filter. A diver could stay underwater almost indefinitely, limited only by fatigue, hunger and the capacity of the carbon filter.

Kumodan selected two of his least experienced men. He didn't believe there was any real danger and these two could use the experience. The young seamen had returned late from a visit to the bordellos of Hangzhou. They had also missed the briefing on the installation's revised defensive information. It was unlikely they would need the information before the next briefing in two days. Sending them off for a few hours of underwater maneuvers would teach them a lesson in military discipline.

"Gattis! Sadmere! Report to the dressing room!" boomed the familiar voice over the public address system. Bartolomew Gattis and Morovan Sadmere were the least experienced divers in the underwater platoon, but they were no raw recruits. Even the least experienced had to prove himself worthy of the honor of this assignment.

Though delinquent in their obedience to the curfew they knew full well the consequences of less than immediate response to Captain Kumodan. It was late and they were preparing to retire to their bunks. They were dressed only in their dark military pants and T-shirts.

"What could he possibly want at this hour?" grumbled Gattis while he and Sadmere rushed to the dressing room. They both knew that to be summoned in this manner meant certain underwater duty. So far, of the twenty-seven times frogmen were sent into the water during the past two months, they were always assigned the false alarms.

"Just another chasing after ghosts, I'll bet," Sadmere dissented. "I'm beginning to wonder if we'll ever see real action."

Although seasoned in combat, Gattis and Sadmere had quickly rubbed Kumodan the wrong way shortly after his arrival at Hangzhou Base. Full of the youthful exuberance characteristic of young men of any nationality in their mid-twenties, they frequently played jokes on the other men and women in the platoon. Kumodan considered them pranksters who needed to be honed before he could trust them.

Arriving in the dressing room the Captain briefed them on their mission. "The General is concerned about a blip on LOFWAR. Treat it as though it was an invasion by the AWF's most advanced underwater equipment. Here are the coordinates. We will be monitoring your every heartbeat, so no horseplay."

No horseplay indeed, thought Gattis, not wanting to speak aloud and raise the Captain's ire. *Just who does he think we are, children?*

Each diver's gear had a monitor that measured his heartbeat. A radio transmitter sent this information to the base station. While the signal remained within the diver's specific rhythmic pattern, the observers at the base would take no notice. However, if the signal suddenly changed rhythm or stopped the base would send out reinforcements to determine what caused the change.

The two divers put on their scuba gear and climbed into the small power launch that would take them beyond the entrance to the harbor. They settled in, double checking their equipment. The roar of the motor sounded and the nose of the craft lifted out of the water from the acceleration. *Five and a half hours of oxygen, we'll be back in two,* mused Gattis. He anticipated a restful night after this drill.

They sat in silence during the fifteen minute trip from the dock to the harbor entrance. It was a beautiful cloudless night. Their wetsuits protected them from the chill. A sliver of a crescent moon low in the eastern sky was just beginning to peek over the horizon. Sadmere nudged Gattis and pointed to the west. "Look, I see a HORS over there. They chuckled at his play on words, but sat in awe contemplating the power of the advanced satellites that would be launched in just three days.

At the entrance to the harbor they passed over the huge submarine gates six meters below them. Only the smallest craft could enter or exit the harbor with the gates closed. Another three kilometers and the engine sputtered to an idle. The nose settled back down. The two frogmen eased silently into the water and switched on their heart monitors. *Let them read this*, thought Gattis, *they won't notice a hiccup.*

Chapter 3
Enemy Frogmen

Suddenly, Tom was shaken from his mental wanderings. The interior lights of NUMSUB dimmed. Danger approached in the dark water. NUMSUB's sensors had detected an external threat.

He swung his feet over the edge of the bunk and looked at the clock. He had dozed off and slept for almost an hour. Rubbing the sleep from his eyes, he quickly made his way to the conn.

The metal skin of the sub was made of a polymer bonded over the light titanium alloy structure. The compound had several unique properties. One gave it a chameleon-like capacity to change color and texture. While sitting on the bottom, the skin of the outer hull began to change color and shape to imitate its surroundings. Slowly, the outline of the hull vanished into the surrounding seascape.

Another feature allowed portions of the skin to become as transparent as glass from within. The occupants could see out as clearly as though they were looking through the walls of a huge aquarium. This visual effect was unidirectional; someone outside the sub could not see in.

Now, nestled snugly on the ocean floor, NUMSUB looked like the coral and sand surrounding it. When the interior light faded, the only illumination was the eerie red and aqua glow of the instruments. Large windows seemed to appear before the crew's eyes. As each man and woman's sight became accustomed to the reduced light, they could make out forms and movement in the water.

They could see the wave-like motion of schools of small fish that changed direction in unison as though signaled by some unseen force. Within a few minutes one of the crew pointed to starboard. Faintly, Tom made out the form of two frogmen.

In the distance their dark figures were difficult to see in the dim light. As they approached, they became more distinct. It was obvious they were looking for something. They glided through the water as effortlessly as sharks searching for prey. They wore light magnifying infrared goggles in their facemasks. With their black wetsuits and swim fins they seemed as if they were supernatural creatures from some alien undersea world. No bubbles escaped their breathing apparatus.

They stopped near the sub and looked around as if searching for something. One signaled the other, pointing in the direction of the bow.

They seemed particularly interested in something and they focused their search in that area.

Tom and Al stood next to the wall of the control room watching the divers.

"If they detect the sub they'll signal the base. Do you think they'll have heart monitors, too?" asked Al.

"I'm sure of it. Two years ago the NWO required all divers on hostile or potentially hostile assignments be equipped with them."

"What do you think we should do about them?"

"We need to get them on board. We could use an update to the intelligence we have."

"Do you have a plan?"

"I'm working on it."

Both frogmen had to be captured simultaneously and incapacitated quickly to keep them from alerting the base. To complicate matters, the frogmen had to return to the base within a couple of hours unaware of what happened to them. This operation would be tricky.

Tom had to come up with a plan quickly. His mind raced through the capabilities of the crew he had selected for this mission.

"Get Pete and Robin up here."

Al picked up the intercom in the captain's chair and called Lt. Pete Wilson and Lt. Robin Buckner, two highly skilled underwater combat veterans.

Pete was a body building champion who had recently competed in the Armed Forces Amateur Body Building Finals in Fort Lauderdale, Florida. At six foot four, he was almost too tall for the confines of the sub. He had won his weight class at 225 pounds. He was slated to advance to the World Free Style Championships but had declined when the opportunity to serve on this mission came up.

A strikingly handsome man of twenty-eight years, his chiseled features were highlighted by dark brown hair and contrasting blue eyes. He moved with the grace of a tiger. His broad smile put at ease anyone in his presence. He exemplified the definition of humility; great power under perfect control.

He could have handled both frogmen by himself with ease were it not for the sophisticated electronic transmitters they wore and the need for simultaneous incapacitation.

Robin Buckner, though physically much smaller than Pete at five feet four inches and over a hundred pounds lighter, was definitely his mental equal. She had a stunning figure that was difficult to hide under her service uniform. She kept her jet-black hair short in a military cut. Her dark eyes could both enchant and intimidate depending on her mood. Her size was an advantage in hand to hand combat. She could defeat much larger male opponents with her lightning quickness. She held a third degree black belt in martial arts. Watching her apply her skills with men twice her size was like watching a cheetah battle a rhino.

"Pete, Robin," began O'Donnell. "You know how quickly the NWO changes the defensive codes of its installations?"

Pete said, "Yes," while Robin nodded affirmatively. She seemed preoccupied with looking through the hull at the two figures gliding silently near the sub. She knew the enemy had no idea they were within touching distance of a secret AWF submarine. Still, it gave her an eerie feeling just watching them come so close.

"We need the information in their heads," said Tom.

"That should be easy," piped in Robin. "We use Trascan."

They were all aware of the power of the hypnotic drug. Injected into a subject, the drug would block all sense of reality within seconds.

She continued, "We get them under the drug and into the infirmary. They'll tell us anything from highly classified information to what they had for breakfast three days ago. The subconscious is photographic, recording the exact details of anything processed by the conscious. Once they come out of it, they'll not remember a thing."

"We're ready to bring them in," responded Pete. "What's the plan?"

"You two will slip into the aft torpedo tubes and wait until they are near the stern. Then you'll exit the tubes and take them by surprise. You'll have to silence their transmitters and heart monitors."

"Won't the base become suspicious if the heart monitors stop?" questioned Pete.

"They won't know the monitors have stopped. NUMSUB's computers have picked up the monitors' transmission frequency and have duplicated both heart patterns. We'll transmit signals with the same rhythm and characteristics while we have them in custody."

"They'll remember their last conscious thought. You'll have to inject the drug before they discover your presence. The second you turn off their transmitters, we turn on the false signals. The base will never know what happened."

"Let's go, Pete," said Robin. "You take the big one and I'll take the other big one." Her obvious attempt at comedy produced a guffaw from all three men. Robin hardly weighed more than a hundred and fifteen pounds soaking wet, literally. Yet, Pete completely trusted her with his life in this situation. He had been with her in action before.

There wasn't enough space in the sub to accommodate separate dressing rooms for men and women. Pete and Robin quickly stripped to their underwear and began putting on their wet suits. Though they both maintained a professional demeanor, the physical attractiveness of the other was not lost on either. They dressed in forced indifference to the other's presence.

They had developed an iron bond of honor that would not allow physical appetite to displace the urgency of the assignment. In silence they quickly donned their scuba gear and checked each other's equipment.

"All set, Lieutenant?" asked Pete.

"All set." She looked up at him. Pete thought he caught a glimpse of softness he'd not noticed before. He quickly dismissed it, but vowed he'd pay more attention in the future.

13

"Let's go."

The only combat weapon they carried was a seven-inch knife attached to their right calf. They also carried the drug injection guns they would use to incapacitate the two frogmen. They waited in silence, each contemplating the task at hand.

Somehow, simultaneously, they had to sneak up behind each enemy frogman undetected and inject the drug. If either frogman discovered them, he would immediately signal the installation and their attempt at secrecy would be in vain. They would then have to engage in underwater combat.

Since one tube wasn't large enough for both of them at the same time, they slipped into the two aft torpedo tubes. They emerged from the tubes and stayed hidden beneath the stern.

The frogmen glided past with their backs to the sub. Pete and Robin looked at each other and nodded their heads. Quickly and silently they fell in behind their targets. Ordinary sailors would have adrenaline pumping and hearts racing in anticipation. Not these two. They were as calm as if they were sitting down to play a game of chess.

Gattis and Sadmere swam to the coordinates given them by Kumodan. Looking around they saw nothing but coral and sand. *Just as I thought, nothing!* Sadmere complained to himself. *If anyone was here it's unlikely they'd be sitting around waiting for us to find them.* He signaled to Gattis that he wanted to do a little exploring. Since they were already in the water they should make it seem like they were spending their time constructively.

Two hundred years ago the harbor had been home for bands of Pirates who used the security of its protected waters to hide from British patrols. Storms had caused several shipwrecks in the bay and the seafloor was the site of an occasional rare find. Sadmere and Gattis had small collections of artifacts smuggled into their lockers and living quarters.

Seeing was not difficult with the low light eyepieces attached to their scuba masks. This spot was particularly interesting. In the dim light the motion of the sea plants in the underwater currents cast an eerie backdrop to the scene. Curious fish darted from among the tentacles of a field of sea anemones daring the divers to reach out and touch them before disappearing instantly into their hiding places. Small coral mounds broke the smoothness of the seafloor.

A large outcropping of coral lay directly in front of them. It must have measured forty or fifty meters in length and at least ten meters high. Gattis wondered how long it must have taken the tiny residents of that reef to grow to that size - perhaps a hundred years or so, he thought.

The far end of that outcropping of coral seemed to be a likely place to begin their search for treasure. Upon arriving at the end of the reef, Gattis noticed that the sand under the coral appeared to have been recently disturbed by the motion of something big on the ocean floor. *Probably just a large fish or a shark trying to find a morsel for dinner*, he thought.

Finding nothing of interest, the two divers turned to explore the other end of the coral reef. They were swimming in that direction, when they sensed a strange presence. Perhaps it was just a disturbance in the water or maybe that shark returning for a larger morsel for dinner. In a fraction of a second the adrenaline began its course through their bodies, but before they could react they felt an odd prickling in their necks. Almost immediately the sea began to grow darker about them until they were engulfed in total blackness.

Pete and Robin had practiced underwater ambush until they could do it in their sleep. Many times each had engaged an enemy and overpowered them before their targets knew what had happened. Surprise and quickness was their advantage.

If something went wrong, either of them could draw his knife and sink it deep into an enemy's heart, stopping it before it could register an alarmed beat.

Gliding gracefully through the water, keeping an eye on each other, they reached their targets at precisely the same instant. They pressed an injection gun against the neck of each frogman, just below the facemask, and squeezed the trigger. The drug quickly entered each man's system. Within seconds, the drug began working on their brains. Each man noticed just a prickly sensation in his neck before losing consciousness.

The heart monitors were switched off and at the same time the sub's computer started the false monitor signal.

TOM HAYNIE

Chapter 4
The Stage

The crew of NUMSUB watched in silence while the brief drama unfolded before them. Pete and Robin appeared at the rear of the sub. Within seconds they were upon the frogmen and had immobilized them with the drug. They were now towing them back to the aft underwater transfer chamber.

A transfer chamber located at each end of the sub is used to enter and exit while submerged. To exit, a diver enters the chamber and seals the door. Water is pumped into the room until it's full. The diver opens the hatch and swims out. To enter, the process is reversed.

Tom watched from the control room. He knew it would take at least a half an hour for Pete and Robin to come through the aft chamber, expel the seawater and prepare the frogmen for interrogation. He returned briefly to his wardroom.

He looked at one of his few personal possessions on NUMSUB; an old photograph of a submarine returning to port in Pearl Harbor, Hawaii. Her commander and crew are standing on deck. Written in the upper right corner of the photo are the words "*USS TANG, 12 September 1944.*" The commander of the submarine was Tom's great grandfather, Commander Richard H. O'Kane.

Under Commander O'Kane, the *TANG* began her fifth war patrol from Pearl Harbor on 24 September 1944. After 30 days at sea, *TANG* had fired twenty-two of the 24 torpedoes in her arsenal and had sunk 12 enemy ships. On the night of 24 October, the officer on duty on the observation deck spotted a transport that had been hit, but not sunk, in an earlier attack.

Under cover of darkness, *TANG* launched a surface attack and fired the first torpedo. When it was observed to be running true, the second, her last, was fired. From the observation deck the crew saw one of the most dreaded sights of submarine warfare. The second torpedo curved sharply to port, broached, porpoised and circled. In bars over a beer, stories of renegade torpedoes summon silent dread among submariners. Little prepares a man for the sight of his own torpedo turning and coming dead on.

Commander O'Kane called for emergency speed. The rudder was thrown over and in agonizing slow motion the ship began to turn. A surfaced submarine is still 80% underwater and the physics of turning a heavy steel hull submerged in the sea is never so apparent as in a crisis.

The evasive measures resulted in the torpedo striking the stern. Ten officers and men were thrown into the cold water of the Pacific. Only four were able to survive through the night.

TANG came to rest on the bottom at 180 feet and the men inside crowded forward when her aft compartments flooded. Thirteen men escaped from the forward room. Only eight reached the surface, and of these but five were able to swim until rescued. Ninety-two officers and men were aboard *TANG* for that last patrol; 83 were lost. Commander O'Kane with the other eight survivors were picked up by a Japanese destroyer escort and held in Japanese prison camps until the end of the war.

The loss of *TANG* by her own torpedo, the last one fired on the most successful patrol ever made by a U.S. submarine, was a stroke of singular misfortune. *TANG* had fired her entire arsenal of twenty-four torpedoes in four attacks. Twenty-two found their mark in enemy ships, one missed, and the last torpedo turned on her like an avenging angel.

In her five patrols she sank 31 ships and damaged two. This record is unsurpassed among American submarines. She was awarded the Presidential Unit Citation twice and her Commanding Officer was awarded the Congressional Medal of Honor. Commander O'Kane has been called the Submarine Force's most outstanding officer.

With the blood of Commander O'Kane coursing through his veins, Commander O'Donnell was no stranger to risk and daring.

After he entered the Naval Academy, he drove himself like a man possessed, leaving little time for a social life. By his third year at Annapolis his dedication and efforts had earned him a commission as the third highest ranking student officer in the school. It was then that he met Bree Taylor.

Al Hunslinger introduced Tom and Bree to each other. Bree had briefly dated Al during his second year at the Academy. Their relationship never blossomed into romance but they remained close friends.

Tom and Bree had something more in common. The same internal forces that controlled him drove her. She was the daughter and only child of a wealthy politician, Senator Chance Taylor from Dallas, Texas. During the years following the nuclear conflict, terrorism increased greatly in the United States. Political figures were favorite targets and Bree's father was no exception.

One summer, while congress was in recess and most politicians had returned to their home districts, her father had been targeted by a terrorist group from Iran. He had been championing legislation through congress that would reduce the U.S.'s dependence on Iranian crude oil. Unhappy with his political philosophy, a terrorist group known for suicidal attacks on prominent figures placed a bounty on his head.

One evening Bree and her parents were driving home from her father's campaign headquarters. A terrorist pulled alongside of them on the freeway. In the trunk of the terrorist's car was a bomb rigged to explode with the flick of a switch by the driver.

Warned that Senator Taylor was a terrorist target, the President had assigned Secret Service bodyguards to him and his family. Two Secret

Service agents were guarding them. One was in an automobile directly in front of and another directly behind the Senator's car.

The terrorist pulled alongside the Senator's car and reached for the switch. The agent in the car behind the Senator recognized what was about to happen. He radioed a warning to the lead agent. With little time to do anything else, the lead agent slammed on her brakes, forcing the Senator to do the same to avoid ramming her from behind.

The terrorist was unable to react as quickly. By the time he hit his brakes his car had moved ahead of the Senator. The force of the sudden braking threw him forward and his hand triggered the switch. The bomb exploded beside the Secret Service agent's vehicle, destroying it and killing her instantly. The Senator lost control of his automobile, spun and flipped over, sliding several hundred feet upside down before striking an overpass support.

Bree and her father received only minor injuries, but her mother suffered a massive head injury and died on the way to the hospital. The loss of her mother left Bree empty and angry.

When she and Tom met in Annapolis, they connected immediately. By the time Tom graduated from the Academy, they were talking of marriage. They decided to wait until their lives were more settled before they made that final commitment.

Shortly thereafter, the structure of world governments began to change and Bree's father became deeply involved in the creation of the Allied West Federation.

Following the nuclear war between MANTRA and SOWPANC, the leaders of the world's major powers realized they could not contain the spread of nuclear weapons under the world's fragmented political infrastructure. There were too many weak governments with religious and geographic axes to grind. If a subversive element, driven by world domination or a thirst for power, could gain control of just one, the horrors of nuclear warfare might be repeated.

The only way to avoid that possibility would be to unite all nations into one world government that could not be overthrown. The North and South American continents had dissolved international boundaries to form the Allied West Federation (AWF). Most of the former European and Asian free world allies of the Twentieth Century also joined the AWF. Although the Alliance dissolved political boundaries, each nation elected to maintain geographic boundaries to retain their social and cultural identities. Accordingly, there remained the United States, Canada and Mexico and all of the other countries in the Alliance. However, the laws, taxation, currency, military and all features of government were combined.

Opposed along ideological and political lines, most of the historical enemies of the West similarly united to form the New World Order (NWO). The NWO did not dissolve boundaries, but formed an alliance governed by a treaty that provided for a single military machine. Within a few years of formation, the military had become so powerful that no single or collective government within the NWO had the ability to control it. The military leaders took advantage of the weakness of the political infrastructure and formed the High Command, naming a Supreme Commander from among their ranks. The governments of the NWO became mere puppets of the new military oligarchy.

Washington, D.C. would have been chosen the capital of the AWF were it not for the political climate. Many of the members of the new Federation did not want U.S. politics to dominate the alliance. In a compromise, Montreal was selected as the capital city.

Bree's father moved to Montreal to assume a major part in the formation of the AWF. He was elected to a seat in the new Senate and became a powerful political leader. Bree spent much of her time working in her father's office.

Tom dedicated himself to his work in the Navy. He rose quickly in rank and drew the attention of some of the most influential men in the Department of Defense, Secretary George Warnick being the most powerful. His involvement as a senior military officer in sensitive highly secret projects consumed him. His latest project, code-named the Dogfish Project, had taken him underground for the past eighteen months.

Because of the turns in their careers, Tom and Bree had little time to nurture a budding romance. Their relationship waxed and waned like the phases of the moon. Still, there never was a time when either felt the relationship was over. The bond that had developed pulled at them like the silent force that holds the sun and the earth, never releasing them, yet never bringing them closer together.

Just before Tom's assignment to work on the Dogfish Project, they tried to revive their relationship. Tom had been assigned a tour in Montreal as a deputy military advisor to Secretary of Defense Warnick. Their relationship flourished, but they had never dealt closure to the pain of their losses. Try as they could, something always stood in the way of a complete release of their emotions. They simply could not bring themselves to reach that level of devotion that would result in a melding of two souls into one.

When Tom received the assignment to command the Dogfish Project, they realized they would see little of each other until it was completed. Without constant involvement, they also knew that their relationship would never survive. They had tried to make it work from a distance, but that lasted barely a year.

After much soul-searching they decided to do what they thought would be the right thing. They said goodbye in a tearful farewell and severed the bond that had held them together for so long.

Chapter 5

Summons

Tom recalled that day, a little over three months ago. He was summoned to the office of Secretary Warnick. He had been on leave for fifteen of his thirty days of well-deserved rest.

The pressures of developing the Navy's newest top secret underwater project had not allowed more than a day or two's time off in a year and a half. Dogfish had taken that long to develop and test and was nearly complete. Final non-combat trials had proven successful. The Top Brass was anxious to see what it could do in an actual live engagement situation.

The summons was innocent enough. Just a telex with a short statement,

> "TO: COMMANDER THOMAS O'DONNELL
> FROM: GEORGE WARNICK, SECRETARY OF DEFENSE
> DATE: 27 SEPTEMBER 2055
> YOU ARE HEREBY INVITED TO ATTEND A BRIEFING IN THE OFFICE OF SECRETARY OF DEFENSE GEORGE M. WARNICK.   YOUR ATTENDANCE IS REQUESTED AT 0900 HOURS ON MONDAY, 30 SEPTEMBER 2055."

Secretary Warnick was the President's appointed civilian chief of the Dogfish Project. He was the one who had handpicked Tom for the top military position. Together they had selected the military and civilian experts who would develop the program. They met often regarding the project and a telex was frequently how the Secretary called Tom to a briefing. It was the same kind of telex the Secretary used when he summoned anyone to his office. Except for one small detail. The word "hereby" was a code. Whenever it was included in the message, Tom knew it was serious.

Because the invitation appeared innocuous and was delivered via unsecured telex, it did not raise suspicion from the usual eavesdropping of NWO intelligence. It seemed these days in Montreal, as in other major cities in the AWF, that every other stranger was an NWO operative. You didn't talk to strangers unless the conversation was baseball, soccer or, in Montreal, ice hockey.

Tom liked Montreal. September was particularly pleasant. The weather was changing. The leaves on the trees throughout the city were getting dressed in their fall colors. The crisp, frosty nights brought out the most brilliant hues of reds, yellows and oranges. The night cold turned the evening dew to ice that melted quickly when the morning sun cast its rays through the chill.

Tom knew that to receive an urgent summons, even if disguised as an invitation, to the Secretary of Defense's office meant that something was afoot. His mind raced while he shuffled through the crowded sidewalk conveyors. The moving sidewalks whisked him and a multitude of other pedestrians over city streets and through buildings to a myriad of destinations. He was so engaged in thought that he didn't feel the stranger in a dark overcoat gently brush by him.

He was more interested in the dark sedan that was following him. The windows were tinted so he was unable to distinguish the vehicle's occupants. It stayed about a half city block behind him and moved in concert with the conveyor. It seemed unusual that they weren't making much of an attempt to be covert. He had gotten used to being followed. Still, his subconscious was prepared for flight at the first sign of danger. He was unaware that the sedan was merely a decoy to draw his attention while the silent stranger completed his task.

Tom wasn't in uniform, but his picture was in every NWO agent's portfolio in Montreal. He had been a nemesis to the alliance since it was formed. They knew him well and they knew that whatever he was about spelled trouble. He was rarely able to avoid their watchful eye when he was in a populated area. Only when he was assigned duty somewhere in the world did he become invisible.

For much of the past year and a half, no NWO agent had seen him. This fact caused great anxiety within their intelligence operations. They knew that when he was not under surveillance, somewhere in their world something was about to go wrong. He had been gone for eighteen months and nothing had happened. This disturbed them greatly. They had to find out what he was up to.

The stranger paused briefly. With the skill developed through years of practice, he attached a midrange radio transmitter no larger than the tip of a fingernail along the out seam of Tom's trousers. The stranger then disappeared in the crowd and within a few seconds the sedan was gone as well.

Tom looked at his watch, *Eight-forty-nine,* he thought to himself. *I wonder what the Secretary wants. It would be nice to get back into action, but it's probably just some political PR surrounding Dogfish.*

Tom arrived at a complex of small one-story buildings surrounded by a ten foot high iron fence topped with concertina wire. He approached a guard post. An elevator would whisk him eight hundred meters straight down to the Secretary's office. The AWF government complex was built completely underground to be secure from a nuclear attack and to prevent eavesdropping from NWO intelligence forces. It was hard to imagine that nearly half a mile below the surface, a bustling city of government offices, shops and complexes, inhabited by 15,000 people, was governing the free world.

Tom showed his credentials to the guard and entered the guard station. He stepped into a soundproof, cylindrical Plexiglas booth. The door to the booth closed behind him. In front of him at waist height was a pair of pads in the shape of hands. Before his face was an instrument that would examine his eyes.

A soft green light glowed and a calm computer-generated female voice recited instructions. "Place your hands directly on the hand pads with outstretched fingers. Rest your chin on the pad in front of your face and look at the red spot behind the lens," cooed the voice.

He placed both hands, fingers outspread, on the pads at waist level on either side of him. He rested his chin on a small pedestal and leaned his forehead against a cushion. He looked directly into what appeared to be the lens of a camera. The pads under his hands registered the fingerprints of all ten fingers and the rhythm of his heartbeat. The lens registered the patterns of his irises and the vision cells at the back of his eyeballs. These tiny optical cells, which allowed humans to see in color, are arrayed in slight variations unique to each individual.

Eight long thin fingers of steel descended from the ceiling of the booth and gently touched his head in different locations. Two rested on either side of his forehead, two on either side of his crown, one on each temple and the final two at the base of his skull. A mild electric pulse passed from a node in each steel finger to all of the others and to nodes located in the chin and forehead pads. From these ten positions, the computer measured the dimensions of Tom's head, the final procedure for positive identification.

A ring slowly descended around him, scanning for unauthorized eavesdropping devices with both a laser beam and an electronic sensor. The device seemed to miss the tiny transmitter placed on Tom's trousers by the stranger. The transmitter was designed to remain dormant until activated by the change in temperature from the cool September air on the surface to the warmth of the office structure below.

The computers took less than a second to verify Tom's identity. "Thank you Commander Thomas Fredrick O'Donnell," announced the voice with characteristic serenity. "You may exit the booth now." The door opened and Tom stepped back.

The guard, in crisp Marine brown and blue uniform topped by a white garrison hat, greeted him with a salute. "Welcome to the Secretariat, Sir. Secretary Warnick has been expecting you. Level twenty-three, Sir."

Tom walked quickly through the entrance of the building and faced a bank of elevator doors, silently opening and closing for the passengers. Level twenty-three would be twenty-two floors below level one. Level one was the length of three football fields straight down. The elevator would take a mere sixty-eight seconds to descend to the Secretary's level.

Exiting the elevator, he was met by another guard station and repeated the routine just completed at the station on the surface. Security was tight around the Secretariat, and no unwelcome visitor had ever penetrated its defenses.

This time the Marine guard was a female. No less official than her male counterpart on the surface, she greeted Tom with a brisk salute when he finished the process. "Thank you, Commander," she said. "Please continue through the double doors to your right."

Fifteen seconds after passing through the second check station, the transmitter on Tom's trousers began operating. Every word spoken within ten meters was clearly transmitted to the surface and the listening ears of the NWO intelligence agent disguised as a cab driver waiting for a fare.

Tom stepped into the front room of the Secretary's office. This was the reception area. There were four chairs for waiting guests. There was no direct overhead lighting. The light emanated from the walls as well as the ceiling. It was hard to distinguish the color but the walls seemed to glow with a faint tinge of yellow. There were no wall hangings or pictures. A small black Plexiglas dome in the ceiling subtly announced that the area was under surveillance. The only other furniture in the room was a sleek white desk.

A young receptionist in her late twenties sat at the desk. She was a striking brunette with steel blue eyes and a statuesque figure. Tom entered and she rose to greet him.

"Good morning, Sir," acknowledged the receptionist. "I'm Kate Mosley. The Secretary will be with you momentarily. Would you please have a seat? May I get you anything? Coffee, water, juice?"

"Nothing, thank you. I'm fine."

"How's the weather on the surface? I haven't been up there in two weeks."

Tom instantly realized that the receptionist was a resident. A resident was one of the people who lived as well as worked in the government complex. It was more economical and secure to limit the number of times a person passed through the security check stations. It was rumored that the NWO was working on semi-cloning certain body parts from a few cells of one individual and grafting them onto another. The harvest cells could be obtained from such unobtrusive sources as discarded fingernails, Kleenexes or even semen. The possibilities for breach of security were frightening.

To enhance the comfort of residents, the complex was built to nearly duplicate living conditions on the surface. Wide streets separated the shops and offices. Electric cars and moving sidewalks provided transportation. With lights and electronics, the illusion of day, night and weather conditions were created. All offices and living quarters had windows that looked out upon beautiful scenes of seacoasts or mountains and valleys all created for residents. Some people actually preferred life in the complex to life on the surface.

"The weather's a bit chilly for this time of year. I think we're in for a hard winter," replied Tom.

"I guess that means I'll have to break out the overcoat and gloves fairly soon. They try to duplicate surface conditions as much as possible in the complex," added the receptionist wistfully.

The soft bell of the intercom built into the receptionist's desk interrupted their conversation. At first Tom hadn't noticed that the desk was strangely void of any visible signs of work. Everything was electronic and operated by pressure pads that recognized the receptionist's physical characteristics, her voice, her body temperature, and her heart rhythm.

"Kate, will you show Commander O'Donnell in, please," called another soft female voice from no apparent source.

"The Secretary will see you now," instructed the receptionist. "Go through that door on your right."

Tom entered through the door into a room about fifteen by fifteen feet square. The walls were covered in heavy dark drapes. There was a single overhead light with a cover that diffused light into the room. To the right were several hangers with white shirts and trousers. To the left were hangers that contained street clothing. The hushed sound of conversation between three individuals, two males and one female, was in progress.

The conversation sounded like idle talk about nothing in particular, as if the people were just meeting and opening with a few obligatory salutations. He was quite startled to hear what appeared to be his own voice, greeting the three others.

In front of him a video monitor flashed instructions. Above the monitor was a sign. "BE COMPLETELY SILENT AT ALL TIMES WHILE IN THIS ROOM" was printed in large letters. "READ THE INSTRUCTIONS ON THE MONITOR."

Tom moved to the monitor. The instructions were simple. "Remove all of your clothing, including undergarments, watches and jewelry. Hang them on the rack to the left. Put on the white clothing to the right. When you have finished dressing, pass through the door behind the monitor."

Obeying the instructions, Tom removed his clothing and put them on a hanger before noticing another small surveillance camera behind him near the ceiling. *I wonder who's getting a show,* he thought to himself. *I hope they're enjoying it.* Tom chose a shirt and trousers from the rack and slipped his trim, well-muscled torso into them.

He approached the door behind the monitor and noticed there was no doorknob. When he was near, it opened silently, then closed just as silently after he passed through.

On the other side was another female, this one blond, short, middle aged and a little pudgy.

After the doors had closed, she greeted him cheerfully, "Good morning, Commander O'Donnell. I'm Mary Petersen, Secretary Warnick's Administrative Assistant. I trust your garments are comfortable."

"Quite," responded Tom. "By the way, why the change of clothes?"

"New security procedures, of course. The Secretary had them

installed since the last time you visited. Never can tell what one can pick up on the surface."

The assistant continued, "By everyone leaving their street clothes in the same room a computer generated conversation of each person's voice will keep any possible eavesdroppers busy."

Tom was curious. "But I heard my own voice join the conversation. How did that happen?"

"The central computer was listening to your conversation with Kate. While you were talking, it duplicated your voice patterns and structure. You were inserted into the conversation you heard in the room at just the right time. We've created some pretty fascinating scenarios for anyone with itching ears to hear," explained the receptionist.

"In fact," she continued, "we can usually tell after someone has listened. Within a few days, whatever plot we have created will play out somewhere in the world. You should have seen the satellite activity over Area 51 in the Nevada desert after the Secretary had a meeting with the Armed Forces Alien and Space Research Director last month."

"The Secretary requests that you immediately join him in his office, through that door." Ms. Petersen nodded toward the door to Tom's left.

Tom entered the room and saw three individuals. One was the Secretary of Defense, a somewhat short, stocky man of about five feet seven inches and 220 pounds. The top of his head was bald with a few long strands of hair combed across in a futile attempt to cover the shiny dome. The dark hair around his temples and the back of his head gave away the fact that, at the age of sixty-two, he colored it. The Secretary was dressed in a navy blue business suit with a white shirt and open collar. He kept a closet full of spare clothing to wear in his office.

Tom didn't recognize the other two people in the room, a man and a woman, both late forties and slender. Both were dressed in the same white clothing as he.

"Tom, it's good to see you again, my boy!" exclaimed Secretary Warnick cheerfully, rising from his seat. "Come on in, I have a couple of folks I'd like you to meet."

Chapter 6
The Mission

The Secretary's office was elegant. A large mahogany desk stood in the center of the room. The high-back executive chair and the pad on the desk were covered in dark green leather. An eight-foot mahogany conference table and eight swivel chairs covered in the same dark green leather stood to the left of the desk. A crystal pitcher of ice water and eight crystal glasses turned upside down on a cloth sat in the center of the table.

A portrait of General George Washington in his uniform, kneeling in prayer in the snow at Valley Forge, his gray steed standing silently behind him, hung on the mahogany paneled walls. A cloud of breath from the horse's nostrils gave life to the portrait. Pictures of famous Prime Ministers, Kings and Presidents adorned the other walls.

Hidden ceiling lights illuminated the room with a diffused glow. A brass lamp with a translucent green shade sat on the desk beside pictures of the Secretary's wife and two grown sons, with their spouses and children. Altogether, the Secretary had six grandchildren. The papers that Secretary Warnick had been working on when he arrived at work around 6:00 this morning were neatly stacked on the desk.

"You always look great in white, Tom," said Secretary Warnick. "It's good we made the clothing change standard procedure. We detected a bug on your trousers when you came through security. Our systems have detected an increased NWO effort to penetrate our top-secret installations. We think something's up. Right now we're entertaining whoever is listening with the details of a wild goose chase. I hope they like it in the Himalayas this time of year."

Tom chuckled at the prospect. George Warnick was a master when it came to counter-intelligence.

"I'm not even going to ask what highly confidential mission could be about to take place in such forbidding surroundings. Knowing you they'll be sending some of their top scientists along with the infiltration team," said Tom with a wide grin.

"I see a couple of folks I've not met before. George, are you going to introduce us?" Tom turned toward the two strangers. He extended his hand to the woman first.

"Commander Tom O'Donnell, AWF Naval Underwater Operations, meet Margaret Cranston, Director of Space Surveillance, and this is Roy Constance, Vice-Chairman of the Federation Intelligence Agency."

Tom recognized the names. He was right earlier. This was not going to be a political PR meeting to satisfy Secretary Warnick's curiosity about the status of Dogfish. He wondered what space surveillance and the FIA could have to do with him.

Margaret Cranston had graduated Cum Laude from Cal Tech with a Ph.D. in space engineering. She had worked her way up through the ranks at the Space Surveillance Agency. She began her career as a research assistant and quickly caught the eye of then Director, Terry McNeal. McNeal was a crusty disciplinarian who demanded long hours and dedication from his staff. Margaret was the kind of person he liked. She was sharp and a quick learner. Not a socialite, she didn't mix well with the other staffers. Her rise to the top was legendary.

Cool-headed and calculating, she now ran the agency with determination. Her staff respected her authority and head for details.

Roy Constance, a Canadian, headed the world's most sophisticated intelligence gathering agency. The FIA was the successor to the U.S. CIA and FBI and their counterparts in each country that had joined the AWF. The Agency had combined all of the technology and skills of a dozen highly developed foreign organizations.

Roy was nearly the opposite of Margaret in character and personality. He was amicable and put on a front of boyish enthusiasm. He was black, a descendant of American slaves who had escaped into Canada from the South during the U.S. Civil War.

Underneath that amicable exterior, beat the heart and soul of a highly competent leader. It was no secret he was being groomed for chairman of the agency, and some believed he would some day be the President of the AWF.

"Good morning, Ma'am, Sir," acknowledged Tom, slipping into formal military demeanor. "I'm very pleased to meet you both. I've heard a lot about you." He shook their hands, noticing that they both had a firm, warm grip.

"Nothing good, I hope," chortled Vice Chairman Constance, withdrawing his hand from the greeting.

"Nice to meet you as well," responded Director Cranston. "Your reputation certainly precedes *you*, Commander." She nodded her head and peered at him over the top of her glasses. Tom couldn't help but think about one of the librarians at the Academy many years ago who used to look at him the same way.

Margaret was tall for a woman. She stood about six feet and had jet-black hair. Not overly attractive, she was wearing no makeup and her hair was cut in a straight, shoulder-length style.

"Thank you, Ma'am," he responded politely. Tom could instantly put on the charm of an officer and a gentleman.

"First off, let's dispense with the Ma'ams and Sirs," interrupted Secretary Warnick. "I have a feeling we're going to get to know each other very well. Let's move on to Tom, Margaret and Roy. Or would you prefer 'Peg,' Margaret?" Secretary Warnick chided with a gleam in his eye.

"Sounds good to me," said Roy.

"O.K. with me, too," added Tom.

Margaret gave George a dirty look. "Margaret will do," she said with the hint of a chill in her voice. He knew she hated the nickname 'Peg.' George had known Margaret since she was a little girl growing up in Washington, D.C., the daughter of a congressman from California. Her father had given her the nickname. She always thought that it was childish.

During the preliminary introductions, Tom noticed that Roy was an inch or two taller than Margaret. His hair was cut short and he wore a well-trimmed moustache. There was a hint of gray beginning to show around his temples. Tom had a feeling that he took a lot of pride in the way he dressed.

"Well, now that we've got the niceties out of the way, let's get down to business," began George. "Why don't we all sit down around the table? Tom, do you have any idea why you're here?"

"Uh…, well…, no, Sir," stammered Tom, caught a little out of focus while he was sizing up his new acquaintances. "I thought it might have something to do with the project I've been on for the past eighteen months. But if it involves Space Surveillance and the FIA here, I assume it's something else."

"Actually, you're right, Tom. It has a lot to do with Dogfish. And Dogfish has a lot to do with Margaret and Roy being here. Before you arrived, I brought them up to speed on how you became involved in the project. I'll let them fill you in on their involvement."

"Margaret, why don't you start?" George turned to Margaret and gave her a nod of endorsement.

Margaret cleared her throat quietly.

"You're familiar with Horizon Dawn, aren't you, Tom?"

"Certainly," Tom nodded. "It's our system of secret surveillance satellites. They blanket the earth with high-resolution cameras and electronics. I believe they're disguised as weather satellites."

"Right. About six months ago, we observed a buildup of pre-launch activity at Hangzhou Base. That's where most of the NWO space launches take place. You may be aware, Commander, Hangzhou Base is the largest of the military installations in the NWO's defensive system. It covers an area of approximately 200 square miles, being roughly ten miles wide and twice as long."

She looked at George and gave him a slight nod of her head. George pushed a button on a console on the table near his seat. A panel in the far wall opened up to reveal a flat video screen about ten feet square. A satellite image of Hangzhou Base came up on the video.

"Yes, I'm familiar with it," replied Tom sitting back in his chair and crossing his arms and legs. "I've studied it from the intelligence Roy's people have gathered and the photos taken by your satellites."

"Then you're aware that it houses several garrisons of military and civilians. The population is estimated at nearly sixty thousand."

Tom pursed his lips and let out a low whistle.

"They are mostly the defensive forces, scientists, educators and families of the permanent residents. The military conducts training at several locations within the base for their army and sea-going personnel. There are all of the necessary support activities, commissaries, hospitals, and so forth. A large air field used by their high altitude reconnaissance aircraft and a contingent of jet fighters and bombers occupies the northwest quadrant."

Margaret used a small laser pen to point to the section of the image she was discussing. Instantly the section magnified and showed greater detail. Tom could clearly see the aircraft neatly lined up along the runway of the airfield.

"Adjacent to the airfield is a battery of anti-aircraft missiles." The airfield faded out and the missiles faded in. "The harbor on the east is home to six nuclear assault submarines, two aircraft carriers, four heavy cruisers, a dozen battleships and the necessary support vessels." The video faded through each element while she described it.

"However." She paused and stared directly into Tom's eyes, her face changed expression. "What has interested us the most is the activity at the space launch facility."

Noting her facial emphasis, Tom leaned forward to listen carefully.

"Ever since the launch of their High Orbiting Reconnaissance System, also known as HORS, we've been wondering when they would finish the job."

"Finish the job?" Tom glanced at George and Roy.

"Yes. Finish the job. HORS was designed to be the most advanced satellite surveillance system ever put into orbit. Its purpose is primarily defensive. Its sophisticated electronics can detect, from an orbit 1,000 miles high, movement of a large dog."

A computer image of one of the HORS satellites appeared and phased through each part of her description.

"It's able to detect any electronic or electromagnetic shielding - which renders useless most of the defensive shields of our naval vessels and all aircraft. And, it has the capability to detect and identify any sea-going vessel on the surface of the water."

"On the surface of the water?" Tom did not let that subtle comment pass without notice.

"Exactly, and I'll get to that momentarily. HORS has a couple of inherent weaknesses that we've known about ever since they launched the project. One is that they were able to successfully launch only two satellites. The program called for four, but two of the launches failed on liftoff and self-destructed over the East China Sea."

"But the NWO has much more territory around the Northern Hemisphere than can be covered by two satellites."

"I told you our boy was sharp, Marge," piped in George.

"No one challenged you on that, George," Margaret quipped with a smile. That was the first time Tom had seen her smile and he noticed a touch of warmth peeking through the veneer of her professionalism.

"With only two satellites, they are unable to cover all of the territory under their control. For that reason, they have assigned vigilance primarily over the three main military installations."

"And they can't even see all of those simultaneously," added Roy enthusiastically, anxious to tell his part of the story.

"Right," said Margaret. "They had to synchronize the orbits over the installations to get as much coverage in a 24-hour period as possible."

"Exactly how much coverage is that?" questioned Tom.

"It varies among the installations. We're most interested in Hangzhou Base at the present, and they have coverage for about fourteen hours a day. The cycle is pretty constant at three hours with surveillance and two hours without."

"That's one weakness. You mentioned there were two."

"At least two that we know of. There may be others yet undetected. The second weakness is that HORS is unable to "see" underwater."

"From a submariners point of view, I'd say that's pretty substantial, wouldn't you?" interjected Roy as though that fact would be lost on Tom.

Tom nodded in response to Roy's question. "So what's the deal with finishing the job?"

"This is where the AWF is getting a little nervous," added George.

"I'll let Roy get into the details about that," said Margaret. "But like I mentioned, we've been concerned with the buildup of activity around the launch site. We knew they weren't preparing for a routine weather satellite launch. They have too much security surrounding the site. Most of the activity takes place at night."

"Can't our satellites see at night?" asked Tom.

George reached over and poured himself a glass of ice water. "Water?" He motioned around the room. Tom's throat was a little dry so he looked at George and nodded. Margaret and Roy shook their heads.

"Yes, they can. However, the night image is not nearly as clear as during daylight. Still the night activity is a bit more suspicious. They're moving what seem to be large modular containers at night. That activity has never been observed during daylight hours."

"Your turn, Roy," said George. "Fill us in on what your folks have found out."

Margaret passed the laser pointer to Roy.

He took the pointer in his right hand and began tapping it against his left. "Well, we've known since right after HORS was deemed less than a total success, that the High Command has been anxious to move on to the next phase."

"How do you know that?" asked Tom.

"I'm not at liberty to say, security of our personnel, you know. Let's just say that not everything at the High Command is what it might seem."

"O.K. then, what's the next phase?" Tom asked, affirming his attention.

"I was just getting to that. The next phase is HORS II. HORS II will make HORS look like a toy. HORS II will blanket the earth with a system of thirteen satellites with both offensive and defensive capabilities."

"How many launch vehicles will they need to launch all thirteen satellites?"

"Only one. We know that they're going to use their largest liquid fueled launch vehicle, the Serpico.

"Miniaturization has enabled satellite technology to build into a box the size of a golf cart more electronics than could be squeezed into one the size of a semi-truck in use five years ago. All thirteen satellites will be launched with the same vehicle." A schematic image of the launch vehicle appears on the screen with the thirteen satellites neatly arranged in the nose cone.

"The launch vehicle will dock with their unmanned space station. The space station will place all thirteen satellites in strategic orbits around the world." The image on the screen flashed through the sequence of placing the satellites in orbit.

"Once in place, every square inch of the earth's surface will be under constant watch. Nothing can be hidden."

"Nothing?"

"No, nothing. The engineering will make it possible for each satellite to see up to a half mile below the surface of water, including under the surface of the oceans and lakes. Not even our most sophisticated shielding will thwart HORS II's penetration."

"So how does that involve Dogfish? When these satellites are in orbit won't they be able to see subs, too?"

"Yes, I'm afraid so," answered Roy with a sigh. Then he leaned forward, "And that's precisely why the capabilities of Dogfish are so valuable to us right now."

"You've got my attention."

"We need to get a team of personnel inside Hangzhou Base and take out HORS II before they can launch it. We need a vehicle small enough to avoid detection, yet large enough to do the job. Regardless, we can't use any of our current submarine fleet."

"Why's that?" asked Tom with a frown.

"Because, NWO intelligence has identified every sub in our Navy and would be suspicious if any of them disappeared during their preparations to launch HORS II. As far as we know, they know nothing of the subs in the Dogfish Program."

"I'm fairly certain of that. Dogfish has been surrounded by the highest level of security and secrecy I've seen during my career. In fact, I understand my disappearance from NWO surveillance for the past year and a half has caused a bit of a stir in their organization."

"That's for sure," brought up George with a look of satisfaction on his face. "Our moles have reported that you've been the subject of more than one highly secret meeting. I'll bet they're happy to see you surface again."

"No doubt. Since I've been on leave for the past couple of weeks, I've had company almost everywhere I go. They're not even very covert about it anymore."

"They don't have to be. We know they're watching you, and they know we know they're watching. Why go to all the bother and effort to conceal their activities when both sides know what's going on."

"Well, they were able to plant a bug on me without me knowing about it," replied Tom with a shrug of his shoulders.

"True, that part probably did require some stealth. Since their presence has been so obvious to you, you most likely let your guard down a little. They were counting on that."

"By the way, Tom. What can you tell us about Dogfish? Even the FIA has limited knowledge of the program," asked Roy, a look of boyish interest on his face.

Margaret interjected, "We've never been able to find your project with our satellites. I don't know of any time Dogfish has ever been observed. We've certainly been trying. Instructions from the Secretary and the President have been to do everything we could to spy on the program. Whatever you've got there seems to be working well."

Tom looked at the Secretary for permission to continue.

"Go ahead, Tom. Margaret and Roy are both cleared. They're in on this and have a need to know," said George spreading his hands open in front of him.

"O.K., George. I'll be brief, though. "Dogfish" is the code name for a top-secret project that was first developed for underwater research. When they realized what they had, the military potential attracted a lot of attention from the top. It quickly went underground - or, should I say underwater?

"We have three prototype mini-subs. They can out maneuver any known sea-going vessel in existence. Each sub's on-board computers have more computing power than all computers in existence at the beginning of the current century. The computers virtually control everything and record every movement. They could maneuver the sub, completely unmanned, to or from any water destination on the face of the earth."

It was obvious Tom was proud of the program.

"The computers are in constant contact with the central mainframes here in Montreal and are updated with current information in a continuous stream. The technology is so secret that only a handful of scientists and government officials are even aware it exists."

Tom looked at George again for permission to go further.

"Tell us about the metamorphosing and holographic capability, Tom," said George acknowledging Tom's unspoken question. He looked at Margaret and Roy. Their expressions indicated rapt attention.

"Yes, two of the most unique capabilities of the program," continued Tom. "The sub's outer skin is composed of a material that can actually take on the look and feel of its surroundings. It can literally metamorphose into the terrain and seem to disappear. It's one of the most fascinating things I've ever seen.

"The holographics are also amazing. The computers can create a holographic duplicate of the sub so realistic that electronic surveillance can't tell the image from the real thing. The image can be projected through the water for a hundred miles. Couple that with the shielding and you can send a snooper on a chase that will leave them empty handed a hundred miles away. In tests, sonar homing torpedoes have actually passed within a few feet of the real sub and chased after the image five thousand yards away."

"Incredible," sighed Roy.

"No wonder we couldn't find you," said Margaret.

Tom was understandably nervous about talking about the program to two people who, a half-hour before, were complete strangers to him. He had to rely on the assurance that the Secretary had properly screened Roy and Margaret and that they could be trusted. One would think so considering their positions in their respective agencies.

Unfortunately, that hadn't always been the case. A couple of years ago, the heads of two of the most critical defensive departments in the AWF had been convicted for espionage.

"Now, what does all you've told me have to do with Dogfish? Dogfish is in development and has never been tested in an actual confrontational situation."

"Basically, Tom, we have a mission that we believe can only be accomplished by Dogfish," responded George. "Like Roy said, NWO intelligence keeps an eye on every submarine in the AWF navy. We would have no trouble taking one or all of our subs out of sight. However, I mentioned before, if even one were to disappear for any length of time it would tip our hand that something was up."

"We have to destroy HORS II and we have to do it quickly. We have a little less than four months before they launch the system," interjected Roy. "Our intelligence has discovered that they've targeted January 17th for launch. That doesn't give us much time for preparation."

"January 17th? You're right. That isn't much time."

"There's a trick to it, though."

"Which is?"

"Which is that we have to destroy it without the NWO ever knowing we did it. It has to look like an accident."

"No bombs, lasers, explosives?" asked Tom, eyebrows raised.

"No. The destruction must look like a natural occurrence, a malfunction in the launch."

"How are we going to do that?"

"One of our intelligence agents has infiltrated the design team of the HORS II launch vehicle. We know everything about it. The brain of the rocket lies in a small computer located behind the payload. That computer is controlled by the main computer in the launch command center."

"Go on. I'm with you so far."

"It's simple. All we have to do is get into the command center and replace a small circuit in the main computer. The circuit contains a computer chip programmed to interrupt the launch sequence just when the rocket engines have reached full capacity and the vehicle has lifted off about a hundred feet or so. The interruption will appear to the computer that the vehicle is six miles high and the engines have malfunctioned. The self-destruct sequence will automatically engage. Then BOOM! The entire system will disintegrate, including the command center and most of the scientific brains behind HORS II."

"Simple?" said Tom incredulously. "We just walk in, replace the circuit and that's it. Should we ask their engineers to give us a hand?"

"Actually, that's closer to the truth than you realize, Tom. This particular circuit has been known to malfunction before. They keep spares on hand in case of emergency."

"And how do we create an emergency?"

"That's been taken care of. The mole on the design team has inserted a small bug into the countdown sequence. At exactly one hour prior to launch, the program will duplicate a malfunction in the computer circuit. The computer will automatically stop the countdown and display a malfunction warning. That will prompt an engineer to replace the circuit with a spare. Your team's job will be to provide the spare."

"Well, you seem to have everything figured out. I suppose you've already planned how we are going to do that, too."

"Exactly. One of your crewmembers will be Jorge Rojas. Jorge is one of our most proficient agents. He is one of only two individuals in all of AWF with complete knowledge of Serpico and the launch command center. He could take the command computer apart and put it back together again in his sleep."

"I've heard of him. Isn't he the computer genius that practically invented fourth generation computer viruses?"

"He's the one. We're lucky he outgrew his propensity for crime. When he was twelve he invented the virus that took Washington, D.C. to its knees right after the nuclear war. You may remember, that was the year the IRS refunded the entire national debt."

"I remember it well. Every hobo in town was driving a new Mercedes back then." Laughter erupted around the room. "How's he going to get in? Security must be extremely tight."

"Jorge's developed a way to hack into the installation's main computer from any workstation or terminal connected to it. He'll be carrying a miniature disk with all of the team's data. Once in he can upload personal demographic and physical information into their security system. All security checks are run through that system. You'll pass through security as though you were supposed to be there."

"You said Rojas was one of two. Who's the other one?"

"That's Major Sara Brauer. She's Jorge's equal when it comes to technology. She'll be back here at the Operations Center where we'll monitor every move of the mission."

"She's an AWF Air Force major. She earned her wings flying combat fighter missions over Australia during the War," said George referring to the cleanup effort after the nuclear conflict.

"I've received assurances from the highest levels of the military command that Dogfish is quite combat ready and capable. Do you agree?" asked George, knowing what Tom's answer would be.

"Of course, George. I know everything there is to know about Dogfish. There is one concern, though."

"What's that?" asked Roy, raising his eyebrows so high the creases in his forehead became furrows.

"The people who've been developing the program are scientists, engineers and computer geeks. None of them have any combat training and even if they did I wouldn't want to take any of them on a mission like this."

"So, where are you going to find your crew?" asked Margaret.

"They're around. I know just who I need. Leave that to me."

The four of them sat for a moment in total silence, contemplating the drama that was about to unfold. They had barely three months to prepare an untested submarine system, gather together an elite crew of highly trained men and women and infiltrate one of the most heavily secured installations in the world. They were to sneak in undetected, replace a small circuit in a highly sophisticated computer and slip out without being noticed. If they were successful, they would have to get away without being blown to pieces by the exploding launch vehicle. If they were not successful, their world would look very different when and if they returned.

George broke the silence. "Well, folks. That about sums it up. We all have work to do. Roy, your people have to make sure we have the latest intelligence on Hangzhou Base. Margaret, no need to tell you how important it is to keep surveillance current in case there is a change in activity. Tom, you'd better get on that elite team you're going to need to make all this happen. Any questions?"

Glances were exchanged. No one spoke.

"Good. Tom, you've got the most to do. Let me know what I can do to help. The receptionist will show you all out."

35

Chapter 7
Idaho

Tom had a difficult job ahead of him. In a matter of days he had to assemble two crews; one to operate the sub, another with the talent AND the courage to pull the mission off. They would have less than three months to train. The submarine crew must become thoroughly familiar with NUMSUB. He had been working on the project for a year and a half and some of the systems were so new and untested that even he wasn't sure of them. The infiltration team must know every detail and every scenario that could happen on the mission. The task seemed impossible.

His job would be easier if he could get Navy Captain Al Hunslinger to help him. Al was one of the best submarine CO's in the Navy. Tom knew if he could get him, the chances of success increased dramatically.

Al and Tom had distinct similarities. They were both dedicated to their Navy careers. Both had graduated with distinction from the Naval Academy. However, that's where their similarities ended. Unlike Tom, Al did not come from a line of submarine veterans. His roots were firmly planted in a small farming community outside of Grangeville, Idaho. Before his father died, Tom grew up all over the world in a military family, seldom living more than a couple of years in the same place. Al never left the farm where he was born.

Al shared farm chores with a large family, six brothers and two sisters. They were church going, God-fearing and hard working. Al was the third of the seven boys. Life on the farm meant long hours baling and stacking hay in the summer, planting corn in the spring, harvesting it in the fall and milking the cows twice a day every day of the year.

While most of his brothers and sisters were content with staying around home, Al had a wandering spirit. He would rather race the tractor than pull the wagon with it. He spent long summer afternoons lying by the creek under the shade of a broad oak tree dreaming of the day he would leave the farm. He knew his ticket out of Idaho was an education, so he worked hard at his schooling. He graduated from high school with a high enough GPA to earn an appointment from his Congressman to the Naval Academy at Annapolis, Maryland.

The night before he left home, the family held a farewell for him. When a farm boy leaves home in Idaho, a farewell is a community event. All of his friends and some folks he didn't know showed up. His mother and sisters cried. His brothers kept him up all night in the barn telling him what he ought to do about tattoos and things.

His father, a large, powerful man with hands like meat hooks and shoulders you could stack hay on, took him aside. "Son, I've always taught you the value of hard work and dedication. You can do anything you want to in this life if you want it bad enough and are willing to work for it. The farm's been good to us. It's been in the family for generations past and I suppose it'll be that way for generations to come. You have a rich heritage and a proud name. Never do anything to dishonor it. Now, you go out there to Annapolis and do your best and I'll be as proud of you as I am of any of your brothers and sisters."

After speaking, his father reached out with hands that had seen years of hard work. They were brown and prematurely wrinkled from the hot sun and cold winters. He placed his hand on the back of his son's neck. Al could feel the hard calluses against his skin. He could feel the power in arms that could toss hundred-pound bales of hay the width of the barn or cradle a newborn kitten that had strayed from its mother. When his father drew him close for a manly embrace, Al felt a small shudder from the large man's frame. He noticed the glistening of moisture in the corner of his eye. He had never seen his father cry and he wasn't sure that's what was happening now, but he felt the emotion that welled up inside and he cherished it.

The next morning Al was on his way. His family drove him to the airport outside of Boise to bid him good-bye. When the plane backed away from the gate, he looked out the window at his family standing in the terminal. They were all waving and smiling as though they were sending him off to conquer the world. He felt a little like they were.

Al was two years older than Tom so, when Tom entered the Academy and began his first year as a Midshipman Fourth Class, Al was beginning his third year at the Yard. Upper class Midshipmen usually take an interest in new Plebes. Al and Tom met one evening at the Nimitz Library. During the first year at the Academy, there is very little free time and most Plebes spend the long weekend hours studying. Tom was no exception.

The two became close friends during Tom's second year and developed a bond they would carry with them throughout their military careers. Al graduated and went on to submarine school. They kept in contact over the years after Annapolis and occasionally spent furloughs together.

Al saw considerable combat action and was awarded the Silver Star and the AWF Supreme Medal of Honor for an engagement in which his sub, the *USS Interloper,* slipped behind enemy lines and rescued seventeen FIA operatives in an extremely dangerous operation.

Tom requested access to a secure terminal in the government complex. Searching the military database in the central computer, he found that Al was on leave and was spending a couple of weeks on his parents' farm in Idaho. Turning to the televideo console on the desk, he called the private number listed in the computer. Al's mother answered and her image immediately appeared on the screen.

"Hello, Mona, this is Tom O'Donnell."

"Tom!" exclaimed Mona Hunslinger. "I haven't heard your voice or seen your face in nearly two years! How have you been?"

"Just fine, Mona. I've been hiding out for the past year or so on an assignment. How's Levi?" Levi was Al's dad.

Mona knew that it would be futile to ask about Tom's assignment, so she moved on. "Levi's doin' just fine. He's getting ornerier the older he gets. Now that most of the boys are grown up and gone, he's running the farm by himself with a couple of hired hands. When Jacob and Joseph, the two youngest, graduate from Boise Agricultural College, they'll lend much needed help. When are you going to come and see us again? There's always a place at our table for Albert's best friend."

To Tom, an invitation to Mona's table was not to be taken lightly. He had never met anyone else who could prepare a literal feast and call it 'just some old scraps I could scrape together in a hurry.' "Well, that will depend on Al. I'd like to speak with him. Is he there?"

"Yes, he's here. He's been working the farm with his father for the last couple of weeks. He says he comes here to rest and relax, but he has a funny way of showing it. We've just finished breakfast and he's getting ready to go to work. Hold on and I'll get him."

"Thanks, Mona. Great seeing and talking to you."

Shortly, Al's image appeared on the screen. "Tom, is that you? I'd heard you were on a top-secret project. Didn't know when I'd hear from you again. What's up?"

"Well, I'm in the mood for some great Idaho fly fishing. I've got a couple of weeks left of my leave and I was wondering if you'd be interested in some backcountry camping. I've got a taste for some of those great Rocky Mountain brown trout." Even though the televideo at the complex was secure, Tom did not want to reveal anything about his new mission over the airwaves on the chance that it could be intercepted. No telling when NWO intelligence would break through the latest AWF scrambling technology.

He and Al had previously worked up a code between them. Any time either mentioned fly-fishing in Idaho it meant that something extremely important was about to occur and they had to meet in private as soon as possible.

Al caught on instantly. "Excellent idea, Tom. The fish are really biting in the mountain streams. I've been working so hard on the farm I need a break. When can you come out?"

"I'll be there in the morning. I'll catch the first flight out of Montreal to Boise tomorrow. Grangeville, it's still about a two-hour drive from the airport, isn't it?" asked Tom, expertly covering the anxiousness in his voice.

"Yep. Two hours. Last I checked they haven't moved us. It'll take you longer to get here from Boise than it will for you to fly from Montreal. We'll see you in the morning."

Tom clicked off the televideo. He really would like to do a little fly fishing in Idaho. The brown trout were excellent eating. Too bad there's so little time to prepare for the mission. He was looking forward to seeing his good friend again after these past couple of years. They'd have some catching up to do.

He rose early in the morning and took the supersonic shuttle from Dorval International Airport outside of Montreal into Boise International Airport. There wasn't enough traffic between Montreal and Boise to warrant a commercial airliner, so Tom was flown by National Guard shuttle, a four-passenger jet used by the military. The supersonic flight lasted about an hour and forty-five minutes, just barely enough time to read the newspaper on the video monitor in the seatback in front of him.

The headlines were innocuous enough. Inner city crime hadn't changed much in the last hundred years in spite of the government's efforts. Politicians were still corrupt and elected office always seemed to create a case of amnesia in a person when asked about events in their past.

At the airport, Tom stopped at an auto rental counter to pick up a vehicle for the drive to Grangeville. The young woman behind the counter was very attractive. She was tall, blond and architecturally correct. *Good job, Idaho!* he thought to himself.

"First time to Boise, Sir?" asked the rental agent.

"No, I used to come out often. This is the first time in a few years, though."

"Well, not much has changed if you're familiar with the area," she said politely, noticing how attractive this visitor was. "Please place your wrist into the tube in front of you."

Tom placed his hand into the tube and heard a click and then a short series of beeps. All of his personal information was in a chip located in the wristband of his watch.

His driver's license and credit information from the tiny chip were transferred into the auto rental company's central computer somewhere in South America. The information instantly identified Tom as a frequent driver, and his car preference and rental agreement came back immediately.

Tom digressed from his usual automobile preference and selected a Jeep Wrangler for the trip. The Jeep was the kind of vehicle they would need to get into the backcountry of the Idaho panhandle. The Wrangler still carried the basic design of the 4-wheel drive sport utility vehicle that was still popular after the past seventy years or so. It was small, versatile and could go almost anywhere.

Unknown to Tom, the girl typed a code into the computer that also directed his information into the NWO's data banks. Within seconds the nearest NWO intelligence office was notified of Tom's whereabouts.

So, that's what the famous Tom O'Donnell looks like in person, she thought. *His pictures don't do him justice.* She may have been an NWO operative, but she was also a woman. When he picked up his paperwork, he noticed her looking him over.

"So, Mr. O'Donnell, where will you be staying during your visit to Boise?" she concealed the real intent of the question with standard auto rental protocol.

"Actually, I'll be staying with friends in Grangeville," he replied. "We'll be going up into the mountains to do a little fly fishing." This charming young woman had briefly caused him to let his guard down a little. *Darn!* he thought. *Be careful, Tom, old boy. You can get in trouble like that.*

Tom was used to attractive women coming on to him. He had to be careful, though, because vanity had lead to the downfall of a number of individuals in his position. Still, he thought that before he left Boise, it might be fun to see if there was anything interesting in town, and an attractive companion could make things even more interesting. He decided to remember her face and he tucked away the name on her nametag for future reference. *Shawna. Nice.*

NWO agents were assigned to every major airport in the free world. They could be janitors, skycaps, ticket agents, security officers, ground crew or any other airport employee. They were instantly ready to carry out ant order, be it espionage, assassination or simply to keep a subject under surveillance.

Tom knew the NWO had operatives in Boise. They had them everywhere. That's why he had to get Al to an isolated place where they could talk. He went to the lower level of the parking structure to pick up his vehicle. He wasn't aware of the tiny transmitter in the plastic logo on the head of the ignition key. Shawna had signaled the key attendant, also an NWO operative, to give this VIP driver a special set of keys. The transmitter with its miniature microphone could pick up a conversation within twenty-five feet and transmit it clearly a distance of five miles. A transmitter in the gas cap sent a signal to a satellite. The NWO could track the movement of the vehicle and pinpoint its location to within a few yards.

Chapter 8
The Farm

Tom arrived at the Hunslinger farm just past noon. Al and Mona were waiting for him on the porch of the farmhouse when he drove up. He parked the Jeep in front of the house and stepped out, slipping the keys into his pants pocket.

"Tom!" exclaimed Al, rising from his seat on the edge of the porch and taking long strides out to meet him. The two friends embraced. "How was the trip?"

"Uneventful," replied Tom. "I see one of your sisters, where's Mona?" Tom asked with a twinkle in his eye.

"Tom, you young spit," said Mona. "You always were the kidder."

She, too, put her arms around him in a welcome embrace. "Are you going to come in and set a spell?"

"I'd love to, Mona. But I need to chat with Al for a minute first. Al, let's take a walk."

Al was anxious to find out what Tom was up to and why the urgency in meeting. He and Tom walked toward the barn.

"Al, yesterday morning I was in Defense Secretary Warnick's office in Montreal. I met with Margaret Cranston, Director of Space Surveillance and Roy Constance, Vice-Chairman of the Federation Intelligence Agency."

"Wow, Space and FIA! Something big must be cooking. What's that got to do with me?" Al knew his friend would get right to the point. Tom rarely beat around the bush about anything.

"You're right, it is big. There is a highly sensitive situation and I need your help. The NWO are ...."

He was about to divulge the purpose for this urgent meeting with Al when Levi burst around the corner of the barn.

"That you, Tom?" interrupted Levi, taking giant steps toward the two men.

Levi was dressed in his trademark faded blue jeans, plaid red flannel shirt and western boots. He had been out in the back pasture baling the fifth cutting of Alfalfa hay when he noticed the white Jeep Wrangler coming down the driveway.

Even though he had passed his 65th birthday, Levi was as strong as a bull. The sinews on his neck were as tight as violin strings and his chest was as solid as granite. Long hours and hard work running a farm raising cattle and hay gave a man little time to get soft.

Throwing his arms around the younger man, Levi picked him up in a big bear hug.

"Good to see you, boy. What's kept you away for so long?"

"Government stuff, things like that," answered Tom. "Levi, you're still as solid as a rock."

"It's the farm. You work hard, you play hard. Not a life for everyone. Never ceases to amaze me those city-folk who're always saying they plan on retiring to the farm. When I retire I'm going to get me a city apartment so I can die fat, dumb and happy."

"Yeah, sure. That'll be the day. The minute you keel over, they'll have to rip out your heart and beat it to death with a stick."

"Damn!" exclaimed one of the two men parked five miles away in a tan Hummer. He threw his headset on the console.

"We almost had him, Ira. He was that close to spilling his guts when that damn farmer interrupted." He held up his thumb and forefinger about a quarter inch apart.

Ira Bonslick and Martin Morgan were NWO operatives. They had lived in Boise before and were familiar with the countryside. The NWO had sent them to many parts of the world, and they were used to working together on highly sensitive assignments. O'Donnell was at the top of the NWO's list of AWF figures to watch. Ira and Martin had worked everything from surveillance to assassination. This time, all eyes and ears at NWO intelligence would be on them.

They were born in the United States before the Nuclear War and grew up in the Rocky Mountains, where small radical groups that opposed the government formed pockets of influence. Ira and Martin joined one of these groups and developed strong opinions about the power government should have over them.

The radical group they joined was formed by a career U.S. Marine colonel who had earned several decorations commanding an elite Marine combat unit called Red Patch. Members of Red Patch were highly trained in fighting terrorism.

After the colonel retired he found that peace and the changing world political climate made returning to civilian life unbearable. Out of desperation he moved to a remote location in the American West and formed a paramilitary splinter group. They called themselves the American Freedom Army or AFA. Like most militia groups, they were more of a platoon than an army.

The formation of these militia groups became a popular counter culture for radicals, racists, anti-government militants and just about anyone who couldn't mold themselves to mainstream society. Many claimed to be patriots who were going to rise up and save the country from a mega-corporate conglomerate made of a few very powerful and very rich individuals.

Their revolution never came and the powerful central controlling faction of the rich never materialized. As a result, many of the militias simply got bored and disbanded. A few extremists survived. The AFA fortified themselves in the mountains and conducted training exercises and war games. This lifestyle appealed strongly to Ira and Martin. Like the colonel, they found it difficult to rejoin civilian life.

The AFA vigorously opposed the formation of the AWF. Some of the more radical members had bombed government buildings in Portland, Seattle and San Francisco. Several of its leaders, including the colonel, were arrested and sent to prison. Others fled deeper underground maintaining a loose network of communication that spread across the country.

They were ripe for recruitment by the NWO. It was not difficult to locate the scattered members of the AFA through their secret network. Playing on the politics to which they were attracted in the first place, the NWO easily convinced Ira and Martin to cross over and become agents.

The NWO had decided that it could no longer just watch O'Donnell. He had been the cause of significant discomfort to them too often. They would try to find out what he was doing and then they would do away with him once and for all. They couldn't chance any more disappearing acts. Whatever it was the AWF was up to, it would be infinitely more difficult without Tom O'Donnell at the helm.

The agents chosen for this task were two of their best. The Hummer was literally a small fortress. Their arsenal included a shoulder held ground-to-ground anti-tank rocket launcher, automatic rifles, 9 mm automatic hand guns and laser scope mounted sniper rifles.

The Hummer was equipped with a radio receiver to listen in on conversations picked up by the Jeep keys. It had a console that showed a satellite map of the area. They could pinpoint exactly where their targets were at all times from the signal emitted by the transmitter in the gas cap. A long-range radio kept them in touch with the High Command leadership via satellite.

They had no idea where their NWO commander was located. They only knew that he contacted them via secure radio transmission and identified himself as "Silent Owl." Their code name was "Red Fox." They never used names over the radio or in any other transmission.

"Silent Owl ordered us to intercept O'Donnell's conversation and find out what they're doing. The High Command doesn't really believe he's going to the Himalayas at this time of year, even though they've sent a team, just in case. If it wasn't for your wife sleeping with the Colonel we'd be on snowshoes carrying a tent and packing climbing gear at forty below zero right now," cracked Martin with a chuckle.

"Don't push it, pal," warned Ira. He glared menacingly at his companion. "Yvette doesn't think I know what's going on. When I get back to Tehran I'm going to put an end to that relationship. The Colonel will be looking for a new kitten to play with."

"What are you going to do, kill her?"

"That would be too easy. I've slit the throats of a hundred agents. I can do it so fast they don't even feel pain. No, she'll learn the penalty for taking me for a fool. Have you ever seen what nitric acid can do when dripped slowly into body cavities?"

Martin didn't respond. He knew his companion was serious.

Back on the farm, Levi walked between Al and Tom with a big arm around each of them.

"Really good to see you, Tom. I hear you and Al are planning a little fly-fishing up the Panhandle."

"That's right Levi, we need to do a little planning before morning," said Tom, not really disappointed that the great man had interrupted them. He had liked Levi ever since he first met him during his second year at the Academy. Al had invited Tom for a visit over Thanksgiving and a bond had instantly formed between his friend and his father. Levi reminded Tom of what a father would have been to him had his lived. With seven sons, Levi had no trouble accepting Tom as an unofficial eighth.

"Well, boys, not until after we have a little dinner. Mona has thrown together a few scraps she scraped up around the kitchen and she's ready for us now."

After dinner and some friendly conversation, Tom went to the guestroom to unpack his things. He tossed the keys to the Jeep on the dresser and went downstairs looking for Al. He found him on the porch.

"Let's go for that walk now, Al."

Chapter 9
NUMSUB Gets a Captain

Early October in northern Idaho means crisp nights. This evening was no exception. Tom and Al deeply inhaled the chilly night air. They could see their breath by the light of the nearly full moon high in the eastern sky. They walked in silence through the pasture where Levi kept his horses this time of year.

Levi's dogs, an eighty-five pound male German Shepherd mix named Cisco and a thirty-five pound female Australian Cattle Dog named Sam, accompanied them on their walk. Not only were the two breeds excellent watchdogs, Sam made herding the farm's livestock much easier. The dogs darted around, sniffing the ground and checking out each bush, determined to discover a smell they hadn't noticed before.

Tom took in a deep breath. "Man, I nearly forgot how good fresh air smelled." The smells of newly mown hay mixed with that of the first bite of frost signaled the onset of autumn. The maple and oak leaves were beginning to turn the forest into brilliant hues of reds, oranges, and yellows interspersed with the deep green of the tall Douglas Fir trees that dotted the landscape. They could almost hear the frosty dew settling on the ground around them. In the distance the plaintive wail of a coyote interrupted the stillness.

"Al, how long's it been since your last classified mission into NWO territory?" Tom asked contemplatively.

Al spoke softly as though not to disturb the stillness around them. "A little over eighteen months. We had to smuggle a team of FIA agents through the Bosporus into the Black Sea and pick up the team they were replacing."

"Would you say that mission was routine or dangerous?"

"A little of both, I guess. Routine because we'd had assignments like that a dozen times before. Dangerous because any slip up and both we and our 'cargo' would not have returned alive."

"I mentioned this afternoon that I had met with Secretary Warnick, Director Cranston and Vice Chairman Constance. You know about the NWO's High Orbiting Reconnaissance System?"

"HORS? Yes, I know about it. I understand that it's used mainly for defense, right?"

"That's right. They were supposed to launch four satellites but two didn't get off the ground."

"O.K.?" said Al, waiting expectantly for Tom to explain what this had to do with secret missions and especially what it had to do with him.

"They've apparently perfected their system. In about three months they'll send up thirteen more satellites in a single launch that will make HORS look like weather balloons. Once in orbit and operational, these thirteen will cover the earth with the most sophisticated electronic surveillance ever known. They'll be able to see through solid concrete. Nothing could stop their snooping," Tom went on.

He stopped and sat on a log near the edge of the field. Cisco and Sam vied for his attention while he petted their heads and scratched their ears. Though the night was cool, they were panting from exertion. They looked like they wore smiles on their faces.

"That will mean the Federation will be at the mercy of the NWO. We could never mount a defense to anything they decided to throw at us," speculated Al.

"Exactly, and it's worse than that. Not only would they have supremacy over our military, they could control every financial, medical, government, university and transportation system in the world. They could disrupt the food delivery process throughout AWF. They could interrupt airline schedules, telephonic communications, everything that depended on electronics."

"They could destroy the AWF without firing a single shot. We would have no choice but to surrender," added Al, his jaw set and his eyes tight. He slammed his fist on the log they were sitting on. "You didn't come here just to tell me the end of the world was near. How can I help?"

"Have you heard of the Dogfish Project?"

"I know it's a highly sensitive project. Security is so tight that I've not heard anything more. There are rumors that it has something to do with submarine intelligence."

"It's been my project for eighteen months now. I've lived and breathed it."

"So that's where you've been. You disappeared from sight about a year and a half ago. I thought maybe the NWO had gotten you and the usual cover up was going to be reported. Nothing came so I guessed you were up to something."

"When Dogfish started out it was a project designed for civilian research, but when they discovered what they had, the military jumped on it. What could you do with a sub that could not only become invisible to any known electronic surveillance, including radar and sonar, but could disappear from visual sight and send a holographic image of itself up to a hundred miles away?"

"I'd say that's impossible, but my reason tells me you wouldn't be asking unless it was possible. If I had a sub like that, I could control the oceans. Hell, man, I could control the world."

"That's exactly what you could do. I haven't told you half of what the sub is capable of doing though. It's also small enough to infiltrate nearly every NWO harbor on the map and can be operated by a crew of seventeen."

"Seventeen! How large is this thing?"

"One hundred forty foot keel with a fifty-one foot beam. The sub is nearly all computer controlled. It could maneuver unmanned, but then I guess they don't want to render all submariners obsolete just yet."

"I hope not. I'm not ready for retirement. I've got a lot I want to accomplish first. I'm hoping I know where you're headed with this."

"I'm here to ask you to help me put a crew together to run the boat. I want the best in the Navy. They will have to be willing to risk Their lives with no questions asked. Once briefed on the mission, they will not have the option of backing out."

"I'll do that on one condition."

'What's that?"

"I command the crew."

"I was hoping that was the condition, my friend," said Tom gratefully. "I'll be putting together a team of the best intelligence operatives in the AWF. We don't have much time to plan."

"Then I'd say we'd better get going," said Al firmly. "What's the next step?"

"The next step is to get some sleep tonight. We'll head up into the mountains tomorrow where we can be sure we're out of NWO earshot. I don't want to spend much time on your father's farm. The NWO thinks I came out here on a fishing trip and we'd better make it look like that's what we're doing. If we stay here it might endanger your family. Let's head out early in the morning and I'll brief you further on the way up."

The two men headed back to the farmhouse wrapped in the same silence they brought with them to the pasture. The only sounds were those of their footsteps crunching the early fall frost just forming on the grass.

When they arrived at the farmhouse, the lights in the living room were on. Levi and Mona were still up, waiting for the two younger men to return. The living room was small, but comfortable. A room where guests could be invited to relax and visit. The worn carpet and well-used furniture indicated that many had taken advantage of the hospitality offered there.

Levi sat in his favorite recliner, boots off and feet propped up on the footrest. He scrolled through the newspaper displayed on the flat screen television monitor built into the wall of the room. Newspapers made of paper had pretty much been replaced by the electronic version. They could be delivered instantly, saving gas and postage. Gone were the huge printing presses required to print them and, most importantly, they used no wood that depleted the forests. When he clicked the remote, the pages flipped on the screen to the sound of turning pages emanating from the speakers.

Mona sat beside him on the divan. She was busy working up the finances of the farm on the laptop. She was connected directly into their bank in Boise, where she was transferring receipts from the sale of cattle and hay into the loan distribution account from which the bank would extract the seasonal loan payoff funds.

Tom and Al entered the room. Levi looked away from his reading. "You two have a chance to catch up?"

"Always good to see Tom again, Dad. Our work always seems to take us to different parts of the world and we need some time to stay in touch."

"Come on in and have a seat," said Mona. "I've got some fresh apple pie cooling in the kitchen just itchin' to get eaten." She rose to get it and Al accompanied her into the kitchen, leaving Tom and Levi to talk.

"Nothing like fresh apple pie," began Tom. "Especially Mona's. I'm sure glad they don't have to freeze dry everything we eat."

"No doubt. The farm's about the only place where you can get real food anymore. Last week we were in Boise and stopped by one of those steak and seafood restaurants. I get all the steak I want here so I ordered up one of those lobster tails. Wheeoo! You'd a thought it was soaked in gold by the price. So I said, what the heck? I only get into town once or twice a quarter, let's splurge a little. It didn't' taste too bad, so I asked the waiter where it came from, Atlantic or Pacific. You know what he said?"

"No. What?"

"He said it didn't come from either one. Grew 'em right up the road in Twin Falls. Seems there's a corporation that's built a lobster ranch. A bunch of salt water tanks full of lobsters. Seems like nothing's for real any more.

"Tell us what you've been up to, Tom. We haven't seen neither hide nor hair of you in, what's it been, goin' on two years now?"

"Oh, not much to talk about. Just working on the usual secret military projects trying to stay ahead of the NWO. Seems like there will always be a job for the military no matter how advanced the world becomes. Always going to be two opposing sides."

Levi knew that Tom was up to more than he could talk about.

"Been that way since the beginning of time. Seems that there will always be opposites, good and evil, freedom and slavery, one side that wants man to do for himself and the other to force him to do things the way they want," reflected Levi. "Scares me sometimes that peace is so fragile."

"I know, and with technology advancing so rapidly today, the balance of power could shift with just the flick of a button or the creation of new and more powerful tools."

"You and Al going to get to see more of each other?"

"Yeah, I think so. We might actually get to do a project together shortly. It would be good to …."

Al and Mona interrupted their conversation by entering the living room each carrying two plates of warm apple pie. "Hope you've got a hankerin' for some great baking," said Mona.

"Always," responded Tom. "I can never get enough of the treats that come from your kitchen, Mona." He sat up and took a plate from Mona, lifting it to his nose and taking a deep whiff. "My mouth is watering so much my teeth are about to melt."

"Oh, Tom. I can never get enough of your compliments. You're enough to make an old girl blush."

"Old? Seems to me the only one getting old around here is this crusty old farmer kicking back in his easy chair. Levi, how on earth do you keep your wife looking so young?"

Levi scratched his chin and put on a look of wisdom. "The secret is in the manure. Every morning I scratch a little off my boot and drop it in her juice. Keeps her young and just ornery enough to make her toe the line."

The conversation continued in small talk, catching up on news and discussing the politics of the day for another hour when Tom rose and stretched out in a big yawn.

"Guess I need to be hitting the hay," he said rubbing his eyes. "The time zone change still catches up to me even with the light bars they give us to counteract jet lag. Al and I want to get an early start and I'm anxious to smell the woods and feel the tug of a big brown hitting my line. I'll see everyone in the morning."

"Morning seems to come earlier every year," said Levi. "It's time we all turned in for the night. You all get a good night's sleep."

Mona and Levi climbed the stairs to the master bedroom and Tom went into the guest bedroom down the hall from the living room.

Retiring to his bed, Al was glad they were going to get an early start in the morning. He knew he wasn't going to get much sleep. He lay awake, contemplating the names of the men and women who had served with him. Men and women who had freely risked their lives protecting their families and their freedom.

Some had died in the effort; others had been less fortunate and had fallen into the hands of the NWO.

Those unlucky enough to be captured had the worst of it. The men were usually tortured to extract whatever information they would give up before being executed. The women were victims of additional atrocities before they met the same fate as the men. He had lost only a few during the missions under his command. But even a few were too many.

He thought of their names and began to form his crew from the best. There were many more names than seventeen. It would depend on what their duties would be on this incredible submarine. He could hardly imagine how only seventeen people could operate a sub with such capabilities.

Al was still wide awake when he heard a rooster crow in the barnyard. *Good grief,* he thought, *I've been awake all night.*

Chapter 10
Fly Fishing

Tom woke a half-hour later to the aroma of bacon frying and coffee brewing. He dressed and came downstairs. Al was packed and ready to go. Fishing gear, supplies and camping equipment were stacked neatly on the porch ready to be loaded into the Jeep. In the corner was a rifle with a scope mounted on it. It was five a.m.

"What's that for?" asked Tom, yawning and nodding toward the rifle.

"Bear," replied Al matter-of-factly. "I've heard there's a Grisly up in the mountains that's been giving some campers a scare. You want some breakfast?"

"Smells fantastic," said Tom. "Nothing like a country breakfast to get me in the mood for fishing."

The two men hurried through breakfast in relative silence, their minds on the discussion of the previous night. Finally they finished and packed their gear into the Jeep. Al said good-bye to Mona while Tom, leaning on the Jeep, briefly discussed fly-fishing strategy with Levi.

"Best stream fishing this time of year will be in the Bitterroot," explained Levi, speaking of the Selway-Bitterroot Wilderness area about sixty miles or so due East of Grangeville. "The streams are full and the trout are lively. Best luck I've had fly-fishing was with the Mayfly larva. If that doesn't bring in your limit, get out your spinning rod and drop a night crawler behind a rock. Wish I could go with you, but I know you boys want some time alone. You all have a good time, O.K.?"

"Will do. Thanks, Levi," responded Tom, glad the older man had enough chores to do that he had to stay on the farm.

Tom and Al headed east to the Bitterroot through the Clearwater Mountains of the Nez Perce National Forest. The drive through the mountains was awe-inspiring. The stately Douglas Fir trees shrouded the mountains and cast a beautiful emerald green color into the scenery. Now and then they would see a large Mule Deer buck watching over his harem, head erect, ears forward, eyeing them suspiciously as they passed by.

On the way, Tom briefed Al about the mission and filled him in on the details he had discussed in the Montreal meeting with Warnick, Cranston and Constance. Fortunately, the Jeep had a canvas top. The wind noise and the roar of the off-road tires on the pavement made it impossible for the microphone in the keys to pick up their conversation.

Martin and Ira had gotten an earlier start and had set up a camp on the trail Tom and Al were going to take. They had overheard Tom talking to Levi and knew which turnoff of the main road to take. They were now trying to listen to the conversation in the Jeep. They were picking up nothing. They were beyond the five mile range of the transmitter and what little they could hear over the static was drowned out by the wind noise.

"I'm going to wring Shawna's neck when I see her," said Ira. "She should have given O'Donnell a Jeep with a hard top. I can't hear anything with all of the wind noise."

"The only thing we've been able to make out is that something is planned that has to do with a 'dog'," said Martin. "Maybe High Command can make something of it." All communication received or transmitted from the Hummer was relayed via satellite to an offshore location somewhere in the Pacific..

"That must be a code name for something. It looks like they've turned off on to the trail," observed Ira while he and Martin eyed the satellite tracking monitor. "They should come by in about twenty minutes. Start acting like we've been here all night."

Tom and Al stayed on the main road until they were about half way between Grangeville and Missoula, Montana. Then they turned south onto a backcountry trail. Tom shifted the Jeep easily into four-wheel-drive. The deep tire tread dug into the soft dirt of the trail, giving them the sure-footed traction they needed.

This was pristine wilderness. Majestic mountains on either side of them, an occasional stream rushing down a valley, untouched meadows opening to the warmth of the sun. A bald eagle soared overhead, wings motionless, riding the updrafts created by the sun breaking over the mountain ridges and warming the cool valley air. Tom wondered why anyone would ever leave the country and move to the city.

They rounded a switchback and cleared a ridge. Tom pointed down into the valley below. "Looks like someone beat us up here," he said. Smoke from a campfire listed lazily above the treetops next to a mountain stream.

The Jeep lurched along the narrow trail until they came to the clearing where the smoke had alerted them to the presence of others. They approached the camp and noticed two men, dressed in waders and flannel shirts, getting ready to start the day's fishing. "Any luck?" Tom greeted the men with the basic fisherman's salutation.

"Limited out yesterday," responded one of the men. "Just getting started today," he added eyeing the Jeep curiously. The other man said nothing but went about his preparations without looking up.

"Guess we'll head up the valley a few more miles. We'll try our luck upstream." Tom tried to sound nonchalant.

They turned and headed away from the fishermen's camp. While they were leaving, Tom and Al eyed the campsite. Dark green tent, campfire with a Dutch oven hanging on a spit, fishing gear leaning against a tree and various items of trash strewn about the area. Parked off to one side, partially concealed by some bushes, a tan Hummer.

Once out of earshot, Al spoke up. "Those guys aren't here to fish," he said.

"I got the same impression. What makes you think they have something else on their mind?"

"They aren't serious about what they're doing. It's 9:30 in the morning. More than likely the fish have stopped biting. Most of the serious fishermen who come up here this time of year and camp overnight would have been in the water and nearly limited out by now."

"Yeah, that's true. They also said they limited out yesterday. Did you smell any fish for breakfast?"

"No, I didn't. But, I did see half-burned breakfast wrappers from the Burger King we passed back in Lowell this morning."

"Right, they weren't camped overnight. From the looks of things they arrived early this morning and set up to make it look like they'd been here a while. The campfire was fresh, no ashes from the previous day's cooking," responded Tom. "The windows on the Hummer were clear. Parked under that tree the sun hadn't hit it yet. There wasn't any moisture from the frost that would have formed on them last night. I wonder what they're up to."

"Either they're running from something, or, in light of what we've been talking about, you don't suppose they're NWO, do you?"

"If I had to choose I'd go with NWO. Suspicious campers are too much of a coincidence. I wonder how they knew we'd be coming to the Bitterroot on this particular trail?"

"The only time we mentioned anything was back at the farm when you were talking to Dad, and on the road up here. You and Dad were standing next to the Jeep. Do you suppose the Jeep is bugged?" Al began looking apprehensively around the interior of the vehicle.

"We have to assume that's what it is. I wonder how much of our conversation on the way up here they heard."

"I don't know. It was so noisy I had trouble hearing myself. Thing is, if they are NWO and the Jeep is bugged, they know we know who they are by now. Keep a look out."

"We've been made!" said Ira, removing the headset from his ears and lowering the volume of the radio receiver. "I told you they'd never go for the innocent fishermen bullshit. I don't know why I listened to you."

"It's too late to worry about that now. Since they figure the Jeep's bugged it's unlikely we'll hear any more. Our job just took a giant leap forward. Now we gotta finish them off." He reached in the back of the Hummer and opened the case containing the rocket launcher and five rockets. He placed a semi-automatic rifle between them. "Let's get this over with."

Ira switched on the ignition of the Hummer and the engine roared to life. He gunned the accelerator and all four over-sized tires dug into the soft soil at the same time. The tires threw up dust and dirt as the big vehicle lurched into motion.

"There they go!" shouted Martin over the engine while Ira steered the truck onto the trail recently taken by Tom and Al.

Looking back over his shoulder, Al spotted the Hummer crashing through the brush about a half mile behind them. "Gun it! Here they come!"

Tom pushed his foot to the floorboard and the Jeep sprang forward. Staying on the twisting trail was useless. Now they would have to take their chances by running cross country.

"That way!" Al pointed to a stand of fir trees off to the right that appeared to have solid ground beneath them.

The Jeep spun and headed toward the trees. Bullets from an automatic weapon whizzed around them. Unseen by the two men, the stand of firs was on the crest of a steep embankment leading into a deep ravine.

"We'll never get through!" yelled Al. He saw the fir trees were growing too close together.

"Watch out for your mirror!" yelled Tom as he ducked his head into his shoulder. Al did likewise. Both mirrors simultaneously slammed into trees and were ripped from the doors. Broken glass sprayed the inside of the vehicle. Tom skillfully maneuvered the Jeep between the closely spaced trees with just enough room on either side to clear the wheels.

The Jeep cleared the edge of the embankment and became airborne immediately. Tom gripped the steering wheel tightly and held on while Al grabbed the roll bar with his right hand and the dash with his left. The Jeep came down hard on the front tires. When the rear tires struck the ground the front bounced up again. Al was nearly thrown from the vehicle. The embankment was steep and it was all Tom could do to keep the Jeep facing forward. He couldn't stop or slow down and he prayed that he could keep from rolling. They bounced and crashed through brush and small trees all the way to the bottom of the ravine two hundred yards below the ridge.

Following behind in the more powerful Hummer, Ira and Martin were closing in. Martin had pushed the windshield down and was trying to get a bead with an automatic rifle. The terrain was too rough and the bouncing made it all he could do to hold on as he fired wildly around the fleeing Jeep.

The Jeep did a quick turn and darted toward a stand of trees. "We've got them now!" cried Ira, with a wry smile on his lips. He knew O'Donnell and Hunslinger wouldn't make it through and they'd be trapped like sitting ducks. The smile quickly faded when the Jeep disappeared through the thicket.

"After them!" yelled Martin. 'We'll get through, too!"

Accelerating toward the opening through which the Jeep had just gone, their faces registered alarm when they realized that the much wider Hummer would never make it between the trees. With a bone-crunching thud, each end of the Hummer's bumper crashed into a tree and the vehicle shuddered to a complete stop. Ira lunged forward and was restrained by his seatbelt. Martin had removed his seatbelt to use the rifle. When the Hummer stopped suddenly, he was thrown over the hood and landed in a pile of leaves and mud. The rifle was hurled from his hand and slammed against a tree, bending the barrel.

"Damn!" yelled Ira, throwing the vehicle into reverse and backing off the trees. He jumped out and found that the bumper was badly bent, but the vehicle was drivable. He rushed over to Martin, who was slowly picking himself up off the ground. He was covered in leaves and mud.

"Are you all right?"

Cursing and spitting dirt from his mouth, Martin didn't answer.

"We've got to find a way around these trees!" Ira cried wildly.

At the bottom of the ravine, the Jeep had finally come to a stop straddling a log. It was high centered and unable to get enough traction in any of the wheels to pull itself off, despite Tom's efforts at rocking it back and forth.

Martin had run forward to the edge of the embankment to see where their prey had gone. He saw them at the bottom of the ravine about a quarter-mile away. They appeared to be stuck. Running back to the Hummer he shouted, "Quick, the launcher!"

Retrieving the rocket launcher and two rockets, he ran back to the edge of the embankment. He hurriedly loaded a rocket into the launcher and cocked the mechanism. Taking aim through the sights, he squeezed the trigger.

With a loud WHOOSH, the rocket was sent screaming toward its target.

Al had looked up the embankment and saw what was happening. Time seemed to stand still when he saw the fiery tail of the rocket pushing its deadly payload directly at them.

"Incoming!" he screamed. He and Tom ducked their heads in a futile attempt to hide from the inevitable.

The rocket missed and whistled over their heads. It exploded with a deafening blast when it struck a large boulder a hundred feet ahead. Pieces of rock and dust rained down on them.

In his excitement to launch the rocket, Martin hadn't taken his time. He was panting hard from the exertion of running with the heavy weapon to the edge of the embankment. His chest was heaving, causing the sights of the launcher to sway above and below his target. At the instant he pulled the trigger, the sights had moved through the target and the rocket was launched high.

When he saw that he had missed and cursed again and scrambled to load the second rocket.

"Move!" Tom shouted at the Jeep, gunning the engine one more time. The shock wave from the explosion had turned the log just enough to change the angle of the vehicle. The wheels dug into the ground and hurled them forward off of the log.

Tom slammed the transmission into second to give them more speed. They disappeared behind another large boulder when the second rocket exploded, showering them again with dust and rock fragments.

Martin threw the launcher to the ground when he saw his second shot miss and the Jeep disappear further into the ravine.

He picked the launcher up and ran back to Ira and the Hummer. "Did you get them?" questioned Ira. The look on Martin's face gave him the answer he didn't want to hear.

"Let's go," he said. "We can get around this stand of trees over there." He pointed to a break in the trees about two hundred yards to the left.

Tom and Al were moving up the ravine as quickly as they could. The sides seemed to be closing in on them and were too steep even for the Jeep to climb out. Finally they reached the end of the ravine. The banks on all three sides hovered menacingly above them.

"We can't go back and we can't go up," said Al with dismay in his voice.

"No, but we can pull ourselves out with the winch," offered Tom.

Al leaped out of the vehicle and unfastened the hook. The soft whir of the electric motor sounded as Tom reversed it and played out the cable. Al climbed the steep bank in front of the Jeep.

"Attach it to that tree behind you!" shouted Tom.

Al pulled the hook around the tree and fastened it back on the cable.

Tom switched the winch motor into forward and the cable pulled taut. The motor ground slowly and the Jeep shuddered forward a few inches.

"It's too steep!" he exclaimed as the winch motor tried and failed to pull in any more cable. "We'll burn up the motor!"

"I'll help," said Al. He jumped into the Jeep and dropped the transmission into low 4-wheel drive.

"Watch yourself!" yelled Tom. "If that cable snaps it will backlash right through the windshield and knock your head off!"

Al had to take that chance; the only way they were going to get out of that ravine was if he could assist the winch with the Jeep's own power.

Slowly the wheels dug in and between the winch and the low gears, the vehicle climbed up and out of the ravine. Tom unhooked the cable from the tree and rewound the rest onto the winch.

He jumped in just as they saw the Hummer clear the ridge to the left.

"Go!" yelled Tom. All four wheels caught at the same time.

They crashed through brush and small trees then bounced onto an abandoned logging road. "That way!" shouted Tom pointing down into the valley.

As they sped along the road, the more powerful Hummer was closing behind them. "We'll never outrun them!" cried Tom.

He reached into the back of the Jeep and grabbed the hunting rifle. "Time to hunt bear!" he exclaimed. "When you round that turn up ahead next to the ridge, slow down and let me jump out."

They had to cross a small stream that was coursing across the logging road, making it slippery. Al maneuvered the Jeep through the water and over the rise beyond.

Following behind, Ira misjudged the stream and the Hummer fishtailed into a skid and slid off the road into the side of a bank. The engine stalled and took a couple of tries before Ira could start it again.

Martin saw that the road forked and one arm went above the other. "Up there!" he pointed. "We'll get in position above them and take them out from high ground."

Al rounded the turn Tom had pointed out and slowed down. Tom leaped from the moving vehicle, holding the rifle above his head to avoid damaging it. Rolling on the ground to break his fall he quickly ran into the brush and started to move up the hill. He reached a vantage point on an outcropping of rock where he could see the winding road below with the valley spreading out into the wilderness.

He also saw what Al couldn't see and his blood turned cold. A larger stream had completely washed out the logging road a couple of hundred yards ahead. It had cut a wash fifty feet deep and a hundred feet wide across the road.

Al saw the road disappear. He slammed on the brakes, and the Jeep skidded to a stop inches from the edge where the road dropped off to the stream below. He couldn't go back because the Hummer was behind him, and he couldn't go forward. He was a sitting duck.

Tom looked around and saw that the Hummer was stopped on a higher road above Al, just a hundred and twenty yards away.

Ira pointed below. "Look! There they are! They've stopped!"

Martin grabbed the rocket launcher and the three remaining rockets. He moved to the left front fender of the Hummer and placed the rockets on the hood beside him. He loaded one, aimed the weapon at the Jeep stopped below and pulled the trigger.

In disbelief Tom watched the fiery tail of the rocket make a straight course toward Al and the trapped Jeep.

Again, Martin's aim was high and the rocket exploded in a tree above Al.

Tom was desperate. He had to do something quick. He aimed the deer rifle toward the Hummer and looked through the scope. He saw the man with the launcher reach up on the hood, pick up one of the remaining two rockets and load it into the chamber of the weapon. The man was crouched behind the front of the vehicle and Tom didn't have a clear shot at him. He had to do something fast or the next rocket might not miss. He looked through the scope and had an idea.

He would get only one shot. If he missed he didn't want to think about the consequences.

He settled the crosshairs of the scope on the nose of the last rocket on the hood of the Hummer and slowly squeezed the trigger. The recoil of the rifle pushed hard into his shoulder as it sent the projectile on its way.

Martin was taking his time now. He wasn't going to miss this one. He rested the rocket launcher on the corner of the bumper and held his breath. He slowly squeezed the trigger and held the sights steady on the Jeep. As he squeezed, he noticed that there was only one man in the Jeep. *Where's the other one?*

Then darkness.

Neither Martin nor Ira heard the report of the deer rifle or the impact of the 30-caliber 150 grain bullet strike the nose of the last rocket on the hood of the Hummer.

Tom saw the Hummer explode in a fiery ball. The fourth rocket never left the launcher.

Somewhere in the NWO's world, a radio receiver went blank.

Chapter 11
Laying Plans

Al knew the next rocket might not miss. He was about to drive the Jeep over the edge of the wash out. He would rather take his chances riding the Wrangler down the near vertical bank than face another missile. He slammed the transmission into low and his left foot began to engage the clutch. He took one last look over his shoulder. The Hummer disappeared in a fiery explosion. One word crossed his mind. *Tom.*

He backed up the road and met Tom at the site of the explosion. All that was left was a crater and scattered fragments of shattered metal and debris. The rear axle of the Hummer was hanging from a large fir tree about 150 feet away. The engine had been blown down into the crater and was nearly submerged in the mud. The passenger compartment was upside down in front of a large rock near the rear axle. The sides and top had been peeled back like the skin of a banana. Nothing recognizable was left inside.

There was little trace of the two men who had been chasing them except a few scattered body parts. Against a tree a few yards away was a forearm and hand with a finger still on the trigger of a piece of twisted metal that was once a rocket launcher.

"I see you've mastered the finer points of bear hunting," said Al with relief.

"It's got one helluva kick, too," said Tom.

"There's usually enough left to eat, though."

"Yeah. It looks like our relationship with the NWO has just reached a new level. Let's finish what we came up here for and head back in the morning. We need to contact Warnick and decide where this thing is heading."

The two men climbed into the Jeep and turned back up the logging road. After a few miles, they pitched camp by the side of a rushing stream and started a campfire. Fly fishing was the furthest thing from their minds.

"Tom," Al broke the silence. "Stop me if I'm out of line. But how are things between you and Bree? The last thing I'd heard she was having trouble with you and the Navy. I saw her about six months ago on a trip to Montreal. We had gotten together like old friends do. Eventually the subject got around to the two of you. I got the impression that she's not quite over you."

"No, you're not out of line."

He knew that he and Al had too close of a relationship for Al not to have asked about this sensitive part of his life. Tom and Bree had developed a strong love for each other. He had met Bree through Al, who had been their greatest fan. During periods of highs and lows of their relationship they both would confide in Al.

"We thought we had the thing licked, the Navy part. It just didn't gel. Something always got in the way. When Dogfish came along we knew we had to make a choice. We made it and I've lived with the torment of that decision for nearly two years. I can't get her out of my mind, but I can't think of a way to make it work."

"Do you still love her?"

Tom paused for a couple of minutes before answering.

"Is it love that tears you up inside when you think of what could have been? Is it love that leaves the last image of her permanently etched in your mind's eye? I can see what she was wearing the last night I saw her. I can still smell her hair and feel her tears on my shoulder." Tom's voice trailed off for a moment.

"But there's nothing I can do about that now."

He stared into the burning embers of the fire as though watching a vision from the past. Silence settled like a blanket over the campsite, broken only by the crackling of the fire or an occasional hoot of an owl.

Al knew his friend needed a little time to think.

Tom was reliving in his mind, as he had a thousand times before, the last time he had seen Bree. They had parted nearly two years ago, but he could see it like it had been just last week.

It was the final night of his leave and they had spent the last couple of days deciding that their relationship was not progressing. She was sitting on the couch in her apartment, her hair pulled back, her brown eyes reddened from crying.

"I understand," she was saying bravely. "It isn't fair for me to expect you to give up your career and I can't live not knowing whether you'll go away some day and never come back."

He reached out to her and pulled her into his arms. He could still smell the sweet fragrance of her hair as she buried her face against his neck. His arms ached at the thought of letting her go, but he had to answer his heart. His father's honor and his own self respect hung in the balance.

"I know," he said softly. "I can't promise you I'll always return, but I couldn't live behind a desk. I wish there was another way."

They spent the rest of the night in a tight embrace; he caressed her hair and shoulders and kissed her cheek. She snuggled close as though she could melt into his chest.

Slowly the night passed and the first light of morning began to appear at the window. Finally he put his hands on her shoulders and pushed back. "I've got to leave now."

She nodded, her face twisted with emotion. He kissed her deeply and held her tight, then released her and stepped back.

"Goodbye," he said out loud. *I love you.*

"Goodbye," she said, holding her fist against her lips to hold back another sob.

He picked up his hat and closed the door gently behind him. The click of the latch added what seemed like a period at the end of a sentence. That was the last time he saw her. He had thought about calling her a couple of times when he was in Montreal, but he couldn't bring himself to do it.

Finally, as if emerging from a trance, Tom spoke. "We need to move on. I need your help to develop NUMSUB into a tactical operating battle-ready warship."

Al leaned back against the log next to him and focused on Tom's words. His non-verbal assent was visible in the expression on his face.

"We have barely three months to transform the Dogfish Program. For the past couple of years we've been developing and testing, developing and testing. All systems are functional and have tested well under laboratory conditions. There's no reason to believe they won't perform as expected in combat. We have to pick our crew, train them and be prepared to put them behind enemy lines by the second week of January."

"That doesn't give us much time."

"No it doesn't. That's why we need to act now. There will be two teams. The crew that will operate the sub will consist of you, an executive officer and fifteen submariners, allowing for twenty-four hour operations in twelve-hour shifts. I'll find five of the best counterintelligence operatives and anti-terrorist infiltrators in the AWF."

"Myself, an XO and fifteen crewmen? I'm still amazed. Tell me again, what kind of submarine can be operated by a crew of only seventeen?"

"A sub like none you've ever seen before. NUMSUB is the most sophisticated underwater vessel in the history of the world. She can outperform anything we've ever produced. There are times when I felt she could actually think for herself. If the entire crew were incapacitated, she could make it back to any port in the world without further human intervention, and take out a few thousand tons of hostile shipping on the way."

Al let out a low whistle. "Give me the operational requirements and I'll have the crew ready to start training inside of a week. The hardest part will be choosing only sixteen out of the best who have served with me. I could find a hundred if you needed them."

"Great. I knew I could count on you." Tom turned to the fire. His face changed expression. "Don't forget, there's a catch."

"Oh-oh. What's the catch?"

"On any other mission, failure meant you might be able to return home to try again. If we fail there won't be much of a home to return to. Can you handle that?"

"Then I guess failure isn't an option."

"Not for us it isn't."

Al dismissed the possibility of failure with the same aplomb as though swatting at an annoying fly buzzing around his head. "How are you going to get inside the installation?"

"That's where you come in."

Tom picked up a stick for a stylus and scraped away leaves to clear a drawing board on the ground. He began by drawing a rectangle.

"Hangzhou Base is roughly twice as long as it is wide. It has about ten miles of frontage on the Hangzhou Bay, near the East China Sea, and extends inland for nearly twenty miles. The Fuchun River runs through the center of the base essentially dividing it in two halves, north and south."

He drew a meandering line through the center of the rectangle to represent the river.

"In the northwest corner of the complex are the airfield and missile batteries. At the northeast corner the river widens to form a harbor about eight kilometers wide where the flotilla of naval vessels is located. Immediately to the west of the naval complex is the command center and headquarters."

As he drew the features of the installation on the ground, he tapped his stick to emphasize a point or location.

"Over here in the southeast corner is the space facility. That's our target. The rest of the base houses the residential and commercial centers necessary to support over sixty thousand inhabitants. Directly to the north near the harbor is the old Chinese city of Hangzhou."

Tom laid down his stick and sat back on the log. "You're going to float us right up to the space facility and drop us off."

"No problem. Should we ask the NWO to have a band play and an honor guard accompany us through the security checkpoint and into the space facility? We could just hand them our I.D.'s and they'd escort us right in."

"You're actually closer to the truth than you realize. One of the members of my team will be Jorge Rojas. Have you heard of him?"

"Isn't he the computer geek that brought the IRS to its knees several years ago?"

"His reputation with the IRS overshadows everything he's done since. He'll get our personal stats into the computer database at the installation and we'll use fake identification to pass through security checkpoints."

"That's great if you can get that far, but how will we get you up the river? It must be heavily guarded." Al folded his arms and leaned back on the log.

"Actually, the only security on the river is at the mouth where it enters the harbor. A minefield blocks all underwater access and most surface ships. The NWO figures that if they secure the mouth, the rest of the river is safe. The only other risk is an occasional patrol boat. The trick will be to get through the mines. Once past those we'll be relatively home free. Most of the river has been dredged to at least 120 feet. There's just one short section with a shifting sandbar that will be risky to navigate."

"What'll keep us out of the harbor?" Al leaned slightly forward.

"There's a heavy steel and concrete antisubmarine gate at the entrance to the harbor. The bay is about eight to nine kilometers wide at that point. There's an underwater concrete wall built from both shores to the center of the bay with the gate closing off the middle kilometer. The water over the wall and gate is only twenty feet deep. Anything larger than a patrol boat can't enter or exit the harbor with the gates closed. The gates open only under very tightly controlled conditions.

"Inside the harbor an electronic field sets up an invisible net that crisscrosses the entire length, width and depth of the water. Any questions?"

"So when does it get difficult?" chided Al. "Sounds to me like they're pretty serious about keeping unwelcome guests out of their house. I suppose this miracle sub can get through all of that without being seen or blown out of the water?"

"Well," began Tom.

"Oh, no!" interrupted Al. "You're going to tell me that NUMSUB *can* get through all of this."

"Almost. We can get through the gate if we're lucky enough to be there when a ship at least the size of a cruiser enters or leaves the harbor. The electronic net should be no problem for the sub's shields. The problem is the minefield. We'll have to figure a way to get through that."

"What you're saying is that the extremely difficult we do immediately, the impossible takes a little thought?"

"I knew there was a reason you finished at the top of your class at the Academy."

"Let's say we get through everything and get to the space facility. What happens next?"

"The river runs from southwest to northeast. There are two ninety-degree bends."

Tom picked up the stick and returned to his crude map.

"The second bend, farthest from the mouth, is about a mile and a half from the security checkpoint at the entrance to the space facility. There's a park that's unoccupied at night. We'll put ashore there where a grove of trees and brush will provide a place to hide. The road between the barracks and the checkpoint weaves through the trees where it can't be seen from either direction.

"There's a nearby motor pool where we'll requisition a vehicle to take us to the checkpoint. We'll go through like we were part of a regular shift change. We'll present our fake identification and pass through the security booths about four hours before launch."

"Only four hours before launch? Does the NWO change out all of their launch personnel just four hours before a launch?"

"No, only non-essential personnel will change shifts. Critical personnel will have been there for several hours and will work through the launch. Non-essentials aren't directly related to launch systems or the countdown. They're back up personnel, system maintenance, testing, observation and so forth. Still, there'll be several hundred personnel changes as well as day shift workers who aren't replacing anyone. We shouldn't have any trouble blending in."

"How's Jorge going to get you into the computer?"

"Good point. I forgot to mention that detail."

"Which is?"

"Before we leave the harbor and enter the river, Jorge will slip into the headquarters command center and upload the data from a disk he'll be carrying. We'll find an empty berth big enough for NUMSUB to stay submerged and out of sight. Jorge will have about two hours to find a terminal and upload the data into the main computer."

"Won't the command center be heavily guarded?"

"Yes, but he can hack into the main computer from just about any workstation. The easiest is the accounting section, which is located away from the command building. Even the NWO has to have someone juggle the numbers and balance the books. The accountants wrap things up around 6 p.m. and go home. It isn't very exotic, but it'll work."

"No way. We're going to penetrate one of the most sophisticated security systems in the world by slipping through the general ledger?"

"Like I said. It isn't exotic. That time of year it gets dark around 5:30. We'll sit off the dock and wait for everyone to go home. Then Jorge will go ashore and do his magic."

"O.K. We get through the sub gates, through the harbor net, Jorge does his accounting thing, we skirt the mines, grab a vehicle, you slip through security and blow up the rocket. Have I left anything out?"

"Nope. That about covers it."

"Good. I was starting to think this was going to get complicated somewhere. I don't even want to know what has to fall in place to get the launch to blow. What happens after the Big Bang?"

"We have to be back in NUMSUB before it explodes or we become part of the fireworks. After the explosion, we make a run back through the river to the harbor and out to sea. The commotion should cover our escape. If everything goes as planned we'll be back in the open sea while the NWO is still trying to figure out what happened."

"Goes as planned. What ever goes as planned? I suppose we'll have a back up plan."

"We've only got three months. There won't be much time for back up plans. If anything goes wrong we'll have to improvise as we go along."

"Somehow, I figured there'd be a 'seat of the pants' part in there somewhere."

"That's why I chose you. When we get to that part I want the best floating the boat."

The conversation slowly died along with the crackling of the fire. There was a lot to think about and many plans to make. Somewhere during the night, Tom and Al managed to doze off. Thursday would start very early in the morning.

Chapter 12

Deafening Silence

.

Sturgaard Ivanovich stood next to a radioman in the communications room of the attack submarine, *Lone Wolf*. He had a worried look on his face. The sub lay five meters beneath the surface of the Pacific Ocean, two hundred and two miles off the coast of Washington State's Olympic Peninsula.

The radioman adjusted the receiver on his equipment. He had listened to the transmissions from Bonslick and Morgan. Ivanovich anxiously watched his effort to restore the signal that had disappeared without warning.

"Silent Owl to Red Fox, do you read me," he repeated over and over. His calls were answered by silence.

"What happened? How can they just disappear like that? Could the battery in the vehicle have gone dead?" demanded Ivanovich.

"I don't believe so, Sir. The signal was strong, there was no interference, no indication of power degradation. Their radio seems to have simply stopped transmitting."

"Could the AWF have jammed their transmission?"

"The instruments indicate no AWF interference. This is a secure frequency. The transmissions are scrambled. No one could have been listening nor could they have identified the source of the signal."

"The last rocket went wide and they were about to launch another. Was there any indication of trouble? Replay the last few minutes of the recording."

The radioman reset the recording and they both listened carefully to Ira and Martin's last words. Martin had sworn profusely when the rocket missed its target. He had reloaded the launcher and assured Ira that this time he would not miss. He would rest against the fender of the Hummer to steady his aim and take his time. Ira was describing the scene in a hushed voice as though announcing a golfer's attempt to sink a critical putt for a tournament lead.

"Martin is taking his time now, the Jeep's a sitting duck. Steady . . . steady. In a few seconds we . . . ."

There was a sharp crack, not unlike the snapping of two fingers, and the transmission instantly went dead.

"Can you tell what that was?"

"No, Sir. It sounded almost electrical, like the flipping of a switch or a spark. Their equipment must have malfunctioned. Perhaps firing the rocket so close to the radio? I have no other explanation."

Unwilling to accept the obvious, Ivanovich stumbled through his course of action.

"Well, then we'll have to assume that we've simply lost contact with our agents and we'll keep trying to raise them. We'll assume they completed their mission and eliminated O'Donnell and Hunslinger. We'll know for sure in a few days. They'll be missed. Our intelligence network will hear the news that will race through the AWF. We will report to the High Command *after* we determine for certain what happened."

He was reluctant to admit that Morgan and Bonslick may have failed. That something unimaginable could have happened and they, not the two naval officers, were dead. He would wait until absolutely certain to inform headquarters of any possible failure in the mission.

Ivanovich's official duty aboard the submarine was as its political officer. In reality, he was an NWO intelligence agent. His dark navy blue uniform jacket was buttoned to the neck. A line of five brass buttons rose from the center of his waist to the collar beneath his Adam's Apple. His plain black oxford shoes were polished to a high gloss. His hair was cut short and he was clean shaven. His crisp uniform confirmed the fact that he was not a regular submariner.

His assignment as the political officer aboard the submarine was to observe the captain and crew and provide the required twice-weekly propaganda briefings. It was not a particularly exciting assignment for a highly trained intelligence officer. Their original orders had been to conduct a routine surveillance patrol off the west coast of the United States. They were to intercept military radio transmissions and relay them back to NWO Encryption and Deciphering Command for analysis.

Fate placed the *Lone Wolf* off the coast of Washington when Bonslick and Morgan received their assignment. Ivanovich's new orders were to direct his full attention to the interception and assassination of Tom O'Donnell. The submarine was placed at his exclusive disposal.

The captain had made no attempt to conceal his location. He knew the AWF had been tracking him since he left Hangzhou Base three months ago. While he remained alone and stayed outside the 200-mile international boundary, the AWF would take little interest in him.

NWO intelligence activity had picked up significantly when they learned that O'Donnell had surfaced after eighteen months. Their interest increased when he was summoned unexpectedly to Montreal during a routine leave.

A simple spur-of-the-moment fly fishing excursion to Idaho appeared too suspicious. Had O'Donnell returned to his normal rest and relaxation, they might have dismissed the visit to Montreal. However, an abrupt change of plans after a meeting with the AWF's senior defense official demanded further attention.

They had intercepted O'Donnell's televideo call to the Hunslinger farm. The NWO routinely tapped the home telephones of family and friends of military and political figures. Listening to hundreds of innocuous telephone calls is tedious work, but occasionally they hit pay dirt.

Reacting quickly to O'Donnell's plans, the *Lone Wolf* had arrived at its current location the night before. Martin Morgan and Ira Bonslick were already in Boise on a routine surveillance assignment. Their new orders were to find out where O'Donnell had been for the past year and a half and what Hunslinger had to do with his plans. The final phase of their mission was to assassinate the two Americans.

Sturgaard Ivanovich, as with other senior officers of the NWO Intelligence Agency, was well educated in politics. His father was raised in Moscow during the dissolution of Communism, when Boris Yeltsin was elected President of the Soviet Union. His grandfather, a high-ranking member of the newly elected government, opposed the attempt to bring democracy and freedom to Russia. His grandfather's views were popular to many and his influence blossomed. When the differences between those who favored democracy and those who pushed for a return to communism escalated to civil war, those who favored communism seceded from the new government and formed an alliance with the NWO.

During Sturgaard's pre-teen years, while his father attended to political business, his mother influenced his moral education. As a child she would hold him on her lap and teach him.

He remembered her words well. "Power can create or destroy. It is the nature of almost all men, when they rise to power, that they will exercise unjust domination over the people. Consider power a privilege. When one assumes it is a right, the people will suffer."

Shortly thereafter, his father took an interest in his upbringing. He took Sturgaard with him to observe government in action. His father made him a steward, where he ran errands and did favors for other congressional officers.

His father's influence gained Sturgaard admittance to the University of Moscow, where he studied politics. Upon graduation, he received an appointment to the intelligence agency where he soon rose to the rank of a senior officer.

Now, to fail at such an important task would not be looked upon with much favor. When the High Command made an assignment, success was the only acceptable measure of performance. An officer's career could be made or broken by the results of just such an assignment. Bonslick and Morgan were well trained and dependable. Failure was the last thing in Sturgaard's mind when he received his orders. Although his involvement in the mission was simply to monitor, there was no other upon whom the wrath of the High Command could be administered. While he could share in commendation for the success of their mission, he would also assume blame if it failed.

He instructed the radio operator to continue trying to make contact with the two agents. Then he returned to his stateroom. NWO submarines are not known for their accommodations. This one was designed after the old *Typhoon* class of Soviet submarines developed near the turn of the century. Though technology had achieved significant advancements and the submarine's capabilities were state of the art, creature comforts had not kept up. The stateroom was barely large enough for the officer's folding bunk, a chair, a desk, a small wardrobe and a few personal belongings.

On the desk was a photograph of his wife and two children. He had not seen them for three months. He missed them terribly but dared not return in disgrace. He opened the drawer in the desk and pulled out a 9 millimeter Ruger automatic pistol. He would have preferred a much lighter weapon of smaller caliber. It was easier to conceal and in close quarters was just as effective.

Weapons were permitted to only a few on board an NWO submarine. The possibility of a man becoming depressed after long periods in such cramped quarters was a matter of some concern. Weapons had no legitimate function, since there was little chance that anyone would have occasion to engage an enemy face to face in armed combat.

Accordingly, no sailor below the commander and a select few of the high ranking officers on board were allowed to possess a weapon. These officers would be required to quell any disturbance, and a weapon was a necessary tool for such a task. Visitors and passengers with no assigned duties critical to the operation of the sub were seldom allowed firearms. NWO intelligence officers were among the few exceptions.

Sturgaard checked the clip. It was full. He pulled back the action and chambered a round. With his finger on the hammer, he squeezed the trigger and then carefully allowed the hammer to move forward to rest against the firing pin. He set the safety and placed the pistol under the pillow on his bunk.

Chapter 13

After the Hunt

Early the next morning, Tom and Al broke camp and returned to the farm. They drove up the entrance road and met Levi leaving the barn.

"Hey! Looks like you two've been rode hard and put away wet. How was the fishing?" Levi looked them over curiously. The state of their clothing and the condition of the Jeep indicated that they had had a pretty hard time.

"Bear," answered Al in one word.

"It turned into more of a hunting trip than a fishing trip and we were the prey."

"Bear? From the looks of you two I'd hate to see the condition of the bear."

Al couldn't relate the events of the previous day to his father without causing unnecessary alarm. "We have to contact Montreal. There's a new project brewing that we need to get briefed on."

Levi detected that Al wasn't telling him the whole story, but he knew from experience that it was best not to pry. If his son was secretive about something, there was good reason.

Tom and Al went into the house and passed Mona in the kitchen.

"You two look a bit tuckered and hungry. Supper will be ready in about an hour. Why don't you settle down and rest for a while before you wash up."

"Thanks, Mona," said Tom. "We need to finish something and we'll join you then."

He and Al went into the guest bedroom, where Tom picked up a tan leather briefcase. They left the house, climbed into Levi's pickup truck and drove toward a remote grove of trees about three miles from the farmhouse.

"I don't want to take a chance that a bug is planted anywhere on your parents' property. We need to contact Secretary Warnick and let him know what's happened."

They parked the pickup by the grove and walked a hundred yards to an open field. Tom placed the briefcase on the ground and opened it. It contained a miniature antenna, a video monitor and a two-way radio.

"This will create a secure satellite hookup with the Secretariat."

Tom powered up the transmitter and the video screen flickered and came to life. He keyed in the code to connect to the Secretariat and almost immediately, the face of Secretary Warnick appeared on the screen.

"George, we've had some trouble."

George's face took on a serious look and he leaned closer to the video camera in his office that transmitted his image across the country to the screen in front of Tom and Al.

"What kind of trouble?"

"The NWO tried to take us out. We nearly didn't make it back. Have you heard any word they may be on to Dogfish?"

"None. But we did pick up they were watching you in Idaho. Since they're always watching you whenever they can, we assumed that it was just routine. Everything else has been quiet. Almost too quiet."

"What do you mean?"

"One of our moles informed us that the NWO was interested in what you were doing in Idaho and were going to tail you. I tried to get in touch with you but you and Al had already left for the woods. We intercepted a series of garbled transmissions that originated somewhere in the Northwest area of the U.S. Since it was the only unintelligible transmission in that area during the past two days, we assumed that it had something to do with you. There was something else unusual about it, though.'

"What was that?"

"The transmission was pretty steady for most of the morning, yesterday. Then about 11:15 a.m. your time, all of a sudden it stopped and we haven't been able to pick it up again. Do you know anything about that?"

"It definitely had something to do with us. They sent a couple of goons who used us for target practice with a rocket launcher. We were lucky their aim was off. We'll tell you about it when we get back to Montreal."

"Good, I'll call a session of the Command Staff and we'll be here when you arrive. I take it Al's on board?"

Al leaned over in front of the video lens. "Turn down a chance to get in on Dogfish? This is a once in a career opportunity. You couldn't keep me away."

"Great, with the three hour time difference between there and here, we'll see you tomorrow afternoon. 1300 hours, sharp."

"Count on it."

After a dinner of roast beef, farm fresh peas and baked Idaho potatoes, topped off with more of Mona's apple pie, Tom and Al spent the evening in quiet conversation with Al's parents before retiring to bed. They had to be at the Boise airport to take a military shuttle to Montreal by seven o'clock in the morning.

At 6:45 a.m. Tom stood at the auto rental counter to return the Jeep. Shawna was assisting one other customer ahead of him when she looked up. He caught her eye. There was a momentary blank gaze followed

69

by recognition and then a brief but perceptible look of shock. Shawna tried to control her expression, but for a fraction of a second her eyebrows raised and the white above the iris in her eyes betrayed her. This was not lost on Tom. She had given herself away. At that moment he knew for certain she was working for the other side.

He approached the counter and dropped the keys in front of her. He looked straight into her eyes.

"Surprised to see me?"

She tried to cover herself. "N..no, not at all. H..how was the vehicle?"

"Fortunately more maneuverable than a Hummer," he answered with a steel edge to his voice. He turned to leave.

She watched him walk away, knowing that she would soon be leaving Boise. She had been made, which meant a quick transfer to some remote part of the NWO world. Not something a girl really wanted to do with her life.

Chapter 14

Return to Montreal

The flight to Montreal was uneventful. At the altitude they flew there was little turbulence. The cargo bay of the aging Air Force C-171 Stratolifter had been modified to hold a passenger cabin. At the request of the Secretary, there were no other passengers on board. Tom and Al used the time to discuss their plans before the meeting. They went over the list of names Al had compiled of the best individuals he knew with the skills they would need on the mission.

Approaching the airport, the big cargo plane dropped sharply out of the sky and landed smoothly on thirty-six wheels. A cloud of blue smoke briefly announced the initial contact with the runway. The time was 12:30.

A black limousine waited at the end of the taxiway to pick them up. The driver gave a crisp salute and opened the rear door. The trip to the Secretariat was about fifteen minutes through light traffic. The driver took an indirect route through less traveled parts of the city. Tom noticed that there were two cars directly in front about seventy-five yards and two more following at the same distance. The limo's windows were bullet-proof tempered glass, and Tom guessed that the doors were well armored.

They hurried through security and met in Warnick's office wearing the customary white outfits. The other members of the Command Staff, General Abram Wainscot, head of the Joint Chiefs, Margaret Cranston, Roy Constance, and Admiral Dirk Beaumont, Commander of the Navy's Submarine Fleet, were already assembled and awaiting their arrival. The white clothing everyone was wearing gave the meeting a somber, almost hallowed atmosphere.

General Wainscot was a graduate of West Point, Class of '26. He was the Chairman of the Joint Chiefs because of his political savvy in addition to his military experience. During the war he had organized the Southern Pacific Allied Forces into a smoothly operating unit. Coordinating the efforts of British, French, Mexican and Australian militaries took an iron will and a keen sense of politics. He was hard, but usually considered fair in his dealings. The only fault he acknowledged having was an occasional streak of stubbornness.

Admiral Dirk Beaumont had been seasoned in Her Majesty's Royal Navy. A descendant of a line of British nobles, Admiral Beaumont was a model of protocol. He began his career in the surface Navy and served for six years aboard one of Great Britain's three nuclear powered aircraft carriers. The Royal Navy was small, with a total uniformed contingent of less than 50,000 men and women. When an opportunity to serve in the submarine corps presented itself, he jumped at the chance. He earned distinction as the commander of one of the Royal underwater vessels.

Upon formation of the AWF and the combination of the military forces, Beaumont was selected to oversee the free world's fleet of submarines, a position sought after by several senior naval officers from a variety of countries. Some, like the United States, had considerably larger fleets of submarines than Britain. However, the intensity of British submarine training unquestionably qualified him for command. His selection had first brought skepticism from U.S. submarine officers who considered the British submarine fleet to be less technologically advanced than its U.S. counterpart.

Beaumont quickly won over the minds if not the hearts of the American naval commanders when he lobbied a key spending bill through congress that nearly doubled the size of the Navy's underwater fleet budget. This was no small task. The world's civilian leaders believed that the military focus of the AWF ought to be concentrated in the air and space programs, not the oceans, and in particular, not under the oceans.

Tom and Al entered to a hubbub of conversations in progress. At the top of each person's mind were questions regarding the incident in Idaho.

Secretary Warnick rose to meet them. "Gentlemen, we're glad to see you! Come on in and sit down. Tom, I think you know everyone here. This must be Captain Hunslinger."

Tom nodded a greeting to each person while he approached the table. "Nice to see you again General, . . . Margaret, . . . Roy, . . . Admiral Beaumont. We're not only glad to be here, we're lucky, too. Let me introduce Al Hunslinger to you."

Al looked around the room at the assembled individuals. He shook hands with each of them. When he came to Admiral Beaumont, he greeted him with recognition, having met him previously.

"Nice to see you again, Admiral. How's Martha?"

"Doing well, Captain. You've developed quite a reputation for yourself. Proud to have you in the fleet."

"Thank you, Sir. I echo Tom's comments. It's good to finally be here."

Al was feeling a little strange being the newcomer to such a collection of powerful individuals. The magnitude of what he was about to do was beginning to weigh on him and his adrenaline was pumping.

Secretary Warnick sat in his usual place at the head of the table. Tom and Al took their places in the two seats immediately to his left with Roy next to Al and General Wainscot, Margaret and Admiral Beaumont directly opposite them. Tom reached for the pitcher and poured himself a glass of ice water.

"We've been anxiously awaiting your arrival. I understand you had a bit of difficulty on your trip to Idaho. Why don't you brief us on it?" began George.

Taking a long sip on his glass and then placing it in front of him, Tom glanced around the room. "I wanted to enlist the aid of Captain Hunslinger, here, to command NUMSUB. In my opinion, Al's the best sub commander in the fleet. I knew him at Annapolis and have followed his career since. You won't find a better man in the Navy."

Tom paused to emphasize the point.

Admiral Beaumont interjected, "I can vouch for that. Al is one of our best officers."

"When I heard he was on leave at his parent's farm in Idaho, I went out to talk over the mission with him. Naturally, he's more than willing to come aboard."

Each head around the table nodded approval.

"Knowing the NWO would be watching everything I do, I felt we needed to get away from the farm to find some privacy. I was wrong. Apparently, they tracked me down through a rental vehicle and assigned a hit squad to conduct an assassination."

"We knew they'd located you when we intercepted your demographic data being transmitted to the NWO," explained George. "However, we had no idea they were going to resort to violence. We had no forewarning of that."

Tom reviewed the details of their experience in the panhandle with Al adding a comment here and there. Al ended with a simple explanation of the outcome. "We're fortunate Tom has talents other than jockeying research submarines through dangerous waters. He's quite the marksman. One shot with a 30-30 and he took out a rocket launcher, two assassins and a Hummer."

"I'll bet there will be sleepless nights for some NWO intelligence officer. They're not quite as forgiving as we are," said Roy.

George broke in. "Let's look at the plans you've come up with. Do you have your teams identified?"

"Yes. Al has identified his XO and the fifteen crewmen he wants to run NUMSUB. He'll go over their names with Admiral Beaumont. I have the team I want to put together. They're on this list. I've worked with them all in the past and as far as I'm concerned, they're the best in their league."

Tom passed the list of names around the room. It had the words "TOP SECRET" handwritten in bold letters across the top and contained the names of the following individuals.

Lieutenant Pete Wilson, USN, Navy SEALS

Lieutenant Robin Buckner, USN, Navy SEALS

Lieutenant Mark Ganon, USN,

Lieutenant Marne Armstrong, USN,

"With myself and Jorge Rojas, these four will round out my team of six. Lieutenants Armstrong and Ganon will team together and

Lieutenants Wilson and Buckner will make up another team. Their duties and responsibilities will be redundant to cover all contingencies. Wilson and Buckner will make up the "A" team with Armstrong and Ganon as their backups. They should all be relieved of their current assignments immediately and brought to Montreal for briefing within forty-eight hours. They'll need no explanation until they arrive; they're all used to changes in plans. Does anyone see any problems?"

Secretary Warnick responded, "Dirk, you can handle the details I trust."

"I'm not sure where they're all located off the top of my head, but I'm familiar with them. You've certainly picked the best. They'll all be here the day after tomorrow," responded Admiral Beaumont.

"Good, that's settled. We have some new developments identified by our satellites. Margaret, do you want to brief the rest of the staff now?"

"Certainly."

Chapter 15
New Dangers

Margaret moved to the wall and opened the doors covering the monitors. She flipped on the console. One of the large screens flickered and lit up. She keyed in a few commands and an aerial picture came into focus. It was a military rocket launch facility.

"This is live surveillance of the space facility at Hangzhou Base. We moved one of our satellites into a stationary orbit over the base. We've been keeping constant observation both day and night. As you can see, it's still night over there. We're monitoring the activity by high resolution, low light photography. Let me focus in on this section for a better look."

The activity on the screen showed movement of vehicles and personnel. She moved her fingers across the screen and flicked up the magnification. The screen quickly enlarged an area of activity near a new building.

"What do you gentlemen see here?" she asked.

Everyone leaned closer to the monitor to get a better look at the image.

"I see a building," said General Wainscot, leaning back in his chair. "What are we supposed to see?"

"Look closer. Concentrate on the relationship to the launch control center building and the rocket launch pad." She used a small laser pointer to outline the objects she had just mentioned.

"It looks like a duplicate of the control center in size and distance from the pad," said Al.

"Exactly. We were curious because none of their other launch sites have anything like it. I asked Roy if any of his people had any information. Tell us what you found out, Roy."

"Our mole at the facility says they're taking no chances on a malfunction. They're building a duplicate control center to run parallel with the first. Each center's computer will double-check the other to assure any problems are corrected. If one develops a malfunction, the other will take over."

"Wow! What does that do to our plans to create a malfunction?" asked Tom.

"Basically, it makes the job much more difficult."

"Do we replace circuit boards in both locations?"

"I'm afraid not. The security database for the second control center has identification for only the technicians assigned at the time of launch. No one else will be allowed in. Even with your demographics in the database, you couldn't get access."

"You must have thought this through before you brought it up. I've never known FIA to bring up a problem without a solution. What do you have up your sleeve?"

"You know FIA better than I thought, Tom. Jorge will have to program the circuit board to send a self-destruct command to the onboard computer while at the same time masking the command from the backup system."

"You make it sound simple. My guess is that it's not."

"You guessed right. Programming that level of complexity into a simple chip on a small circuit board might be more than either he or the chip can handle."

"What kind of odds are we talking about? What are the chances he can do it?"

"Right now, I'd guess about 60-40."

"And what happens if it doesn't work? Will the self-destruct sequence be aborted?"

"Yes. In that event we'll have to blow our cover."

"What do you mean 'blow our cover'?" asked Al.

"For a backup, NUMSUB will carry two Diamondback water-to-air missiles capable of overtaking the launch vehicle and destroying it. They're to be used only in the event you are unable to carry out the mission as originally developed."

"Not only will that blow our secrecy, it will leave NUMSUB exposed deep inside the base. Our chances of escape, without the benefit of surprise, drastically diminish," observed Tom. "If that's the case, why not simply sit outside the installation and launch a few missiles from offshore? I can see why we couldn't launch from any distance or from a higher altitude without alerting their ground to air defenses. But a low level attack from a short distance wouldn't give them time to react. Seems to me that would be much simpler and a lot less risky."

"Let me show you why that won't work." It was Margaret who spoke. She adjusted the satellite view of Hangzhou Base and moved the visual display to the perimeter of the base. Directing the cursor to one of several small buildings ringing the installation, she enlarged the view to show details. The building was apparently made of thick concrete walls with a dish antenna on the roof. The only opening was a slit in the side about a foot high and four feet wide.

"This is one of a hundred and sixty new defensive devices built around Hangzhou Base in the past six months. They're spaced about a quarter of a mile apart. At first we were baffled. The secrecy was so tight not even our deepest mole could find out anything about them. This made us even more curious. Apparently, we were dealing with something more sophisticated than a simple anti-aircraft defensive system."

"Apparently," echoed Tom. "Why would you need a hundred sixty of them if they were merely for air defense?"

"Exactly. It took us a couple of months to break the silence, but we finally found out what they are. They're an interconnected anti-missile laser defense system. Each bunker contains a high-energy laser generator that can take out an incoming missile."

"Anti-missile lasers. Sounds a little like the defunct Star Wars defensive system the United States tried to get off the ground seventy or eighty some years ago but could never get congressional funding for it."

"That's pretty close, Tom. There are similarities, more in concept than design. A low flying missile, even at subsonic speed, originating from a nearby source would be difficult to identify, track and lock onto. A single laser would be trying to hit a target in a rapidly changing two-dimensional sight picture. The chances of a miss, regardless of how low, are unacceptable considering the consequences."

"Right, all it would take is for one to get through. Apparently, they've overcome that obstacle."

"They have. The proximity of the laser bunkers allows multiple locks onto the same target. Each bunker contains a computer controlled guiding system that is interconnected to the bunker to either side of it. They act in tandem, like they were a pair of eyes. Now you have a three-dimensional sight picture with from two to four lasers aiming at the same target. Together they make an impenetrable barrier. The chance of a missile penetrating that defensive network is close to zero. Now the odds of failure shift to our side, and those consequences are unacceptable to us."

"Do you see why we had to put you inside the installation?" asked George.

"Yes," answered Tom. "We can't take them from outside the installation, so we have to get inside the laser ring."

"Correct. And another reason for the secrecy, the attempt to create an "accidental" malfunction, is to allow you to escape undetected. However, that failing, the risk to the world is too great to take the chance. We had to consider a backup plan."

"A backup plan that lifts the shroud of secrecy?"

"Unfortunately, there's no other way. Once inside the installation, the mission must be successful at any cost."

"Even if it means sacrificing NUMSUB and her crew." Tom stated.

"That would mean NUMSUB could possibly fall into enemy hands," said General Wainscot. "Wouldn't that be just as bad, letting them have the technology?"

"No, there's a contingency for that," answered Tom. "NUMSUB is designed with its own self-destruct capability. As long as the crew hasn't been incapacitated, NUMSUB will obey the commands of the captain. If the crew is incapacitated she'll take over control and bring herself back. If she's trapped, for example, in the bay with the sub gates closed, and can't escape, she's been designed to destroy herself. There wouldn't be enough left for the NWO to build a row boat."

"Are you saying she's a floating explosion waiting to happen? What about an accidental self-destruction? How would you make certain that all of her critical components are destroyed?"

"There's redundancy built into the back up computer to prevent an accident. The sequence begins in the nuclear reactor. The program would create a massive melt down, turning the equipment and many of the systems into unrecognizable hunks of metal. The interior would burn in a fire so hot that the superstructure would melt. The job would finish with a high explosive detonation that would destroy the computers and the remaining systems."

"Sounds like you've covered everything," added Roy.

"I think the men and women in the crew need to know that going in. The choice whether to begin the assignment has to be made with complete knowledge of the risk. Only those willing to take the risk should be asked to go."

"Our sentiments exactly, Tom," said George. "That same decision has to be made by the two of you. Now that you both know the potential and the possibilities, what are your choices?

Tom and Al exchanged glances. The unspoken communication between the two friends was clearly evident on their faces. Neither had to ask the other what they felt.

"Are the odds insurmountable?" Tom's question was directed at Al.

"Nobody told me they are," answered Al.

"We're in," said Tom.

"Good. Let's get those teams together for orientation. We'll start at 0800 hours the day after tomorrow. We've all got jobs to do. Let's get on it. Any questions?"

Chapter 16

Choose Your Team

Monday morning, 0748 hours.   The briefing room in the Secretariat was down a long corridor from George Warnick's office. The room was plain, with white walls and a tile floor. There were thirty classroom chairs arranged in five rows facing the front. The front of the room contained a whiteboard and two large flat video monitors built into the wall. One of the monitors displayed a map of the world and the other was on, but had no image. There were eight chairs to the left of the monitors facing the classroom. A small podium was set up on the right.

Twenty men and women were assembled in the room. Everyone wore the same white shirts and trousers.

The conversations were marked with excitement. Old friends and acquaintances exchanged handshakes and greetings. Many of them had served together on other missions. They were anxious to find out what brought them together today.

"What about these white duds?"

"I thought I could hear myself talking in the changing room."

"Hey! Bob! Where you been keeping yourself?"

"It's good to see you Marne. What do you think O'Donnell has up his sleeves?"

"I don't know, Mark. I heard some buzz about a top-secret mission and a top-secret weapons system.   Something about the Himalayas. That's all I could find out. Security around this is tighter than I've ever seen before."

Of the twenty military personnel from the Navy, sixteen were highly skilled submariners. The other four were specialized in various aspects of counter intelligence and anti-terrorism.

"Himalayas? Everybody here is Navy and most of these guys are submariners. I have a sneaky suspicion that this has nothing to do with mountains."

Suddenly, a brisk command from somewhere in the room.

"Ten-hut! Officer on deck."

Instantly the hubbub gave way to the staccato sound of heels clicking together that signaled twenty people coming to rigid attention.

Secretary Warnick quickly strode to the front of the room followed by Admiral Beaumont, Captain Hunslinger, Commander

O'Donnell, Roy Constance and Margaret Cranston. All except Warnick were wearing white.

George stepped to the podium. "At ease. Please take your seats."

Everyone quickly relaxed and took a seat. Their attention was focused on the Secretary.

"Ladies and gentlemen, I'd like to get directly to the point. We're assembled here because of a grave global situation. We have a mission to accomplish that will require the utmost secrecy and highest level of risk. You have all been hand picked because of the skills you possess and your potential value to the mission."

He paused briefly and observed the expressions on each face. They looked like they had expected him to say that. Some leaned forward to hear what he would say next. These were unique individuals. They were used to danger and risk and accepted it as matter-of-factly as though they were being briefed about the opposing team before a baseball game.

"Let me introduce those assembled at the front of the room before I relinquish the podium. You all know Admiral Beaumont. Captain Hunslinger and Commander O'Donnell will give you the details of the assignment. Seated next to them are Roy Constance, Vice Chairman of the FIA, and Margaret Cranston, Director of Space Surveillance."

As each was introduced, they turned to the assembly and nodded. Twenty pairs of eyes followed George's introduction from person to person.

"Tom. The floor's yours."

Tom stood and approached the podium.

"Thank you all for accepting the invitation to come here on such short notice. Naturally, we were unable to advise you of either the nature of the assignment or the reason for your selection. Al and I selected you because you represent the very best in your field. I could go on with superlatives, but that would serve only to swell your heads. After all, much of what we'll do will take place under water. The ability to walk on water could seriously jeopardize the mission."

A round of laughter relaxed the atmosphere.

"Suffice it to say we have a mission to accomplish and you will be instrumental to its success.

"First, though, before I disclose the nature of the assignment I must advise you of the dangers and risks. You have to choose whether you can accept them. We know that some of you have families and you must consider them in your decision. You will be given the opportunity to pass on this assignment and if you choose to do so, no one will hold it against you. You'll simply be asked to leave before we disclose the nature of the mission.

"If you commit, you'll be held to the strictest confidence and will be removed from society until the mission is over. This mission will be completed in approximately three and one-half months, during which time you will have no contact with your families and friends.

"The assignment is such that the continued safety of the free world will rest on its successful conclusion. Failure will bring the greatest potential for worldwide domination by an evil power in the history of mankind. Success will mean simply that we will have delayed that conquest to be fought again another day. If we succeed, no one, save a small number outside this room, will ever know what you did. There will be no parades, no returning in glory. You'll have only the self-satisfaction of a job well done in a world that will never know how grateful they are to you.

"You will risk your lives on this mission. I can't tell you exactly what the degree of risk is because it depends on too many factors. If the mission goes as planned, the risk is low. However, if anything goes wrong, and there are many elements that could, the chances we will not survive may be as high as 90 percent."

A hand went up in the back of the room. Tom acknowledged it.

"Yes, Lieutenant Ganon. You have a question."

Lieutenant Mark Ganon stood. "Yes, Sir. So what you're telling us is that if we fail, the NWO will rule the free world, and if we succeed, the free world remains the free world."

"That's correct, Mark"

"Well, let's say we fail and come home, assuming there is a home to come to. What happens to us in this room?"

"You are all highly trained and loyal to the AWF. I would assume that if you are captured you would be executed as a danger to the NWO."

"So, if we fail, we're a hundred percent dead and if we succeed, worst case is .. say …. 90 percent, and the odds get better from there?"

"That's one way to look at it."

With a shrug of his shoulders and a look of confidence around the room, the hint of a smile on his face, he sat down. "No further questions, Sir."

"Does anyone else have any questions?"

Tom looked around the room. Each face showed signs of deep consideration. A few traded glances, each individual looked around at those with whom they had risked their lives before. They exchanged nods. This was not a group of strangers. They had trusted each other with their lives. They had chosen their profession for a variety of reasons. There was a bond of loyalty and patriotism exceeded nowhere in the free world.

All eyes were back on Tom. The expression on each face was that of confidence and determination.

"If there are no further questions from the group, I have to ask, does anyone wish to withdraw from participation? If you do, you may stand and exit the room."

Tom again looked around the room; the only movements were a few leaning back and folding their arms to punctuate decisions to commit to the assignment. No one was going anywhere.

"Thank you. We are proud to serve with you. I'll now advise you of the nature of the assignment.

"I assume that everyone in the room is familiar with the NWO's HORS satellite surveillance system. Is there anyone who is not?"

He looked about the room. No one raised a hand. He continued.

"HORS was originally designed to provide a defensive system for their three main military installations. Failure to launch two of the four satellites put a damper on the system's effectiveness. We wondered why they have never attempted to replace the two satellites lost during launch. We believe we have discovered the reason."

The room remained silent.

"The NWO has developed a new, more dangerous system named HORS II. A series of thirteen satellites will ring the earth with the ability to see through solid concrete and disrupt all electronic systems. They intend to launch HORS II from Hangzhou Base located on the northeast coast of China."

He turned to the monitor with the map of the world. Quickly the image of the earth rotated until China was centered on the screen and highlighted. The map focused in on the northeast coast. The map focused until the Hangzhou Bay filled the screen. Shortly Hangzhou Base was clearly visible.

"If HORS II is successfully launched, no movement in the free world will go undetected. It will be as though the NWO had a camera in every governmental and military briefing room in the world. There will be no secrets from them. It will also be capable of penetration and control of all electronic systems. They will control banking, telephonic, transportation and all other systems.

"Does anyone doubt the necessity to destroy HORS II before it gets off the ground?"

A seaman's hand went up. "Why don't we just take it out with one of our missiles?"

"A good question, sailor. One I had myself. Hangzhou Base has a new laser defense system that will make any attempt at a missile attack useless." Tom clicked the screen controls again and the image of the laser defense system became visible. "This new system will destroy any missile attempt from any direction. We have to penetrate this perimeter and attack from the inside."

Another hand went up. "How do we get inside? The security systems surrounding the main installations make them nearly impenetrable."

"We're going in with a new, secret submarine. One you have never seen before and perhaps never even dreamed could exist."

Tom continued the briefing for approximately an hour, describing every detail of the Dogfish program and the mission. At the end of the briefing, he asked, "Are there any more questions?"

"Just one, Sir. When do we get started?"

"Immediately. We will take a short break and assemble back here at ten hundred hours in two groups. The members of my team and I will meet in the room across the hall. The only civilian on the team, Jorge Rojas, will join us. We'll go over the details of the mission and each person's assignments. The sub crew will meet in this room with Captain Hunslinger for a briefing on the logistics of the installation.

"Upon completion of the briefings, you will have twenty-four hours to put your affairs in order for the next three and a half months. You will then be taken to the secret research facility we call Dogfish Base, where you will spend the next three months in intensive training for the mission on board the submarine. Submariners will train under Al and the staff at the facility. My team will train with me. We will exercise every possible scenario that might take place once we've penetrated the installation.

"If there are no other questions, let's take a break. Be back here at 1000 hours. The restrooms are down the hall; refreshments are in the next room."

Chapter 17

Commitment

At precisely 1000 hours Tom entered the smaller briefing room. The room was similar to the one they met in earlier except for the size. Each man and woman was already seated and ready to begin; no stragglers in this group. Tom passed out a red three-ring binder with the words "DOGFISH PROJECT - TOP SECRET" printed in large black letters across the diagonal. No one opened a binder until instructed to do so.

"Before we get started, I'd like to introduce the person responsible for cracking the security code in the NWO main computer at Hangzhou Base. He's also the one who designed the program that will create a false malfunction in the launch vehicle and cause the system to self-destruct. This is Jorge Rojas. Jorge, would you like to say anything?"

Jorge was a handsome man, approximately five feet four inches tall. He appeared to be in his mid thirties. He had jet black hair and a mustache of the same color. His dark eyes and medium brown skin accented his Hispanic features. He approached the podium beside Tom.

"Just that I'm honored to be here among such an elite group of men and women. I'm proud to be a part of the mission." He returned to his seat.

"Truly a man of few words," remarked Tom.

"In front of you is the culmination of eighteen months of hard work. The contents are so highly classified that, outside of the personnel assigned to the project, not more than a handful of highly placed government and military personnel are even aware the project exists. What you are about to see is the existence of a weapons system so highly evolved that it doesn't even exist in the science books.

"When you review each page, you will initial the bottom right hand corner and the person to your immediate left will also initial to witness yours. When you leave here today, you will return the binders and they will be locked in a vault at an undisclosed location in the Secretariat."

He pressed a button on the podium and a cover on the wall retracted to reveal a large screen. "I'll project visuals on the monitor while you follow in the binders. If you have any questions during the presentation, feel free to interrupt. Are there any questions before we start?"

No hands were raised.

Tom clicked on the monitor and an image of NUMSUB appeared. He would spend the next two hours going over the sub's capabilities. A similar scene played out in the room across the hall where Al familiarized his crew with more detail about some of the sub's standard operating systems. He was unable to go into detail on the unique capabilities of NUMSUB's new systems.

At noon both teams broke for lunch and reassembled at 1300 hours. The instructions diverged. Tom reviewed the tasks his team would face and Al briefed his crew on the defenses at Hangzhou Base.

Tom began the afternoon with an aerial photo of the installation, which he enlarged to focus on the headquarters complex.

"Jorge will disembark the sub at one of these docks, navigate himself around this guard tower and enter the accounting building at this point." He traced the route with a laser pointer.

"Once we arrive at the park about a mile and a half from the space facility, Robin and Pete will be responsible for obtaining a vehicle from the motor pool at this point. Jorge and I will use the vehicle to drive to the security gate. We'll be less suspicious if we arrive in a vehicle rather than on foot. Several hundred personnel will pass through the checkpoint during the shift change so we should be relatively inconspicuous.

"Once inside, Jorge will place a computer circuit board in spare parts to be used when the main computer detects a false malfunction in its circuitry. When the malfunction occurs, an engineer will replace the circuit with the spare we supply. A chip on the spare circuit is programmed to cause the rocket to self-destruct on launch."

The briefing continued for the rest of the day. Each detail of the installation and the tasks to be accomplished were reviewed. Questions were asked and details were repeated. At the end of the day the binders were collected.

Aboard the *Lone Wolf*, Sturgaard Ivanovich had heard the radio report from NWO agents assigned to the AWF Central Command Headquarters in Montreal. The news was not good.

Commander O'Donnell and Captain Hunslinger were seen entering the Secretariat earlier that morning. That confirmed his suspicions that Bonslick and Morgan had failed. It also meant that since no one had heard from the two assassins, there was a high possibility that they may have met the fate they were supposed to have inflicted on the two AWF naval officers.

Ivanovich was concerned. His orders came directly from the High Command. They would not be happy. He had to redeem himself in the eyes of his superiors or he would lose his commission and be banished to an insignificant desk job in a remote outpost.

He sent a coded message over a secure satellite connection to the High Command headquarters, "Aware that guests failed to dine.

Waiters dropped the entrée. Table has been reset. Dinner will be served before celebration." NWO intelligence knew that AWF intelligence was as adept at cracking codes as their own agents were. Most codes were good for no longer than a couple of weeks at the most.

The message was scrambled aboard the *Lone Wolf* and sent to a communications satellite in a fixed orbit above the Pacific. The satellite scrambled it again and relayed it to a second satellite in a stationary orbit above NWO territory. The message was then relayed to the High Command headquarters where it was received and descrambled. A radio operator handed it to an intelligence officer. Since the message was not labeled "Urgent," he did not deliver it immediately to the Chairman. Instead he added it to the agenda for the next High Command meeting the following day.

The news that Morgan and Bonslick blew the operation swept through the High Command. Ivanovich's reputation and past performance bought him time. He was to coordinate the surveillance of O'Donnell and Hunslinger and report on their activities. He would remain aboard the *Lone Wolf*. If the two men dropped out of sight he was to search until he found them. He was unaware that they were about to disappear for the next three and a half months.

"O'Donnell and Hunslinger have been in and out of the Secretariat in Montreal for the past three days now," Ivanovich observed to Captain Porknoi, commander of the *Lone Wolf*.

Porknoi simply listened, completely uninterested in the details of the surveillance. He was bored to death with intelligence activities. He was a submarine combat veteran. His ship was an attack submarine. He would rather be following AWF surface maneuvers while playing hide and seek with their warships and sub chasers. This activity of making five hundred mile diameter circles in the Pacific while Ivanovich played spy was driving him crazy. Every time a ship passed by he wanted to pop up to periscope depth, catch it in his sights and sink it with an imaginary torpedo.

Ivanovich droned on. "There has been much activity at the Secretariat. At least fifty naval officers and seamen have been there at the same time. The AWF probably knows that we have noticed. I imagine the activity is related to O'Donnell. We're not taking chances. We'll have agents assigned to watch them to see if there is any coordinated effort involved."

At the Secretariat, O'Donnell wrapped up his presentation.

"Gentlemen, and ladies, you are now to take care of your affairs. We will meet back here the day after tomorrow at 0600. You will be assigned military air transportation to Dogfish Base. You and the crew under Captain Hunslinger's command will go to the air base in groups of two or three at various times during the day. Your planes will depart at irregular intervals and will fly to several different military installations in the U.S., Canada and South America. All of you will change planes during your trips.

"We have provided for the possibility that the NWO will be watching your departure with a degree of interest. We're relatively certain that they'll notice so many new faces at the Secretariat at the same time. To add to the confusion, we have an additional thirty personnel waiting in a classroom down the hall. They're not involved in the mission, though their travel plans are similar to yours. They'll also be leaving at irregular intervals for various destinations. The one significant difference will be that their final destination is not Dogfish Base. Most of them, however, will be taking differing routes to a half dozen destinations on the East and West coasts.

"When you leave this secure facility, you are not to discuss the mission or refer to it in any manner, not even with each other. Total silence by each and every one of you is the only way we can be sure that there will be no leaks. The NWO are sure to do everything they can to find out what we're up to. It will drive them nuts until they find something out about the operation. Watch your backs; getting to Dogfish could be a hazardous trip for those who aren't careful. Are there any questions?"

A hand went up. "Lieutenant Armstrong, you have a question?"

"Will the NWO resort to violence on AWF soil?"

"It's been relatively rare. However, they made an attempt on Al's and my life last week in Idaho. Our intelligence reports that they have increased hostile activities against our foreign operatives in the past few months. Three agents were car bombed in Madrid in July and two more were trapped in a hotel fire of suspicious origin last month in Tokyo. We believe this escalation in violence is related to the activities surrounding HORS II."

"What should we expect while making our way to Dogfish Base?"

"You'll travel in relatively secure surroundings. However, be on the lookout for any kind of suspicious activity. Watch for strangers who may be following you. If you see the same strange face twice in an hour, consider him or her to be a tail.

"Any other questions?"

Another hand in the back. Tom pointed to the raised hand, "Pete."

"Yes, Sir. Will we be doing all of our training at Dogfish Base?"

"During the first few weeks you'll become familiar with the operation of NUMSUB. At that point we'll go to a secure training facility where we've built a replica of some of the key sites at Hangzhou Base. By the time we're finished you'll be so familiar with the installation you'll think it was your permanent duty assignment. You'll spend two months training there, and then return to Dogfish for the final few weeks to coordinate with Captain Hunslinger's crew.

"Are there any other questions?"

No hands.

"Within the next several days we'll all be at Dogfish Base, where you'll receive your dormitory assignments. You'll have a few days to relax and become familiar with the facility. Beginning early next Wednesday morning you'll be on an intensive training schedule.

"See you at Dogfish. You are dismissed. As has been the practice the past couple of days, please go to the surface one or two at a time."

Pete Wilson grabed Robin Buckner's arm. "Robin, have you had a chance to look around down here. It's like a real city. I'm thinking about grabbing some dinner before leaving. I hear there's a great Italian place just up the street. Want to join me?"

"Sounds like a great idea. You buying?"

Chapter 18
Dogfish Base

With tremendous excitement, Al anticipated his first look at the mysterious submarine. Nicknamed NUMSUB, the vessel was like no other in the rest of the world's submarine fleets. Most submarines were classified into broad categories with similarities such as size, mode of power, function, etc. NUMSUB did not fit into any known class. It was the first of its kind and would create a class of its own.

All three of the vessels in the NUMSUB program were still designated experimental and had not been officially christened. Therefore, they did not have names associated with them. They were simply NUMSUB I, NUMSUB II, and NUMSUB III. NUMSUB III, the most advanced, was the one chosen for immediate service and would simply be known as NUMSUB during the operation.

The secret location of Dogfish Base was on the Pacific Coast seventy miles west of Portland, Oregon near Tillamook Bay. The site was ideal because of the relatively sparse population and the rugged cliffs and headlands that made up the shoreline. The Army Corps of Engineers had excavated a huge cavern and built a large underground complex into the cliffs accessible from underwater on the seaward side. Land access was through an old farm that stood immediately above the underground chamber. The farmhouse and barns concealed the security checkpoints and elevator shafts through which personnel and equipment entered the complex.

The facilities housed the three thousand men and women carefully chosen for their expertise, skill and ability to pass a rigorous background investigation. The secrecy shrouding the program rivaled any other in the history of military weapons development.

Tom and Al arrived early in the morning in an inconspicuous pickup truck. The truck looked like an ordinary farm vehicle, complete with rust, mud and old tools in the back. No entourage of security vehicles accompanied them and no conspicuous military uniforms provoked suspicion from the keen eyes of satellite surveillance. The two navy officers were dressed in coveralls, flannel shirts and farm boots. Tom wore a faded green baseball cap with the John Deere logo. They looked like they were reporting for a day of farm work.

The long driveway from the paved county road was covered with gravel. The tires picked up small rocks and pelted the inside of the fenders as Tom steered around potholes full of rainwater from the previous night's thunderstorm. The truck jostled and bounced alongside a barbwire fence surrounding a pasture with a herd of Holstein cows that had just been milked. The cows serenely chewed their cud. A few watched the truck with blank stares.

Past the end of the fence, they came to a large red shed. The doors were open and Al could see several pieces of farm equipment inside; balers, tractors and windrow machines were neatly lined up and put away for the winter. Most of the baling had been completed and the farm was settling in for the cold weather. A couple of farmhands busied themselves next to a tractor whose motor they had taken apart for repair.

On the left, near the end of a curve in the driveway stood a large, two-story white farmhouse with green shutters and smoke billowing lazily out of the chimney. The house was nearly surrounded by tall Douglas fir trees that provided a break against the frequent winter winds.

Opposite the farmhouse, a large barn occupied a prominent position among several other outbuildings.

The scene reminded Al of the farms around Grangeville.

Tom parked the pickup between the barn and a tool shed. They stepped out of the vehicle and entered the barn.

A few minutes later, two men of similar build, dressed in similar clothing left the barn. One mounted a tractor hooked to a baler and headed for one of the last fields of mown hay waiting to be baled and stacked. The other picked up a pitchfork and began feeding a half dozen head of cattle in a holding pen.

The inside of the barn looked much like any other Al had seen back home in Idaho. They approached what appeared to be a tool room. A farmhand dressed in familiar coveralls, seated by the door, abruptly rose and greeted the two officers with an outstretched hand.

"Good morning, Commander. Good to see you again, Sir. How was that leave?"

"Very good, Corporal, and much needed. I see nothing has changed around here."

"No, Sir. Everything's as it was when you left. Captain Fullerton is anxious to see you. I'll alert the Captain that you've arrived." The Marine guard eyed the visitor accompanying Commander O'Donnell and reached out his hand in the same gesture he had offered Tom. With a grin he greeted Al, "You must be Captain Hunslinger. We've heard much about you, Sir. Welcome to Dogfish Base."

"Thank you, Corporal?" Al looked at Tom and cocked his head quizzically, noticing the Marine guard's strange appearance and the digression from formal military protocol.

Noting the look, Tom explained, "We've dispensed with the usual military attire and protocol for security purposes. We don't want to give anyone an idea of what's going on here. But, don't worry, the security is tight. One hint of trouble from this Marine and he'd be joined by a hundred others who are doing farm chores nearby. Helicopters would rise out of haystacks and a platoon of highly trained forces would literally emerge out of the ground."

The Marine guard opened the door to the tool room revealing the same sophisticated security booth installed above Secretary Warnick's office at the Secretariat in Montreal. One at a time, Tom and Al entered the booth and cleared security. Behind the booth was a bank of elevator doors. Upon entering an elevator, Al noted that there were only two buttons on the wall. There were no markings on the buttons. Tom pressed the lower button and the elevator began its descent.

"Only need two buttons," remarked Tom. "One for down and the other for up. The elevator shaft is a little over five hundred feet deep. We'll be at the bottom in less than a minute. If your ears get plugged, just yawn and they'll pop." It wasn't necessary for Tom to remind Al how to clear his ears as the atmospheric pressure changed slightly with the rapid change in elevation. Nevertheless, it was small talk that paved the way for further discussion of the underground facilities.

"As I mentioned before, we have close to three thousand people in the program. All of their needs are met within the complex itself. In addition to residential facilities that would make a four star hotel blush, there's a commissary, a fully staffed infirmary, movie theaters, a library, chapels for religious services of various denominations, a small synagogue and mosque. The athletic and sports complex has a full complement of intramural programs.

At the bottom of the elevator shaft, the doors opened to reveal another security checkpoint. A female Marine sat behind a desk and greeted the two men. Al noticed a video monitor that showed the checkpoint on the surface. He hadn't seen the hidden camera. Apparently this marine had seen and heard them pass the booth topside.

"Good morning, Commander, Captain," she said nodding to the two men and motioning them to approach the security booth next to the desk.

"Good morning, Sergeant," replied Tom. "Al, I'd like you to meet Sergeant Jessi Granager. Jessi's been with the program since it started. She's responsible for base security. One of the best security specialists in the Program. I think she knows everyone down here by first name. Nothing gets by her team."

"Good to meet you, Sergeant," responded Al.

"Thank you, Sir. You're cleared to proceed."

Passing through the final checkpoint, Tom led Al through a door marked "Restricted Area, Authorized Personnel Only."

Al thought it was a little strange to have a restricted area inside one of the most secure facilities in the free world. He had a funny look on his face, so Tom explained, "Even in here there are places where the equipment is so sensitive that access has to be limited."

On the other side of the door they entered a well-lighted control room that was a hive of activity. Neat rows of consoles made parallel lines through the room. At each console was a technician busily working at his or her station. The constant murmur of quiet conversations filled the room. At the far side was a large bank of Plexiglas windows angling forward to allow an unobstructed view of the activity below.

When they entered the room a tall, attractive woman in a white lab coat looked up from her discussion with one of the technicians working one of the consoles.

"Tom!" she exclaimed, striding quickly toward them. It took Al about two seconds to take in her features from head to toe with the eye of an experienced male observer. About five ten, blue-green eyes, blonde hair just over shoulder length, weighing in at perhaps 130, even the lab coat couldn't hide ample curves in the right places, well-turned ankles that rose to calves of a runway model.

"Good to see you're back," she said. "We've been perfecting some of the tools on NUMSUB and I wanted to go over them with you."

Tom turned to Al. "Al, I'd like you to meet Captain Monica Fullerton, USAF. Monica is responsible for the technical development of NUMSUB. She's quite an expert in her field, graduated magna cum laude from MIT with a Ph.D. in about everything they have to offer. I never could figure out why she chose a career in the Air Force over a civilian job that would pay her ten times her military salary."

"It's the benefits, dummy, the benefits," she said, coyly elbowing Tom gently in the ribs. "Where else but the military could I get an unlimited budget and play with the most technologically advanced toys in the world?" She smiled at Al and she squeezed his hand firmly.

Hmmm. About six feet, maybe six one. Nice build. Good looking features. Eyes to melt in.. Looks like a real hunk, she thinks to herself while greeting him. Al wasn't the only one in the room with the ability to inventory a person's assets with a skillful eye.

"Good to meet you, Captain. Tom tells me you're the Navy's best sub jockey and you're going to be the first to drive NUMSUB in live combat conditions."

"From what I hear, I wonder who'll actually be doing the driving, me or NUMSUB. Sounds like she has a mind of her own."

"She can return home on her own. She'll need you to get her out of the neighborhood. By the way, what neighborhood are you going to invade, if I may ask?"

"Sorry. We can't even tell you where we're going," said Tom. "The secrecy around this one matches that around Dogfish."

It didn't escape Al's observation that Monica stood a little closer to Tom than he would have expected from a fellow officer. She occasionally touched his arm gently during the conversation. The gesture could have been unconscious and without meaning, however Al sensed vibes that seemed to say otherwise. He imagined that working closely with such an attractive woman, in nearly isolated conditions, would create some degree of chemistry. *Funny how people get hormones and chemistry mixed up sometimes.*

Monica led Tom and Al to the windows. The console room was constructed high on the wall of a cavernous chamber carved out of the solid rock. The chamber appeared to be at least a quarter of a mile long and three hundred yards across. The ceiling of the chamber glowed with the yellow-white luminescence of an artificial lighting system that illuminated the entire area. The floor of the chamber buzzed with activity. Scientists and engineers moved about, engaged in a variety of tasks.

A hundred and fifty feet below the room in which they stood, the sea water gently lapped against three dry docks, each containing an unusual looking vessel. They resembled nothing Al had ever seen in his career with the Navy. The vessels looked more like the Nautilus of the 19th century Jules Verne novel "20,000 Leagues Under the Sea." They were completely out of the water, suspended within the dry docks in huge cradles.

They looked to be about half the length of a football field and about a third as wide giving them somewhat of a cumbersome shape. The sail was much abbreviated from those of traditional submarines. It resembled a dorsal fin, tapered on both ends and rounded in an arch at the center. Instead of the black of most underwater vessels, the color of these ships appeared to be a pale blue, almost translucent to the eye. One nearly had to look away to see it clearly. The color appeared to emanate from inside the sub, as though generated by some mysterious source or power.

There was minimal activity around two of the subs, but the third seemed to be the object of significant attention. The interior of the dry dock was brightly lit and several technicians were working on various sections of the hull.

Mounted at the stern was a single propeller, offset from and below the central plane of the vessel by at least fifteen feet. The oddly shaped stern tapered gracefully from the sail to end bluntly with an opening that appeared to be approximately six feet in diameter. A circular hydrofoil surrounded the opening. The tapered bow gave the vessel an overall shape not unlike that of an overweight swordfish without the sword. Faintly etched into the skin, both fore and aft were two sets of torpedo tube doors. Immediately behind the abbreviated sail were a series of parallel doors in the position one would expect to find missile launch tubes.

"Al, it's time for you to meet NUMSUB," commented Tom with obvious pride in his voice. "I'll let Monica describe her to you while we go down to take a cook's tour."

They all returned to the rear of the console room and entered another elevator. The elevator had glass doors and sides. When it cleared the floor of the control room, Al was surprised to see there was no shaft. The car was attached to a track on the wall behind it. The glass doors and sides allowed a complete panoramic view of the chamber. While they descended to the dry dock level, Monica described the sub in more detail.

"NUMSUB will be operated by your crew of seventeen. It has room for up to eight additional passengers. In this case those passengers will consist of Tom and his team of experts. Its dimensions measure a mere 140 feet long by 51 feet at the beam. The odd shape is due to the newly

93

developed and highly secret propulsion system, which we'll discuss later when we examine the propulsion room."

"It carries fourteen of the Navy's most advanced torpedoes. Hidden beneath retractable doors on the deck are forward and aft facing Gattling guns which can fire 6,000 50-caliber rounds per minute at incoming aircraft or missiles. Each gun is aimed by a computer controlled radar system that can knock the whiskers off of a fly at five thousand yards."

"Seven nuclear warhead tipped missiles can be launched on the surface or from a depth of 1,500 feet. The missiles have a range of 750 miles and the multiple warheads can strike four targets each. The warheads are smaller, yet punch more power than those five times their size. The range is significantly less than those carried by conventional boomers because of space limitations. They contain less propellant to fit in the smaller space. However, because NUMSUB is capable of approaching closer to enemy territory without being detected, range is not an issue."

Nearing the level of the submarines, Al began to feel a sense of excitement rise within his throat. He was about to examine close up one of the most sophisticated weapons systems in the world. *Not everyone gets to do this.*

Chapter 19
NUMSUB

Al remained silent throughout Monica's narrative, he listened intently, his eyes fixed on the vessel through the glass walls of the elevator. Upon reaching the lower level, they exited the elevator and walked across scaffolding to the dry dock. There they entered an enclosed walkway that led to the sub's main entry hatch. Al stepped out of the walkway and onto NUMSUB. When his foot touched the surface of the vessel, he noted that the translucent glow did indeed come from within the hull. The skin felt oddly flexible under his foot, not the rigid metallic characteristic that he expected. He knelt down and ran his hand over the surface. The texture was much like soft leather.

"What you are feeling is a new poly-bonded alloy of five different metals and plastics," explained Monica. "Five years ago, this material didn't even exist in computer models. It was discovered quite by accident in a chemistry lab at a major private university in Utah. A lab assistant was helping a professor with research for a material to make snow skis. They wanted something that would combine the strength of plastic with the cold endurance of metal. They created a compound that exhibited the desired characteristics, but wouldn't stay rigid and kept changing shape. They tossed it in the trash at the end of the day. When they returned the next morning the material had molded itself to the surface of the trash can and was nearly indistinguishable from the container.

"With a little more research, the material was refined to change shape on command. It was married to a computer and viola! We have NUMSUB's skin. It can assume the physical characteristics of its surroundings. We call it a morphing process. The hull can change color and shape to make it blend in perfectly. Should it come to rest on sand it could be made to look like a sandbar. Put it on a coral reef and it will assume the shape and color of an outcropping of coral."

"No kidding? This stuff can actually change shape? That's amazing."

"Before we go below, let's walk the hull." Monica led them to the bow.

"The bow is tapered sharply to provide a smooth contour to slip easily through the water. While under conventional nuclear power, she can attain a top speed of 42 knots submerged. She's not the fastest sub in the fleet but she'll outrun most. When we switch over to hydraulic power, she'll run circles around anything either we or the NWO has at sea."

"Tom told me a little about the hydraulic propulsion system. I understand she'll do 60 knots," interjected Al.

"That's about as fast as we've taken her. We believe she's capable of more with a few modifications we're working on. Did you see those two oval doors about six feet back of the tip of the bow?"

Al nodded the affirmative. The doors were approximately eight feet long and six feet wide. The seam they formed with the hull was nearly invisible.

"When we go to hydraulic propulsion, they open to suck in seawater, which serves two purposes. It reduces resistance by reducing the amount of water the hull has to push out of the way and it assists forward thrust by sucking water into the system. Let me give you a quick and dirty sketch of how the system operates."

She pulled out her pen and flipped the top piece of paper on her clipboard over to the blank side and began to sketch the hydraulic propulsion system. First she drew the outline of the hull. Running parallel through the center of the ship were two elongated chambers, each roughly a quarter of the sub's width at its beam. The chambers tapered rapidly to join together at the blunt end of the tail.

From the two forward openings in the hull she drew tubes that ran parallel to the chambers and connected to the bottom of each. In the right chamber she drew a piston positioned near the bottom of the chamber with directional arrows indicating that the piston was moving aft. In the left chamber she drew another piston near the top of the chamber with arrows indicating movement toward the bow.

"This is rough but it'll give you a good idea of how it works. Do you know what happens when you fill a balloon with air and then let go of it?"

"Sure, it takes off around the room," responded Al.

"Why?"

"Because the pressure inside the balloon is equal on all walls. When the air can escape through the opening, the pressure on the other side of the balloon propels it forward. Simple physics."

"That's exactly how the hydraulics works. The piston draws back and water is sucked into the chamber through the tubes. Once the chamber is full of water, the piston reverses creating tremendous pressure on the water, forcing it out the aft end of the sub, creating forward motion just like that balloon.

"While the right piston forces the water out of the right chamber, the left piston retracts, pulling water in from the front and refilling the left chamber. Working together and alternating, they create a smooth forward motion that is literally silent."

"When the piston pushes the water out, what prevents the build up of a vacuum behind it that creates negative pressure and reduces efficiency?" asked Al, rubbing his chin.

"I see you know your physics, Captain. I didn't draw it, but there's a tube that connects the top of each chamber. Behind each piston is a column of pressurized air. As one piston retracts, the air is forced over into the adjacent chamber behind the other piston, eliminating the vacuum." She quickly sketches in the necessary connecting tube.

"At each point where intake and exit tubes join, we've installed baffles which open when water is being sucked in and close when water is forced out. We have a very simple and very efficient propulsion system."

"What powers the pistons?"

"The same oil hydraulic system that raises and lowers the lift at the garage where you take your automobile to be serviced. An electric motor moves the oil behind each piston. Because the volume of water in the chamber is being forced out through a relatively small opening in the stern, the pistons don't have to move very rapidly."

"That's absolutely amazing. Why didn't someone think of it sooner? This principle has been around for centuries."

"Who knows?" responded Tom. "Sometimes people think technological advances are only achieved by new theories. We step over the answer to create the question."

"Let's move on back, behind the sail." Monica turned and walked away from the bow and the two men followed obediently.

Directly behind the sail, they walked between two rows of parallel doors a little larger than manhole covers.

"These are the missile launch doors. Nothing particularly exciting here except that you may notice the rather small size and wide spacing. As I mentioned before, the missiles are small compared to those carried by conventional boomers. We sacrificed distance for space in order to accommodate sufficient firepower. We're not really trying to make NUMSUB a substitute for our fleet of ballistic missile submarines, just a supplement to them."

Moving toward the stern, the three approached the circular hydrofoil that surrounded the aft opening of the hydraulic propulsion system.

"The hydrofoil provides sound deadening and rudder assistance. When the water is forced through the opening it creates a slight whooshing sound that could be picked up by listening sonar, if they knew what to listen for. The hydrofoil acts like a silencer, blocking and reversing any sound. It also assists steering. By rotating it right or left, up or down, it forces the water coming out to change direction, thus turning or raising or lowering the sub. Remember your vector physics from undergraduate school?"

Both men nodded. Al was obviously impressed with the simplicity of the design. He could only imagine how the vessel would perform. He knew he would soon have the opportunity to find out.

"Let's drop through the forward hatch and take a look around. Tom, you go first," instructed Monica.

Slipping through the hatch one at a time, they entered the control room directly beneath the sail. The room was approximately twenty-five feet wide by twenty feet long. Its size was deceptive because every spare inch was crammed with electronic equipment. Technicians were seated at each of four stations. Each wore headphones and was intently focused on the monitors and banks of indicator lights arrayed in front of him. Hands skillfully moved across the keyboards and switches, quietly testing the sub's systems.

Near the center of the room was a large plate of clear acrylic mounted perpendicular to the floor. It measured eight by eight feet. A topographic map of the coast of Oregon was clearly outlined down the center. A few green, yellow, white and blue dots gradually moved across it in various directions and speeds. The yellow and white dots moved much faster. At the center of the map was a green square about a half an inch on each side. Al moved toward the map to get a closer look.

"This is DEFSIM, a Digitally Enhanced Flat-Screen Imaging Map. It was recently developed for the Navy's newest ships. The location of NUMSUB will always be the green square directly in the center. As the sub moves about the surface of the earth, the map will move with it, always staying centered on NUMSUB. The operator can change the scale of the map to show detail in a radius as close as a few hundred yards to more than 1,500 miles."

She spoke to the computer, "SupCom, phase to five hundred miles."

Instantly the map faded out and came back in with the West Coast from Canada to northern California running through the center. The green square remained right in the middle.

"The blue dots are civilian surface vessels and the green dots are military vessels. The yellow and white indicators are airplanes. White for civilian and yellow for military. You can see that most of the military vessels on the map are ours. An enemy aircraft, ship or submarine shows up as a red indicator. Squares are airplanes and circles are ships. If there are any submarines they'll show up as triangles, however, subs must be close enough to be picked up on sonar. Fortunately, we've deployed a ring of sonar buoys along both coasts to a distance of three hundred miles."

Al noticed that there were a couple of red circles and triangles several hundred miles off the coast.

"We picked up this red triangle a few weeks ago." She pointed to a triangle about 300 miles due West. "It's an NWO attack submarine called the *Lone Wolf*. It was sitting on the sea floor off the coast of Washington for several days. About a week ago it moved south and started sailing in a large circle. It's still doing it today. That's a little unusual and we've been watching it closely. It doesn't appear to be a threat so we're leaving it alone. If we need to we can send a couple of surface ships and submarines out to investigate. They usually just high tail it back to wherever they came from when we do that.

"We don't show all submarines that could be in range of the map because we haven't developed the technology yet to see everything underwater. Occasionally, when one approaches our coastline, like the *Lone*

Wolf, a sonar buoys will see it and SUPCOM III will pick it up by satellite transmission from the central system in Montreal."

A swivel armchair dominated a position in the center of the room. It was mounted on a raised platform to the right of the map and in front of four video monitors.

"This is the Captain's chair," explained Monica. "NUMSUB doesn't have a conventional periscope. The periscope on this vessel can see in all directions at the same time. Video cameras mounted on the periscope shaft show a view from all directions on the four monitors above the chair. The captain can see everything around the ship instantly. Digital video technology with enhanced night vision capabilities and fog piercing radar will show a perfectly clear image in any weather and under any lighting conditions. A readout on each screen shows distance to any object in yards, and if the object is moving, it indicates the direction and speed.

"There are four additional video cameras mounted on the periscope a few feet under water. With a click of a button on the captain's armrest, one or all of the video screens will show a clear view of subsurface conditions."

"Whew!" Al blew out his breath. "No more hunching over the periscope handles and squinting through an eyepiece. There goes the whole reason I became a sub commander. I guess this means an end to the command, 'Up periscope.'"

"Pretty close," responded Tom. "You'll still need to raise and lower the scope, but you'll control that yourself with switches on the chair. Monica, show him the optics. Are you ready to be blown away, Al?"

"At this point I'm not sure you could surprise me with anything else she can do."

Monica picked up a telephone set and dialed two numbers. She gave instructions. "Dim the main lights, leave on just moonlight, we're demonstrating the optics."

Al folded his arms and waited for the next trick to unfold. He wasn't ready for this one.

An engineer on the dry dock moved to a large rheostat dial on the main electrical console. He briskly turned it down and the exterior lighting in the chamber dimmed to a faint glow. Inside the sub the interior lights gradually darkened. The only remaining illumination was the faint glow of the instruments.

After Al's eyes adjusted to the low light condition, his jaw dropped open and he gave out an audible gasp. Catching his breath, he said, "I guess I was wrong. You've completely floored me."

The exterior skin had become transparent and the occupants of the interior of the vessel clearly saw everything outside the sub. It was so realistic that Al waved to an engineer standing on the dry dock.

"Don't bother," explained Monica. "He can't see you. The optics are mono-directional. You can see out, but no one can see in. The exterior looks exactly like it did when you last saw it."

TOM HAYNIE

"Unbelievable! Tell me that's all. I can't imagine what else she's got up her sleeve."

"There is another major capability, but we'll wait until we're outside to show you that one. First, let's finish the tour."

Monica led them to the port side of the room to a console with a label that read, "SHIELDS." She pointed out the controls as she explained the function.

"You're familiar with the shielding capability of the Navy's surface ships and submarines?"

"Definitely. The technology was developed right after the nuclear war. A central harmonic generator can enwrap the vessel in an electronic sine wave that effectively makes it invisible to probing electronic detection devices such as radar and sonar. The electronic waves generated by the external source literally combine with the shields and pass completely around the vessel as though it wasn't there. There is no reflected image. If we'd possessed the technology before the war we wouldn't have lost so many ships and lives."

Immediately after speaking, Al realized his mistake in referring to the loss of life in the war. He saw the slight expression change on Tom's face. His father was the commander of a nuclear submarine that was sunk near the end of the fighting. The sub had devastated the enemy with torpedoes and missiles. His arsenal depleted, Commander O'Donnell was directing his boat back to base when they were discovered by an attack sub. Unable to outrun the smaller and faster vessel, Tom's father had desperately attempted to hide among the canyons in the Marianna Trench. The ploy nearly worked except for the pursuer's sonar. One errant ping had reflected off of the larger vessel, disclosing its location. The attack sub launched one torpedo that struck the rear of his father's vessel, destroying the engine room and flooding the aft third of the sub. They were too deep to escape and all hands on board perished.

"Sorry, Tom. That was a stupid blunder."

"Don't worry about it. You didn't mean anything. I've got to put the past behind me and get on with life. Let's continue with the tour. Go ahead, Monica."

Monica continued. "Directly forward of this compartment is one of two computer rooms housing the brains of NUMSUB. A redundant computer is located aft that will take over in the event of a failure of any kind in the main computer. The computers are identical SUPCOM IIIs, which stands for SUPer COMPuter, third generation. Their power is equivalent to three of the old bulky Crays that were the rage at the turn of the century, and they're no bigger than a Volkswagen. They're the closest thing to artificial intelligence we've been able to come up with.

"We control them by voice command. They recognize the voice patterns of the operator and won't respond to a person whose voice isn't in their memory banks. Later on today we're going to have you give us a voice print to load into memory so you can operate NUMSUB. Without it you wouldn't get out of the harbor. You could talk to SUPCOM and it would talk back, it might even do what you ask if it felt that your request was logical and reasonable, but there'd be no doubting who was in charge."

"I thought the crew controlled the sub," interrupted Al.

"They do. The commander gives verbal orders and the crew carries them out. SUPCOM listens to each order and if it comes from the commander's voice, allows the order to be carried out regardless of what the order is. However, if the computer does not recognize the voice giving the order, *and* the order is not logical, for example, directions to enter an enemy harbor on the surface with shields down, the computer would take over and override the command. It might even decide that it should return to a friendly port."

"How would it know it was entering an enemy harbor?"

"Remember, its memory has the entire ocean floor and all coastlines including ports, harbors, inlets and all other features. It knows exactly where it is at all times. It knows the difference between a friendly port and an unfriendly one. The feature is designed to prevent a captured sub from falling into enemy hands. Consider the remote possibility that an enemy could overpower the crew and take possession of the sub. Could you imagine the expression on their faces when they show up at Norfolk Naval Base instead of one of their installations? They would literally become prisoners of NUMSUB and would be delivered into the hands of our military.

"Directly behind the control room is a bulkhead that encloses the front of the two hydraulic propulsion chambers. Below us are the officer's quarters, the wardrooms and the crew's mess. A small kitchen serves up tasty freeze-dried food at the selection of a button. While there is a cook on NUMSUB, all crew members are schooled in the culinary art of freeze-dried food."

Al chuckled. "Lest we think that the Navy will ever change too fast or become too technologically advanced, there's one thing that will never change - the food."

"Amen to that," added Tom.

"Don't be too hard on the Navy," added Monica. "While the normal daily fare is freeze-dried, there are specials for certain occasions and for morale. The kitchen includes a small walk-in freezer containing some of the finer delectables: real steaks, roasts, chicken and vegetables.

"To the forward torpedo room now, gentlemen."

Descending stairs toward the bow of the sub, Monica led them into the forward torpedo room. Tom and Al both had to duck their heads to pass through the watertight door to the room. Neatly stacked along the walls were eight of the fourteen torpedoes in the sub's arsenal. Four were attached to each wall. The other six were in the aft torpedo room. The torpedoes were about eight feet long and eighteen inches in diameter. Each was secured to the wall by a bracket with quick release locks. Resting in front of each torpedo tube was a cradle on a track. If the command to load a torpedo into a tube were given, the cradle would move beneath the torpedoes and it would grab one from the wall. The cradle would carry the

101

torpedo to the tube door and automatically load it. Other than added automation, the process hadn't changed in seventy years.

The tour continued with a walk through the wardroom, mess, recreation room, engine room and ended through the aft hatch on the top of NUMSUB's hull.

"Let's return to the briefing room up top for any questions," instructed Monica. "On the way we'll take a look at that last feature I promised you, Al."

"I can't wait." Al ducked his head to pass through the entrance to the walkway that led back to the side of the dry dock.

Monica picked up a phone handset on the wall and spoke to an engineer inside NUMSUB. "Take it through the imaging cycle. Back her out of the dock and do a run through the tunnel." Hanging up the phone, she turned to the two men. "Pay close attention to this, Al."

Al and Tom turned toward NUMSUB in the dry dock. They could hear a low whine that sounded like electric motors starting up. The skin of the sub seemed to shimmer and the color became iridescent. Slowly, the upper gates of the dry dock opened and NUMSUB began to back out of its harness. The sub raised in front of them as though lifted by some invisible hand to clear the lower gates, the tops of which were flush with the surface of the water in the channel. Al assumed there was some powerful electromagnetic field generated to carry the vessel up and over the gates. When the sub passed by the three onlookers, it came so close that Al was tempted to reach out and touch it.

Passing over the lower gates, NUMSUB gently lowered into the water, creating a small wave that lapped over the gate and spilled seawater into the dry dock. Floating three-quarters submerged in the water, the sub backed away from the dry dock and turned toward the sea tunnel that led out of the chamber into the ocean.

Making her way toward the tunnel, she began to submerge, and the water slowly crested over her bow. The sail finally disappeared beneath the surface and the water became still again.

Al turned to Monica and Tom with a quizzical look on his face. "O.K.? What did I miss? Looked like a normal launch to me. Was there something in the water or something about the color change? I didn't notice anything I'd consider unusual. However, at this point, nothing would surprise me."

"Well, let's take a look," said Monica. "Follow me." She went back to the middle of the dry dock and entered the walkway that had previously led to NUMSUB. The walkway was still in place, suspended over the empty dry dock.

Approaching the end of the walk, Monica motioned for Al to move to the front and look down. "What do you see?"

Peering over the edge of the walk, Al looked down to the bottom of the dry dock, holding on to the railing to keep from falling to certain death or serious injury. "I see the bottom of the dry dock about sixty feet down," was his reply.

"Really, let me take a look." Monica leaned over the edge, and catching her foot on a loose cable, she lost her balance. She reached out and grabbed Al's shirt, forcing him through the opening, both of them falling out of the walkway.

Al reached for the railing and missed. His face showed terror. Monica screamed. Tom reached out his arms, but too late. Al and Monica were already falling out of the entrance. Al let out a short yell. Then there was a loud THUMP as he and Monica fell against something solid.

Both Tom and Monica immediately began to laugh hysterically. Al's look of terror changed to one of shocked surprise. He and Monica were lying flat on their backs suspended in mid air by some invisible solid surface.

"What the h...?" began Al. "What's going on here? What is this? Why aren't we falling?" The questions came fast and furious as he spread his hands to feel the transparent object. The texture of the surface was identical to that of NUMSUB. *But that was impossible.* He had seen NUMSUB leave the dry dock. He'd seen the waves, had seen it disappear beneath the water.

Finally Tom and Monica's laughter calmed enough for Monica to explain. "You're lying on NUMSUB. What you saw leave the dry dock was a holographic image.

"The computer generated the image at the same time it encased NUMSUB in its electronic shields. The shields not only pass electronic signals through but can also bend light around an object to make it seem to disappear. The principle is a little like moving an object through water. Instead of the light being blocked by the object, like the water it bends around the object and comes together on the other side as though the object never existed."

"But I saw the water move. It crested over the bow and spilled into the dry dock. Was that real?"

"No, that was holographic also. The image has all of the characteristics of the submarine. It appears solid and can be seen on a radar screen, but it doesn't interfere with the natural elements. We call it a solid imitating holographic imaging system. It can create a ghost with all of the structural and visual characteristics of the real thing."

"I've never heard of that before. Is this something new?"

"Newer than you might think. That's what we've been working on while Tom was on leave. We had the holographics down, but couldn't get it to solidify. We mastered that just in the last few days. It's still fairly well untested."

"Well, you surprised me, too," commented Tom. "Is this what you were so excited to see me about topside?"

"Exactly," Monica replied with a look of satisfaction. "We knew we were close and we worked around the clock to get it ready for your return. We put the finishing touches on it the day before yesterday and tested it with the program you just witnessed. We're working on creating more features and the computer is learning fast. Within a few weeks it will have learned to create and carry out just about any scenario you can think of."

"Let's go topside and talk," Monica suggested. She turned and walked back through the walkway with Al and Tom following close behind.

Exiting the walkway, Al looked back over his shoulder at NUMSUB. She was dropping her electronic shields and rapidly became visible again, appearing to materialize out of thin air. Within a few seconds everything was back to normal in the dry dock.

Chapter 20
Dogfish, It's Farther Than You Think

Tom, Al and Monica entered the elevator and returned to the control room. Monica led them to her office at the back of the facility and they sat around a small table.

"Would anyone like something to drink?" asked Monica, opening a small refrigerator against the wall. Inside were several bottles of water, soft drinks and tea.

"I'll just have a water," answered Tom.

"Make mine a diet," said Al.

She returned carrying the beverages and set them down in front of each man. Twisting open the cap on a bottle of iced tea, she took a long drink and turned to the men.

"I understand the operational crew will arrive in a few days to begin training on NUMSUB. We're quite excited to know that she'll be getting some serious experience for a change. You can only train and test so much before it gets a little boring."

"Al's crew will arrive in groups of two or three over the next several days. We don't want to attract any attention to the farm by having a large number of farm hands arrive all at once."

Tom turned to Al "When we first staffed the base it took us over six months to get everyone down here."

"I imagine building the place was quite a covert operation, too."

"Exactly. The equipment was brought in by pieces on large tractor-trailer rigs disguised as hay trucks. Bales of hay were stacked around the pieces and the trucks were backed into the barn. Fortunately the NWO didn't get suspicious of so many hay trucks dropping off loads of hay. If they would have counted they might have noticed that, had the trucks really been loaded with bales of hay, we could have fed all of the cattle in Oregon for a couple of years.

"We sunk large elevator shafts first. The dirt was mixed with cow manure, loaded on manure spreaders and the mixture was spread over the fields. When the fields started to look like hills, we converted large milk tanker trucks with false tops to haul it to a fake milk processing plant.

"By the time we'd sunk a shaft below sea level and bored a tunnel out to the ocean they pulled a half dozen old nuclear boomers out of mothballs and remodeled them into underwater dump trucks. The missile bays were large enough to hold quite a cargo of dirt. When they were full they didn't need much water in the ballast tanks. After they finished the cave, they used the subs to haul in the building materials. You're right, it *was* quite an operation."

"And continues to be so. When will your team be here?"

"They'll all arrive by Monday evening. We'll start training on Wednesday."

Mark Ganon and Marne Armstrong had picked up their gear at the air base in Montreal and were waiting to board the C-231 cargo plane sitting on the tarmac. They had been waiting for approximately an hour for the ground crew to repair the landing gear on the big plane.

The C-231 was the largest airplane in the AWF Air Force. Even sitting at rest beside the runway it was ominous. Its big olive green tail reached fourteen stories in the air. Each wing was the length of a football field. The eight Pratt and Whitney jet engines under each wing had enough thrust to propel the giant aircraft at nearly the speed of sound. The landing wheels were fourteen feet in diameter and there were forty-eight of them. There was enough rubber under the plane to provide four tires on each of two hundred passenger automobiles. It required a runway five miles long to gather enough speed to get the plane airborne.

Marne paced back and forth in the officer's lounge while Mark sat reading the morning edition of the local newspaper on the monitor mounted on the arm of his chair.

"I'd rather be walking than sitting around waiting for a plane. I hate delays," she muttered to herself. "Seems like this happens all the time to me. Maybe I'm just cursed with bad luck."

Mark peered over the top of the monitor at her. "Take it easy on yourself, girl. We'll get there in plenty of time. They won't start without us."

"Maybe not, I'd just as soon be there early than late."

As though someone was reading her thoughts, an airman entered the lounge and announced, "Lieutenant Armstrong, Lieutenant Ganon?"

Mark looked up from the monitor and caught the airman's eye. "Over here, what's up?"

"Change in plane. The 231 won't be ready until tomorrow morning. Seems that the only place they can get the replacement part is out of Athens supply depot."

"Athens, New York?"

"No, Athens, Greece. You've been assigned the H-1627. It's a rusty old bucket but it'll get you to where you're going. By the way, where are you guys going?"

It was a dumb question and both Mark and Marne knew it. It was customary not to ask where military travelers were going from Montreal. Many had secret assignments and couldn't discuss them anyway. However, they chalked it up to an inexperienced airman and Marne gave a non-committal answer.

"Routine training down at Lowry Air Force Base in Denver. They reactivated the old base for pilot training after the war." It wasn't entirely a lie. They were going to Denver on the first leg of their indirect route to Dogfish Base in Oregon. From Denver they were scheduled to go to Oakland, California and then to Portland.

The airman had taken a chance on asking the question and knew that the answer was a hoax. These were Navy SEALs, they weren't pilots. Turning to leave the room, he nodded to the bartender, signaling that these two officers were likely part of a suspected secret operation involving suspicious activity at the Secretariat.

The airman was an unwilling participant in espionage. He was married with a couple of children and liked to party with the guys. He had a good marriage and had been faithful to his wife, at least until a couple of months ago. While out with a couple of friends they had a few too many when they met up with three attractive young women seated at the bar. A stray glance had turned into flirting and before he knew what happened he woke up in a motel room with one of the women.

He was devastated. If his wife ever found out he'd lose her, his children and everything he had. Little did he know the entire episode was a set up by the NWO. Before long they contacted him with incriminating videotapes. They promised him that his wife would never find out if he followed a few simple instructions. At first all he had to do was keep a count of how many passengers passed through the officer's lounge.

It didn't seem like such a big deal. The information couldn't be significant, and if he kept his blackmailers happy he'd stay out of trouble. This time they told him what question to ask departing passengers traveling in small groups. Anyone who gave a deceptive answer was to be identified to the bartender.

The bartender had been screened by the FIA for his position in the officer's lounge. They ran a limited background check and he was judged loyal enough to mix drinks behind the bar. He, too, had been turned by the NWO in a blackmail scheme. All he had to do was make sure the pilot of the H-1627 was offered a drink before leaving the base. Of course, the drink would contain a sleeping potion that would activate about an hour into the flight.

Just then an Air Force pilot swaggered into the lounge. He was dressed in a worn leather flight jacket and khaki flight suit. On his feet he wore cowboy boots. On his head, tilted at an angle, was a western hat. He had a gold leaf sewn into each shoulder on the jacket, indicating his rank. The major was the pilot of the H-1627. He was an experienced helicopter pilot who had thousands of hours of flight time in his aircraft.

He entered the lounge confidently and looked around. He asked for Lieutenants Armstrong and Ganon by name. They identified themselves to him and he introduced himself in a thick Texas drawl. "I'm Major Bill Worty, Abilene, Texas. I've got your flight plans to Denver. We'll be takin' off in fifteen minutes, just as soon as they've juiced the goose and kicked her in the pants."

The local custom before pilots and passengers left the lounge required the bartender to offer the three officers one for the road, on the house.

"Make mine orange juice," replied Major Worty. "Y'all know the rules."

"I'll have a Scotch and Soda," said Marne. "I'm just along for the ride."

"Draft beer," said Mark.

Unknown to the Major, the bartender slipped a few milliliters of a clear fluid in his orange juice. As far as he knew it was simply supposed to make the pilot sleepy enough to force an unscheduled landing. That's all that had happened on previous occasions when he did what he was instructed to do. He was unaware that those exercises were merely covering for a bigger ploy when the time was right. Today the time was right. The liquid he gave to the pilot was much stronger than anything he had used before.

After downing his juice, the Major stood and said to the bartender, "Great juice. Best I've had in a while. Has a really sweet flavor."

Turning to Marne and Mark, "You folks ready?"

Marne nearly leaped off her stool. "Let's do it!" she said anxiously.

Mark chugged down the last swallow of his beer. All three left the lounge and walked to the waiting H-1627.

The H-1627 was a ten-year-old jet-assisted helicopter affectionately nicknamed the *Honey Bee*, or *Bee* for short. It could carry six heavily armed soldiers and their gear. Exceptionally fast and trustworthy, the *Bee* was ideally suited to get a strike force to a target area quickly and quietly. This one had seen plenty of combat action in the cleanup after the war, but now was used mostly for ferrying passengers between military installations. The *Bee* was considered one of the safest aircraft in the military.

The single main rotor provided vertical takeoff and low speed maneuverability. The twin Pratt & Whitney turbofan jet engines mounted beneath the rotor produced a combined 40,000 pounds of thrust for supersonic speed. The aircraft had wings and a rudder for lift and control. The small fixed wings were attached under the twin jet engines, and the vertical rotor was mounted inside the rear vertical stabilizer. Upon reaching sufficient forward speed to allow the wings to provide lift, the pilot would stop the main rotor and fold it into an aerodynamic compartment parallel to the fuselage. At high speeds the relatively flimsy rotors could disintegrate. The *Bee* had a top speed of just over mach one with a full load. For this trip, though, with only one-third the payload, it would reach an airspeed of nearly eight hundred seventy miles per hour. The trip to Denver would take about two hours.

Major Worty completed the customary walk around inspection required of all pilots before they accept their aircraft from the ground crew. He climbed through the side door of the *Bee*, tossed his western hat in a rack above the console and plopped down into the pilot's seat. He slipped on the head set and pulled out his preflight checklist. Beside him was an empty copilot's seat. On domestic passenger flights of fewer than three hours, there was no copilot.

Lieutenants Armstrong and Ganon followed the Major through the door. There were two rows of three seats each behind the pilot. They sat in the front of each row directly behind the pilot and copilot seats. The ground crew had removed their gear from the 231 and stowed it behind the rear seats in the *Bee*.

While Major Worty worked through his pre-flight, Marne looked around the interior of the *Bee* with interest. She was an avid amateur pilot when off duty and had taken an interest in helicopters before she entered the Navy. The *Bee* was a little different than the non-military choppers she had flown several years before. The basics of helicopter flight were the same, but the jet assist required more sophisticated controls than she had seen before.

After the Major had completed his checklist, she asked, "Do you mind if I sit in the copilot's seat? I'm fascinated by the instrumentation and characteristics of these unique machines." What she meant was these "old" machines, but she didn't want to offend the Major.

For safety reasons, rules of flight dictated that non-trained personnel were not allowed to sit in the pilot or copilot's seat. However, Major Worty had determined that Lieutenant Armstrong was a fine lookin' little filly. He was a red-blooded Texas male with appropriate hormonal balance and loved to show off his skills and his aircraft. The flight would be routine and he wouldn't mind conversation with someone, especially an attractive woman.

So he broke the rules. "Sure, climb in, just don't touch nothin'. We'll be airborne shortly."

Chapter 21
That Was Some Orange Juice

The air traffic controller in the tower gave the *Bee* clearance for takeoff. Major Worty pulled back on the throttle and adjusted the trim of the rotors. The *Bee* quickly rose vertically to five hundred feet.

"We'll fly by normal 'copter power using just the rotor for lift and forward 'til we hit six thousand feet. Then we'll switch her to jet power and climb to twenty thousand for the rest of the flight."

During the five minutes it took to reach the desired altitude, the Major described the operational characteristics of the *Bee* while Marne listened intently. Until now, the flight was pretty much the same as any other helicopter she had flown. The altimeter climbed steadily and leveled off at six thousand feet.

"The transition to jet can be a little bumpy. Kind of like that first kick out of the chute while the bull's still a little frisky. Hang on to your seat." The Major had a little bravado in his voice.

Marne watched the Major throttle up the rotors to bring the aircraft to sufficient forward airspeed for the wings to take over. At one-eighty knots, he reached over to the console and lifted a clear plastic cover. On the left side of the cover was a label with the letter "H". On the right was the letter "J." Under the cover was a red handle that was pointing to the "H". The Major pulled the handle back and turned it to point to the "J". When he let go of the handle the *Bee* shuddered slightly and rapidly dropped about a hundred feet. Marne heard and felt the jet engines ignite. She was thrust back slightly in her seat when the forward speed of the aircraft picked up.

Worty explained, "Don't you be scared now, y'hear. The rotors and wings both gave lift until I shut down the rotors. Then it's just the wings. We dropped altitude on the change until airspeed picked up and the wings could handle things by themselves."

While he was talking, Marne could hear the metallic sounds of the rotors folding into the storage compartment for supersonic flight.

During the conversation, Mark was half listening, half looking out the windows at the passing scenery. He settled comfortably in his seat and leaned his head back to take a nap.

"Hold on while I kick 'er in the ass. She'll burn 'til we break sound."

Worty pulled back to full throttle and the afterburners exploded to life. The *Bee* leaped forward. The sound of the engines over their heads burst into a loud roar. This time Marne was pushed hard into her seat.

The altimeter began to climb again, more rapidly than before until it read twenty thousand feet. Major Worty leveled the aircraft. The airspeed continued to rise. Near the speed of sound the *Bee* began to vibrate. The vibration increased in intensity. At 700 miles per hour, Worty punched the throttle. The *Bee* pushed through the sound barrier and the vibration suddenly ceased, replaced by a serene smoothness.

Marne looked back at Mark. He barely stirred when they broke the sound barrier. He was deep in a mid-morning nap. She envied his ability to relax and take things as they come. Nothing seemed to bother him. She turned back to the controls, a hundred questions raced through her mind, and a few spilled out of her mouth. Major Worty was more than happy to explain anything she wanted to hear.

Gradually the conversation turned to a more personal nature.

"So, Lieutenant Armstrong, tell me a little about yourself. What's a good lookin' filly like yourself doin' in the Navy, and the Navy SEALs at that?"

Ordinarily, Marne might be offended by the patronizing, sexual overtones in the Major's comments. However, she passed it off as just his way of talking, a throwback to his Texas roots.

Loosening her seatbelt to be more comfortable, she leaned back in her seat. "I guess I was always a tom boy. I grew up in a little town in Southwestern Pennsylvania in a family of five kids. I have four brothers, three of them older than me. I was playing football by the time I was seven. Boy, talk about survival of the fittest, I had to learn to fight like a boy. I don't think my brothers knew I was a girl before I turned sixteen and had my first date. That's when they realized it. From then on there was no more rough housing. They screened every boy who took an interest in me.

"When it was time to choose a college, I didn't want to stay around home and I didn't want to go to some run-of-the-mill coeducational school. So I went to the Citadel. When I graduated I wanted to get into an elite combat unit and an opportunity with the SEALs came up and . . . ." Her voice trailed off. Something was wrong. Worty hadn't responded to anything she was saying.

The altimeter was descending rapidly. She looked over at the Major. He was seated upright with his hands on the stick, but his head was slumped over, his chin rested on his chest. He looked like he'd fallen asleep.

She reached over and poked him in the shoulder. "Major, are you O.K?"

When he didn't respond she poked him harder and spoke loudly, "Major! Wake up!" Still no response. Now the aircraft was tilting forward into a dive.

She shouted at Lieutenant Ganon, "Mark! We have a problem! Wake up!"

Lieutenant Ganon opened his eyes and shook his head to clear the sleep out of his mind. "What's happened? What's wrong with Worty?"

By this time the *Bee* was in a steep nosedive toward the earth. The altimeter read fifteen thousand feet and was dropping rapidly. The angle of the dive now caused the Major to slump forward against the stick. The weight of his body pushed hard against it.

Marty grabbed for the stick in front of the copilot's seat. "I can't pull it back! He's too heavy! Help me move him!"

She released her seat belt and grabbed Worty. At the same time Mark came over the back of the pilot's seat and put his hands under the sleeping man's arms. He slipped his arms around the limp body and pulled him back against the seat. Marne grabbed for the stick in front of her. The altimeter read seven thousand feet.

She pulled back as hard as she could with no apparent effect. Then she remembered that she'd read that at the speed they were traveling, in an aircraft designed like the *Bee*, the controls work backwards. Fighting back logic and forcing her mind to control her actions she pushed forward on the stick. At first there was no reaction, then slowly the nose of the diving aircraft began to rise.

She looked out the front canopy; the ground was closing fast. They were lucky they were over the plains of northern Iowa. If they were over the Rocky Mountains, they would be scattered over a dozen square miles of mountainside by now.

She leaned hard into the stick. The ship vibrated violently. The gravitational stress on the superstructure was tremendous. The *Bee* wasn't built to withstand this kind of pressure for long.

The nose continued to come up, but it was too slow. They were about to hit the ground. At this speed there would be nothing left larger than a softball. Gritting her teeth, she let out a scream and put every ounce of her strength into the stick. The G-forces on her body were tremendous as she fought to stay conscious.

The trajectory of the dive flattened out at the tops of a stand of oak trees next to a wheat field. The undercarriage of the *Bee* clipped the top of a tree at the instant it careened off the bottom of the dive. The shock wave from the speeding aircraft flattened the trees and most of the wheat in the field. The *Bee* shot forward and up like she'd been ejected from a slingshot.

Marne let off on the stick. The *Bee* was still traveling faster than sound. She pulled into a moderate climb, both to gain altitude and to absorb some momentum. With the altimeter climbing, the airspeed began to drop. During the dive they had reached a speed of over twelve hundred miles an hour. They were lucky that she had held together. Marne silently thanked the engineers who designed her, the assemblers who put her together, the ground crew who maintained her.

Mark released his grip on the Major. He had no idea how he was able to hold him during the dive. The adrenaline in his body was beginning to subside and he was drenched with perspiration. He looked at Marne. She was as white as a ghost. Her quick action had saved all three of their lives. Never had anyone looked more beautiful to him.

She leveled the *Bee* off at eighteen thousand feet and began to relax again. Then she heard the radio for the first time. A voice had been frantically calling them for several minutes. "*Honey Bee seven-three*, do you read me? Come in?" The message was repeated over and over.

Finally she pulled the headset from Major Worty and put it on. "This is *Honey Bee seven-three*. Over."

"*Honey Bee seven-three*, this is Omaha air traffic control. What happened to you? We lost you when you went into a dive and we thought you were gone. Then you came up again. What's going on? Are you all right? Over."

"This is Lieutenant Marne Armstrong, U. S. Navy. The pilot of the *Bee* is unconscious. We don't know what happened to him. He lost control and we were barely able to regain it before we hit the ground. We seem to be O.K. now."

"Who's flying the *Bee*?"

"I am. I've never flown one of these before, but I'm starting to get the hang of it. I've jockeyed a few Sikorsky's and am pretty familiar with small fixed wing civilian planes. I think I can handle this O.K."

"Do you want to bring it in to Lincoln A.N.G.?"

"No. I think we can keep going on to Denver. It'll give me time to figure out how to bring this thing back under sound. I'll need someone to walk me through reentering chopper phase, though. Can you let Denver know we're coming and that we need help?"

"Will do. Looks like you're about forty minutes out of Denver. I'll let them know what to expect."

"Thanks, Omaha. *Honey Bee seven-three*, out."

The tower at Lowry Air Base in Denver received a call from Omaha. Within minutes, fire trucks and emergency vehicles surrounded the landing area. Activity in the tower picked up quickly. An air traffic controller watched his radar screen intently while the *Bee* came into his range.

A few minutes later the radio in Marne's headset came to life again. "*Honey Bee seven-three*, this is Lowry tower. Over."

"Go ahead, Lowry tower."

"We have you on radar. You're about fifteen minutes out. What's the status of the pilot?"

"He's still unconscious, but his vitals seem to be normal. Pulse is fifty-five and respiration is about six. He's in a deep sleep. He acts like he's been drugged."

"We'll check him out as soon as you touch down. We have a doctor and an ambulance standing by at the pad. It's time to reduce speed and convert back to helicopter."

"Sounds good to me, Lowry tower. Do you have someone there who can walk me through this? I watched Major Worty make the change to jet. Do I just reverse the procedure?"

A new voice came over the radio. "Lieutenant Armstrong, this is Captain Ryan, Air Force. How's the flying up there?" Captain Bill Ryan, an air force pilot with much experience flying the *Bee* was on the radio. He wanted to assure himself that Marne was calm and in control of herself as well as the aircraft.

"Pretty smooth, Captain. I'm surprised that I've picked it up so fast. It's a little like flying a Cessna but there are significant differences. I am a bit nervous about bringing her back to 'copter mode."

"You're doing fine, Lieutenant. I don't know of anyone who could have done better. The transition back is almost as simple as going jet. Do you remember that lever that the pilot turned when he made the change?"

"The red one under the plastic cover with the letters "H" and "J"?"

"That's the one. Drop your airspeed to two-one-zero, then turn the lever to the "H" position."

Marne let out on the throttle and the airspeed began to drop. Passing through the sound barrier to subsonic speed was smoother than going through the other direction. After a couple of minutes, the airspeed indicator read two hundred ten knots.

Marne lifted the cover and turned the lever back to "H". Immediately she heard the sounds of the rotor coming out of its compartment and unfolding. The jet engines were still powering the aircraft, though.

"Captain Ryan, rotors are extended. What do I do now?"

"If you look up you should see the rotors slowly turning above you. The motor needs to be started and the transmission engaged to allow rotor power to take over before you shut down the jet engines. Above and to the left of the red lever you should see a toggle switch labeled "Rotors." Flip it on and the motor should start."

She flipped the switch and the motor started. "Done. Rotor motor started."

"Now, to the left of the toggle switch is a handle. Pull it toward you to engage the rotor transmission. You will see and feel the rotors take hold."

"Done. Rotors engaged."

"On the right side of the console will be a toggle switch labeled "Jets". Flip that switch and the jet engines will flame out. At that point the *Bee* should again be a helicopter."

Marne followed his instructions and the jet engines shut down. She noticed how much quieter it was with only the rotors on. She was much more familiar with the operation of the *Bee* at this point.

"Everything seems to be normal here, Captain. I have the base in visual. I think I can bring it down, now. Thanks for the lesson."

She saw the landing pad clearly. Emergency vehicles with red and blue flashing lights surrounded it. Three paramedics in white uniforms stood beside an ambulance. She gently put the helicopter down in the middle of the pad and turned off the motor. Before the rotor stopped turning, the paramedics had opened the side door and removed the Major from the *Bee*.

She and Mark unbuckled their seatbelts and jumped out. The solid ground felt really good under them. A man approached. On each shoulder of his uniform were two stars.

"I'm General Marshall, base commander. Welcome to Lowry. I understand you had a rough go of it, Lieutenant. We're relieved you made it."

Mark and Marne presented a crisp salute. He returned it. "There's a briefing room in the terminal. You have an hour before you leave for Oakland. Let's talk."

They followed the general into the briefing room. There were three officers seated at a table. The general sat at the head of the table. Marne and Mark took chairs to the right of the general.

"Let me introduce Captains McDowell, Murphy and O'Callahan. McDowell is base security. Murphy and O'Callahan are military intelligence. Gentlemen, they have only forty-five minutes to answer questions and they have to be on their way. Let's get started."

The briefing went rapidly. Marne explained that she thought the pilot was drugged. She reviewed the events leading up to their change of plans. The maintenance on the C-231. The reassignment to the *Bee* and the traditional drinks at the bar.

"Major Worty commented about the difference in taste of the orange juice. I thought nothing of it at first, but now I wonder if there was something in it."

"We're doing blood tests at the hospital. I rather doubt we'll find anything, however there will be a complete investigation. I'm sure that if there is something going on we'll uncover it in Montreal."

The general looked at his watch. "Well, we appreciate your report. It's time for you to go."

They picked up their gear and left. The remainder of the trip to Oakland and then on to Portland was uneventful. They arrived at Dogfish Base just two hours behind schedule.

Chapter 22
A Time to Train

By Tuesday morning all personnel had arrived safely at Dogfish Base, although three of Al's crew were delayed about twelve hours. Al and Tom were in Tom's quarters.

Tom's unit was a one bedroom apartment similar to most of the other personnel quarters. The base was designed with little difference between the officer's, enlisted and civilian living facilities, except that the enlisted personnel were doubled up. Most of the men and women assigned to the Dogfish Project would be committed to at least three years of intensive research and testing. Quibbling over privilege and status would only disrupt.

The apartment was relatively large, approximately fourteen hundred square feet. It included a kitchen, two bathrooms, a living room, dining room, master bedroom and small office/library. A large flat-screen TV occupied one wall of the living room and the office was equipped with appropriate computer and technical equipment. The kitchen was stocked with cookware although many of the tenants chose to eat at the cafeteria. The cafeteria was open twenty-four hours a day to accommodate crews working in three shifts around the clock.

The telephone was strictly for internal use. No calls to the outside were permitted from living quarters. Each person assigned to the base could communicate with family members over secure outgoing lines once a week. In an emergency, a family could contact someone at the base through a secure number. The number routed to an operator in Montreal who would connect the call to a special trunk line. The line branched around the country taking a different route each time it was used. The operator did not know where the trunk line originated and was not informed of the nature of the security nor the reason for it.

"We know the NWO is nervous about something," said Al. "The incident with Armstrong and Ganon was a blatant attempt to keep them from getting here. The other aircraft accidents and the deaths of two of the decoy teams leaves little doubt that they believed something was up at the Secretariat."

"We lost five good people," responded Tom. "The only thing that's come of it is that NWO intelligence had to tip their hand. The FIA will have a field day with all of the evidence. I understand they've already arrested the bartender at the officer's lounge in Montreal. He's singing like a bird."

"If FIA can't sniff them out, no one can. They have to be nervous to come out so openly like that. Do you think they caught on to Dogfish?"

"I rather doubt it. We found a couple of homing devices planted in duffel bags meant to follow the owners to their final destination. We picked one up in Portland and one in Mexico City. Right now they're on their way to the Himalayas in separate aircraft. They'll be attached to parachutes and dropped over Tibet. By the time this is all over, the NWO should have quite a mountain expedition going."

"Is everything ready for tomorrow?" asked Al.

"All set. I'll run my crew through NUMSUB I so you can have NUMSUB III. They're identical for all practical purposes. We'll spend a couple of weeks training onboard and in classrooms, then we'll move to the mock up of Hangzhou Base. We built it at the old Nuclear Test Site in the Nevada desert north of Las Vegas."

"So that's where the mock up is. I was wondering where you hid it."

"Yeah. The Test Site is ideal. After the U.S. government finished the underground nuclear tests they found that some of the detonations opened up fairly large subterranean caverns. Most of them collapsed, but a few of the larger ones held. Imagine the hole created by a 100 megaton hydrogen bomb detonating a mile or so underground. It's going to push some dirt and rock out of the way."

"I imagine the compression would be terrific."

"Exactly. The blast pounded out a hole and the heat from the fusion reaction melted the rock around it. When the molten rock cooled and solidified it formed a wall more dense and stronger than concrete. We lined the chamber with lead to shield the radiation. Then we simply dropped a couple of elevator shafts and added a level floor. We use a couple of the chambers to build mock ups of foreign government facilities. We use them to train intelligence agents so they're familiar with the surroundings. Nothing like a spy who can act like a tourist."

"Or a tourist who thinks he's a spy."

"Yeah. We've had a number of them mucking up the works when we're trying to get a job done. Seems like everyone wants to get into the act nowadays."

"You'll spend a week here at Dogfish, a month and a half or so at the Test Site then another couple of weeks back here coordinating with my crew, right?"

"That's right. By the time both crews are done training they'll be able to do this in their sleep"

"Speaking of sleep. I haven't gotten much over the past couple of days. I think I'll go back to my room and turn in. I can't get over these accommodations. They're great."

"Yeah, makes the job a little easier. Get a good night's sleep. See you in the morning at breakfast."

The next morning Tom and Al assembled the crews for their initial briefing at Dogfish. Then they split up to review their assigned tasks. The two crews spent the next three months in intensive training.

The captain of the *Lone Wolf* was going crazy. For the past three months, since O'Donnell and Hunslinger had disappeared, he had to listen to the nightly intelligence reports dictated by Ivanovich. Oh, to be doing war drills rather than these monotonous games of hide and seek, especially when he knew full well that he was never really hidden. The only relief came on the monthly rendezvous with their submarine tender to take on fresh supplies and allow the crew a couple of days of relaxation in the tender's larger quarters and recreational facilities.

Even then the occasional news from some of the other sub captains passed along by the officers of the tender made him yearn for this mission to be over. There were tales of cat and mouse games played with merchant ships and occasionally with military vessels. Both sides tolerated these games because they knew no one dared start any serious shooting.

Nevertheless, he would obey his orders. He would provide a moving base of operations so Ivanovich could be the pivot point in a global search for the two Federation officers.

Sturgaard Ivanovich was no happier with the turn of events than was the captain. He felt alone and isolated on the submarine. Although the crew included a hundred ninety two officers and men, none of them held anything in common with him. In fact, most of them distrusted him immensely. The enlisted men never dared associate with an officer and the officers avoided contact with him as much as possible. They had heard of or witnessed many of their colleagues' careers come to an abrupt end at the hands of the NWO intelligence corps.

Sturgaard felt particularly isolated. Unlike many of his profession, he did not revel in the power that fed their egos. Were it not for the benefits afforded his family, he would have left the intelligence ranks years ago. He would have loved to serve in the regular navy aboard a battleship or aircraft carrier.

The solitude, boredom and frustration at losing his prey made him irritable. He frequently let his guard down in front of the captain. The captain was the only officer who took the time to listen to him, and then it was out of sheer duty.

They had lost O'Donnell and Hunslinger in the early days of October. The weeks of searching had taken them into November and through December. It was now early January. They had missed the turn of the New Year, Sturgaard's favorite holiday. He was usually able to spend the passing of the old year into the new with his family. The discouragement mounted. One day he vented his frustrations in front of the captain.

"Damn the High Command! We've been out here searching for O'Donnell for over three months and there's no indication that we'll ever find him. The last time we lost him he didn't surface for nearly two years. I'll die if I have to spend two years in this god-forsaken tin pipe under four hundred feet of water. If I had half the courage of my father, I'd quit the service and escape to the West."

Captain Porknoi felt the same about spending a prolonged search with little sight of the end, but he never held any thoughts of defection. Those were treasonous words, regardless that they were spoken in abject frustration.

"Sturgaard, get hold of yourself! The men! They shouldn't hear these words from someone of your position. You endanger yourself as well as the *Lone Wolf.* I'll have no more of this kind of outburst on my ship. Do you understand?"

Ivanovich knew the captain was right. Had he been any other intelligence officer, he would not have stood for a captain to correct him. But then, had he been any other intelligence officer, he might not have spoken out like that. He left for his stateroom and threw himself on his bunk. Before long he drifted off into a fitful sleep.

Captain Porknoi pulled down a small volume which he had hidden behind some of the ship's logbooks. He opened it and began writing with determination. The date he entered at the top of the page was 14 January 2056.

Chapter 23
Interrogation

Pete and Robin eased the two unconscious bodies of the enemy frogmen through NUMSUB's double hatch and into the waiting arms of Lieutenants Ganon and Armstrong. Ganon and Armstrong were the two members of Tom's team with medical training. It was their job to prepare the frogmen for the interrogation.

Mark carefully removed the scuba gear from the divers and placed it in the corner of the infirmary. The infirmary was a ten by fifteen foot room. In the center of the room stood two collapsible gurneys that could double as examination tables. Against one wall were three supply cabinets and a refrigerator for medication that required cold storage. A locked vault containing narcotics for pain relief and the powerful poisons team members could use in the event of capture stood in a corner of the room.

The frogmen were placed in semi-reclining positions on the gurneys. Restraining straps were secured across their arms, legs and chests. The restraining straps were similar to auto seatbelts with quick release buckles that snapped when the male end was inserted into the clip. As a precaution, a tray with additional doses of Trascan was set up between the gurneys. In their hurry to secure the divers, Ganon didn't notice that the buckle of the right arm strap on one frogman had not engaged properly.

When the subjects were prepared for the interrogation, Ganon went to the intercom on the wall. "Commander O'Donnell, we're ready to proceed with the interrogation."

"Thanks, Lieutenant. We're on our way."

Tom and Al were with Jorge Rojas.

"I'd like to conduct the interrogation," requested Jorge. "The answers they give to the basic line of questions might lead to other questions about the installation's security."

"That's O.K. by me, if you want to. How do you see it proceeding?" asked Tom.

"Well, first I'll ask some relatively innocent questions to keep them comfortable. Even though they're in a semi-conscious state, it's a little like being hypnotized."

"What do you mean, like being hypnotized?"

"Some folks believe that if you're hypnotized you'll do anything you're told. It doesn't quite work that way. If you put a person under hypnosis and ask them to do something repulsive, say like asking a teetotaler to drink whiskey, he'll object and probably won't do it. The mind still has to be receptive to the suggestion. Being under Trascan is a lot like that. I'll have to lead them into the questions we really want answers to by asking benign ones up front."

"O.K. Let's go. We have only an hour or so before the Trascan wears off. We can risk one more injection, but we have to have them back in the water in no more than two hours."

Tom, Al and Jorge filed into the infirmary. Tom approached the two figures and with his thumb and forefinger opened the eyelids of each. He examined their pupils to assure himself they were completely comatose. Satisfied, he turned to Jorge.

"They're all yours. I think you can begin."

Jorge took a position on a stool between the two frogmen. Everyone in the room ceased talking or making any sounds. Speaking softly to the one on his right he began the interrogation.

"My name is Muhammad Repoman." He used a fictitious name in case they remembered anything later. "You are in a secure room among friends. Do not be alarmed. You will not be harmed. I only wish to ask you some questions. If you understand say 'Yes.'"

Without moving any other facial features, the frogman opened his mouth slightly and said, "Yes."

"Good. If you are comfortable say 'Yes.'"

"Yes."

"Good. What is your name?"

"Morovan Sadmere."

"May I call you 'Morovan?'"

"Yes."

"How old are you. Morovan?"

"Twenty-six."

"What is your rank?"

"Seaman First Class."

"What does a Seaman First Class do?"

"Underwater naval combat duty."

"Who is your companion?"

"Bartolomew Gattis."

"Is he a Seaman First Class, too?"

"Yes."

"What were you doing in the water?"

"We were sent on a wild goose chase."

"What were you chasing?"

"A ghost ship that appeared on LOFWAR."

"Who sent you?"

"Captain Kumodan." Sadmere's face showed the first sign of emotion as he pursed his lips with displeasure when he said the name of his commander.

"Ah, you do not like Captain Kumodan?"

"No. He is an ass."

"What makes him an ass?"

121

"Unfair. Arrogant son-of-a-bitch."

Jorge could see by the expression on Sadmere's face that this was an uncomfortable conversation. He changed the subject.

"What do you and your friend, Bartolomew do together?"

His face softened. "We go into Hangzhou to the bordellos." A wide smile crossed his lips.

"Do you attend briefings at the installation together, too?"

"Yes."

"What do you discuss at the briefings?"

"Security. Changes in location and schedules."

"Do you discuss passwords for the computer systems?"

"Yes."

Jorge looked at Tom and Al and nodded with a smile.

"When was the last time you went to a briefing?"

"Tuesday."

"Damn!" Jorge reacted to the answer with an involuntary expletive. No one noticed a slight eye movement by the frogman named Gattis.

Tom and Al knew exactly why Jorge reacted. Tuesday was five days ago. The installation changes security procedures and passwords every two to three days. The two frogmen had missed the last briefing and did not know the correct passwords. Any information they had would be useless.

Gattis blinked his eyes. He thought he heard people talking. One of the voices sounded like Sadmere. *What is he saying? Who is the other voice? Where am I?* The questions raced through his mind. He opened his eyes slightly. The room was fuzzy. He could make out four, no five people. They were all strangers. Four were standing across the room; the other was seated beside him. Sadmere was lying on a table in front of him. He could see the back of the stranger seated next to him. He was talking to the others. They didn't sound pleased. *There is danger. I have to act.*

He tried to move. His arms and legs were tied down. He began to panic. *What are they doing to me? Are they torturing Sadmere?* Slowly he turned his head. There, on the tray, a scalpel. He tried to move again. His right hand was loose. In one motion he grabbed the scalpel and lunged for the figure beside him.

Marne was the first to see a quick movement from the frogman behind Jorge. Instinctively she jumped forward. She saw the scalpel in his hand.

"Watch out!" she shouted.

He swung the scalpel wildly at Jorge. Surprised, Jorge turned to see what was happening just as Sadmere's right hand slashed across his neck and severed his jugular.

Jorge screamed and grabbed for his neck. A bright torrent of blood squirted between his fingers as he fell to the floor.

Marne grabbed the hand with the scalpel. Using her body for leverage against his one free hand she pushed his arm against the edge of the gurney. In the struggle, she was cut on the right shoulder, but she managed to subdue him.

"Mark, the Trascan!" she shouted.

Lieutenant Ganon was already in motion. He grabbed a syringe of Trascan and injected it into the leg of the struggling frogman. Almost instantly Gattis relaxed and fell back into unconsciousness.

Tom and Al had grabbed sterile gauze pads and were frantically applying pressure to the wound on Jorge's neck to stop the bleeding. Jorge was lying on the floor, a pool of deep red blood spreading out beneath him. His eyes were wide open in a look of terror and he was gasping for breath.

His legs began to spasm and his body involuntarily shook as his life drained from him. With one last violent shudder, his body stiffened and went limp. Within a few seconds he was dead.

Mark checked his pulse. There was none. He looked at his pupils. They were dilated.

"He's gone," he said in disbelief. "My God! What happened?"

Everyone in the room fell back in shock. Marne knelt on the floor, her hands limp in her lap. Tom sat beside her, the pool of blood soaking into his pants. His hands and arms were covered with blood. Al knelt on the other side of Jorge, blood soaking his shirt and pants. Mark stood beside the frogmen. His knees had nearly buckled and he was leaning against the wall.

There was blood all over the room. It had spattered on the walls and on the wetsuits of the unconscious frogmen.

For a moment no one spoke. Silence shrouded the room like a cloak.

Marne spoke first. "What are we going to do?" She knew how vital Jorge was to the mission.

Tom answered, "Let's be calm. We'll have a backup. We have to contact Warnick. Mark, Marne, start cleaning this place up." He knew they had to keep occupied. The worst thing to do in combat was to take time to think about tragedy.

For the next fifteen minutes they busied themselves with the clean up. They wrapped Jorge in a body bag and placed him in one of several cold storage compartments behind the freezer adjacent to the infirmary. The sub was equipped with a small morgue. Jorge's body would be kept nearly frozen until they returned home for a proper burial.

Tom went to the control room and called George Warnick at home. It was nearly three o'clock in the morning in Montreal. Warnick was asleep, his wife beside him in the bed when the secure phone rang. He struggled to open one eye and look at the clock. The digital readout read 2:52. Groggily, he reached for the red handset on the nightstand beside the bed.

"Hello?"

"Secretary Warnick?"

"This is George Warnick."

"This is the secure operator, Sir. I have an emergency call from Commander O'Donnell."

Instantly, Warnick's eyes opened and he was wide awake. He sat up in bed and swung his legs over the edge. "Tom. Is that you? What is it?" He expected the worst. To receive an emergency telephone call from NUMSUB at three a.m. could not mean good news.

"I've got some bad news, George. We lost Jorge. We had taken two prisoners for interrogation and one of them broke free. In the struggle, Jorge's throat was cut. He died quickly."

Warnick paused until the impact of what Tom had just told him had a chance to sink in. His mind was still foggy from sleep. Still, he knew what to do.

"I'll call an emergency meeting of the command staff. I'll have them assembled in one hour. I'll call you back from my office."

By this time Warnick's wife was awake. She rubbed her eyes and asked, "What's the matter, George?"

"Nothing, dear. Just a little fire that I have to put out. I have to go to the office early. Go back to sleep. I'll call you later."

George had been spending a lot of extra hours at the office the last week or so. His wife didn't ask and he wasn't going to tell. She turned over and went back to sleep.

Chapter 24
An Absurd Plan

The Warnicks' home was on the eighth level of the underground complex that housed the government offices and the residential facilities. The section of the complex where they lived was patterned after the closely built brownstone houses neatly lining the streets of mid-twentieth century Philadelphia. Their house was about ten minutes away from George's office on level twenty-three.

Before he finished dressing, George called for his military chauffeur to bring his electric transport to the front of the house. The transport was not much larger than an enclosed golf cart with room in the front for the driver and space for four passengers seated on two bench seats facing each other. The passenger compartment of the vehicle was enclosed for privacy. High-level government officials had chauffeured transports. Most other workers and residents used smaller vehicles they drove themselves or travelled to work on moving sidewalks or public units that carried up to twenty passengers.

George used the televideo communicator in the transport to contact each member of the Command Staff on his way to the office. Since the other members of the Command Staff lived on the surface, it would take most of them at least half an hour to arrive. That would give him time to contact Tom for a briefing.

By 4:30 a.m. Montreal time, members of the Command Staff began to arrive. George was already on the phone discussing the situation with Tom and Al. First to arrive was General Abram Wainscot, and his two aides, Colonel Alexandria Rosewood and Colonel Montgomery Farnsworth. In close succession Margaret Cranston, Roy Constance, Admiral Dirk Beaumont, and Major Sara Brauer, Jorge's back up, followed them.

Major Brauer, a petite brunette about five feet four inches tall, had large brown eyes and short hair that she wore cropped close to her head. She was staring blankly at her hands. They were clasped in front of her, her knuckles nearly white from her grip. Silent and stone-faced, she contemplated the loss of her friend and compatriot. Tears from the emotional shock had dried. Her composure gave way to solid determination. She had experienced pressure many times before, but pressure drawn from tragedy brought out unfamiliar emotions within her. Hers would be a monumental responsibility, though one she would have gladly taken given different circumstances.

125

The soft hubbub of voices filled the room. Some of those present had been briefed on the purpose of the emergency meeting when they were contacted, others were not yet aware of the situation. The faces of those who knew told the others that this was a serious matter.

General Wainscot's face was drawn into a frown, the wrinkles on his brow and around his mouth belying years of dealing with international crises.

Secretary Warnick called the meeting to order.

"Gentlemen, and ladies, let's sit down and I'll tell you why I summoned you here on such short notice."

The room instantly became quiet. The only sounds were chairs scooting across the carpet and creaking under the weight of the occupants as each person took a place around the conference table. Warnick pressed a button on a console by his seat. A wall panel opened to reveal a monitor with Tom and Al's image transmitted from NUMSUB's wardroom.

All eyes focused on the screen.

Tom's face was drawn, his lips tight, brow furrowed. Leaning back in his chair with his left arm draped over the back, he was facing to his right. Al, seated next to him, appeared equally stressed. Yet there was an air of quiet strength that emanated from them to everyone in the Secretary's office.

"Tom," said George. "You're on. I've given some of the folks here a very brief rundown of the situation. I'll leave it up to you to fill in the details."

Tom and Al immediately turned toward the camera. On the sub's monitor, the image of the eight people seated in Warnick's office appeared

Tom leaned forward in his chair. He cleared his throat. His voice was strained.

"Apparently, the NWO have improved LOFWAR and they were able to penetrate our shields. Before the computer could adjust the resonance, they detected a brief signal and sent a couple of divers to check it out. We captured them with Trascan and brought them into the infirmary.

"Before we knew it one of the frogmen came to and grabbed a scalpel. He lunged for Jorge and severed his jugular. In spite of everything we could do, Jorge died within three minutes."

Silence shrouded the room like a heavy blanket, broken only by the audible gasps of those who were unaware of the extent of the tragedy. Sara's shoulders shuddered again at the confirmation of what she already knew. Her emotions boiled into anger and she slammed her fist on the table.

"What was Jorge doing in the infirmary?" she demanded.

"He was conducting the interrogation," answered Tom. "He felt he needed to find out what the frogmen might know about security and passwords."

"Were there any other casualties?" asked George.

"Lieutenant Armstrong was cut on her shoulder. There were no other injuries."

"What about the frogman who woke up? What did you do with him?" inquired General Beaumont.

"After we subdued him, we gave him another dose of Trascan. The only thing he'll remember will be a bad dream. We have to release them both soon, before they're missed."

The shock of losing Jorge was giving way to the impact his absence would have on the mission. He was a critical link in the chain of events. Without him, or someone to fill his role, the mission would be impossible.

A visible transition was taking place among the occupants of the room. When they heard the news they were shocked. They had lost a friend, acquaintance, mentor, valuable member of the team and compatriot. In their own way, they each felt Jorge's loss differently. They had allowed themselves the luxury of sorrow, but now it was time to get to the business at hand. They had all experienced tragedy before. They had learned to put it behind them and move on.

One result of the white clothing requirement was that it reduced the impact of rank. Everyone looked the same. At this level, each person had to feel his or her input was as valuable as anyone else's.

They were each aware of what must now be done.

Admiral Beaumont spoke up. "We have to get Major Brauer on NUMSUB quickly."

"That's right Dirk, she has to take Jorge's place. She's the only one left who can do the job," confirmed George. "Now all we have to do is figure out *how* we're going to do it."

Colonel Rosewood asked, "Can we do an underwater sub to sub transfer?"

"No, the NWO knows every one of our subs. If one disappeared this close to launch time, even for a few hours, they would become suspicious," responded Margaret. "We have to do it so they won't suspect."

Several conversations broke out in the room, each person coming up with ideas to get Sara on the sub, then dismissing them as unworkable. This was going to be no easy task.

Roy spoke up, "What about another NUMSUB? Could we use one of the others to get her over there and on board?" He looked around the room. Anxious nods indicated the others thought it might work.

"That would be a good idea if we had more time," said Tom. "Unfortunately, we have only two days. Even at top speed it would take more than that to get Major Brauer to Dogfish Base and across the Pacific. I'm afraid NUMSUB's sister boats aren't a solution."

The room settled into a few minutes of silence.

Finally, it was Sara, herself, who spoke. "I know how we can do it," she said calmly.

All eyes turned in her direction.

"I'll just drop in."

"You'll just drop in?" questioned Tom from the monitor.

"Yes. In fact, we'll need the help of the NWO. They'll play an important part in the operation," she continued.

The room was filled with curious expressions.

TOM HAYNIE

"This sounds like it ought to be good," chuckled General Wainscot, a touch of sarcasm in his voice. "I can't wait to hear how you're going to pull it off."

"Roy, you're still using high altitude reconnaissance planes, aren't you? The ones that fly over enemy territory at altitudes in excess of 100,000 feet and take pictures," she asked.

"Occasionally we'll use one to augment the surveillance we get from Margaret's satellites. They do a pretty good job, but they haven't been very effective."

"And why not?" Sara asked, with a note of confidence in her voice.

"Because the NWO usually shoots them down with a surface-to-air missile. They've developed some pretty sophisticated ground to air technology."

"Exactly."

"What does that have to do with getting you on board NUMSUB?" insisted General Wainscot.

"Everything. I'll fly in one of the planes at high altitude, say, 120,000 feet over Hangzhou Base. The NWO will think we're trying to take reconnaissance photos of the launch site. They'll shoot me down with one of their missiles."

"Oh, that sounds effective. I still don't follow, and I don't know where you're going," said General Wainscot, sounding a little irritated at this point.

"Well, let me put it this way. When they shoot the plane down, it's going to contain a little surprise in it." She was playing with him now.

"And what's the surprise?"

"Me."

"You! That's ridiculous. What good will that do?"

"The onboard radar will detect the approaching missile. Just before impact, I'll eject and free fall to NUMSUB. While in free fall, their radar may pick me up, but while I'm falling, I'll look just like debris from the exploded plane and missile. Near the surface of the water, when I'm below their radar, I'll deploy my parachute. Bingo. NUMSUB picks me up, mission accomplished."

"Do you realize that even though you'd be falling at over 200 feet per second it would take you almost ten minutes to fall from 120,000 feet? You'd have to pull your ripcord in the last few hundred feet, assuming you were still conscious. Miss by a second or two and you'd hit the water like a watermelon hitting a sidewalk. It's too dangerous. The idea is absurd."

"Then you come up with a better idea, General." Now it was Sara who was getting irritated. "I've experienced high altitude free fall and I think it's the only way I can board NUMSUB without being detected."

"That's right, Major. But your high altitude acrobatics was a controlled event with plenty of safety nets from a balloon at 90,000 feet and you didn't try to become a fatality," boomed the General, preparing to pull rank.

It was George, though who pulled rank first. "Calm down, now, Abram. Major Brauer is right. We don't have time to come up with a better alternative. I say we give it a try."

"Well, I just want to go on record saying I don't think it will work," declared General Wainscot firmly.

Roy turned to the video monitor. "Tom, what do you think? Can we pull this off?"

"It's feasible. We can have NUMSUB waiting. We'll have to be able to pick her out from among the rest of the debris so we'll know where she'll land."

"I have an idea for that," answered Sara. "I'll let you know when I confirm the availability of some equipment."

"Then it's settled. She goes up tomorrow. Abram, in spite of your misgivings, if you don't mind, I'll contact Colonel Osgood and we'll set this in motion," answered George. "Once plans are set, I'll recall all of you and brief you on them. Make sure everyone is available at a moment's notice."

General Wainscot gave a grudging but affirmative nod in response.

Turning to Sara, George put his hand on her shoulder, more a vote of confidence than a gesture of comfort.

"Major Brauer. I'll need you to stay here while I get hold of Colonel Osgood. I'm going to have him come to Montreal today to discuss strategy and how we're going to pull this off."

He didn't wait for her to respond. It was a foregone assumption that he was in complete charge of the plan.

Pressing the button on the intercom, he spoke to his secretary, "Mary, find out where Bill Osgood is and get him on the phone. This is extremely urgent. Use the code word."

George Warnick was a study in efficiency when he was on a mission, and right now, this was one of the most important missions of his life.

He turned to the others. "Thank you all for coming. We'll assemble back here tomorrow to watch the events relayed from NUMSUB. Mary will call you to let you know when to be here."

Everyone but Major Brauer exited the room and returned to the surface or in other parts of the underground government complex.

A few minutes later, the bell on the intercom sounded. Mary's voice came over the speaker. "I've located Colonel Osgood. He's in Arizona testing a new high altitude plane. I've given a message to a member of his staff for immediate delivery."

"Good," responded George. "We should be hearing from him momentarily. Would you like something to drink? Coffee, tea?"

"Yes," answered Sara. "I'll have a glass of ice water if I may, thank you."

Chapter 25
Release

Tom switched off the video connection with Montreal. He knew the next thing they had to do was put the two frogmen back in the water. The incident was unfortunate, but to take revenge on the frogman who had killed a valuable member of the team would jeopardize the entire mission and serve no purpose. He couldn't blame the diver. He was only doing what he was trained to do. No, the only solution was to put this behind them and finish the mission.

In the control room at the base, the technician monitoring Gattis and Sadmere's life support signals studied his monitor quizzically. He was holding the ear piece of the headset tightly against his ear. His look was not lost on Captain Kumodan.

"Corporal, you seem to be a bit disturbed. Is there something wrong?"

Kumodan moved to the console where the Corporal was seated. He stood behind the technician and leaned over his shoulder.

The corporal didn't remove his eyes from the monitor nor the headset from his ears.

"I'm not sure, Sir. It just seems that Gattis and Sadmere have been out there a long time and there has been no change in their signals. No indication of effort, surprise, relaxation, nothing. Just steady, constant signals. You'd think there would be some slight changes just from normal exertion. It seems strange to me."

"Let me listen," said Kumodan. He removed the headset from the technician and put it over his own ears. He listened intently to the signals for a couple of minutes. "You're saying that this is how the signals have sounded? How long has it been like this?"

"For almost two hours, Sir. I couldn't pinpoint exactly when it started because it didn't seem strange at first."

"Well, knowing those two boneheads, they must be up to something. I'm going to send a team and find out what they're up to." Captain Kumodan turned and walked toward the locker room.

Toweling off in the locker room, having just finished a workout on the free weights, were Lieutenants Yong Ling and Brut Hammergren, two of the most experienced divers on the team. Ling, a Chinese, and Hammergren an Austrian, were frequently teamed together on assignments. They were perfectly matched in underwater combat skills.

On land, Ling, a martial arts expert, was quick and light on his feet. He had never lost a fight. Hammergren could bend a horseshoe with one hand and frequently entertained other members of the crew with feats of strength. The two were considerably different in physical size. Ling, at five feet eight inches tall, was lean and lithe. The muscles on his body were as tight as bowstrings. Hammergren, on the other hand, stood six feet six inches and had shoulders you could land helicopters on with arms to match. His narrow waist made his shoulders and chest appear even broader.

Kumodan entered the room. "Ling, Hammergren. Suit up and go find out what Gattis and Sadmere are up to."

"What kind of horseplay are they into now?" asked Ling. "I thought they were in the bay chasing another phantom radar signal," he said, looking at Hammergren with a broad grin.

"Very funny," said Kumodan. "They've been out there for nearly three hours and something doesn't seem right with their life support signals. Find out if they're in trouble. If not, and they're screwing around, I'll have them pulling disciplinary guard duty for the next forty-eight hours."

The divers under Kumodan dreaded disciplinary guard duty. When the Captain decided that someone on the team needed a little reminder of who was in charge, he would make him or her stand guard, wearing wetsuits and heavy scuba tanks, for forty-eight hours straight. To add humiliation, they usually stood guard over the trashcans outside the base kitchen. They were allowed a ten-minute break every four hours for relief of bodily functions and two thirty-minute meal breaks a day, but they were permitted no other rest. Anyone who fell asleep at his post was given three days in solitary confinement.

Ling and Hammergren winced in mock pain at the thought of disciplinary guard duty. Very few of the platoon's frogmen had escaped the wrath of Captain Kumodan. He had not endeared himself to any of them and seemed proud of it. Frequently, he found it necessary to prove his authority over each man and woman on the team. They obeyed out of fear rather than respect. Even Hammergren, who could have crushed Kumodan with one hand, maintained a cool distance from him.

Tom called Al, Robin and Pete into the infirmary where the two frogmen were still unconscious. White tape reinforced the straps that held them to prevent another tragic incident should one or both wake up again. The blood had been cleaned off of their wetsuits. Unnoticed, though, was a small cut on Gattis' right hand between his thumb and forefinger that he received in the struggle to take the scalpel from him.

Speaking to Robin and Pete, Tom gave instructions on how they were to release them.

"Inject them with the antidote for the Trascan. You'll have fifteen minutes to put them in the water and get back to the sub before they wake up."

"Will they be able to breathe through their mouthpieces while unconscious?" asked Al. "I've not seen how this Trascan drug works before."

Robin responded first, "No problem there. The drug won't interfere with their muscular activities or with their motor functions. It simply puts their minds on hold for a while. When they wake up they won't remember anything since the last time they were conscious."

"How sure are we that Gattis won't remember waking up during the interrogation?" Al asked.

"Well, we're not. In tests, the subjects rarely woke. Those few that did reported remembering only bits and pieces, sort of like a dream that you just couldn't put your finger on. Ever had one of those, Captain?"

"Oh, yeah. You know you dreamed something, but it just doesn't come back. The harder you try, the more fleeting the memory becomes. Let's get these boys back into their tanks and get them out of here before they're missed."

Pete carried one of the heavy tanks in each hand. He handed them to Al and Tom, who had to use two hands to take them from him.

"Show off!" chided Robin with a grin.

Ling and Hammergren put on their wetsuits while Kumodan continued to instruct them on their mission.

"Find those two playboys and bring them back to me. I'll expect a full report when you return, and it had better be a good one.

"Approach the area with caution, in case there's something wrong, but don't expect any real danger. I wouldn't have sent two cut ups if I thought Battarian had any sense about him."

General Battarian was tough at times, but he was always fair. He evoked the opposite of Kumodan from those under his command. The men in the platoon would do anything for him out of respect and esteem. Everyone knew of the General's disdain for the High Command and they respected him all the more for standing up to what they perceived to be an invincible, frequently unreasonable force.

Many suspected that Captain Kumodan was a High Command mole. They believed he was planted to undermine the General so they could remove him from command of Hangzhou Base. This suspicion further flamed the fires of hatred the men had for Kumodan.

On the way to the drop zone, Ling and Hammergren, out of earshot of the boat driver, commented on their feelings for the Captain.

"One of these days that snake will meet his justice," said Hammergren with a tightly set jaw and cold stare. "I'd give an arm to be the one to administer it."

"Careful, my friend. To gain that privilege you might have to. We're near the drop zone. Get ready to get wet."

The two divers fell off of the boat backwards into the water and began their search for Gattis and Sadmere.

Pete and Robin pushed the limp bodies of the two frogmen through the airlock's outer hatch. NUMSUB still sat on the bottom of the sea floor in the shape of the coral reef that had fooled the frogmen a couple of hours before. They had just a couple of minutes before the sleeping men regained consciousness. It was necessary to put them near the stern of the vessel where they had captured them.

Placing them gently on the sea floor and turning on their heart transmitters, Pete and Robin turned to reenter the sub when Pete grabbed Robin's arm and pointed off in the distance. Robin could see the excitement in his eyes as she followed his gaze past his extended arm.

She saw the distant forms of two more frogmen swimming in their direction. They had not given any indication that they had seen Robin and Pete.

There wasn't time to make it back to the hatch. Quickly, Robin signaled toward the stern of the sub. Pete saw that she was motioning toward the torpedo tubes. They swam quickly to the tubes. Fortunately, the outer doors were still open. They lowered themselves inside just as Ling and Hammergren arrived near Gattis and Sadmere.

Hammergren was the first to spot their errant comrades. He motioned to Ling and they both swam toward the two drugged frogmen.

The effect of the drug was wearing off and Gattis and Sadmere came out of their stupor just before the other two divers arrived. They hadn't noticed Ling and Hammergren approaching. Gattis was rubbing his neck where he felt the sting when Robin injected him with the Trascan. In his mind the sting had just occurred. He was still groggy when he felt the presence of Hammergren behind him. He turned with a start before he recognized him. Could Hammergren have stung him on his neck? All he could figure otherwise was that he must have come too close to a small stinging fish or some other kind of marine animal.

Ling poked Sadmere on the shoulder and pointed toward the surface. Sadmere nodded affirmatively and all four divers began to swim upwards. Within a few moments they were bobbing on the waves and Ling waved for the boat to pick them up.

After climbing into the boat, they all removed their masks and tanks. Ling turned to Gattis, "What the Hell have you two been up to? Kumodan is as mad as a hornet!"

Gattis looked quizzically at Sadmere. "What do you mean? He's the one who sent us to search for a ghost. We've been gone only an hour."

"An hour! More like three!" barked Hammergren. "What did you do? Fall asleep down there? Look at your watch!"

Gattis looked at his watch in the dim light. His eyes grew wide with amazement. Somewhere they had lost two hours. How could that be? They had just started searching around the reef when Ling and Hammergren showed up. He instinctively tapped on the face of his watch when he felt a stinging between the thumb and forefinger on his right hand. He hadn't noticed a cut there before.

"I don't know," he said furtively. "It seemed like we were only down a short while when you arrived. It doesn't make sense."

"You bet it doesn't make sense. And it will make less sense while you're guarding the trash for the next two days," replied Ling.

"What!? Guard the trash? We haven't done anything wrong!" shouted Sadmere. "What is that mealy son of Satan trumping up on us now?"

Ling felt sorry for Gattis and Sadmere. In their minds they had done nothing wrong, but Kumodan would take little note of that. He was always looking for someone to make an example of. Ling was just glad it wasn't himself this time.

The driver opened the throttle and the small boat picked up speed. They passed easily over the submarine gates at the entrance of the bay. The bow of the boat made a direct line to the dock by the base approximately six miles away.

The four frogmen spent the rest of the trip in silence; each lost in his own thoughts. Gattis tried to remember when he had cut his hand. Fleeting images of a struggle passed through his mind. There was a dimly lit room, four or five strange people; one was talking to him in a muffled voice. There was the struggle again; he was lashing out with something in his hand. Then nothing. He could not, no matter how hard he tried, put any order to this vision.

Something else bothered him about the whole incident. While checking his equipment, he noticed that the meter on his tank indicated that he had used little more than an hour of oxygen. *Impossible*, he thought. *There must be a malfunction.*

He was wrestling with his thoughts when they approached the dock where they would meet their fate with Captain Kumodan. Nearing a berth, they noticed a commotion. Several men were running across the dock toward the divers' quarters.

"What's the matter?!" shouted Hammergren to one of the men running past the boat.

"There's been an accident in the locker room!" the man shouted back before he disappeared through the door.

The driver quickly tied the boat to the mooring and all five men leaped onto the dock and joined those running for the door. Inside the locker room they saw fifteen or twenty men huddled around a corner of the room. They recognized General Battarian's voice.

"Looks like someone took issue with his style of command." Battarian was speaking to the officer next to him. "I'll notify the High Command. They'll want to be informed immediately."

Sadmere, Gattis, Ling and Hammergren approached the crowd. Several of the men parted enough for them to see the object of everyone's attention. There, lying in a spreading pool of deep red blood, a fishing spear piercing his chest and pinning him to the wall, lay the lifeless body of Captain Kumodan. In his hand, the spear launcher.

In stunned silence, the four divers stood for a moment and took in the sight of the dead Captain. Soon the shock on their faces melted into expressionless stares, nearly revealing a hint of satisfaction.

"Looks like you won't have to worry about guard duty," Ling said to Sadmere and Gattis, without looking away from the scene or showing emotion.

"Yeah, and I guess the four of us are the lucky ones," Gattis said with a smile.

"What do you mean, lucky?" asked Hammergren.

"We've all got alibis," he replied, with a smug satisfaction in his voice.

TOM HAYNIE

Chapter 26

High Dive

Colonel William Osgood, Commander of the Allied West
Federation Air Force High Altitude Reconnaissance Squadron, was at the
Desert Staging Area outside of Phoenix, Arizona. He was attending a
briefing on the newest addition to his fleet of spy planes, the XU-71.

The XU-71 had just been released from experimental status after
eighteen months of testing. It had a maximum ceiling of 157,000 feet, a
range of 16,500 miles and a top speed near Mach 2. It could fly manned or
unmanned, could refuel in midair and could jam an enemy's radar if
detected. Its shape was similar to its predecessors: an unusually large
wingspan compared to the length of the fuselage.

The briefing officer described the role the plane would fill and the
results of the latest tests.

"We anticipate that within the next two years, the XU-71 will
replace all of the aging pre-twenty-first century aircraft. NWO advances in
defensive systems render our older planes useless. Every time we send one
of them over hostile territory, their missiles shoot it down. It is of little use
to us to provide them merely with target practice. The advanced electronic
technology on the XU-71 will outsmart their most sophisticated missile
tracking systems. It will give us back high altitude superiority. Next month,
the plane will be officially removed from experimental status and will be
designated the U-71."

The atmosphere above 130,000 feet verged on the edge of space.
At that altitude, wings of a normal span were basically useless. The XU-71's
long wings took advantage of what little air there was. Navigation was
made possible by means of thrusters. Outfitted with the latest in electronic
equipment, the XU-71 was a formidable spy plane.

A sergeant slipped quietly into the briefing and handed Osgood a
folded note. "It's from Secretary of Defense Warnick," he said in a hushed
voice. "He instructed me to interrupt you and deliver the message
immediately."

"TO: COLONEL WILLIAM OSGOOD,
COMMANDER, HIGH ALTITUDE RECONNAISSANCE.
FROM: GEORGE WARNICK, SECRETARY OF DEFENSE.
YOU ARE HEREBY REQUESTED TO CALL
SECRETARY GEORGE WARNICK WITHIN THE HOUR AT
514-555-7676."

Familiarity with the Secretary's unique use of the word "hereby" prompted the Colonel to leave the briefing immediately and go to the nearest secure telephone. He dialed in his classified code and the number to Warnick's office.

"Hello, George. This is Bill Osgood. How are you doing?"

"I'm doing fine, Bill. How's the weather in the desert?"

"Weather's great. If we could have Januarys like this in Montreal, I'd take up permanent residence. What have you been up to?" he asked, anxious to know what could be so urgent.

"I can give you only sketchy details on the phone, Bill. We have a critical need for one of your spy planes by tomorrow. I need you here in Montreal by 11:00 this morning and I'll give you the complete story. Can you make it?" George's last question was not a request, and Bill knew it.

"Let's see, that's three hours from now. I can take an F-1114 and make it by then, no problem," he responded matter-of-factly.

"Good, I'll see you then."

George hung up the phone. He pressed the button on the intercom on his desk.

"Mary, Bill Osgood will be here in a couple of hours. He's flying in from Phoenix. Could you alert security to be expecting him, please?"

Two and a half hours later, Mary buzzed the intercom on George's desk and announced that Colonel Osgood had just passed through security at the street level and would be in the office in a matter of minutes.

Shortly, Osgood walked through the door to George's office, dressed in the customary white shirt and trousers.

"Bill! Good to see you again." George rose from his desk and walked toward the Colonel, hand extended.

"Same here, George. How long has it been? Two, maybe three years? You haven't changed a bit, not a gray hair on your head. I want your secret." Bill warmly clasped George's hand in a firm handshake.

"Nothing to it. It comes in a plastic bottle," joked George. He put his arm around Colonel Osgood and guided him to a seat at one end of the conference table.

"Well, order me a case of the stuff. Looks like you could use a little Rogaine, though," he chided. George chuckled.

The smile quickly faded from George's face as he leaned forward in his chair. Bill knew he was about to learn something of utmost importance.

"Bill, we've been working on a highly classified mission these past few months and we're about to reach critical mass. We have a serious situation that could destroy the entire effort and we need your help."

Bill leaned forward in his seat, resting his right elbow on the table, his right hand folded across his chin. His left hand was on his hip.

"You know you can count on me for whatever you need, George."

"I know I can, Bill. I can't tell you exactly what we're up to, the mission is so highly classified that very few people are even aware it exists.

137

Except for the President and a handful of folks here, no one else is in the circle.

"The mission includes about fifteen or so highly skilled individuals who have specific responsibilities that will impact the positive outcome of the effort. Most of the men and women are cross-trained and can carry on in the event of an unforeseen mishap. Only a small number have unique skills that no other member of the team possesses."

Bill furrowed his brow and squinted. He knew that George hadn't asked him to fly all the way to Montreal at the drop of a hat just to sketch out the skeleton of a top-secret mission. There must be a critical piece that included him and he sensed that George was about to drop a bomb.

George continued. "Early this morning, Montreal time, one of those mission-critical individuals was killed. I can't go into details; they aren't important at this point anyway. The important thing is that we have only one other person in the Federation with the same skills and we have to get her into the mission tomorrow. The lives of a lot of people depend on it."

Bill broke his silence. "Where do I come in on this?" he asked.

George went on, "She's an experienced pilot and I'm going to need one of your planes to fly her at high altitude over Hangzhou Base. Do you have a plane available?"

"Hangzhou Base? Eastern China."

"Yes. On the coast of the South China Sea."

Bill thought for a moment.

"We could use any number of planes, however, the best one I can think of off the top of my head is the new XU-71. There are three operational today. Two we've been testing in Phoenix and another in the Philippines about three hours from Hangzhou. We can have it ready in six hours and can have her over the target three hours later."

"There's a wrinkle," cautioned George. He searched Bill's face closely for a reaction.

"Oh-oh. I'm afraid to ask. What's the wrinkle?"

"We have to let the NWO shoot the plane down with a missile." He saw the expression he was expecting.

Bill's face briefly showed a look of shock that quickly changed to a frown.

"Shoot her down?! That's a two hundred and forty-two million dollar aircraft. How is shooting down an airplane worth nearly a quarter of a billion dollars going to get your pilot where she needs to go?"

"She has to be seen without being seen, if that seems possible. This has to look like a routine surveillance flight over the installation. Since the NWO has warned us that any high altitude flights over their territory will be considered hostile, they've threatened to shoot down any plane we send over them.

"She'll eject just before the missile explodes. Then she'll free fall 120,000 feet and deploy her chute just before striking the water. The mission will pick her up in the water."

"That's awfully dangerous," responded Bill. "Very few people have ever free fallen from that altitude and lived to tell about it. She'll be killed if she misjudges her velocity or distance from the surface by mere fractions. Is this woman crazy?"

"We're all a little crazy right now. It's not like we have much choice. We have to get her into the mission within the next twelve hours or the results will be catastrophic to the free world. We have no other alternative at this time."

"I see. Well, if there is no other way, who is this female daredevil?"

"Let me introduce you. She's waiting in the next room. You've probably heard of her."

He turned to the anteroom next to his office and opened the door.

"Sara. Come on in and meet Colonel Osgood."

Sara walked into the room and stepped over to the Colonel.

"Bill, this is Major Sara Brauer"

"Thanks for your help, Colonel. George told me we could count on you in a crisis."

"Nice to meet you, Major. So you're the angel who's going to fall out of the sky?"

"In a manner of speaking, yes, Sir."

"And you're confident you can do this?"

"About as confident as I can be."

Bill could tell right away that this was a determined young woman. She didn't seem to be the type who'd be happy hiding behind a desk in some dingy military office.

"George here says that you're out of alternatives. So, I guess we'd better figure out how to make this happen. I can't believe we're talking about sacrificing an aircraft just ready to come out of experimental status. Are you familiar with the XU-71?"

"Not really," she answered. "I haven't kept up on the high altitude reconnaissance aircraft. I'm more familiar with the combat fighters. That's where I've concentrated most of my flight training and experience. Is the XU-71 manned or drone?"

"It can go either way. If there's a high possibility of casualty, we can send it up unmanned. We won't always get the best shots that way. It takes a pilot to make decisions based on visual criteria. We still haven't figured out a way to take the place of human thought and logic."

He continued. "The XU-71 has some advanced capabilities that make it superior to anything we've got so far. The electronics can fool the radar homing of a missile's guidance system. It creates a false sense of closeness to the target. The missile will actually "think" it's closer than it is and will detonate at least a mile away."

"Does it work like the scrambling devices on fighter aircraft?"

"No, not really. The scramblers actually confuse the radar by seeming to make the target disappear, or at least fade into a background of interference. The NWO has developed counter measures. Their radar

139

transmitters rapidly vary the frequency of the signal. The frequency changes are random, making it impossible for a scrambler to keep up. We're close with the ability to match instant frequency changes, but we're not there yet. Let me show you on the video how the new technology works."

He sat down at the conference table and turned toward the still visible screen in the wall. The screen was part of an interconnected computer system that linked the Secretary's office to the main computers deep within the AWF. This was a highly secure and highly classified government equivalent of the publicly accessed Internet.

He punched a few codes into the keyboard in front of him and an image of the XU-71 appeared. He ran through a simulated missile attack, showing the missile's radar and the XU-71's response.

"Here we have the missile locking on to the target," he explained as he worked the keyboard.

"The onboard computer senses the location of the approaching threat and sends out an electronic image of the aircraft in the direction of the missile. The missile's radar detects the signal, thinking it to be the real thing, and explodes harmlessly, far enough away from the aircraft that not even a shock wave is felt. The computer has the capability to create up to five images at the same time in the event of multiple missile attacks."

"Pretty amazing." Sara replied with appropriate awe for the Colonel's new plane. He was obviously very proud of the technology. "Unfortunately, though, it sort of defeats what we'll be trying to do."

"Yes, I know," Bill replied with a dejected look. "I hate to even think of the opportunity to try it out in an actual combat situation and not be able to throw the switch. We won't even have time to take the hardware out of the plane. We'll end up losing it all."

"I'm sure you'll get your chance to try out your new toy in the very near future," interrupted George. "Where are we going to originate the fly over from?"

"The aircraft is in Manila. It'll be ready to go as soon as Major Brauer gets there. First, though, she'll stop off in Phoenix for some quick training on one of the other two. I believe that she'll have enough time for about two hours in the cockpit before she'll have to leave. She'll need to make the drop during daylight hours, so she'll have to leave the Philippines in the morning. The flight to the China coast will take about two hours at the altitude and speed she'll be flying. Then it's another hour to Hangzhou."

Colonel Osgood turned to Sara.

"You'll approach from the South. The NWO will have you under surveillance from the time you leave Manila. You won't make a direct bearing toward Hangzhou Base until you're close. We don't want them to figure out that we're going to do a fly over too early. They could shoot you down so far from your target zone that you'll never reach it.

"We have to hope they wait until the right moment to launch a missile. Timing throughout this whole event will be critical. A few minutes too soon or too late and you'll land miles from your intended drop zone.

"Timing of your ejection from the plane will also be critical. If you eject too soon, you'll show up on their radar and could arouse suspicion. Eject too late and . . . well, I don't need to go into that. I think you get it.

"Your altitude will be right at 120,000 feet or nearly 23 miles above the surface of the earth. The atmospheric conditions will be extreme. You'll be in the upper half of the Stratosphere. The atmospheric pressure will be approximately one-one hundredth that at sea level. The temperature will approach 100 Fahrenheit degrees below zero. You'll be wearing an oxygen tank and pressurized suit: otherwise you wouldn't be able to breathe. Your pressurized suit will be heated to keep you from freezing to death. Essentially, you'll be in near outer space conditions for a while."

"So I'll be wearing a space suit."

"No. Not a space suit per se. It won't be nearly as bulky or as sophisticated. You'll be in extreme conditions for only a few minutes. The outfit will resemble more an inflatable skin diving suit."

He continued, "The temperature will start to climb once you reach the Troposphere at approximately 10 miles up, a little over five minutes into your fall. You'll remain in your pressurized suit, though, until you're picked up. There will be no way for you to take it off in free fall. It will keep you afloat like a life raft once you're in the water. Any questions so far?"

"If you're trying to scare me, you're succeeding. Are there any positives?"

"Yes, of course. If you misjudge your altitude and deploy your chute too late, you'll feel no pain when you hit the water. Imagine a grasshopper hitting your windshield at 100 miles an hour. You'll die so quickly that the pain won't have enough time to travel your nervous system before the brain turns to mush."

Sara gave a nervous chuckle. "You sure know how to comfort a girl."

"You're aware of the dangers. You've been in risky situations before," said George.

"True," she responded. "But, you never get used to it. It never becomes routine."

"It's time for you to get on your way. I have a car waiting to take you and Colonel Osgood to the air base. His plane should be refueled and ready by the time you get there. Good luck. I'll gather the rest of the team together and brief them. I'll give Commander O'Donnell instructions on your pick up. Is there anything else before you go?"

"Not that I can think of. There will be a million things going through my head during the next several hours. Hopefully, by this time tomorrow, I'll be with the mission. Thanks for everything you've done George. Are you ready to go, Colonel?"

"Yes, I'll be right behind you. You go ahead and change. I'll see you topside, shortly."

Sara exited the room to change back into her street clothes. Colonel Osgood turned to George.

"That's quite a brave young woman there, George. Male or female, I'd like to have a dozen people like her in my outfit. She's got a lot of guts," said Bill, obvious admiration in his voice.

"That's why she's part of the team," responded George, a look of pride sweeping across his face.

"I'll get in touch with the mission. We need to let them know the final plan details."

George turned on the video monitor and punched in the secret code to establish secure two-way audio/video communication with NUMSUB. Colonel Osgood departed into the dressing room before George made the connection. Sara had changed and left. She was waiting for Colonel Osgood on the surface.

The video screen flickered, and almost instantly Tom's image appeared.

George began speaking. "Major Brauer is on her way. She just left for the airbase to catch a plane to Phoenix and then on to the Philippines, where an XU-71 is being prepared for her fly-over of Hangzhou Base. She should be in the water at approximately 1100 hours tomorrow morning your time."

Al joined Tom in the wardroom and nodded at George on the monitor.

"Good. We're looking forward to having her on board," said Al.

George continued, "She'll approach southern China in an erratic flight pattern until she's about 200 miles south of the base. Then she'll abruptly change course and head directly for the target area. Both you and the NWO will track her. You'll know when they send up a missile and you'll see the impact with her aircraft on your radar. When the missile is launched, she'll veer to the East in a mock attempt to get away from it. That will send her out to sea and toward your location. It will be critical for the missile to strike the aircraft over water. If she's shot down over land, she'll be captured."

"How will we be able to see her? There will be a lot of junk falling out of the sky," asked Al.

"Once she's in free fall, your radar will be able to distinguish her from the rest of the debris. She'll wear a coded transmitter that will emit a signal detectable on your radar screen as a red dot. The code is synchronized to your frequency and will keep her from being seen on NWO radar. You'll follow her all the way down and adjust your position to meet her. She won't know where you are until you surface."

"We'll be there waiting."

"I know you will. This entire mission depends on it. We'll also monitor the event through your transmissions. The entire team will anticipate a successful pick up. You fellows catch some sleep and we'll talk to you in the morning."

Chapter 27

Disturbing News

General Mustaval Hussein, NWO Supreme Commander and Chairman, was awakened early in the morning by one of the house servants. An attaché waited at the door with a message for the General. His instructions were to deliver a top-secret dispatch directly into the hands of Hussein. The dispatch had just been received from Hangzhou Base. General Hussein quickly slipped his arms into the sleeves of his bathrobe and tied the belt around his waist. He met the messenger at the door.

It was cold and blustery outside. The wind whistled through the barren oak trees by the stately mansion where Hussein lived. Winter was well established in this part of the former U.S.S.R. He had neglected to put on his slippers, and the tile floor was cold against his bare feet. He stepped from side to side, alternating contact between each of the soles of his feet with the floor.

The mansion was lavish, well appointed for the senior member of the High Command. Still, Father Winter had no more respect for Hussein than he did for the beggar huddled in his ragged coat next to the gate that sealed the entrance to the compound. Hussein quickly invited the messenger inside.

"Sorry to disturb you so early, Sir, but I believe you would want to be apprised as soon as possible of this situation. We received this message over secure transmission just moments ago." He handed General Hussein the message.

"TO: GENERAL MUSTAVAL HUSSEIN, SUPREME COMMANDER AND CHAIRMAN,
FROM: GENERAL ACKMED BATTARIAN, COMMANDER, HANGZHOU BASE
DATE: 14 JANUARY 2056
MUSTAVAL, MY DEAR FRIEND AND MENTOR. IT IS WITH DEEPEST SYMPATHY AND REGRET THAT I MUST INFORM YOU OF THE VERY UNTIMELY DEATH OF CAPTAIN ASHOK KUMODAN. IT APPEARS THAT THE GOOD CAPTAIN WAS THE VICTIM OF AN UNFORTUNATE ACCIDENT. HOWEVER, YOU MAY BE CERTAIN THAT I HAVE INITIATED A THOROUGH INVESTIGATION INTO

THE MATTER. YOU WILL BE PROMPTLY INFORMED OF ANY DEVELOPMENTS. THE BODY WILL BE RETURNED TO ROSTOV-NA-DONU FOR A PROPER FUNERAL. WE ARE ALL SHOCKED AND DISMAYED AT THE LOSS OF OUR COMRADE. SINCERELY, ACKMED."

For a moment, Hussein couldn't believe his eyes. He read the message a second time before the full impact of its meaning sunk in.

Kumodan. Dead! How could this be? Is Battarian responsible? Did he suspect anything? "The body?" Why would he refer to him as "the body" instead of using his name? He must suspect that Kumodan was working for me. A dozen questions raced through his mind. Clearing his throat to calm his speech, he turned to the messenger.

"Thank you, Lieutenant. I will come to my office when I am dressed. Summon Generals Wing and Dillgard to an emergency meeting in the High Command Center. I expect them to be there promptly at 6:00 a.m."

Hussein closed the door and turned sharply away. He paused while he gathered his thoughts. *I must discuss this with Wing and Dillgard. They will know what to do. This will not change our plans.*

Returning to his bedroom, he rummaged nervously through his closet for a uniform. He selected one and hung it on a hook near his dresser.

He showered quickly, contemplating the implications of this turn of events. As he shaved before the vanity mirror in his bathroom, he noticed that the razor needed a new blade. He stopped and stared at the image looking back at him.

Some say that he looked strikingly similar to his great-grandfather, Saddam Hussein, who ruled Iraq with an iron fist at the end of the twentieth century. Mustaval was just over six feet tall, with a round face and bushy dark eyebrows and mustache. A slightly bulging middle gave away the fact that he was a little overweight. Turning sideways and looking at himself in the full-length mirror on the door, he reminded himself that he must get more exercise.

He dressed in his normal military uniform pants and brown shirt with five stars in a circle on the collar, a sixth star centered in the circle. He tied the laces of his dark brown shoes and summoned the butler.

"Domingo, get me a light breakfast this morning. Just orange juice, coffee and a sweet roll. I have no time for my usual meal. I will be leaving in fifteen minutes."

In five minutes, Domingo returned with a tray containing the breakfast Hussein ordered.

Gulping down the orange juice and wolfing down the roll, he sipped the hot coffee. He slipped into his uniform jacket and called for his driver. Shortly, his car was waiting at the curb in front of his house. The military driver stood beside the open rear door and saluted crisply.

"Good morning, Sir. To the High Command Center?"

"Yes, Sergeant. And hurry, I have much business to discuss."

He settled into the back seat as the driver closed the door behind him. The car pulled away from the curb. The wrought iron gates swung open. The guard at the entrance snapped to attention and rendered a salute as the limousine sped past. Wind from the rushing vehicle blew up a small cloud of powdered snow.

The drive to the High Command headquarters building took twenty minutes. Hussein's thoughts wandered to the events that brought him to his position. *Battarian has been a friend and supporter. He has been instrumental in my succession to Senior Officer of the High Command. Why is there such a schism between us?*

Born of pure Russian lineage, Battarian's grandfather was a member of the old Soviet Politburo and his grandmother was the daughter of a respected leader of the now defunct Communist Party. Because of his heritage, he was selected to enter the new NWO military training academy at Minsk.

Battarian was driven to prove that he could succeed on his own merits. While others partied, he studied. When others wasted time demonstrating against the imperialistic AWF, he attended meetings held by the military authorities. The civilian leaders of the Third World exhibited foolish reasoning when they created a common military to serve the alliance of independent nations.

To him it was clear and inevitable. Eventually the military would assume complete authority over the NWO. He cast his lot with General Barturial Medovich, the commander of the NWO combined military machine. General Medovich was the Chairman of the military High Command, which included the Army, Navy and Air Force.

An outstanding student with superior potential, Battarian received an assignment as a junior attaché to General Medovich. The General took a special interest in this bright young officer. During the formative years, when the High Command was beginning to chart its course as the most powerful force in the NWO, many power struggles erupted among the senior leaders of the various military factions.

Medovich, a negotiator skilled in political prowess, held the others at bay and solidified his influence and position. He became the undisputed leader of the High Command. It was during this time that Battarian achieved recognition and was assigned command of a series of military units and bases. He carried out his responsibilities with vigor and loyalty, gaining further attention of the military leaders to whom he pledged his unwavering allegiance.

Two years ago, worn by the constant struggle to maintain his position and put down the insurrections that attended the formation of the High Command, Medovich contracted an illness from which he was unable to recover. His funeral was a State affair in each of the NWO alliance countries, and he was laid to rest with full military honors in the new international cemetery in Rostov-na-Donu, a city in southwestern European Russia.

Hardly had the last note of his national anthem faded into history when the political infighting to name his successor began. Battarian was disgusted with the process and wisely withheld his allegiance from all of the candidates until it was clear who was likely to assume the position of authority. Then, like the skilled tactician he had become at the feet of General Medovich, he threw his support to General Mustaval Hussein. Battarian didn't like Hussein, but when it became apparent that the baton of authority would either pass to him or to the incompetent Yo Chi Lee, he chose the lesser of two evils. Because Medovich had been his champion and mentor, Battarian's support was instrumental in Hussein's successful rise to power.

Hussein lacked Medovich's leadership skills and soon maintained his authority by intimidation and subterfuge. He formed a covert group of a few senior officers of the High Command. Those who openly opposed him frequently disappeared under unusual circumstances. Battarian was one of the few exceptions. In a weak-willed attempt at gaining his loyalty, Hussein appointed him Commander of Hangzhou Base. It soon became apparent that this ploy would not produce the allegiance Hussein desired, and General Battarian quickly became a thorn in his side.

Desperate for a solution, Hussein sent Captain Ashok Kumodan, a loyal officer and comrade, to find a way to eliminate this irritant. Whenever a high-ranking officer in or near the High Command had disappeared, Captain Kumodan always seemed to be lurking somewhere in the shadows.

Hussein arrived at the High Command headquarters at six o'clock. As expected, General Wing and General Dillgard were awaiting his arrival.

General Yo Ling Wing, from the former People's Republic of China, was a slight man of five feet four inches, weighing about 120 pounds. His gray hair receded and he had a wisp of a mustache and goatee. Wing was a staunch supporter of Hussein and was also instrumental in winning the oriental factions away from Hussein's opponent, Yo Chi Lee, after Medovich's death. Wing's face disclosed a shifty presence. He would betray his mother, given the reason and the opportunity.

General Ferdica Dillgard, the Deputy Commander of the High Command, descended from French Huguenots who migrated to southern Germany in the sixteenth century. She was an ominous figure of a woman, standing over six feet tall, with broad shoulders and a piercing stare. She wore her black, gray-streaked hair pulled back in a bun. Her dark eyes could drive right through a man and bring him cowering to his knees in an instant. Her sharp tongue was unmatched by any other on the High Command, and she trusted no one, some said not even Hussein himself. She had even had her father executed during the infighting that preceded the rise of Hussein to his position. Many an ambitious young officer with visions of command and a bright military career had crossed her path and experienced first hand the magnitude of her brutality. She was feared by all and despised by most. There was no doubt in anyone's mind that she eyed the seat of Supreme Commander and Chairman of the High Command held by Hussein.

Wing and Dillgard were engaged in small talk. What possible reason could Hussein have to summon only them and not the entire High Command for an emergency meeting?

The command room, the official meeting room of the High Command, was richly furnished with large, high backed, overstuffed chairs, strategically placed to facilitate small group discussions. A large mahogany conference table with twelve hand-carved mahogany chairs, six on either side, dominated the center of the room. At one end of the table a large mahogany and leather chair for the High Commander punctuated his status, and at the other end stood a similar chair, though slightly smaller, for the Deputy Commander.

General Hussein strode quickly into the command room, emphasizing, by his demeanor, the urgency of the subject at hand.

"Wing, Dillgard. We have serious business to discuss."

They turned quickly from their chat and sat down. Wing and Dillgard faced each other and Hussein around a low table in three of the overstuffed chairs. Wing leaned forward, hands on his knees, anxiously waiting for Hussein to continue. Dillgard was relaxed, leaning back in the chair, her long legs crossed, cradling a cup of coffee in her hands. She stared silently at the man she hoped to replace.

"Since the death of General Medovich we have had to tolerate the insubordination and near treason of Ackmed Battarian. You know we have not been able to confront him directly nor summarily remove him from his command. To do so would create a revolt among some members of the High Command. The three of us have found him to be an aggravation and a threat to our control of the NWO. Were it not for his constant challenge of our authority, we would have been able to obtain complete and unlimited control by now. He has too much influence with the others.

"We devised a method to discredit him. By so doing we would gain their support, however grudgingly, in removing him from his command and relegating him to a meaningless position. We sent Captain Kumodan, our most loyal comrade, to Hangzhou Base under the guise of commanding the underwater combat platoon. His mission was to gather intelligence on Battarian until we had sufficient for our purposes."

General Dillgard, showing impatience with this review of the obvious, waved her cup of coffee in the air as though to dismiss all that had been said so far. "Yes, yes. Tell us something we don't already know, Mustaval."

Hussein glared back at her. How he detested this woman!

Pausing briefly, he leaned forward in his chair and announced simply, "Kumodan is dead."

He paused for effect, letting the impact of his words sink into their thoughts.

Wing's mouth dropped open and a look of shock spread across his face. Dillgard was in the process of bringing the cup of coffee to her lips. The cup and saucer slipped out of her hands. The hot liquid spilled into her lap as she attempted to catch them from falling. She jumped to her feet and

147

TOM HAYNIE

brushed at the dark stain that quickly soaked into her white uniform skirt. The cup and saucer crashed to the floor, shattering into pieces.

Ignoring the clamor, Hussein continued, "Battarian reported that he died early this morning of injuries suffered in a fatal accident. I rather suspect that he was murdered and Battarian is hiding something." He had no evidence to support this statement, but with Wing and Dillgard, he needed none.

Wing spoke, "What do you propose we do? Kumodan was extremely valuable. He had reported that he was gathering much information to discredit Battarian."

Dillgard added, "If HORS II is launched successfully, Battarian's popularity will rise even higher. Without Kumodan's data it will be even more difficult to unseat him."

"Our only option at this point is to follow through with our contingency plan," said Hussein. "We have an agent secreted among Battarian's trusted staff. We will instruct him to choose a time when he can terminate the good General. This unfortunate incident may well play into our hands. Done right, we can make it appear to be an insurrection among his troops and he, the unfortunate victim of the hostilities."

"I see we have little choice in the matter. I would prefer to simply walk in and shoot the man. Why take the chance on something else going wrong?" asked Dillgard.

Obviously agitated by Dillgard's remarks, Wing rose to respond. When he was excited, his Chinese accent became pronounced.

"No, no, most honorable General," interjected Wing. He could never understand why the NWO would place a woman in such a powerful position. Where he came from a woman's place was not intended to be above that of men.

"Let *us* take care of the matter. Our methods are clean, like a long knife slipped gently between the ribs and into the heart. Simple, effective, no mess. Your way, blood all over floor. Our way; he just as dead."

Dillgard looked at the Chinese general. She couldn't understand why the Chinese couldn't simply take action and get it over with. They always had to have order and simplicity.

"O.K. We'll do it Wing's way," said Hussein. "General Wing, get the message to our agent in Hangzhou Base. Go over our plan, and when the time is right, take care of Battarian."

"Yes, General. It will be done."

"Good. In the meantime, we will send our own team of investigators to the installation. I do not trust Battarian."

"Do you mind if I conduct the investigation?" asked Dillgard, her eyes narrow and piercing, lips set and brow furrowed. Hussein knew it wasn't really a request, but a statement of what she intended to do. It would have been futile for him to object. Certainly he was her superior in rank, but he had no stomach for confrontation with this woman.

"Do as you wish, Dillgard. Just do it without creating a disaster."

Ignoring his remark, she quickly rose and followed Wing out of the room.

Chapter 28
Disaster

Major Brauer belted herself into the cockpit of the XU-71 on the tarmac of the military airstrip near Manila. The sun was still below the horizon. A faint sliver of gold just beginning to outline the eastern ocean signaled the approaching predawn. She had slept very little since leaving Montreal the day before. The brief stop in Phoenix had left no time for sleep while she became familiar with the aircraft. Fortunately, she was an experienced fighter pilot, and the controls of the XU-71 were similar to the ones on planes she'd flown before.

Colonel Osgood had briefed her on the advanced electronic technology although there was not much chance she would use any of it. If everything went as planned, this flight would be nothing more than target practice for the NWO.

The flight crew chief gave her the thumbs up to signal that all was clear and she could start her engines. She flipped on the engine start toggle, and the sound of the turbines began with a low hiss and rapidly increased to a high pitched whine. When the engine ignition light turned green, she could feel the engines ignite with a bang and a loud roar. The aircraft vibrated from the tremendous power building up in the thrusters. The ground crew disconnected the external power supply and unchocked the wheels.

Sara closed the cockpit canopy and the roar of the engine diminished. She could feel the vibrations in every muscle of her body. She relaxed when the onboard computer took control of the plane. All Major Brauer had to do now was sit back and enjoy the flight. The computer would do the rest. The flight plan had been preprogrammed into its memory.

Like a radio-controlled toy, the aircraft rolled down the taxiway to the end of the runway. The voice of the ground controller came over the speaker in her helmet. "Blue Bird, you are cleared for take off."

The brakes held the plane still. The engines' revs increased to take off power and the vibrations smoothed out. The brakes released at the instant the afterburners kicked in. The aircraft leaped forward. She was pressed back hard into her seat. Her heart pounded in her chest as the runway lights moved faster and faster past her. She loved the thrill of take off more than any other part of flying.

She watched the air speed indicator climb rapidly through 120 knots. The nose wheel lifted smoothly off the runway and the horizon disappeared. She felt the main landing gear leave the ground and she was airborne. At ten feet off the runway the wheels folded and the landing gear doors closed with a thump. The nose quickly tilted up until the plane was climbing at a sixty-degree angle. Airspeed zipped through two hundred, then three hundred knots. Even at the steep angle of climb, the powerful turbo-boost engines pushed the aircraft as though it was made of paper.

Shortly after takeoff, the sun broke over the horizon behind her. The stars disappeared and the cloudless sky turned a brilliant blue. She would maintain radio silence for the remainder of her flight. Watching the altimeter climb through 30, then 40, then 50 thousand feet, she thought about the number of times she had flown combat missions in this part of the world.

She had been shot down twice before. That didn't bother her, but this time was different. She had never before flown a mission where the *objective* was to be shot down. In combat you didn't have time to fear, you never knew whether your bullet was coming. This time she knew there was a bullet with her name on it and she knew precisely when it would come. *This must be what it feels like to face a firing squad.*

The altimeter continued to climb. 80,000...90,000. The sound of the air rushing past the cockpit had ceased thousands of feet below. The wings were fully extended to take advantage of what little lift could be obtained from the thin air. She continued to climb. Finally at 120,000 feet, the vibrations of the engines eased back. She had reached the predetermined cruising altitude and speed. The nose came over and the horizon reappeared. The sight was breathtaking. The hazy film of atmosphere refracted the early morning sunlight and divided the indigo blue of the earth beneath her and the deep black of space above her. Even though the sun was brilliant in the eastern sky, behind her the stars had reappeared and were steady points of light. There wasn't enough air to cause them to twinkle.

The computer changed course frequently in response to the flight program. Somewhere down below, she knew that there was activity around a radar screen.

General Ackmed Battarian had been called to the radar room at Hangzhou Base for the second time in two days. This time the subject of interest was not in the water but in the sky.

The Corporal worked the controls of the radar tower and focused on the object that was a bright yellow blip on the screen.

"It's a high altitude reconnaissance aircraft, General. It left Manila about two hours ago and has been flying an erratic pattern. It has been indirectly approaching the installation, however, there has been no direct attempt to indicate that we are its target."

"What do we know about the aircraft?" asked Battarian.

"Very little, Sir. It's a new model. We've monitored the test flights of a new version of the U-70 for several months now. However, NWO intelligence has not yet provided details."

"NWO Intelligence!" boomed the General. "Now, that's an oxymoron if I've ever heard one. They couldn't find their nuts with both hands and a flashlight."

The General's obvious disdain for the High Command was showing again.

The Corporal busied himself with the radar controls, glad that the object on the screen demanded his attention. Everyone knew that the General and the High Command did not always see eye to eye. Nevertheless, the High Command tolerated his insolence because of his extreme value and skill as a military tactician. Men of inferior importance had disappeared into the bowels of the NWO's empire for lesser remarks.

Suddenly, the Corporal's attention became even more focused on the monitor. "General!" he raised the tone and urgency of his voice. "The aircraft has just made a turn and is heading directly toward us. It's approximately 320 kilometers south."

The General peered over the technician's shoulder, a look of concern etched across his weathered features. The intent of the AWF was now obvious. They were going to take a closer look at the activities around his launch site.

"Get me Colonel Barkovich at the missile site, immediately!" he ordered.

Colonel Ivan Barkovich, the commander of the missile site, pushed the button on the televideo monitor on his desk. General Battarian's face appeared on the screen. The Colonel figured he knew what the General wanted because his radar also tracked the Federation aircraft.

"General, we've been watching the radar with some interest for a while. Our missiles are ready to lock on the target and we are prepared for launch. Should we mount a defensive attack?"

"Immediately, Colonel. I don't want that plane to come any closer to the installation."

"Yes, Sir! We launch immediately," Barkovich repeated the command. He pressed the red alert button on the console by the radar monitor. The alert siren at the launch site sounded and the men who were attending the missiles scrambled for the cover of their shelters. A missile rose on its launch cradle and pointed toward the sky.

"Fire when locked on the target!" commanded Colonel Barkovich to the launch control officer.

The launch control officer watched the electronic guidance monitor. It showed the outline of the target and three dancing white concentric circles. Each circle searched for the target. One by one the circles locked on. When all three were locked, they turned red.

The launch control officer repeated, "Target locked. Missile launched." He lifted the safety cover on the launch switch and pressed the switch from "Standby" to "Launch."

In a fiery blast, the missile streaked off its cradle toward the high flying plane and Major Brauer.

Submerged at periscope depth about 20 miles East of Hangzhou Base, NUMSUB monitored the high flying aircraft and the activity at the missile site. Through satellite links, they, too, had been tracking Major Brauer since she left Manila earlier that morning.

The radar room of NUMSUB was quiet. The only sounds were the intermittent beeping of the equipment.

The radar technician, Sonarman First Class Darnell Standing Red Hawk, watched the activity on the monitors. Seaman Standing Red Hawk, a full-blooded Sioux Indian, had served with Al before and had earned his place on the crew. His friends knew him simply as 'Hawk.' He wore his black hair in a single twelve-inch braid tied with an eagle feather, lying against the back of his neck. His obvious violation of the Navy's grooming code was ignored.

He watched as the computer aboard the XU-71 monotonously followed the preprogrammed flight plan. He watched with a bit more interest when the computer turned the plane on a direct course toward Hangzhou Base at the predetermined 200-mile distance.

Suddenly, another blip appeared on the radar screen.

"Is that what I think it is, Hawk?" asked Tom anxiously.

The response brought confirmation of what he feared.

"Yes, Sir. Hangzhou Base has fired a missile at the aircraft."

"No! Those idiots!" yelled Tom. "They've reacted too soon! She'll come down over a hundred miles southwest of us! She might not even make it away from land!" The excitement in his voice matched the activity in the room.

The activity in Secretary Warnick's office came to a standstill. All eyes were on the wall monitor showing the radar image aboard NUMSUB. Looks of horror covered the faces of everyone in the room.

"Is there anything we can do!?" asked General Wainscot anxiously.

"Nothing," responded Secretary Warnick, slumping back into his chair. "All we can do is watch."

"I knew this was an idiotic idea!" bellowed Wainscot. He threw up his hands and stormed out of the room, not wanting to witness the inevitable.

The rest of the team members sat around the table in disbelief, staring at the monitor. Without Major Brauer, they could not infiltrate the launch site. This meant the end of the shroud of secrecy surrounding the mission to destroy HORS II. It was now a suicide mission for the men and women aboard NUMSUB.

In the radar and missile control rooms at Hangzhou Base, all eyes watched the missile and the aircraft come together. No one noticed that the plane seemed to jump slightly on the screen a few seconds before impact. In an instant, a bright flash on the monitor indicated that the missile had found its target. Cheers rang out at both locations. The explosion from the missile sent a brief electronic interruption to the ground-based radar screens, obliterating the image of the XU-71.

In the radar room of NUMSUB and the Secretary's office, the atmosphere was anything but joyous. Heads were bowed in shock. Intense concentration on the radar screen had turned into blank stares when the images converged and then disappeared in a flash.

For a few moments, no one spoke in NUMSUB. The silence was intense. The only sounds were the occasional electronic beeps of the instruments and the subtle groaning of the sub's superstructure as the ocean currents worked against the hull.

"Did she eject?" asked Tom quietly.

"No, Sir. I'm sorry," answered Hawk, watching the screen. "There is no signal from her transmitter registering on the monitor." The silence crept back like a chilly fog.

TOM HAYNIE

Chapter 29
Resurrection

Twenty-three miles above the surface of the earth, Sara Brauer sensed something was wrong. She had been jolted from her thoughts by the sound of a buzzer going off in the cockpit and a warning message flashing on one of the XU-71's radar screens. The digital message read simply "Missile Lock On. Take Evasive Action." A calm computer-generated voice audibly repeated the same warning.

The plane's defensive radar system had been switched from automatic to manual to prevent the computer from activating the electronic image and thwarting the intention of the mission.

Sara scanned the instruments. She was still nearly two hundred miles south of her drop zone.

This can't be happening. They were supposed to wait at least another ten minutes. If this one hits me I'll never make it to NUMSUB. I've got to do something.

Were she in a combat aircraft, she would have begun defensive maneuvers to evade the incoming missile. But now, she could do nothing. She did not have control of the aircraft, and even if she did, she wouldn't be able to outmaneuver a missile in a cumbersome reconnaissance plane.

The warning on the screen and the accompanying computer voice announced, "Missile lock on. Impact in three minutes. Evasive action required immediately."

She thought furiously. *Can I climb to a safe altitude? Should I eject and take my chances on the ground? What about the mission? It can't end this way. Too many people are depending on me.*

"Impact in two minutes. Evasive action required immediately."

A plan quickly raced through her mind. *The defensive radar can be turned on manually. Good thing Colonel Osgood showed me how the radar worked.*

She reached for the console in front of her. There was a switch labeled: "Activate Defensive Radar." It was protected by a plastic cover. She lifted the cover and pressed the switch. Immediately the onboard computer calculated the speed and distance of the incoming missile. It sent a false image of the aircraft directly in the path of the missile.

The missile's radar locked on the false signal and its guidance system adjusted its course for the new target.

154

"Evasive action successful. Missile lock on image confirmed."

Never had a digitized computer voice sounded so sweet in her ears.

A few seconds later, a bright flash signaled that the missile had exploded just under a mile from the XU-71.

In the sonar room aboard NUMSUB, the electronic interference from the explosion had dissipated. The radar screen again picked up a signal.

Hawk broke the stillness. "Sir?" he said. "Take a look at this. This is … odd."

Tom and Al rose from their slumped positions and moved slowly to the monitor. Clearly moving across the screen at the previous location of the XU-71 was a familiar blip.

"Is this possible, Commander?"

With a look of relief, Tom said, "It's not only possible, Hawk, it's real. She turned on the image. The missile blew up an electronic picture. It didn't hit her!"

At once a wave of excitement filled the room. Tom and Al exchanged high fives. Crewmen and women slapped each other on the back or exchanged hugs. Now, it was NUMSUB's turn to cheer.

Tom got on the video to Warnick's office. "George, do you see it?"

A similar gleeful scene had broken out in Montreal. "Yes, we watched the whole thing on the wall monitor. Let's just hope that Hangzhou Base reacts now with the right timing!"

The cheering subsided slowly in the radar room at Hangzhou Base. The intense observation of the radar screen was replaced by celebration. The technician had looked away to join in the festive clamor. Now, he settled back in his seat at the console. He glanced at the monitor. The smile on his face suddenly faded, replaced by a quizzical expression, then disbelief.

"General!" he shouted. "Come quickly!"

General Battarian, engaged in cheerful conversation with the Officer of the Day, turned and walked to the console. At first his expression disclosed no change of emotion. He was used to seeing blips on the screen of a radar monitor. "What do you have?" he asked the Corporal.

"Is it possible that the missile missed? The radar still shows the plane."

"What? It couldn't have missed. These missiles have never missed a target. There must be some other explanation. Let me see."

Battarian thought for a moment. Then he asked, "What was the altitude of the explosion?"

The technician checked the readings on the monitor, "35,000 meters, Sir."

"And what is the altitude of this airplane?"

"Just over 36,500 meters."

The general pounded his fist on the console. "Then there were two aircraft. The Federation thought to fool us by putting a drone between our radar and the real surveillance craft. The second one was hiding in the shadow of the first."

He picked up the receiver of the videophone. "Barkovich. Are you proud of your success?" he said calmly.

"Quite, General," Colonel Barkovich responded. "We've never missed a target and we never will," he said with obvious braggadocio.

"Then I'd suggest you take a look at your radar. You haven't finished the job!" Battarian's voice rose.

The bravado in Barkovich's voice faded when he glanced at the monitor. "Where did that come from?" he said out loud.

"It's obvious," replied Battarian. "The AWF dogs thought to fool us by stacking two aircraft in the air. Did they not think we would shoot both of them down?"

He no sooner asked the question than he answered it himself. *They couldn't be that stupid. Our enemies are not idiots. Surely they would have known we could shoot both down. There must be a reason.*

"Send up another missile and finish the job!" he commanded.

"Right away, General. It will take a moment to arm and lock another." He turned to the control room crew and barked the appropriate orders.

Within minutes the second missile locked on the target and was sent on its way. By this time, though, the XU-71 was near the predetermined drop zone where Major Brauer would begin her free fall to NUMSUB.

Shortly, the familiar buzzer sounded again in the cockpit of the XU-71. Sara looked at the radar screen again to see the warning, "Missile Lock On, Evasive Action Required," flashing on the screen and the soothing voice of the computer repeating the words. This time, though, there was no frantic response. Now, things were going according to plan.

The computer turned the plane out to sea and accelerated in a mock attempt to escape.

Sara checked her gear, located the ejection handle and waited.

The only sound she focused on came from the computer's voice. "Impact in 40 seconds. Take evasive action," it said, almost too calmly.

She imagined the sight of the missile streaking toward her.

"Impact in 30 seconds. Take evasive action," repeated the voice.

She knew she had to wait until at least five seconds before impact to eject from the aircraft. At the speed the plane was traveling and the acceleration of the seat propulsion rockets, five seconds would put her far enough away that she would be safe from shrapnel and the shock of the explosion. It was cool in the cockpit, but she had beads of sweat on her forehead and rivers of sweat running down her neck.

"Impact in 20 seconds. Take evasive action." The computer voice revealed no hint of emotion. She adjusted her oxygen mask and pulled down the dark face shield of her helmet.

I wonder what it will say after impact. Then she smiled. *"Impact has occurred. Too late for evasive action, Dummy!"* She gripped the seat ejection handle tightly. She leaned back and took a deep breath.

"Impact in 10 seconds. Take evasive action."

Steel nerves kept her from ejecting too early. She counted down out loud, "10..9..8..7..6..5." On five she pulled hard on the handle.

The canopy blew away and the propellant beneath the seat ignited, slamming her down hard as the seat exploded out of the cockpit.

Chapter 30

Bad News

The private telephone rang in Colonel Jawar Abdullah's office. Colonel Abdullah was the commander of the security force at Hangzhou Base. He picked up the receiver, "Colonel Abdullah, here."

"Colonel Abdullah, this is the operator at the High Command Center. I have a call for you from General Ferdica Dillgard."

Colonel Abdullah leaned back in his chair. He was expecting to hear from the High Command, although not necessarily General Dillgard.

"Yes, please put her on immediately. Thank you."

A click sounded on the line and a few seconds of dead silence ensued while the call was transferred. Shortly, General Dillgard's voice came on the line.

"Colonel Abdullah, this is General Dillgard. I believe we have not yet met. Is that correct?"

"Yes, General, that is correct. I assumed my station shortly after the last time you visited Hangzhou Base. What can I do for you?"

Though Jawar knew of her reputation, he had been fortunate enough to avoid meeting her in person. He was afraid that his good fortune was going to come to an end shortly. He did know that a member of the High Command seldom made telephone calls or spoke personally to anyone below the commander of a facility. Communication to the lower ranks was usually through an aide or messenger. To hear directly from the General meant this was going to be a serious conversation. In addition, the call was not going through the base commander. This was definitely out of normal protocol.

"Colonel, I would assume that General Battarian has assigned you to preside over the investigation into Captain Kumodan's unfortunate accident?" Her voice was terse and the tone indicated that she did not respect Battarian.

"I will meet with General Battarian this afternoon. At that time I assume that he will turn the investigation over to me. I have already begun interrogating witnesses."

"That is good, Colonel. I will arrive tomorrow morning and will expect a full report. May I assume that your investigation will concentrate on *all* possible suspects?"

He knew by her tone that she suspected Battarian was involved in the matter.

"Of course, General. No one on the installation is exempt. At this point in the investigation everyone is a suspect. The investigation will be quite thorough."

"Yes, I will see to that. The purpose of my trip will be two-fold. I will observe the launch of HORS II in two days and I will conduct my own investigation into the matter."

"Certainly, General. I welcome your support and involvement," he lied.

"Speak to my aide and make arrangements for my arrival." As quickly as she had come on line, she was gone and her voice was replaced by the voice of an aide.

"Colonel Abdullah," began the aide.

"One moment please," answered Jawar. It was one thing to be directly insulted by the High Command with insinuations of his lack of competence, it was quite another to have to speak to an aide to make lodging arrangements. "I will put my assistant on the line and you can make your arrangements with her."

At that point, Jawar turned the call over to his secretary.

I'm afraid that Ackmed is not going to be happy with Dillgard's arrival. Her presence during the launch can only mean trouble.

Chapter 31

Free Fall

The subfreezing temperature of the upper stratosphere hit Major Brauer with intensity. The G-forces of the ejection seat immobilized her completely while the seat lifted her up and away from the plane. Her arms felt like they were molded to the armrests. She saw the XU-71 recede below her, rapidly growing smaller as the distance between them increased.

Then a streak of silver came from below the plane and overtook it. In an instant, a blinding flash completely engulfed the aircraft. She had seen the impact of a missile with an aircraft many times in training films, but she had never witnessed one so close or under such conditions. The sight was one she would never forget.

Far below, many eyes watched the same event simulated on radar screens.

In the radar room at Hangzhou Base, General Battarian, the Corporal and a small group had gathered around the monitor to observe the electronic image of the missile chasing the intruder. No one spoke as the images converged and finally met in the telltale flash. All eyes remained on the monitor while the flash faded to see if yet another blip would appear, indicating another AWF trick.

The monitor cleared, eyes searched, the blip did not materialize. Instead only small points of light scattered across the screen as the radar picked up images of debris falling out of the sky.

There were no cheers this time, only a nod of satisfaction from the General and a pat on the back for the Corporal at the monitor.

"Let that be fair warning to the Federation. We will not tolerate such intrusions into our air space," commented the General to no one in particular. He turned and went about his business. Little did he know that one of those small points of light falling out of the sky was Major Sara Brauer, still strapped into her ejection seat.

Twenty miles to the east as well as half-a-world away, other eyes were also glued to radar screens. As at Hangzhou Base, no one spoke. The converging blips, the bright flash fading to tiny points of light. There was one difference. On these monitors, one of those points of light was red.

A sense of euphoria filled the chests of each of those watching. There were no celebrations, though. Each man and woman knew they had just entered the most critical phase of this part of the mission.

Tom spoke with obvious relief in his voice. "She made it. We pick her up in ten minutes."

He looked at Hawk. "Pinpoint the location where she'll land in the water and let's get moving."

Al was already giving the commands to get NUMSUB underway. The sub slowly moved forward and turned toward the coordinates where the computer indicated Major Brauer would touch down.

Sara watched the fireball that was once her plane begin to diminish. The sound of the explosion was merely a muffled thud. The air was too thin to effectively carry sound waves. The sky filled with burning wreckage and debris that had been flung out in all directions from the explosion and was now beginning to arc gently toward the earth.

She could see the near black sky above her, only the hint of blue against the dark background. The stars continued to shine sharply without twinkling. It was a beautiful sight only a few have witnessed in person.

She was at such a high altitude that at first she had no sense of falling. The stratosphere contains no clouds or weather so there were no reference points to indicate motion. The air was so thin she could not feel herself falling through it. There was no sound of wind rushing past her helmet.

She released herself from the seat and kicked it sharply away. She wouldn't need it anymore. Normally the pilot would remain with the seat, which was designed to deploy a parachute automatically at precisely the right altitude. Naturally, the deployment mechanism had been disabled for this mission.

The seat seemed to hang motionless beside her as it fell at the same rate even though it weighed more than four times as much as she did. *Newton was right. Without air to impede, all objects, regardless of mass, will fall at the same rate.* She chuckled to herself. *This is no time to fantasize about old physics lessons.*

She could see the coast of China over twenty-two miles below. She could make out the Fuchun River meandering to the ocean. From this height, the Hangzhou Bay really did look like a dragon's mouth. The outline of Hangzhou Base was clearly visible. She could almost discern the missile facility with two empty launch pads. The view was majestic.

Caught up in the amazing beauty of the scene, she hadn't noticed the moisture from her breath condensing in the oxygen regulator. The regulator was malfunctioning, and with her back to the sun, it was in her shadow. The condensation began to freeze, cutting off her oxygen supply. Her breathing became labored.

What's happening? I can hardly breathe! Her first impulse was to rip off the oxygen mask attached to her helmet and take a deep breath of air. *No! There is no air.* She forced herself to think. She could hardly move her fingers.

I've got to turn over. The oxygen regulator is freezing up. She struggled to turn her body to face the sun while dropping at more than 200 feet per second. In the weightlessness of free fall turning her body was no

161

easy task. Another of her physics lessons came into play. For every action there is an equal and opposite reaction. If she tried to twist her upper body to the right her lower body would twist to the left to counter the effort. She had to concentrate on slow movements, using the thin air like a fulcrum on which to pivot. Slowly she made small gains. The effort caused further labored breathing. *Not too fast. If I start spinning I'll go out of control.*

Finally she turned on her back. The oxygen regulator faced toward the sun. The heat from the unshielded rays quickly melted the frozen condensation and freed the oxygen. Her breathing was restored and she began to think clearly again.

Far below, in NUMSUB, Hawk watched the red dot move slowly on his screen. His dark eyes were glued to the dot, as though if he looked away it would disappear. He chanced a glance at another screen beside him, this one monitoring the surface of the ocean. He froze at what he saw.

"Captain!" he exclaimed. "We have company!"

Al immediately left his post and moved to the monitors. "What do you have, Hawk?"

Hawk pointed to a blip on the surface scanner. "It looks like a small craft about five miles from Major Brauer's landing zone, Sir. It's about 2,500 yards off starboard."

"Periscope depth!" commanded Al. A seaman keyed the proper codes into the computer that controlled the sub's movement. Within a minute the ship was just a few feet under the water's surface and the periscope broke through.

Al, seated at the captain's chair, flipped a couple of switches that controlled the periscope cameras. He quickly saw the vessel on the forward monitor and magnified the image.

"It's an NWO patrol boat," he said with disappointment in his voice. "Damn! What are they doing here?"

The NWO patrol boat, number YT-791, had been on routine patrol along the coast of the mainland north of Hangzhou Base. When the high flying reconnaissance plane was spotted and shot down, the boat was diverted from its coastal duties to the drop zone where most of the airplane's debris would hit the water. There was an outside chance that they might spot some piece of the airplane large enough to salvage and examine. It wasn't often that one side got the opportunity to grab a piece of new technology the other side was developing.

Al turned to Hawk monitoring the electronic surveillance equipment. "Are they using sonar?"

"No, Sir. I've detected no soundings coming from the vessel. They don't appear to be looking for us."

"Can we eavesdrop on their radio transmissions?"

"One moment, Sir. I'll pick up on their frequency." He worked the keyboard. "Here it is, Captain." Hawk handed Al a headset.

Al put the headset on and listened intently. The computer in NUMSUB translated the conversation from the patrol boat into English.

In the control room of the patrol boat, the senior officer intently watched a radar screen with dozens of small moving dots illuminated across it. Another officer was on the deck scanning the sky with binoculars.

The senior officer spoke into the microphone of the radio. "We should see the first of the wreckage hit the water in about five minutes, General. I don't think we will find anything larger than a small dog. The wreckage will be scattered over at least five hundred square kilometers. We have spotted no parachute. If anyone was on board the aircraft, they surely would have ejected well before the missile destroyed it. Most likely it was unmanned."

Al called Tom to the control room. "It looks like the NWO are searching for wreckage or a survivor. This close to the landing zone they're sure to see her parachute when she opens it. What do you suppose we ought to do?"

"I'm not sure," responded Tom. "We could easily take them out with a torpedo, but that would warn the installation of our presence."

"We could jam their radio and take them captive," added Al. "Unfortunately that would let the base know something was up and they'd be all over this part of the ocean like ants at a picnic. NUMSUB doesn't have a brig, anyway. We'd have no where to detain them."

"We're sort of out of options, Al," said Tom. "I think we're going to have to play this one out the way it unfolds."

Chapter 32

Dangerous Landing

Ten miles above the earth, Major Brauer dropped through the invisible boundary between the stratosphere and the troposphere. Seventy-five per cent of the earth's air and all of its weather are found in the troposphere. She had fallen more than twelve miles in a little over five minutes. The air had gradually become denser but was still too thin to breathe.

At five miles above the water, she noticed the patrol boat and wondered if they could see her. *No time to worry about that now.* She searched for NUMSUB. She hoped NUMSUB had her on radar and would be waiting when she landed.

The sea was a beautiful emerald green. There was not another vessel in sight.

Shortly, Major Brauer forgot about the patrol boat and whether anyone was watching. Her focus was on the rapidly approaching sea. She gripped the D-ring of her parachute tightly while she mentally calculated her speed and distance. She had to deploy the chute at least 1,000 feet above the surface to allow enough time for it to open before she hit the water. At the speed she was falling, she would cover that distance in less than five seconds. There was no margin for error.

Her mind imagined all kinds of disasters. *What if it doesn't open? What if I pull the ripcord too late? What if the sub hasn't picked up the signal?*

She forced these questions from her mind and concentrated on the rapidly approaching sea. At the moment she determined herself to be a thousand feet above the surface, she pulled the ripcord. Instantly the parachute unfolded from her back and reached its full length above her. For a few seconds the sea continued to rush toward her at frightening speed. *Did I pull the cord too late?*

Hawk had calculated the exact location Major Brauer would land. The sub moved into position immediately below the spot and waited. All eyes watched the red dot on the screen, waiting for its motion to slow, signaling that Sara had deployed her chute. At approximately two and a half second intervals, Hawk quietly announced her altitude.

"Twenty-five hundred feet . . two thousand feet . . fifteen hundred feet . . one thousand feet."

No one breathed as she approached critical altitude. There were no other sounds. Sweat dampened the brows of everyone in the room in spite of the cool temperature in the sub.

Hawk announced her altitude more rapidly.

"Five hundred feet. . . four hundred feet. . . three hundred feet. . . two hundred feet. . . one hundred ninety feet."

"Yes!" shouted Al. "She's deployed! Let's get her! Go! Go! Go!"

In an instant, air filled the nylon canopy with a snap. Sara's body jerked hard as it quickly decelerated. After ten minutes of falling two hundred feet per second, she felt like she was hanging motionless in the air, the ocean barely two hundred feet below. Had she waited another second to pull the ripcord she'd have been fish food.

The officer on the deck of the patrol boat scanned the sky with his binoculars. He had spotted a couple of larger pieces of wreckage, but had seen nothing that interested him.

The senior officer at the radar console spoke. "Yuri! Off to the north, about eight kilometers. There is a large piece of debris. Can you see it?"

Yuri pointed his binoculars toward the north and began to scan the sky. His face contained no expression. Then, in disbelief, his mouth dropped open and he pressed his eyes into the eyepieces of the binoculars.

"It's impossible!" he exclaimed.

"What's impossible?" asked the senior officer, running quickly to the deck. He fumbled with his own binoculars tangled around his neck.

"It's the pilot! He must have ejected. But his parachute has not opened."

"Could he be dead?"

"He must be. He has fallen from nearly 37 kilometers. I've heard of no one who has survived from such an altitude," responded Yuri. "Wait! Look! He has opened his parachute!"

"His chute must have opened automatically. I can't imagine he's still alive. Let's go! We'll pick him up."

The sailor at the helm turned the vessel in the direction of the descending parachute and the boat accelerated.

Major Brauer glanced in the direction where she last saw the patrol boat and saw it coming toward her about five miles away. She frantically looked into the water below her for a sign of NUMSUB.

There, directly below her was the shadow of a vessel under the water. The sail broke the surface but the rest of the sub remained submerged to avoid being seen by the boat. Relief flooded over her while she prepared for landing. There was movement in the water. *Sharks!*

Fear gripped her chest at the sight of several large sharks swimming slowly through the water below her. The hatch on the sub opened and five people rushed out on the observation deck.

Tom, Al, Smitty the cook and two other seamen scrambled out of the hatch. They knew there were sharks in the water. One seaman carried a rifle and the other wore a wetsuit. Smitty carried steaks from the kitchen.

They spotted Major Brauer about a hundred and fifty feet directly overhead. Smitty tossed steaks into the water on the opposite side of the sub from where she would land. The seaman with the rifle leveled his sights on the dark shadows gliding through the water.

The sharks' keen sense of smell immediately picked up the scent of the meat and they darted quickly toward the source. A feeding frenzy began on the port side of the sub. The thrashing of the big fish attacking the meat caused the surface of the water to churn and foam furiously. Few sights raise fear in the heart more than the sight of hungry twenty-foot sharks fighting wildly over a hapless victim, even if the victim is just a T-bone steak.

Sara watched the activity aboard NUMSUB. One of the men threw something into the water. Whatever it was, the sharks seemed to like it. They all moved to the port side and began thrashing. Within seconds, she hit feet first and sank. The cold ocean water wrapped itself around her like an icy blanket.

The buoyancy of her suit quickly returned her to the surface. She struck the release latch on her parachute and it floated away. Her arms and legs were stiff from the long fall through the cold air and it was hard to make them start swimming.

The crew saw Major Brauer land in the water twenty yards off starboard. She momentarily disappeared from view, then bobbed to the surface. One seaman immediately dove into the water and swam to her. By the time he arrived, she had released the parachute and was swimming toward him.

"Hurry!" shouted Tom. "The boat will be here in three minutes!"

A lone shark separated itself from the rest at the sound of the Major splashing down. It circled the sail to investigate the disturbance. The seaman aimed his rifle at a point just beneath the fin protruding from the water.

"Don't shoot unless you absolutely have to," said Tom quietly. "The sound of gunfire will carry a long distance over water; the boat will hear it for sure."

The seaman acknowledged with a nod without taking his eye from the sights of the rifle.

The shark moved slowly in an erratic course, investigating its prey. Major Brauer and the seaman in the water were about ten yards from the deck when the shark turned and darted toward them.

The seaman with the rifle squeezed down on the trigger when a splash erupted in front of the charging shark.

The shark immediately turned its attention to the object that caused the splash and attacked it with fury. Smitty had just thrown his last steak between the shark and the two swimmers.

The momentary distraction allowed sufficient time for the Major and the seaman to reach the sail. Tom and Smitty reached down and grabbed Sara by the arms and pulled her up, Al and the rifleman assisted the seaman. One by one, all six jumped through the hatch as the sub began to dive.

The patrol boat arrived within seconds after the sail dipped beneath the waves. The hull's iridescent color kept NUMSUB hidden under the water. The churning of the sharks hid the swirling water that was the only evidence of the sub's presence. After a brief search, the sailors spotted the parachute floating in the water and approached it quickly.

"Where is the pilot?" asked the senior officer.

"We haven't found him yet," responded Yuri.

A junior officer pointed a few yards off the starboard side of the boat. "Over there!"

All eyes searched in the direction he pointed. "Sharks!" cried the officer.

With a look of pity, the senior officer commented, "Yes, sharks. They've been feeding. Poor son-of-a-bitch. I hope he was dead before he hit the water."

He turned to the helmsman. "There's nothing more we can do here. Let's return to port. Yuri, advise base that we are returning."

Yuri picked up the microphone and called Hangzhou Base. "YT-791 returning to port. The plane was piloted. Unfortunately, the sharks got to him before we could. There is nothing left but a parachute."

Two hundred feet below Hawk was listening on the radio.

"Captain, we made it. They're leaving. They never suspected we were here."

Chapter 33

Unwelcome Visitor

General Battarian had instructed his command staff to come to his office to discuss the death of Captain Kumodan. Colonel Ivan Barkovich, commander of the missile site, arrived several minutes before the others. Battarian wanted to discuss the downing of the Federation spy plane.

"This is the first time the AWF has used that tactic," said Battarian. "I wonder why we didn't notice there were two planes while they were many kilometers from the base. Surely our radar would have been able to pick out two planes."

"Not necessarily, Ackmed. If the two planes were flying close to one another and their computers changed course and speed simultaneously, the radar would not have had the sensitivity to separate them at that distance."

"But when we shot the first one down they were nearly two kilometers apart."

"Yes, when their radar detected the missile threat, the drone separated from the second to take the missile. The part I don't understand is why they would do that. Surely the AWF would have known we would shoot them both down."

"My thoughts exactly. They must have had some other purpose than to merely cause us to waste one missile."

At that moment, the receptionist announced the arrival of the rest of Battarian's staff.

"We'll take up this discussion later, Ivan. First I want to discuss Kumodan's death with everyone."

Colonel Vidaj Singh, commander of the space facility, Colonel Jawar Abdullah, commander of the military training unit and the installation security force and Admiral Kwetsi Mufweme, commander of the naval surface and submarine fleet, walked through the door to the office and took seats around the conference table. Captain Kumodan reported directly to General Battarian, who kept the command of the Special Forces units to himself.

They met in the conference room adjacent to Battarian's spacious office. The conference room contained a large circular table around which were ten high-backed chairs. There were twelve large portraits on the wall of the twelve members of the High Command. Chairman Hussein occupied the central position and his portrait was raised slightly above the others. To his right was the portrait of Vice Chairman Ferdica Dillgard. Hussein and

Dillgard's portraits were painted in such a way that it appeared that the two were facing each other, their eyes meeting in a never-ending glare.

"Gentlemen, I'm sure you will echo my sentiments. It was truly unfortunate that Captain Kumodan met an accidental fate so soon in his career. Such a fine officer would have made a great contribution . . ."

"Come, now, Ackmed." It was Colonel Singh who interrupted the General. "We all know that Kumodan was a plant, a spy from the High Command, and that his sole purpose was to discredit you. Let's not eulogize the man with the traditional Party rhetoric."

Colonel Singh was from New Delhi. He was thin and stood tall and straight in his uniform, topped off with the traditional turban required of men who professed his religious beliefs. He had a full black beard and mustache streaked with gray. Singh was also a pragmatist. He was not given to fancy words to tickle the ears with useless propaganda.

Singh continued, "We also know it is likely that Kumodan's death was anything but accidental. He had many enemies among the troops he commanded. Any one of them would have wanted him dead. In fact, were one to list all possible suspects, one could hardly omit the names of some of us in this room."

"Vidaj, we can always count on you to cut through the trivia and get to the point," responded Colonel Abdullah.

Colonel Abdullah sat in his chair with his arms folded, a pensive look on his dark face. Abdullah, an Arab, had earned his commission fighting fiercely in the futile resistance following the Nuclear War between SOWPANC and MANTRA. He was a major in the MANTRA ground forces at the close of the conflicts. When he aligned with the NWO military, he quickly rose to his current position of authority. Of those on Battarian's command staff, Abdullah was the one officer the General was unable to read.

"Do not include me on your list of assassins, Colonel Singh," continued Abdullah. "Praise Allah that I found no fault with Kumodan and do not share your suspicions of him. I have no argument with the High Command. Kwetsi, what is your opinion?"

"Opinion? My opinion, if you must call it that, is that Kumodan suffered the consequences of his actions. Were we at war and had he led his platoon into battle, his death would have been less conspicuous in the presence of an enemy to blame it on. During relative peace, only the appearance of an accident would cast doubt on its origin. Kumodan was an expert with a spear. It is unlikely that he could have shot himself with one. It's unlikely that any bumbling fool would be able to shoot himself in the chest with a spear. The foot maybe, but not the chest."

"Well, then, Abdullah, it looks like this is one for you. Of course, you will lead the investigation," said Battarian.

"I shall not only lead it, I shall conduct it myself. I understand Vice Chairman Dillgard will arrive shortly. She has informed me that she will look into the matter as well."

Battarian's face turned red and he made no attempt to hide an obvious scowl. "Dillgard!" He spat the word from his lips as though expelling a gnat that had just flown into his mouth. "Watch your back, my friend. She may be here under guise of an investigation, but she listens to everything you say and has a memory like an elephant."

"I will handle General Dillgard. I have no fear of the woman."

"You may mark my words. When you know her, the fear will come."

Battarian was so upset by the news of Dillgard that he momentarily forgot about the two spy planes.

That afternoon, a private military jet bearing the markings of the High Command landed at the main airstrip at Hangzhou Base. Three command staff vehicles waited on the tarmac while the plane taxied to a stop. The lead vehicle was a black limousine with flags on its front fenders. On the right was a red flag with a circle of five stars signifying the occupant was a general of the highest rank. The flag on the left was sky blue with gold trim and an eagle with outstretched wings, the flag of an officer of the High Command.

An honor guard of soldiers stood at rigid parade rest and lined both sides of the scarlet carpet laid from the rear door of the limousine. They were dressed in crisp black uniforms with white turtlenecks rising from the open collars of their shirts. Spotless white gloves covered their hands, and red berets sat smartly on their heads. White belts contrasted sharply with black trousers and each had a red sash draped over the left shoulder across the chest and tied at the waist under the right elbow. The pants were bloused at mid-calf above black combat boots shined to a mirror finish.

Each member of the honor guard stood with feet apart at shoulder width. Their left hands were placed in the small of their backs with palms out. Their right hands held the barrels of their rifles at precisely a thirty-degree angle in front of them. The butts of their rifles rested on the ground at the outside of their right feet. Eyes stared forward, focused on an imaginary object in the distance.

A small truck with steps mounted on the back pulled up to the plane and aligned the steps with the door. The door opened and General Ferdica Dillgard emerged from the plane. She stood at the top of the steps dressed in a dark blue military uniform, navy trousers and jacket with a white shirt and navy tie. Her garrison cap was dark blue with a black brim. The brim was covered with the gold braid of a staff grade officer. She carried a pair of white gloves in her right hand, a swagger stick in her left. Her tall frame appeared even more imposing to those on the ground looking up at her.

She paused at the top of the steps and savored the power she possessed. A brisk wind picked up under the clear January sky, and she drew her jacket around her.

The sergeant-at-arms gave the command, "Honor Guard! Ah-*ten*-hut! *Pree*-sennnt . . . h-arms!"

Instantly and in unison, the honor guard came to attention, heels clicked together in one simultaneous sound. They smartly brought their rifles to their left shoulders in three coordinated moves, holding the rifle butts in their left hands, their gloved right hands parallel to the ground across their chests. The tips of their index fingers lightly touched the rear sights of their rifles. Their eyes had not moved from the imaginary focal points.

General Dillgard strutted slowly down the stairs, continuing to savor the power of the moment. At the bottom of the stairs she met Colonel Abdullah.

"Colonel Jawar Abdullah, at your service, Ma'am. Welcome to Hangzhou Base." He clicked his heels and offered a sharp salute.

She sloppily returned his salute by flipping her white gloves against the brim of her garrison cap. Acknowledging his rank, she remarked with obvious dissatisfaction that the base commander had not shown the courtesy of meeting her arrival, even though she was the one who offended by not contacting him directly.

"Yes, Colonel. Show me to General Battarian, I have much to discuss with him."

Her dark eyes darted around the airfield noticing every feature. She slipped easily into the back seat of the limousine for the ride to headquarters. Colonel Abdullah entered the second car in line. Protocol dictated that, unless invited, no one except the highest ranking officer of a facility would ride with a member of the High Command.

The entourage arrived at headquarters. A corporal stepped briskly to the door of the lead limousine and opened it. He stood at attention and saluted as General Dillgard stepped out of the vehicle. She ignored him. Colonel Abdullah escorted her into General Battarian's office.

Battarian rendered a half-hearted salute, which was returned in like manner. The chill in the room did not come from the January wind outside. Not waiting to be invited to sit, Dillgard sat herself in the chair at the head of the conference table.

Common courtesy among officers of their rank required that he offer her something to take the edge off of the journey. "May I offer you something to drink? Perhaps coffee or tea, a little Vodka maybe?"

She ignored the offer and went directly to the point of her visit.

"Ackmed. There is no secret why I am here. The High Command is less than convinced that Kumodan's death was an accident."

"I am aware of the High Command's suspicions, Ferdica. I assure you that we are taking this matter very seriously and no possibility will go unchecked. I have Colonel Abdullah, the head of our security, a competent officer and investigator, conducting the inquiry."

"We shall see what he finds. I will be most interested in the outcome of his investigation. In the meantime, I will monitor the activities at the space facility. The High Command anticipates a successful launch. In fact, I will personally assume command of the launch and take your place in the observation room of the control center. I'm certain that you will have enough to do to assure that the investigation into Kumodan's death runs smoothly."

This last exchange was particularly biting to Battarian. The launch of HORS II would be the highlight of the year for the NWO and a significant event for the base. To be unceremoniously bumped from the senior position at the site was a slap in the face. Something he rather expected from Dillgard, though.

"Yes. A good idea," he lied. "It is very important that we get to the bottom of the Kumodan affair. It could put a blemish on the celebration of a successful launch. We wouldn't want that to occur, now would we?"

"Of course not. Now, if you will instruct the good Colonel to show me to my quarters. I am tired and look forward to a short rest. I have much to prepare before the launch tomorrow."

Of course you do, you slut. He forced the corners of his mouth into a smile, and instructed Abdullah to escort her to the High Command officer's suite in the guest officers' quarters.

So, you want to be sure of a successful launch. We'll see about that. No sense tempting fate, now is there? he thought. He picked up the phone and called Colonel Singh, the space facility commander.

"Vidaj. How are preparations going for the backup control facilities for the launch?"

"Ackmed, you know they are behind schedule. The workmen have labored night and day to have the facility ready by launch time."

"You are still certain that this preparation is of little value, aren't you? You believe that the malfunctions experienced in the launch of stages three and four of HORS have been corrected."

"You know I do, Ackmed. I have opposed the creation of a redundant system. I felt it was wasteful from the start."

"Well, then, my friend, you'll be pleased to know that I've done much thinking about the plan and have concluded that perhaps you are right after all. I've decided that you may cease building the backup system and concentrate your full energies on the primary launch systems. What do you think about that?"

Obviously pleased, Singh answered, "Very good, General. I trust you arrived at your decision with much consideration and I am pleased that you place such confidence in me. Thank you."

"You're welcome, Vidaj," responded Battarian. He hung up the telephone and leaned back in his chair. He raised his arms and placed his hands behind his head, contemplating his last order. A look of satisfaction spread across his face.

Battarian was not really convinced that the malfunction that had caused the failure of the original HORS launch had been corrected. That is why he had wanted a redundant system in case of a problem. Now, he was less inclined to create a fail-safe system. *If there is a malfunction, let Dillgard be the person to take the embarrassment. You want the glory, then take the liability. The Devil will judge between us.*

Chapter 34
Welcome Aboard

Tom quickly escorted Major Brauer to the officer's wardroom. She received a change of clothing and then moved to the infirmary. The ship's medical corpsman examined her to determine if she suffered any ill effects from her high altitude free fall. Her body temperature was slightly low, 92.4 degrees F, so the corpsman gave her a thermal blanket. The blanket was light weight and metallic. It had been stored in a heated compartment in the infirmary. The warmth felt good against her body as her temperature returned to normal. All other vital signs were within normal ranges.

After the examination, she returned to the wardroom where Commander O'Donnell waited for word on her condition.

"Major Brauer is in excellent condition, Sir. Other than a mild case of hypothermia, which should clear in a few minutes, she appears to have suffered no ill effects."

"Good news, Corpsman. Thank you." The corpsman exited and Tom turned to Sara.

"Welcome aboard, Major. You had us on our toes for a while there. Glad you're O.K."

Major Brauer extended her hand to Tom.

"It's good to be here, Commander. Under the circumstances I'd rather be watching this mission, but I'm ready to take Jorge's place. Really sorry about what happened," she said, referring to Jorge's death. "He was a good friend and his death was a terrible loss to us all."

"The loss was devastating, and after this is over, Jorge will receive appropriate recognition for his contribution."

"I plan on being there for that, Sir. Now from what I understand, we enter the harbor tonight. Is that correct?"

"Correct. We've received information that Hangzhou Base will send several of their ships, including submarines, to blockade the bay during the launch. When their ships leave the harbor, we'll slip in underneath them while the gates are open."

"Sounds easy enough."

"We hope so. You never can tell what can happen, though. I thought we'd go over your assignments before we're inside the harbor.

"We discussed the plans in the Secretary's office the other day. I was involved with Jorge and trained with him as his backup. I know them inside and out. Although we prepared for it, we never thought I'd be here under these circumstances."

"None of us did. Have you familiarized yourself with the redundant system they're building at the launch facility?"

"Yes. We took the program to MIT to modify it on their Phase II Supercomputer. It took a while to work out the bugs, but I believe we've perfected it. The program should function properly whether there are one or a dozen backup systems in place. There's just one small problem."

"What's that?"

"It's never been tested except on the Supcom II's theoretical reality."

"Well, there's a lot on this mission in the same boat. No pun intended. If it all goes according to plan, we'll give new meaning to theoretical reality."

"When you get right down to it, Commander, everything we're facing is theoretical. Not even HORS II has been tested under actual space conditions. Theories, reality, there's really not much of a difference is there?"

"If you put it that way, I'd have to agree with you. Now, let's go over what your mission is tonight."

"First thing I'll be responsible for is to upload our demographics into the main data banks of the central computer. I'll do that from the accounting office near the headquarters complex. If that fails, we might as well head for home. We'll never get into the space facility."

"Right. We were unable to extract current data on passwords from the two divers we captured. Unfortunately, that whole episode turned out to be a waste of time as well as a tragic encounter."

"I don't think we'll need current passwords in the accounting office. Bean counters are the same everywhere. They think they have too many passwords anyway, so they usually don't change them unless they have to. When they're required to alter them they change them back to something simple as soon as possible. For people who work with numbers all the time, they don't like to complicate things any more than they have to. It shouldn't be too hard to crack their code."

"Well, I hope not. How familiar are you with the layout around the accounting office?"

"I've studied the photographs taken from the satellites. I also spent a few days in the mock up we built under the Test Site. From what I could tell by the photos, the mock up is fairly close to the real thing."

"Sounds like you're on top of it. Do you have any questions?"

"Yeah. I haven't eaten in a while. What's the possibility of getting a little dinner?"

"I think we can accommodate that. You'll find the food on NUMSUB quite satisfying. Anything in particular you'd like?"

"You got Mexican?"

"Is that a trick question?"

"No. Just thought I'd try you out since you said I could have anything."

"Well, let's see what we can drum up. Mind if I join you?" Tom called for Smitty, the sub's cook.

Smitty entered the wardroom.

"Major Brauer, this is Seaman First Class Jedediah Smith. You may remember him from earlier today."

"Yes. You were the one feeding the sharks. I have a lot to thank you for."

"One of his duties is to attend to the meals around here. That is, when he's not running the forward torpedo room."

"Pleased to meet you, Ma'am," said Seaman Smith, with a deep Alabama drawl. "They gener'ly call me Smitty 'round here. Y'all can call me just 'bout anything you'd like and I'd be pleased to answer. Understand you'd like some fixin's?"

"Definitely, Smitty. I think I could eat a horse right now."

"Well, that might take awhile, but I could prob'ly round one up in a jiff. Might be a little hard to cook all at once though. Would you settle for some fine southern fried chicken instead, Ma'am?"

"Actually, Smitty, Major Brauer and I would like Mexican. What do you have in your kitchen that won't take long to fix?"

"I could whip up some fajitas and a couple of chimichangas in a hurry. Would you like refried beans and tortilla chips? The chips are a bit on the stale side. It's hard to keep 'em fresh down here."

"Sounds great. Include the beans and can the chips. My mouth's watering already. What about you, Major?"

"Sounds great to me. Never thought I'd be eating Mexican in China."

Smitty went to the galley to prepare the meal. Putting together a Mexican dish was really no large task. NUMSUB's galley was well stocked with a variety of freeze-dried meats and vegetables that could be reconstituted in minutes to create almost any ethnic meal a person wanted. Food on a submarine was generally more savory than on surface ships. The Navy felt that confinement in the close quarters aboard a sub should be compensated for with some degree of comfort. The two best places to eat in the military are a captain's quarters and a submarine.

Pretty soon the wardroom filled with the tantalizing aroma of hot salsa and Mexican spices. It wasn't long before Tom and Major Brauer were sitting down to a great Mexican dinner. Add a little hot sauce and you couldn't tell that half an hour ago the ingredients had the look and feel of porous cardboard.

After finishing her meal, Major Brauer said she needed to get some rest. The ordeal of the day had taken a lot out of her. Tom showed her the stateroom where she would sleep. She removed her outer garments and settled back on the bunk. She hadn't realized how tired she really was. The room was small and relatively bare of furniture, but that didn't matter. All she wanted was a comfortable place to rest. The navy blue wool blanket was warm and the white cotton sheets felt like silk on her skin as she slipped between them. Within minutes she was sound asleep.

When Tom left her, he returned to the control room. Al was going over the details of the harbor outlined on the large acrylic map in the center of the room.

"You look like you might be up to something," said Tom, approaching the map.

"There's some activity in the bay. How's Sara?"

"She's doing fine. Taking a nap now. The last couple of hours took a lot out of her. Sounds like she knows what she's doing."

"Good. Take a look at this."

The screen was alive with red indicators. Al pointed to a group of red circles just inside the harbor on the other side of the gates.

"It looks like they're preparing a small fleet to exit the harbor. I count twelve ships at anchor on the surface. Five destroyers, a couple of cruisers, an aircraft carrier, three sub chasers and a battleship. There are at least two submarines, possibly three. Two were surfaced a while ago, but have since submerged."

"Good night! I knew they'd take precautions, but this is serious. NUMSUB's going to get a real baptism of fire. What do they have in the air?"

"So far, just the usual. Nothing out of the ordinary. It does look like they've prepared a squadron or two for immediate take off. Probably relying on their radar to give warning of an approaching threat. The laser defense has been operational for some time now. I'd venture a guess that nothing's able to penetrate once they've deployed the whole enchilada."

"Nothing but us."

"Right." Al's response was cautiously confident.

"We go in in about ten hours. I'm going to grab some shuteye. How about you?"

"You go ahead. I'll turn in shortly. I want to go over the systems one more time to make sure there aren't any bugs."

Al was taking a human precaution. If there had been any bugs in the systems, SUPCOM III would have detected and corrected them by now.

Chapter 35

Enter the Harbor

NUMSUB rested on the sea floor just outside the main submarine gates at the harbor's entrance. They waited for the gates to open. All stations on the sub were manned. Every submariner felt the drama of breaching the harbor's defenses and entering deep within enemy territory. Once inside the gates, there would be no open sea for a quick escape.

Al watched the video monitors. The low lighting in the control room gave the room an eerie atmosphere. The front monitor centered on the impenetrable barrier of huge steel doors. From the bottom of the bay, the doors appeared ominous and forbidding.

Hawk listened intently for a signal that the NWO had started maneuvers. Radio activity had increased considerably.

The gates would open only long enough to allow the vessels to pass through. They would close quickly. The NWO did not want to leave them open any longer than necessary.

Tom sat in the briefing room, arms folded, head bowed, listening. Seated around him were the other members of the infiltration team, each lost in his or her own thoughts.

Major Brauer was relaxed and calm, leaning back in her seat, a cap pulled down over her eyes. She was napping.

Tom looked at her intently. *She has guts. She'll need them when she goes in the headquarters compound by herself.*

"The gates should open any time now, Sir," said Hawk, holding the headphones of his radio receiver close to his ears. "The lead cruiser has orders to proceed."

Al focused on the video monitor showing the mountainous steel doors. Each door was made of four layers of three-inch thick steel plates separated by six inches of concrete between each plate. The gates were two hundred feet tall and weighed 25,000 tons each.

Suddenly, a low rumble, much like the precursor to an underwater earthquake, was felt throughout the sub. The sea floor began to vibrate, almost imperceptibly at first, then rising to a deafening crescendo. A cloud of sand rose at the base of the gates. A thin shaft of light appeared between them and grew wider.

Al imagined how Moses must have felt when the waters of the Red Sea began to part. Within minutes, a two hundred foot gap of open water separated the gates. Two hundred and twenty feet above them, the shadow of the first ship slowly moved toward the opening.

Al gave the command, "Prepare to lift off."

He would wait for the moment when NUMSUB could enter the harbor after most of the ships had passed through the gates. The lead ships swept the sea with sonar. Detecting no intruders, they signaled the remaining ships to proceed.

With only three ships remaining to pass through, Al gave the command, "Lift off! Bring her up five feet. Ahead five knots."

SUPCOM III responded to the commands. NUMSUB slowly lifted from her settled position and began to move forward. Centered perfectly between the open doors, her bow entered the harbor.

Suddenly, a red light on the radar console began blinking rapidly and Hawk froze. The radar monitor showed the unmistakable form of an approaching vessel.

"Submarines! Dead ahead! Collision course! Distance one hundred yards! Impact in fifteen seconds!" he barked.

Three NWO submarines were leaving the harbor in single file. The lead sub was about twenty feet above the sea floor. Normally they would exit the harbor on the surface; however, they were making maximum usage of the space available. By the sub's passing beneath the flotilla of surface ships, the gates could be closed more quickly.

"Reverse engine! Full speed!" commanded Al.

Instantly responding to the computer command, NUMSUB reversed its propeller and groaned under the stress of stopping and changing direction. Slowly her forward motion halted and she began to move backward with the first NWO submarine closing fast. There was a shallow ravine thirty feet deep and longer than a football field about two hundred feet behind her. If NUMSUB could drop into the ravine, they might avoid a collision.

In agonizing slow motion, NUMSUB's reverse speed increased to match that of the approaching submarine.

The bow of the first NWO submarine was within ten feet of NUMSUB's nose as she settled into the ravine. The sail would have to be tilted to avoid being struck when the NWO sub passed over her.

NUMSUB dropped into the ravine and Al instructed the computer, "Tilt forty-five degrees starboard."

NUMSUB immediately tilted sideways when her keel settled into the sand. The first NWO submarine passed within inches of striking the sail as NUMSUB leaned out of the way. The floor tilted and everyone on board grabbed for a handhold.

"Have they seen us?"

"No indication they know we're here. They wouldn't have expected anything to be on the other side of the doors. Apparently, they aren't watching for an obstacle in their path." responded Hawk.

On board the lead NWO sub, the captain spoke to his first officer in subdued tones, completely unaware of the drama playing out just a few feet beneath them.

"This should be an uneventful exercise, my friend. The High Command reports they've been monitoring all AWF surface and submarine vessels. There appears to be no interest in what will happen in less than twenty-four hours. Except for those two high altitude reconnaissance aircraft we shot down this morning, there has been no air activity either. They don't seem to have any idea how little time they have left before we completely control their lives."

Fortunately, the two subs following the first out of the gates were higher in the water and passed well over NUMSUB. Tom moved into the control room and stood beside Al, watching the monitors. The doors would soon close and Al had to act quickly. There was no time to gradually lift off the sea floor and then engage the propeller. He would have to begin acceleration immediately.

"Engine ahead full, come off the floor quickly!" he commanded.

Compressed air was pumped into the ballast tanks and NUMSUB began to right herself in the ravine while lifting off the sea floor. The propeller engaged immediately and the keel drug briefly in the sand. A loud scraping sounded throughout the vessel, like a thousand fingernails scraping across a chalkboard. The doors of the anti-submarine gates had reached their widest open position at five hundred feet and started to close. In a few minutes, the harbor would be sealed shut.

Accelerating quickly, the keel struck the leading edge of the ravine, sending a shudder throughout the vessel. Al grabbed the arms of his chair to steady himself. Tom grasped the back of the chair and fell to his knees. The crew reached for handholds again. Hawk slipped onto the floor with a thud.

The accelerating submarine rapidly approached the closing gates.

"Will we make it?" asked Tom, not wanting an answer. "It's going to be close."

The crew focused on the engine controls as though watching them would make the engine produce more power.

The bow of the ship reached the path of the closing doors and passed through. There was no possibility of turning back now. If the doors caught the submarine between them, the hull would be crushed and cracked open like the shell of a walnut.

It seemed to take forever for the sub's 140 foot length to pass through the rapidly diminishing opening. The doors seemed so close they would touch the hull any second. The port and starboard video monitors showed the onrushing edge of the gates on either side. When they passed out of view, the rear camera picked them up as they came together, missing the rudder and propeller blades by inches.

Al slumped in his seat and gasped for air. He hadn't realized that he had been holding his breath. The tension in the control room vanished and the crew went back to their duties.

"Whew! That was close," said Tom with a sigh. "Sure glad you're the one driving. How'd you know we'd make it through?"

Al looked at him with a funny expression on his face that said simply, "I didn't."

Chapter 36

Plan B

"Electronic surveillance dead ahead." Hawk worked the electronic sensors. A video monitor on his console showed the electronic defenses in the bay as a random series of red lines crisscrossing in front of the sub.

"Engage shields," commanded Al.

SUPCOM III responded, "Shields engaged." Instantly the sub's shields deployed and NUMSUB entered the electronic field undetected.

"Are there any ships in the area?" Al asked Hawk.

"None, Sir. All active vessels have left the harbor. Everything inside the harbor is either tied to a berth or resting at anchor."

"All stop. Come to periscope depth."

NUMSUB gradually moved upward until the periscope extended above the surface of the water. Al studied the monitors in front of him. The starlight gave a ghostly glow to the buildings and docks. He magnified the view toward the docks near the headquarters compound where Sara would hack into the main computer. There were two ships at berth with three empty docks between them. They would slip into one of the docks and put her ashore, then wait for her to complete her task and return.

"We'll wait here for an hour and then move into position. We need to be certain there is no additional activity on the docks."

Al said to a seaman near him, "Ask Major Brauer to join us in the briefing room."

He rose from his chair and descended the steps into the room below. Tom followed him down the stairs, and Sara soon emerged from her wardroom. She was dressed in dark olive green fatigues, black running shoes and a black bandana over her hair.

Al briefed her on the details of the current activity in the harbor.

"The harbor is clear and there are three docks vacant near the headquarters buildings. We'll surface in the center berth around 2100 hours. You'll have two hours to complete your job. We'll need to enter the mouth of the Fuchun no later than midnight."

"Have you come up with a plan to get past the mine field?" asked Tom.

"Not yet, but I'm working on it. Sara, do you have your files?"

Sara pulled two items out of her pocket. One was a disk about the size of a silver dollar. It was encased in a clear, waterproof plastic container. The other was a standard USB storage drive.

"Got them right here. Once I locate a computer it will take me about five minutes to upload the data files. Let's hope the NWO have installed the industry standard two-inch six terabyte laser disk drives in their workstations. If they don't, I've got a backup copy on this ancient 23 gigabyte zip drive, but I'd rather not use it. It'll take at least twenty minutes to upload all of the information from this."

"O.K. Let's go over the lay of the land one more time," said Tom.

He unrolled a large photograph of the headquarters complex adjacent to the bay. The photo was taken by one of the AWF's satellites the day before the mission started. The piers and all buildings were clearly shown, down to the detail of the lettering above the doors on each building. Tom took out a silver pen and traced a route from the piers.

"We'll dock in this location." He pointed to the middle pier. "You'll work your way through these small buildings, keeping out of sight. The darkness and shadows will cover you. This building contains the accounting department. By this time at night it should be unoccupied. We've not detected any significant security near this part of the facility. Our intelligence reports indicate that the NWO don't believe an accounting department represents much of a target. The only guard we know of is located in this guard tower behind the pier. You'll need to be cautious here." He circled the guard tower between the pier and the accounting building.

"The door to the building has a timed lock that can be opened by an access code. Typical of accountants, they haven't changed the code since they received the locks from the manufacturer. At least we don't think they have. The code is the four digits '1-2-3-4.' Any questions?"

Sara shook her head.

"What's the procedure if you run into anyone?"

"Avoid contact if at all possible."

"And if you're captured?"

"Inject this." She held up her left hand and showed a plain gold ring which appeared to be a simple wedding band. If she were to flick her thumb across the underside, a small needle about a half an inch long would snap out of the bottom. The ring contained a couple of doses of a lethal poison that could bring death to a human in fifteen seconds.

"Right. The NWO can extract any information you possess regarding the mission and NUMSUB. Their methods are particularly ugly for a woman. Do you still feel up to the task?"

Sara looked Tom directly in the eyes. "More than ever. I'm ready."

If you don't' return to the sub within two hours we'll have to assume you've been unable to complete your assignment and we'll be forced to leave without you. Understood?"

"Yes, completely."

"Then you'd better finish your preparations. We'll see you in the control room in fifteen minutes."

Sara returned to her wardroom.

Al turned to Tom and said, "We've never discussed what would happen if she didn't succeed. Warnick mentioned there was a backup plan but we never discussed it."

"The backup is that Plan A will be scrapped and we'll immediately go to Plan B."

"Plan B? What is Plan B?"

"Plan B was not to be discussed outside of the harbor. You remember we mentioned it in George's office. Once inside the base it is assumed that the mission will be followed to a conclusion, one way or another."

"Right, we'd go to an alternate scenario if something went wrong at any time in the mission. What's the backup plan?"

"The backup plan, or Plan B, is secured in the aft missile bay. We have two short-range missiles and two torpedoes with low-yield nuclear warheads on board. They were loaded before any of the crew came on board, including you. Only myself, Smitty and two members of my team are aware we have them. We couldn't chance anything happening to any of the crew who might have knowledge of the alternative."

Tom continued, "If any critical phase of the mission fails and we are unable to complete as planned, we are to launch a missile against the space facility and destroy it before HORS II is off the ground. This procedure would be used only if there is no possible way to complete the mission in secrecy. Obviously, a missile rising out of the water in the harbor and destroying the space facility would indicate that hostiles were in the area."

"I can see we'd use the missiles for the launch facility, what are the nuclear torpedoes for?"

"The bay is long enough to fire a torpedo at the underwater gate from a distance of at least five miles. The small nuclear blast would be enough to push the gates aside so we could make our escape. We'd have to be at least five miles away or NUMSUB could be damaged. That distance should be sufficient to protect her."

"*Should* be sufficient?"

"Yes. We've never tested her in an actual nuclear detonation from any distance. Our engineers assure us that five miles is sufficient."

"These are government engineers working for government wages, I presume?" asked Al, with a note of skepticism in his voice.

"Yeah. Let's hope their calculations are correct for the first test."

"It's about time to dock this baby. What say we go topside and get ready to drop our passenger off?"

Al returned to the control room and took his seat. Tom sat beside him.

"Let's park her in the middle dock."

NUMSUB moved into the central of the three empty docks next to the NWO headquarters. With her shields activated, she was invisible to the naked eye. She moved slowly to reduce her wake. Someone watching might wonder what was causing the disturbance in the water. Gradually she rubbed against the rubber covered piling supporting the pier. A ladder extended from the top of the pier nearly to the water's surface.

Nestled snugly by the pier, NUMSUB was ready for Sara to begin her mission. Al checked all directions on the video monitors and determined that there were no sentries or activity on the docks or in their vicinity. Sara had joined them in the control room.

"Are you ready?" asked Tom.

"Let's do it," she responded.

Sara opened the hatch and her head popped out. She looked around. The scene would be startling had there been anyone watching. It would look like a head simply appeared out of nowhere and floated just above the water's surface.

Satisfied that no one was around, Sara climbed out of the hatch and walked across the hull to the ladder leading to the top of the pier.

Chapter 37

Cure for a Headache

The High Command suite in the guest officer's quarters on Hangzhou Base was lavish. Two thousand square feet of opulence, including a master bedroom and bath, reading room and living room. The suite had a secure telephone line that scrambled all incoming and outgoing calls to provide complete privacy.

Following her short nap, General Dillgard was unpacking her travel bag when she received a call over the secure line. She picked up the phone.

"This is General Dillgard."

Even though the line was secure, the caller used a code name and disguised his voice.

"General Dillgard, this is Dr. Sadat. I trust your accommodations are satisfactory."

"Quite, Doctor. They are just as I expected."

"Excellent. Your prescription is ready. The dosage has been carefully measured to assure maximum effect."

"Good. This headache is irritating. I will be happy when it is cured. What time may I expect the prescription to be delivered?"

"You may expect it this evening. My messenger has been especially chosen for her efficiency."

"Thank you, Doctor. You will be adequately compensated for your successful treatment."

She hung up the telephone and continued to unpack her bag; a sinister smile crossed her lips. *Well, my friend Ackmed, the wheels are in motion. Tonight the difficulties you cause for the High Command will fade into history. We shall see who is more efficient in excising this irritant to the High Command. General Wing, or myself.*

A lieutenant approached the door to General Battarian's office and knocked.

"Come in, it's unlocked." General Battarian was seated at his desk signing orders.

The lieutenant entered and walked briskly to the side of the desk. He placed a recording disk in front of the general. "Sir, you were correct.

TOM HAYNIE

She received a coded message over the secure telephone. Here is the conversation."

"Excellent, Lieutenant. You are certain no one else knows that the scrambler has been deactivated?"

"Very certain, Sir. I deactivated it myself this morning before her arrival, according to your instructions. I will reactivate it upon her departure. What do you make of the conversation?"

Battarian inserted the disk into a recorder and listened carefully.

"Obviously it is in code. The caller has disguised his voice electronically. There is no way we could identify him through a voice print. We do know there is no doctor named Sadat either on the installation or in Hangzhou. A headache is an irritant. Someone must be a headache to her. I wonder who it could be."

He and the lieutenant chuckled at the insinuation.

"The prescription is a cure for the headache; it will rid her of the problem. The messenger is obviously the person who will administer the medication. The fact that he said 'her' is meaningless. It could be either a man or a woman. Regardless, I must be alert between now and the launch. Trust no one."

"Should I increase security at your door? I could have a guard here within the hour."

"No, Lieutenant. I wouldn't know which guard to choose. Doctor Sadat's messenger could be anyone. Once I am in my quarters I will be safe for the night. Perhaps you could drive me yourself."

"I would be happy to, Sir. When do you wish to leave?"

"Shortly, I'll gather a few things. Please . . . have a seat while you wait." Battarian pointed to one of the chairs in front of the desk. As the lieutenant sat, Battarian opened the lower right drawer and picked up a small velvet bag. He placed the bag in his lap and reached for the pen lying next to the telephone.

"Lieutenant, you have been exemplary in your devotion to duty these past few weeks. I have been thinking of an appropriate reward. I have decided to grant you two weeks on the Black Sea. It will be a well deserved vacation."

"General. I am most honored. My devotion to you is strictly an indication of my loyalty. You are most generous."

"It is nothing, my comrade. I have already drawn up your leave papers. Simply sign your name right here below my signature." Battarian placed the leave orders in front of the lieutenant and pointed to a line at the bottom of the document.

The lieutenant eagerly signed the paper and handed it back to the general.

Battarian signed a few more documents and looked up. The lieutenant was still seated but had drawn a semi-automatic weapon with a silencer and was aiming it at Battarian's head.

Battarian leaned back in his chair and reacted calmly.

"So. You are the messenger. You are one of my most trusted aides. How did she get to you?"

186

"There are reasons why they pay lieutenants a meager salary. It makes us easy to entice with the right amount of money."

"But you had such a bright future. A career officer gains so much respect and privilege, not to mention the pension." Battarian slowly put down his pen.

"I will still receive the privilege and respect as well as the pension. General Dillgard has promised me a quick advancement. By the way, what do you mean 'had a bright future'?"

A loud shot rang out. The lieutenant fell back in his chair. A small hole appeared in his chest over the heart, and a circle of blood rapidly expanded to cover the front of his shirt. He looked down at his wound in disbelief. His weapon had fallen to the floor. As he looked up at Battarian, his eyes passed the front of the desk, and he saw a small bullet hole where there was none a few seconds before.

General Battarian calmly brought his left hand up from his lap and placed a small nickel-plated revolver on the desk. The barrel was still smoking.

"The key was that a messenger would deliver the prescription. That told me it might be you. Too bad, you really did have a bright future ahead of you."

The lieutenant's head fell limply to his chest and he stopped breathing. His eyes still registered disbelief.

Battarian pressed a button on his desk. Two of his private bodyguards entered the office from a small anteroom to the left. They had been watching through a one-way mirror. Entering the room, they holstered their drawn weapons, which a moment before were aimed at the lieutenant's head. Had he made any motion to pull the trigger, both guards would have simultaneously shot him. They would have shot him when he drew his weapon, except for Battarian's instructions to wait.

"Carefully remove the lieutenant. And try not to get any more blood on the carpet than what is already there. I will notify the High Command that I apprehended Kumodan's killer and had to shoot him when he resisted and drew his weapon. His signed confession is on the desk."

Battarian carefully peeled a sheet off the top of the leave orders. Underneath was a confession to the murder of Captain Kumodan with the lieutenant's signature.

The two guards wrapped the lieutenant's body in a blanket and carried him out of the room. Battarian called for his car and left the office.

When he exited the building, his car waited at the curb; the driver stood beside the open rear door. They exchanged salutes and Battarian entered the vehicle.

The driver sat behind the wheel and asked, "To your quarters, Sir? Have you had an eventful day?"

"Yes, corporal. Take me home. The day was no more eventful than I would have expected when visited by a member of the High Command."

Chapter 38

Uploading

Sara cautiously climbed the ladder and looked over the edge of the pier. *No one in sight.* In one motion she pulled herself over the top of the ladder. Crouching low, she silently made her way toward the guard tower, hiding among the boxes and containers on the pier and between buildings.

She approached the tower using a row of barrels for cover. A low intensity light illuminated the interior of the small guard shack on top of the tower. She watched for a few minutes. Only one guard manned the station and he had a routine. He spent approximately one minute looking out of each of the four sides of his post, moving around the tower in a counter clockwise direction. She would wait until he faced away from her before she moved past the tower on the right.

When the guard turned, she slipped easily past the tower and dropped behind a parked truck. Staying in the shadows she made her way past several single story buildings. Finally, she arrived at the door of the building that houses the accounting department. Exactly as expected, the door had an electronic lock panel.

She stepped forward. Her foot struck a large, soft object. Immediately a soul-piercing scream jolted her and she leapt back, dropping to a defensive stance, adrenaline pumping through her system. From the shadows where she had stepped, a form darted to the right.

She made out the shape of a large cat that had been lying by the door. *Damn! What a time to step on a mousetrap! Enough to give me a heart attack.* Gradually, her heart rate slowed from its racing and the adrenaline faded.

In the guard tower, the sentry jumped at the sound of the screaming cat. "What the ...?" he caught himself in mid-sentence. *O.K. Just a cat.*

The electric lock on the door was exactly like the one in the mock up; a numeric keypad with red, yellow and green indicator lights. The glowing red light signaled that the lock was activated. The green light would indicate that the lock was open. The yellow light would warn that an incorrect code sequence had been entered. If the yellow light started flashing, an alarm would sound, alerting security of a possible intrusion. There was a sixty-second delay to allow a bumbling accountant time to reenter the correct code. A small LED screen showed the time left before the alarm sounded.

Sara punched in the lock code provided by FIA intelligence. Calmly she entered "1-2-3-4" and watched for a steady green light to come on. She froze. The yellow light began flashing. The counter started counting down from 60.

No! They changed the code! Her mind raced. *What do I do?* She fought the instinct to run, and calmed herself for a second. *Ten thousand combinations. Bean counters aren't creative. The code has to be simple.*

She entered a new sequence, "2-3-4-5." The yellow light continued to flash.

Forty-five seconds to go.

Her heart raced. *If I were an accountant, what would I do?*

She keyed in "1-1-1-1." No good.

Thirty seconds.

"2-2-2-2." Still yellow.

Twenty seconds.

"3-3-3-3."

Ten seconds.

This is ridiculous. What would they do with "1-2-3-4?" Then she had an idea.

She tried "4-3-2-1." The yellow light went out and the green light glowed steadily. She slumped against the door and caught her breath, thankful that security was not high on an accountant's list of priorities.

She regained her composure and opened the door. She stepped into the reception area. No computers here, just a reception desk with a phone system and some chairs. She opened a door to the left and entered a room. There were no lights.

She pulled a small pen-sized flashlight from her sleeve pocket. The light was small, but bright enough to allow her to see. There were three rows of desks with papers stacked in piles and a computer workstation on each one. She looked at her watch. *Twenty-one-forty-five. Been gone for forty-five minutes. Plenty of time left.*

She examined the nearest workstation. No drive. She went to the next. The same. She checked each one. None of them had a drive she could use to upload from her disks. *Typical NWO. No trusting anyone.* The drives had been removed to prevent unauthorized upload or download of sensitive financial information or computer games. *There has to be a workstation with a drive somewhere.*

She entered a smaller room with a single desk and workstation. *Supervisor's office.* The workstation had a small drive. She powered up the computer. The screen flickerd and a small dialogue box came up. "Please enter password." She entered the sequence "1-2-3-4." The box changed to say "Password incorrect, please enter password." She typed "4-3-2-1." The screen changed to "Welcome, Gretar Gudmundsson. You have accessed the Hangzhou Base General Ledger system."

Unbelievable! I guess we know who changed the code on the door.

She slipped the two-inch disk into the drive. The disk contained an automatic hacking program that scanned the system for an opening into the main computer databanks.

The process took approximately ten minutes. It seemed like ten hours. Finally the screen began to scroll through the messages, "Main data files located . . . security files opening . . . beginning upload . . . two minutes remaining."

She sat back in the chair. *Almost done. I'll be out of here in two minutes.* She looked at her watch. *Twenty-two-twenty.* She looked at the screen. *Thirty seconds remaining.*

She bolted upright! *A sound! Someone's at the door!*

For several minutes after the guard heard the scream of the cat, he had resumed his monotonous cycle of watching each direction for one minute. His mind kept returning to the sound. *Why just one scream?* If it had been a cat fight, there would have been two distinct screaming felines and they would have carried on for several minutes. *Something else must have scared it. Perhaps something big.*

He knew that if it was something big it would be the first time anything exciting had happened in the eight months he had been assigned to the guard tower. There was nothing over there but the accounting office and other boring departments. The only one that ever interested him was the paymaster, and that happened only once a month.

It was probably nothing, but he decided to check it out. It would beat the boredom of the tower and would give him something to enter into his logbook besides the same statement at fifteen-minute intervals, "All quiet, no activity noted."

He made a new entry, "2205 hours. Suspicious cat scream, going to investigate." *That should please the sergeant of the guard. Always room for an alert sentry to move up in rank.* Of course, the suspicious scream occurred over twenty minutes ago and he had heard nothing since. He didn't mention that detail in his logbook.

Quietly he descended the ladder leading from the guard shack at the top of the tower. Taking his time, he checked each door of each building in the direction he had heard the scream. Coming to the door to the accounting section, he saw that the green light on the electronic lock was on. *Damn accountants, this is the second time this month they didn't set the lock.*

He started to enter the code to activate the lock, and then dropped his finger. *Why not take a look inside. I'd like to see what it takes to run this place.* He cautiously opened the door, which made an audible click. He glanced inside. Out of the corner of his eye he thought he saw a light go out.

It seemed to take forever for the last thirty seconds to pass, but finally the screen read, "Upload complete, remove disk." Sara quickly removed the disk from the drive and hit the power off button on the workstation. The screen immediately went dark. She turned and saw a figure of a man in the doorway to the main accounting room.

The guard found the light switch and flipped it up. The lights in both rooms went on. Sara and the guard were temporarily blinded by the brightness. It allowed her time to drop behind the desk before his eyes could adjust.

When his eyes adjusted to the light, he looked around the room. Nothing seemed out of the ordinary. Then he saw into the supervisor's office. The chair behind the desk was rocking almost imperceptibly.

"Who's there?!" he called in a loud voice.

Immediately the words raced through Sara's mind. *No contact!* She stayed still.

The guard lowered his weapon and pointed it toward the desk, stepping slowly forward. "Who's there?!" he demanded.

Sara looked around the room from where she was hidden. There was no escape. She was trapped.

She called out, "Don't shoot! It's just me."

She stood up from behind the desk. "I was just getting ready to leave. Burning some late night oil. It's January. You know what it's like when the annual budgets are due." It sounded corny, but it was the best she could come up with on a moment's notice.

The guard pointed his rifle directly at Sara. "With the lights out? I don't buy it. Who are you? Show me your identification. Keep your hands out where I can see them."

Accountants are a strange breed. For a fleeting moment he thought she could be telling the truth. He briefly dropped his guard and relaxed his finger on the trigger of the rifle.

Sara knew there was no way to escape. She had a fake identification badge, but it was unlikely the guard would be fooled for long. She could not be taken alive. Slowly, she reached for her false I.D. with her left hand and flicked her thumb across the underside of the ring. The needle immediately sprang out.

She pulled out the badge and handed it to the guard with her left hand. He reached across to take it with his left, holding the rifle on her with his right.

When he took the I.D. she pressed the ring against the palm of his hand. The needle automatically injected a dose of the poison.

"Ow! You scratched me with your finger!"

"Sorry. I didn't mean to."

The guard gave her a frown and looked at the identification card. The picture looked like her, but he was having a hard time focusing. He began to feel faint and the room started to spin. He slumped to the floor.

Sara quickly moved to him and placed her fingers on the carotid artery in his neck. His pulse rapidly diminished. After fifteen seconds, the absence of a pulse indicated his heart had stopped beating. She checked for breath. None. He was dead.

She turned out the lights and listened at the door. No one else was around.

She couldn't leave the guard lying in the office to be discovered when the staff returned in the morning. She placed his rifle on his chest, picked up his feet and dragged him out the door. Outside the main entrance, she reentered the alarm code. The yellow light burned steadily, then turned red.

After setting the lock, she struggled with his dead weight. She'd have to drag him all the way back to the guard tower. He was heavy. She weighed a mere 125 pounds and he must have been at least 180. Nearly exhausted, she made it to the foot of the tower at the bottom of the ladder. The ladder had wooden rungs. She climbed to the top, and with all of her strength she pulled on one side of the top rung. It separated from its support.

At the bottom of the ladder, she turnd the guard over on his face. She lifted his head and turned it to the right, placing her knee against the side of his neck. She sharply twisted his head while at the same time she pressed down hard on his neck with her knee. She felt the snap of his spine. Finally, she took the butt of his rifle and struck him on the forehead where he would have hit in the fall. *Let's hope they think he slipped on the broken rung and fell to his death.*

She looked at her watch, *Twenty-one-fifty-eight.* Two minutes to go and she was at least five minutes from NUMSUB.

In the control room of NUMSUB, the tension mounted at the passing of each minute. Sara hadn't returned and they had no indication whether she had completed her mission or not.

Tom turned to Al. "She's been gone nearly two hours. She should have had plenty of time to get back unless she ran into trouble. We can't wait much longer before we have to go."

Al responded, "It's now twenty-two hundred hours. Her time is up. We have to go. We have to think of the safety of the remainder of the crew. If she's been discovered they'll be looking for us by now. It won't take long to figure she got here by sea."

"Give her just a couple of more minutes. I want to make sure."

"O.K. Two minutes. Then we get the hell out of here."

Two minutes seemed to pass all too quickly. "She's not coming back, Tom. We have to go now."

"O.K. Close the hatch and let's go. We have to get into the bay and execute plan B."

A seaman reached up and closed the hatch.

Sara moved as fast as she could while trying to keep quiet. At last she reached the pier and raced quickly across it. Looking down into the water she saw nothing. For a brief moment her mind told her they'd left her behind. With blind faith she jumped off the pier and dropped the seven feet to the water's surface. Bracing for the impact with the water, she landed with a hard thud on a solid surface. NUMSUB!

Everyone in the conn heard the thud on the top of the hull. Al opened the hatch and Sara quickly descended, panting and sweating.

"Whew! When you guys say two hours, you mean *two hours*," she said between gasps of breath. "Next time let's allow for a contingency or two."

"No problem," jested Tom. "Next time we'll have had a practice run under our belt and we'll know how much time we need. What happened? Did you upload the data?"

"Data is uploaded, we're all in the system. I ran into a friend and had to catch up on old times. You know, this stuff really works." She took the ring off her finger and handed it to Tom.

Al dropped to his seat. "Let's get out of here. Set a course for the Fuchun."

At 6:00 a.m. the next morning, a new guard arrived at the tower to begin his shift and discovered the body. Immediately, he alerted his Captain and called medics to the scene. After a cursory examination of the body, the senior medic pronounced the cause of death as a broken neck sustained from a fall.

The Captain examined the logbook and the broken rung on the ladder. He turned to the sergeant of the guard and said, "Find out when the last time this structure was given a safety inspection and who was responsible for doing it. I'm tired of the sloppy work being done here. Someone's head is going to roll for this."

Chapter 39

The River

NUMSUB quickly and silently slipped beneath the water. Her computer set a course for the mouth of the Fuchun River. She passed through the red electronic defense network in the bay like a spider passing through its web.

They approached the mouth of the Fuchun, and Hawk watched as dozens of small blips began to appear on his monitor.

"We're approaching the minefield, Sir. The first device is dead ahead approximately one hundred yards."

Al flipped on the forward video monitor.

"Let's get a visual."

At first the screen showed only empty water in front of them. He gradually adjusted the magnification, and a small round object appeared and then grew larger with each click of the lens. It was spherical with several protruding knobs. It was tethered to the bottom of the river by a chain.

Al picked up the intercom. "Robin, could you come to the conn?"

Shortly, Lt. Buckner arrived and stood beside Al.

Nodding to the video monitor, Al asked, "What do you make of it?"

She studied the image for a few seconds.

"Standard high explosive mine that's been around for the past hundred years or so. Nothing advanced, but then it doesn't have to be. Each knob contains a sensor that will cause the mine to detonate if it touches a solid object. There's about a hundred pounds of high explosives that packs quite a wallop when detonated. It'll punch a hole through the hull if we bump into one."

"Give me the dimensions of the mine field."

Hawk punched a few keys and read the data on the screen. "The width is bank to bank, depth of the field is approximately one mile with mines set at ten feet to one hundred twenty feet off the bottom. Currently the top of the minefield is seventy-five feet below the surface of the river."

Tom sat in the chair adjacent to Al. "NUMSUB doesn't have any tricks that will take us through the minefield. Any thoughts?"

"We have only one option. Since we can't go through it, we'll have to go over it on the surface."

Al turned back to the tech at the radar screen, "Hawk, you said the top of the field is currently at 75 feet. When will it change?"

"The depth will vary depending on the tides. At high tide the depth should be approximately 100 feet, and at low tide only the smallest vessels with the shallowest draft could pass through."

"Which direction are the tides flowing now?"

"They're receding. We will reach low tide in approximately four hours."

"How long before the tides are too low for NUMSUB to pass over the field?"

"We have about an hour, Sir. After that we'd be taking a significant risk.

"Looks like we'll have to pass over soon then. Tom, what do you think?"

"We can do it with the shields up to avoid being seen, but we'll create a wake that might raise suspicions. The riverbanks along the minefield are heavily guarded. There's a guard tower every fifty yards. They keep a close eye for any surface activity since they are fairly comfortable that nothing will get by underwater. An observer on shore or in a passing boat will wonder what's causing the swells."

"Then we'll have to hide our wake,"

"How do you propose to do that?"

"We wait for a ship to pass over going up river. We surface right behind him and follow him across the minefield. Our wake will mix with his and no one will notice anything out of the ordinary.

Al turned to Hawk, "Any surface activity approaching the mouth of the river?"

Hawk looked at his screen, "Not yet, Sir. I'll keep a watch."

The next twenty minutes passed with no activity. As the clock ticked on, tension mounted in the control room.

"Something had better come along fairly fast or we'll have to risk it on the surface. We give it another few minutes and then we take our chances," said Al.

Hawk sighted activity on his screen. "Sir, there's a patrol boat approaching. Looks like he's going to enter the river before low tide."

"There's our ticket. We'll let him pass over. Then we'll surface right behind him and follow him over the minefield. If we stay about a hundred feet off his stern, the darkness should cover anything unusual in the water that could be seen by the ship. Once we've passed over the field we can submerge and continue following him as far as we need to go."

NUMSUB waited quietly for the boat to pass overhead before surfacing behind it. With shields activated, the sub was invisible to both the naked eye and electronic surveillance. The crew of the patrol boat and the guards on shore were unaware that something was closely following the boat.

Unknown to the crew of NUMSUB, a radar technician seated at a console inside the headquarters complex had a puzzled look on his face. He turned to the officer next to him.

"Sir, there it is again. I'm starting to question if there really is a malfunction in LOFWAR. If there is, it's starting to occur more frequently. I first noticed one occurring at the empty docks when I got a blip. Another one came up in the river over the minefield. At first I thought it was the patrol boat, but there appeared to be two vessels. It looked like something was following very closely behind the patrol boat."

"Contact the bridge of the ship and have them take a look. If it's that close they'll be able to see it."

The radio operator on the patrol boat entered the bridge with a note for the captain. "Sir, headquarters radar has requested that we examine the water off our stern and tell them if there is anything following us. Seems like an odd request, because the ship's radar has picked up nothing either in front of us or behind us."

The captain stepped out of the side of the bridge and turned a large spotlight toward the rear of the ship. "Let's take a look."

He passed the light across the water in a sweeping motion. Nothing.

He turned to the radioman, "Tell radar that they must be imagining things. There is nothing behind us."

The corporal at the LOFWAR screen advised the lieutenant, "Nothing, Sir. The ship reports that there is nothing behind them. Perhaps it was another malfunction after all."

"Perhaps, but keep a close watch and let me know if you see anything else strange."

"Should we alert the General?"

"That's probably a good idea, Corporal. I'll call him."

General Battarian was peacefully asleep in his quarters when the phone rang. Groggily he picked up the receiver. "General Battarian, here."

The voice of the officer from the radar room was on the other end. "Sir, we've been picking up some strange indications on the LOFWAR screen. They're probably nothing, but, of course, we felt it wise to advise you."

Battarian was irritated at the news. He did not have much confidence in the new software developed by the High Command engineers. He did not see the necessity of waking him for this kind of news. The tone in his voice was uncharacteristically terse.

"You're likely correct, Lieutenant. LOFWAR has been acting up for the past couple of days, ever since we installed the new software. I'm going to have a long day tomorrow watching the activities at the space facility from my office. Right now I'm more interested in going to bed than examining a malfunctioning radar system. Unless you discover something factual, I'd prefer not to be disturbed again."

"Uh…Yes, Sir. No problem, Sir. We'll advise you if anything certain appears," stammered the junior officer as he hung up the telephone.

"Damn senior officers, can't be bothered unless there is something important, prefers sleep over …." He continued to mutter to himself and returned to the console.

It took approximately ten minutes to pass over the minefield. There was a bit of excitement when a spotlight appeared on the bridge of the destroyer and swept across NUMSUB. At first Al thought that they had been discovered, but then he remembered that with the shields activated, the sub was invisible. Upon clearing the minefield, NUMSUB gracefully submerged to periscope depth behind the ship and continued to keep a safe distance off the stern.

Hawk kept an eye on his monitor to watch for any objects in the water or changes to the riverbed. "Approaching the sandbar," he warned the commander. "If we follow the patrol boat, though, he should lead us around it safely."

"Good point, sailor. Keep us out of trouble."

NUMSUB continued up the river without incident. Approximately five miles from the river bend where they would put Tom and Sara ashore, Al slowed to allow the patrol boat to pull ahead. Once the water was clear, Al moved the sub closer to shore, staying far enough away to avoid grounding against the shallow river bottom.

A motor pool was near the perimeter road that ran alongside the river, where several vehicles were stored for maintenance and for use by personnel visiting the installation. Pete and Robin would be put ashore to confiscate a vehicle, which they would drive to the park at the river bend and meet up with the sub. They had stripped to shorts and tank tops for the short swim to shore. They carried dry clothing in watertight bags to change into once on dry land. They each carried a 9-mm semi-automatic pistol and the tools to break into the secure vehicle storage area. They wore the poison rings on their left ring fingers.

Sighting around the shore through the video monitors, Al determined that there were no sentries. He called Pete and Robin to the conn.

"Are you ready?" he asked them.

"Let's go," they replied.

"We'll meet you at the bend," said Tom. Pete and Robin slipped through the hatch that was barely above the surface of the water.

Silently they swam to the shore, climbed out of the water and put on their dark civilian clothing. They crouched in the brush near the road and observed the vicinity. There were no streetlights and no moonlight. The only light came from a pole near the fence that surrounded the vehicle compound. Several vehicles of different types were parked inside the fence and one automobile was parked off the road near the back corner of the compound outside the fence.

They started to emerge from the brush to cross the road. Suddenly, the headlights of the vehicle parked outside the fence came on and illuminated the area around them. They dropped to the ground and waited motionless, their chins nearly touching the soft dirt by the side of the road.

There was the sound of faint giggling as the engine started and the automobile was put into gear. When it came out of its parking place, they

197

saw that the driver was a male and his passenger was female. They rose to their knees behind the brush. As the automobile passed by them, they saw the female slipping her arms into her blouse. The occupants of the car did not appear to have seen them. Pete and Robin glanced at each other with relieved grins.

They waited until the sound of the vehicle was gone and quiet returned to the area. Certain that there were no more lovers or other surprises lurking in vehicles, they quickly crossed the road and approached the locked gate of the compound.

Robin picked the lock and they slipped through the gate. They opened the unlocked door of the small office next to the gate and found several sets of keys hanging on the wall next to a desk.

Pete spoke softly, "There's a grey Saab at the back of the lot. See if you can find the keys."

Robin searched through the tags on the keys by the light of a small penlight. Shortly she pulled a set off the rack. "These look like the ones." She tossed them to Pete.

Staying in the shadows, they crouched between the parked vehicles and made their way to the back of the lot where the Saab was parked. Pete opened the door and inserted the key into the ignition. The car's engine immediately jumped to life.

"Let's go," he said. Robin was already in the seat beside him.

When they drove through the gate, Robin jumped out and closed it, securing the lock. If they were lucky, no one would notice the missing vehicle for a couple of days.

Pete switched on the headlights and headed north toward the park.

About two miles down the road, a roadblock appeared in the headlights. Two guards stood behind a barricade with automatic rifles folded across their chests. One of the guards held his hand up, signaling them to stop. He approached the driver's side of the vehicle.

"Where are you going?" he demanded.

Pete thought fast. "We're returning to the barracks," he said nervously.

"You know you're out past curfew," said the guard sternly. He peered in the window and looked Robin up and down, eyeing her suspiciously. Robin pretended to clutch the top of her shirt together with her left hand while her right hand encircled the grip of her weapon in the waistband of her pants.

Pete remembered the two lovers they had almost surprised next to the compound. He smiled and winked at the guard.

"Hey, give us a break, O.K.? We were just trying to get a little privacy."

The guard looked back at Robin with a leer. "O.K. Get moving. And don't let us catch you out here again. You got it?" He slapped the side of the car as Pete sped off.

"Whew! That was close," said Robin. "Good thinking. What made you come up with the story about finding privacy? Was it the two we nearly surprised back there?"

"Wishful thinking, I guess," responded Pete staring straight ahead at the road.

Robin glanced at him. *Is he interested?*

Al checked his watch. *0330 hours.* He slowly guided NUMSUB to a stop in the bend of the river next to the park. The morning shift change would occur in two and a half hours.

Al searched the shore through the periscope monitor. Shortly, the headlights of a vehicle rounded the bend, and then switched off. It pulled off the road and slipped out of sight behind some tall bushes.

Pete and Robin were to remain with the vehicle until Tom and Sara arrived to take it the short distance to the space facility in time for the shift change.

Sitting silently in the darkness, Robin slid her hand across the seat and gently touched Pete's arm. "Did you mean what you said back there about wishful thinking?"

Her question stirred feelings inside him as he looked over at her. She was turned slightly and her eyes were soft and moist. She looked beautiful in the darkness. He knew the dangers of involvement between two people whose lives depended on each other during combat. Emotion could cloud quick thinking and instinctive reactions. That could lead to any number of difficult and dangerous situations.

The moment nearly overwhelmed him. A dark starlit night alone in an automobile with a beautiful woman. Romantic feelings welled up within each of them. He started to respond in the affirmative to her question, but wisdom locked his tongue.

"Nah! I was just joking." The words nearly choked him when he said them.

Robin drew her hand back quickly. "Oh. O.K." she said. She folded her arms and turned toward the window.

They spent the remainder of the night in silence; each lost in the thoughts of what could have been.

Chapter 40

The Space Facility

Early in the morning, Pete dozed and Robin watched for signs of activity. Everything was quiet. She nudged Pete.

"Wake up, Sleepy. It's 5:45. I think they're coming through the bushes now."

Pete leaned forward and stretched his arms out to the sides. He yawned and rubbed his eyes with his fists. The first light of dawn was still more than an hour away.

Tom and Sara appeared next to the Saab with Lieutenants Armstrong and Ganon. Tom and Sara were dressed in white lab coats over their khaki work trousers and shirts, the standard dress of the engineers and scientists at the control center. Mark and Marne were dressed in dark green work clothes and work boots. They would assume the role of custodial workers and grounds keepers around the outside of the building away from the launch site. They were not armed; however, they were all wearing miniature radio transmitters under their collars and each had a poison ring.

Tom opened the driver's door for Pete to get out. "Nice car, Bud. Mind if I take her for a spin?"

"Naw. Go right ahead, sailor. She's a clean one-owner. Try her out and make me an offer."

Tom slipped behind the wheel and Sara entered the front passenger side replacing Robin. Mark and Marne took places in the back seat. Robin and Pete moved into the bushes to wait their return in less than four hours. They would be back at the park at least thirty minutes before launch if all went according to plan. That would allow sufficient time to get back to NUMSUB and disappear in the river before the explosion.

Traffic had picked up on the road as the morning shift workers headed for the facility. Tom slipped the Saab into a line of cars and drove to the parking lot outside the security checkpoint. He parked the car and turned to the others.

"Well, this is it. Let's hope these folks are used to strangers. It's time for the acid test of Jorge's program and your computer skills, Sara. A few minutes from now we'll either be in the control room or facing a firing squad. Anybody up for taking bets?"

"Very funny," commented Sara.

"O.K. Sara, you've got the circuit board?"

She noded in the affirmative.

"Earlier this morning Warnick called to let us know that Cranston's satellites showed that activity at the back up control center had come to a halt. It looks like they've scrapped it for now. Must've been taking too long to complete. Anyway, we won't need to worry about redundancy.

"Mark, Marne, you know what to do. Once inside the facility, look busy on the grounds and keep us informed of any suspicious activity. We'll be inside making the exchange. We'll see you back here at oh-nine-fifteen hours. Set your watches. The time on my mark is five fifty-eight --- mark.

"Let's go. Don't enter the checkpoint together. Space out and mix in with the crowd."

The line of scientists, engineers and technicians moved smoothly through the six booths at the checkpoint. The security system was not nearly as sophisticated as at the Secretariat. Each worker merely slid a magnetic identification card into a card reader and placed his thumb on a screen that read his thumbprint. Once cleared by a green light above the booth, the worker was permitted to pass through.

Tom couldn't help but wonder about the apparent lax security procedures surrounding such an important event. Silently he was thankful.

Sara had preceded him to the gate by about six people. She inserted her card and placed her thumb on the screen. Tom held his breath. Shortly the green light came on and the guard waved her through. Tom relaxed. Mark and Marne were in the next two adjacent lines about ten people back from the booth. Two more to go and he was next.

A voice from behind him spoke. "Say, stranger. I don't recognize you. Are you new?"

Tom turned around and looked into the eyes of a tall Asian who looked quizzically at him. He thought quickly. "Yes, started last week. Singh decided we needed back up in the event of staff shortage on launch day."

"Oh, really? Singh said that did he?"

Tom looked at the stranger and nodded his head.

"Hmm, well, if you say so. I'm Ton Son Nut, electrical engineer." He put out his hand.

In the tension of the moment, Tom briefly forgot the name on his nametag. If he looked at his identification badge it would look suspicious. He quickly fumbled his card and dropped it.

"Oops. Excuse me." He bent down to pick it up and casually read the name as he stood.

"Boris Yankovich, Communications. Pleased to meet you." They clasped hands in a firm handshake.

Tom turned and entered the booth, inserted his card and placed his thumb on the pad. The small screen in front of him read "Boris Yankovich" and the light turned green.

Early in the morning, General Dillgard called Battarian's private line in his office. No one would answer it except him. It rang several times. There was no answer. She smiled and placed the handset back on the receiver. She called for a car to take her to the space facility.

Battarian sat at his desk when his private phone rang. He also smiled to himself as he looked at it. The small screen above the keypad registered the number from her quarters. *Only Dillgard would call at this time of the morning,* he thought to himself. *Let her think her sinister plan has worked.*

Upon arrival at the facility, the chauffeur driving Dillgard's automobile pulled up to the vehicle entrance by the guard post.

The guard held up his hand and firmly ordered, "Security has been tightened because of the launch today. No vehicles are permitted in or out of the facility. You will have to turn back."

The chauffeur said nothing. He merely lowered the rear side window and pointed with his thumb over his shoulder. General Dillgard glared at the guard.

The guard bent over and looked in the window. When he saw the General he recognized her instantly. He snapped to attention and saluted. "Yes, ma'am. Sorry, ma'am. I didn't know it was you." He waved his hand rapidly signaling the driver to proceed quickly. He did not want to deal any more with General Dillgard than he had to.

Dillgard's car entered the compound and stopped at the control center of the facility. The control center entrance was about seventy-five yards inside the main gate. The building was a white two-story concrete structure with no windows.

Waiting to meet the automobile was Colonel Vidaj Singh. A guard moved to the back of the vehicle and opened the door for Dillgard. She stepped out of the vehicle and greeted Colonel Singh.

"Well, Colonel, are we ready for today's launch?" she asked with uncharacteristic pleasantness, including the wisp of a smile.

"Yes, General. I'm certain the activities of the day will meet with your profound approval. The launch is scheduled for ten o'clock this morning. We have a little more than two hours. Perhaps I might give you a tour of the control center during the pre-launch activities."

"I would like that. It's been too long since I visited your operation. The last time was the unfortunate disaster surrounding phase three and four of the HORS program."

"We have made corrections and modifications to HORS II that have eliminated any chance of a repeat of that dreadful day."

Colonel Singh led the way into the control center. They passed through a security checkpoint. The guard was new and did not know General Dillgard. However, Colonel Singh nodded to him and he allowed her to pass through unchallenged. A wise move.

They entered an observation room above the main control center. The subdued lighting and the dark blue fabric covering the walls prevented any reflection and deadened sound. A large window overlooked the floor of the center, twenty feet below. There were three rows of consoles aligned facing away from the observation room. They faced a two-story window that looked out on the launch facility.

Through the window, the sight was breathtaking. A thousand yards away a large tower dominated the launch pad. The tower was twenty stories tall. It surrounded the launch vehicle on three sides, cradling it like a mother would cradle her child. Just before launch, the two sides of the tower would open, and the tower would move back to allow clearance for the rocket during blast off. A cloud of vapor drifted lazily away from the rocket near the nose cone as the cold liquid oxygen chilled the dew laden air. The morning sun glistened off of the white skin of the rocket, causing it to stand out in bas-relief against the dark tower.

The main control room floor was alive with activity. Scientists and technicians busied themselves with the final countdown procedures. A mechanical voice sounded over the speakers, "T-minus one hour forty-five minutes."

A senior engineer entered the observation room. "We have determined that the AWF has moved one of their geostationary satellites directly over the launch site. There is no danger. Our sensors have determined it has no offensive capability. It is merely an observation platform with high-resolution cameras. Should we destroy it with a laser?"

Dillgard answered quickly, "No, let them watch. We will show them the ominous power of the NWO. Let them observe while their last few hours of imperialistic freedom is wrenched from their helpless hands." She looked at Singh with a smug grin.

"Very good, General." The engineer left the room.

Dillgard's keen eyes surveyed each station as though she knew the thoughts of each technician and scientist. Everyone was busy except for two scientists, a man and a woman, standing on the left side of the room near a doorway. They didn't appear to be particularly interested in any of the stations. They seemed to be scanning the room and waiting for something. Now the man looked up into the observation room where she stood. Did she imagine that he made eye contact with her?

Singh interrupted her concentration. "Allow me to show you the command room. That is where we will observe the launch."

She looked at Singh for a brief moment, and then looked back. The two scientists were gone. Looking about the room, she didn't see either of them. Dismissing it from her mind, she turned and followed Singh out of the observation room and into the command room.

The command room was where the installation's senior officers and visiting High Command sat to watch a launch. The control room was to the left through a large windowed wall and the launch site was directly in front of them. A large tempered plate glass window provided an unobstructed view. The glass was six inches thick to protect the room from the shock wave produced when the rocket engines ignited.

There was a row of seven high-backed leather chairs facing the window with a low table in front of each. Dillgard and Singh sat next to each other near the center of the row.

Singh signaled to a porter near the door. "Prepare some refreshments for the General and me. I'll have orange slices and vodka. General?"

"Ice water and a fruit bowl."

When the porter left to retrieve the order, Singh and Dillgard were alone in the room.

"Well, General. Did you take your medicine last night?"

"Absolutely, Doctor. The headache is completely gone. I'm in much better spirits today."

Chapter 41

System Malfunction

One by one, Tom's team passed through security without incident. Tom made eye contact with Mark and Marne. Imperceptibly, they nodded acknowledgement. Recognition complete, they went about their business. They retrieved some gardening tools from a tool shed and began to work on the landscaping near the control center.

Guards were positioned near both sides of the building. The front of the building facing the launch site was off limits today. Workers were allowed only on the opposite side of the building, shielding them from the launch.

Tom and Sara followed a group of scientists into the control center. So far the blueprints of the center provided by the mole had proven to be accurate. Tom picked up a clipboard and began to look busy. The control center was exactly like he expected. Rows of computers and consoles faced a large window. Through the window, the launch pad was about a thousand yards away from the building. Tom made a mental note that it was too close; in the event of a major explosion on the launch pad, the building would provide little protection for its occupants.

Tom and Sara split up. They spent the next ninety minutes familiarizing themselves with the facility. According to the blueprint, and exactly where it was built in the mock up at the Test Site, a room containing spare parts was on the north side of the center. The door was unlocked and at different times during the past hour both he and Sara had entered the room to examine it.

She was on the opposite side of the main room. Three engineers had gathered around her. From the expressions on their faces, they weren't talking about the launch. They looked like typical wolves on the prowl. Tom chuckled to himself. *Single men are the same in any society. It doesn't matter what's going on, catch the eye of a sweet young thing and egos take control.* Then he noticed that one of the men was wearing a wedding band. *Yep. It's the same in every society.*

He got Sara's attention and nodded his head. She excused herself from the three men and walked toward him. Tom checked his watch. The time was 0830. They met next to the door to the spare parts room.

"Have you located the spares storage?" he asked.

"Yes. It's through this door in the next room. A couple of techs are working on a desktop computer near the cabinet. I couldn't put the defective spare in the cabinet without them seeing me. We'll have to wait until they take a break."

Tom looked around the facility. He noticed an observation room behind and above the control room floor. There were a couple of people in the room watching the activity. From their dress, he could tell they were high-ranking officers. One was a short dark-skinned man with the insignia of an NWO colonel. He wore a turban and appeared to be pointing out features of the facility to the other person. She was a tall, ominous looking woman wearing the rank of a general. The man appeared to be explaining the control room to the woman. Suddenly, he noticed that she was staring right at him.

He slowly turned to Sara. "When I give the word, move into the room. I think we've been noticed."

The woman looked away for a few seconds.

"Now."

He and Sara slipped through the door. The room was fairly large. It contained several workbenches with a variety of electronic test equipment and spare parts scattered haphazardly about. Several cabinets lined the far wall. Six had labels describing their contents; three were empty. Two technicians had a computer disassembled between them. When Tom and Sara entered the room, the technicians looked up curiously.

Tom checked his clipboard and moved to one of the cabinets labeled "PC and Peripheral Spares." He opened it and began to examine a box containing a keyboard. The two technicians turned back to their work. Tom took the box to the other table and opened it. He and Sara pretended to discuss its contents in low voices. They waited for the other two to move from the bench or exit.

Several minutes passed.

Sara looked at the clock on the wall above the cabinets. The time was 8:45. The countdown would stop in fifteen minutes and a technician would come in to retrieve a spare circuit board. The two men working on the computer showed no signs of stopping.

Tom and Sara exchanged glances. They knew what they had to do. Tom nodded.

He returned to the cabinet where he obtained the box and caught the attention of one of the technicians.

"Excuse me, I seem to be having trouble locating the right keyboard. Could you give me a hand?"

One of the workmen stood and walked toward him. "What are you looking for?"

When he moved away from the bench, Sara stepped behind the other technician as though examining some equipment on an adjacent table. Tom reached out to hand the box with the keyboard to the tech.

"I need one with a built in mouse," he explained, handing the box to the technician.

Suddenly, Tom stepped to his left, his right forearm parallel to the floor and his hand palm down, fingers together. He swiftly struck a blow with the base of his hand to the center of the technician's throat, instantly crushing his larynx. Stunned, the technician fell to his knees. He grabbed his throat and tried to scream. The crushed larynx blocked any passage of air either in or out. Mercifully, Tom raised the keyboard and slammed it down on the struggling technician, knocking him unconscious before he died.

The other worker rose from his bench and reached for an alarm button. Behind him, Sara picked up a twelve-inch torque wrench and swung it toward the base of his head. The wrench connected at the pivot point where his skull sat on the atlas vertebra. His head snapped back, severing the spinal cord. The shock to his system rendered his lungs useless. No sound escaped his mouth.

"Quick. We've got to get them out of sight," said Tom. "Let's put them in the empty cabinets and lock the doors."

They each drug a dead technician to one of the cabinets and propped him up inside. Closing the doors, they locked the handles and tossed the keys behind a stack of test equipment.

"Now. Plant the board."

Sara removed the circuit board from beneath her shirt. She opened the cabinet, removed the good board and replaced it with the defective one. She closed the storage cabinet, dropped the good board on the floor and crushed it with her heel. She then kicked it under a workbench in a pile of other used electronic parts.

The time was 9:00. The central computer had been monitoring all systems. It scanned all programs and circuits, making certain that any bugs or errors were corrected or fixed. Suddenly, in a small circuit board within the engine monitoring system, the computer detected an overheated resistor that quickly burned in a tiny flame and caused the board to misinterpret data received from the rocket.

Immediately a loud intermittent buzzer indicated a malfunction. An electronic voice announced, "Circuit malfunction in sector C-02734 of engine monitoring system. Countdown halted at T minus sixty minutes."

Tom and Sara moved to the workbench where the two technicians had been pouring over the computer. They busied themselves pretending to work on the equipment.

An engineer in a white coat hurriedly entered the room and walked directly to the spares storage cabinet. He opened the door and pulled out a circuit board. He closed the door to the cabinet and left the room as hurriedly as he came in. Tom looked at Sara with a look of satisfaction on his face. Her expression caused him concern. She looked wide-eyed at the cabinet. She had watched the engineer remove the board.

"What's the matter?" asked Tom.

Sara moved quickly to the cabinet and opened the door. She reached in and pulled out the defective board. "He took the wrong board!" she said frantically.

"What are we going to do?" she asked.

"I don't know. We'll have to go to plan B."

Just then, the door to the room began to open. Sara quickly replaced the board and closed the door to the cabinet.

The engineer had returned to the room. He walked over to the cabinet and opened it. After a brief search, he removed the board Sara had planted. He looked sheepishly at her.

"Wrong board," he explained, and hurried back to the control room.

Sara and Tom collapsed against each other in relief.

Near a sign that said "C Panel," the engineer placed the board on top of the computer. He opened the panel and removed the burned out circuit. He inserted the new one and closed the panel. A button above his head glowed red. He pushed it. The button changed to flashing orange as the main computer tested the new board. Finding no problems, it accepted the repair; the button began a steady green glow.

Tom and Sara heard the voice on the speaker. "Malfunction corrected, countdown resumed. T minus sixty minutes and counting."

The time was 9:10.

They had thirty minutes to return to NUMSUB.

They entered the control room and moved casually toward the exit to avoid attracting attention. Leaving the building, they saw Mark and Marne working among some hedges. Tom again made eye contact with Mark and gave a slight nod, indicating that the mission was complete. Tom and Sara walked toward the guard station to exit the facility. Mark and Marne fell in approximately twenty feet behind them.

Chapter 42
Capture

General Dillgard and Colonel Singh were relaxing with refreshments when the alarm buzzer went off an hour before launch.

Startled, Dillgard rose from her seat and looked out on the control room floor.

"What's that?" she said excitedly.

Singh had a look of impatience on his face.

"Just a small malfunction in one of the circuit boards. This happens frequently to that particular circuit. We simply have not been able to figure out what causes it. We are prepared with a backup for just this situation. The engineers will have the problem corrected within minutes. Then we will continue with the count down."

Dillgard watched an engineer hurry through the door where she saw the scientists standing a while ago. He emerged shortly and ran to a panel on the side of a large computer. Before he opened the panel, he looked at the board and threw it to the floor in disgust. He rose quickly and ran back into the room. Upon emerging again, he had another board in his hand. This time he opened the panel and inserted it into a slot in the computer. He closed the panel and pressed a red button.

Shortly after he pushed the button, a voice over the speaker announced the continuation of the countdown process.

She was about to turn back to her seat when she saw the two scientists she noticed before walking casually toward the door. *I'll have to discuss the redundancy of personnel with Singh after the launch. It seems there are too many people just milling around in the control room.*

Tom and Sara exited the control center and approached the security post. A loud voice called out, "You! There! Stop!"

A guard in the station drew his sidearm and pointed it in their direction. Another guard came out of the booth with an automatic rifle. He dropped to one knee and aimed directly at them. Their hearts nearly stopped. They froze in their tracks.

The guard with the rifle shouted to them, "You in the white coats! Drop to the ground!"

Quickly they obeyed, dropping face first to the sidewalk. The guard stood and ran toward them. When he reached them, he continued past their prone bodies.

Tom looked over his shoulder. Four more guards had appeared and all six surrounded Lieutenants Armstrong and Ganon. Mark and Marne were on their knees with their hands on their heads.

Tom stood and approached them. One of the guards, a sergeant, spoke.

"Show me your identification. I've been watching you for the last hour." He turned to Tom. "They didn't look like they were doing grounds maintenance. They looked more like they were watching for something. They've been acting very strangely."

He turned to the other guards. "Take them to the interrogation room. Hold them there for questioning."

At gunpoint, the five guards escorted Mark and Marne to the interrogation room at the rear of the guard station.

Speaking to Tom and Sara, the sergeant said, "You may go on your way. We have the situation in hand here now. You're fortunate I was watching. I think those two were following you."

Tom thought quickly. There was no possibility that he would leave two of his crew behind in custody of the NWO. Of course, the guards would extract no information from them. Still, he could not leave them behind to be tortured and killed.

"Are you sure they were following us? We've noticed two people stalking us over the past week. I'd like to get a look at them if I may to see if they're the same ones. I didn't see them well before you took them away."

"That would be good. If they are your stalkers, it will make our interrogation easier. Come with me."

Tom and Sara followed the sergeant into the interrogation room. Mark and Marne were seated in chairs in front of the guards, their hands handcuffed behind them. The guards were armed with automatic rifles; the sergeant had only a pistol in a holster at his waist.

Tom looked quickly about the room. It was small, barely large enough to hold all ten people. There was a desk and chair in one corner, and except for the two chairs occupied by Mark and Marne, it was without other furniture. The walls were white. There were no windows and only one door.

Upon entering, Tom noticed the walls were at least eight inches thick. *Insulated for soundproofing. NWO interrogators have unique methods of questioning. No sense letting sound escape to startle passing scientists and engineers.*

Six guards. Too many for he and Sara to overpower by themselves. Mark and Marne would be of no use handcuffed to the chairs.

"Let me see their hands. Two days ago we were eating in a restaurant in Hangzhou. The stalkers were seated across the room. Their faces were disguised but I noticed a tattoo on the back of one's hand. The other one had a crooked thumb. I want to see their hands."

"Remove the handcuffs. Watch them closely," ordered the sergeant.

One of the guards moved behind Mark and unlocked the handcuffs. He did the same with Marne.

"Hold your hands out!" ordered the sergeant.

Mark and Marne held out their hands. They were both wearing leather work gloves.

The sergeant snapped Marne's hand with a strap. "Remove the gloves! We can't see your hands with gloves on!"

Marne flinched and drew back her hand from the sting of the strap. Her movement created a brief distraction.

With lightening quickness, Mark rose from his seat and struck the nearest guard in the throat with his open hand. Then he spun and kicked another in the chest, sending him backward against the wall. The guard struck his head on the wall and slumped to the floor.

At the same time, Tom and Marne attacked the guards beside them. Tom disabled one with a blow to the temple, crushing the soft part of the skull into the brain. From her seated position, Marne leaned back and kicked the guard in front of her in the groin. When he buckled forward, his head came within reach. She grabbed his hair and smashed his face to the floor, knocking him unconscious.

In the brief seconds of surprise, before the sergeant had time to react, Sara reached to his side and grabbed his sidearm. In one motion, she removed it from the holster and placed it against his temple. She pulled the trigger. The bullet entered the right side of his head through a small hole and exited on the opposite through a hole the size of a fist. Blood and brains splattered against the wall.

The last guard leapt for the door. Sara stopped him with a shot to the back of his knee. He spun around, lowering his rifle and pointing it at her. She reeled off two more quick shots. The first struck him in the arm above the elbow and the second struck dead center in his chest. He slumped to the floor without making a sound.

The entire struggle took less than ten seconds. Tom, Sara, Mark and Marne stood amidst the dead or unconscious bodies of six guards.

"Let's see if these walls are really soundproof," said Tom.

He walked to the door and carefully opened it a crack. Looking out, he saw nothing suspicious. A worker had recently exited the security station and walked toward the parking lot as if nothing had happened.

"Let's go," said Tom, opening the door.

Sara put a hand on his shoulder. "Maybe you'd better look at yourself first."

He looked down. His white coat was covered with the sergeant's blood.

"Good catch."

When they left the building, Tom padlocked the door to the interrogation room and put the key in his pocket. They moved quickly to the Saab and left the parking lot for the return to NUMSUB. The time was 9:40. It would be close.

On NUMSUB, Al prepared for their return. They would have to swim out to the sub and take a chance on being spotted.

Tom pulled off the road and hid the Saab behind some brush beside the river. Pete and Robin had been waiting for them.

"How'd it go?" asked Pete when Tom stepped out of the car.

"Piece of cake. We had to convince some guards that they should let us go, but other than that it went like clockwork."

"Sub's waiting. Move out. We'll watch your rear."

They removed loose clothing and waded as silently as possible into the cold water. NUMSUB was invisible with its shields up. Al had placed a small blue buoy near the entrance to the open hatch.

Swimming to the buoy, Tom located the invisible hatch and looked toward the shore. No one was in sight. He signaled for Marne to go in. She grasped the edge of the hatch and jumped in feet first. Sara followed, then Mark and finally Tom. Pete and Robin waited until everyone disappeared through the hatch before they swam to the sub and followed.

The time was 10:05. The rocket would launch in five minutes.

Chapter 43

Lift Off

Dillgard and Singh leaned forward in their seats to watch the activity on the launch pad. Only a few minutes were left in the countdown. Movement on the launch pad signaled something was about to happen. The sides of the huge tower had opened and the tower had moved back from the launch vehicle.

The rocket stood like a white sentinel on the cradle that supported it above the concrete and steel pad. A solid stream of smoke billowed out from the bottom of the rocket. The engines ignited and burned at idle, waiting for the computer to signal them to burst into full power.

The voice on the speaker announced, "T minus sixty seconds and counting. All systems are green."

The electric power cable attached to a long steel arm disengaged from the side of the rocket and dropped away. The rocket was completely under its own electrical power.

"T minus forty seconds and counting. All systems are green."

The computers throttled the engines up to one-third power. The smoke rushed aside to reveal three bright red flames erupting beneath the three powerful engines. The rocket shuddered as the force of the engines strained against the explosive bolts holding the rocket to the cradle.

"T minus twenty seconds and counting. All systems are green."

The computers increased power to two-thirds. The control room vibrated and the windows shook. The engines complained violently at being held fast to the ground.

"T minus ten... nine... " The central computer signaled the onboard computer to begin increasing power. At T minus one second the engines would be at maximum power.

"eight... seven... " At five seconds to lift off, the onboard computer would take over complete control of the engines.

"six... five... " The onboard computer now controled the engines. The main computer in the center monitored engine systems and performance.

"four... three..." The heat from the flames began to vaporize the reinforced concrete pad below the cradle.

"two... one... Lift off."

Dillgard stood as if to help the huge rocket rise.

The onboard computer immediately throttled full power to the engines. The roar was deafening as the engines reached their maximum power. Simultaneously, all six restraining bolts exploded apart and the rocket was free.

Imperceptibly at first, the rocket began to rise when the thrust of the engines equaled the weight of the rocket and its payload. At equilibrium, it lifted a few inches off the pad, slipped a few feet to the side then stabilized and rose slowly. The onboard computer maintained full power from the engines, making minute adjustments to keep precisely the same thrust from each so that the rocket would rise perfectly perpendicular. The central computer detected no indication of any problem. However, the chip in the circuit board began feeding false altitude data to the central computer. The altitude sensed by the computer rose rapidly to two miles.

The engines struggled to lift the rocket. The lower two-thirds of the cylinder disappeared in a tremendous cloud of smoke. The rocket seemed to hang in mid-air. Then, as though emerging from a cloud, the white body steadied and rose, glistening in the sun as it cleared the cloud of smoke.

Dillgard, standing in front of the window, smiled broadly, her eyes fixed on the sheer power she witnessed.

The central computer detected no indication of problem, but believed the rocket was now at an altitude of five miles.

The base of the rocket rose above the smoke and appeared to sit atop three columns of fire level with the top of the tower. The onboard computer was functioning perfectly. All engines were tuned.

Dillgard involuntarily urged the huge beast on, "Go! Go! Go!"

The chip on the circuit board told the central computer that the altitude was six miles. Then it sent a false signal that one of the liquid fuel tanks had ruptured. One of the engines was overheating from an oxygen-fuel mixture that was too rich in oxygen. Meltdown of the malfunctioning engine would unbalance the thrust and cause the rocket to spin out of control toward the heavily populated city of Hangzhou.

A loud buzzer sounded intermittently. The ominous computer digitized voice on the control center speaker announced, "Engine malfunction, engine malfunction, self-destruct sequence initiated."

Instantly, the central computer signaled the self-destruct system to activate. The self-destruct system must disintegrate the rocket into millions of pieces that would rain harmlessly down on the bay and farmland.

Dillgard's smile faded when she saw a spark near the base of the engines blossom into a brilliant flash and run up the length of the rocket. The rocket disintegrated in a tremendous explosion as the self-destruct charges instantly ignited all liquid fuel and oxygen in the tanks.

The powerful shock wave from the explosion covered the thousand yards from the launch pad to the control center in less than a second. Dillgard had no time to react when the shock wave, followed by the fiery explosion, blasted through the six-inch glass window as though it was paper. Within microseconds, her skin melted and her bones charred. The heat from the blast screamed into the room and vaporized her so quickly she had no time to fall.

Singh and the scientists and engineers in the building met a similar fate.

The shock wave from the explosion spread in all directions for five miles. It flattened the huge launch tower as though it were constructed of toothpicks. The guard post and interrogation room were obliterated. Cars in the parking lot were picked up like toys in a giant hand, crushed beyond recognition and tossed miles away.

Total destruction occurred in all directions within a half mile of the launch pad, diminishing to minor damage at five miles. Pieces of rocket were scattered over fifteen square miles. Flaming debris landed in the leafless woods surrounding the facility, and a multitude of fires sprang up in the brush and trees.

General Battarian had been watching the launch on a TV monitor mounted in a wall in his office. He stared in disbelief at what he saw. *This could not happen. The system was foolproof.*

From all directions, fire trucks and ambulances rushed to the space facility to put out fires and search for survivors. When they arrived, the firemen and rescue personnel saw that destruction near the launch site was nearly total. The intensity of the blast left nothing but charred earth where the control center once stood. There was little hope that they would find anyone alive.

Al, Tom and several crew members stared at the periscope monitor. They watched in awe the destruction they had brought down on the NWO. It was time to make a run for the bay while confusion covered their escape.

The Command Staff assembled In Secretary Warnick's office had been watching the launch beamed to them from a satellite camera orbiting high above Hangzhou Base. In the room with George Warnick were Margaret Cranston, Roy Constance, Admiral Beaumont, General Wainscot and his aides, Colonel Rosewood and Colonel Farnsworth.

The satellite camera brought the launch site into clear focus. They watched the rocket engines ignite and the lift off begin. The rocket disappeared in a fiery explosion and a visible shock wave emanated from the site at supersonic speed in all directions, closely followed by the fireball. The shock wave and fireball destroyed everything in their path near the launch site. A cheer rang out simultaneously from all in the room.

"Excellent!" cried General Wainscot. "I knew they could do it."

The others looked at him suspiciously.

"Now, let's hope they can get out without incident. The explosion should allow them time to get away," said George. "We'll try to raise them first chance we get. They're sure to maintain radio silence until they're clear of enemy territory."

TOM HAYNIE

Chapter 44

Back Through the Minefield

From the air, all one could see of the launch site was a blackened crater. The tower and launch vehicle were gone. The explosion had created a hole a hundred yards wide and forty feet deep where the launch tower had stood. Everything within two thousand yards was nothing but rubble; not a structure was left standing.

The control center was silenced at the instant of the blast by an electromagnetic pulse created by the exploding rocket. The shock wave and fireball that destroyed the structure followed the pulse. They hit the building like a 1-2-3 punch.

Six miles from the blast site, debris fell while NUMSUB made her way back to the center of the river. The sandbar had shifted to create a tight bend barely large enough for NUMSUB to navigate. The side of the hull scraped against the bar when she passed through the bend. There was little danger of damage to the hull; however, had the sand made the river any shallower, the sub might have grounded and would have been stuck until the current eroded the sand sufficient to free them.

As NUMSUB approached the minefield, Hawk studied his monitor closely.

"Sir," he spoke to Al. "We can't make it through submerged. We're too close to low tide, and the depth of the minefield is only forty feet."

"All stop," commanded Al.

To stop NUMSUB in the current, the computer had to reverse the propeller enough to offset the speed of the current.

"How long until the tide comes in enough for us to get through under water?"

"At least four hours," replied Hawk.

"We can't wait that long. We have to come up with an alternative." He and Tom studied the video monitor. The closest mines stood as silent sentinels. They may as well have been an impenetrable concrete wall.

Shortly, Tom said, "I think I know how we can do it. Al, get Lieutenant Buckner up here."

Al picked up the intercom. "Lieutenant Buckner, report to the conn ASAP."

Robin appeared almost immediately.

"What can I do for you, Commander?"

Tom pointed to the video monitors.

216

"Take a close look at the minefield. You said you were familiar with this type of mine."

"Yes, Sir. They're pretty common. Not much to tell except that they're very effective. That's why the design hasn't changed in so long."

"We can't go over them on the surface during daylight, and we can't go through them underwater. I'd like to bounce an idea off of you."

"Shoot, Commander."

"The mines are tethered by chains at depths of ten to one hundred twenty feet off the river bottom. The surface of the river is currently forty feet above the tallest mines. We need a depth of at least sixty feet to get through and we can't wait for the tide to come in."

"I see where you're going. Since we can't raise the level of the water, we have to lower the minefield."

"Exactly. Hawk, chart a course through the field that would hit the fewest mines at sixty feet below the surface and tell me how many mines are in the way."

Hawk studied his screen intently. He adjusted the controls to examine the minefield from different angles.

"Sir, if we move sixty yards to starboard and take a course bearing one hundred sixty-two degrees for eight hundred twenty yards and then change course to one hundred ten degrees, we would contact eleven mines."

"How fast is the current moving?"

"The tide is changing, so that effect is variable. The current is now flowing at seven knots."

Tom turned to Robin. "Can you do it?"

"It'll be tricky with the current that fast, but I can do it."

Al had been listening to their conversation intently. He had a puzzled look on his face. "What are you two cooking up?"

Robin answered, "I've done this before. We have to remove those eleven mines so we can pass through the minefield. I'll swim ahead of NUMSUB with an underwater cutting torch and cut through the chain beneath each mine. Once free, the mine will float to the surface and be carried out into the bay by the current."

"How long will it take to get through all eleven?" asked Al.

"I should be able to do it in about two hours, give or take. Five to six minutes cutting time per chain plus set up and swim time between them."

"I don't know that we have that much time."

Pete had entered the control room and was listening. "How long would it take if there were two of us cutting chains?"

Robin looked up and met his eyes. "It would cut the time in half. Have you ever worked with mines?"

"No, but I've used an underwater cutting torch and I don't see where we have much choice."

"He's got a point," said Al. "I think you two had better get started before much more time runs out."

Pete and Robin went to the locker room to change into their scuba gear. While they changed, Robin gave Pete some final words of caution.

TOM HAYNIE

"Make sure you stay clear of the mine. If one of the sensors contacts the metal in your tank, you could set it off. There won't be enough left of you to fill a coffee cup."

"Those are confidence building words of encouragement. Don't forget to carry a coffee cup," he said with a grin.

"Also, be careful of the chain. Once the mine is cut free it will rise rapidly to the surface. The lower part of the chain will drop to the river bottom and take anything with it that's attached. You'll want to stay clear."

"It'll be tricky but thanks for the advice."

Meanwhile, Al maneuvered NUMSUB to a location ahead of the first mine and aligned her on a heading of one hundred sixty-two degrees.

Pete and Robin entered the transfer chamber carrying cutting torches and oxy-acetylene tanks. They adjusted their facemasks and checked each other's equipment before water filled the chamber. When the chamber was full, Pete reached up and opened the hatch and they slipped out into the river.

The current immediately grabbed them and pulled them toward the minefield. They grasped handholds to keep from being swept away. They would have to let the current carry them in the direction of each mine while they swam to alter their course. When they reached a mine they would grab the chain about six feet beneath the head and attach themselves with a safety hook. Then they would cut through a link above the hook to free the mine. Just before the mine was free, they would unhook their harness from the lower chain to keep from being pulled to the river bottom when the chain dropped.

Robin let go of the handhold and guided herself to the first mine. She grabbed the chain and pulled herself in. Pete released his grip and glided past her to the next mine.

Robin attached her safety hook and harness to the chain and pulled the cutting torch out of its holster. She adjusted the flow of gases and pressed the striker. Instantly the ignited gases created a yellow flame that vaporized the water at the nozzle tip, sending a stream of bubbles toward the surface.

She carefully held the tip of the torch near one of the links in the chain and pressed the oxygen lever. The burning torch burst into a hot blue-white flame. The metal glowed red, then white hot as it melted away from the flame. When the molten metal flowed out of range of the flame it instantly solidified in the water and fell to the river bottom.

Slowly, the torch cut through one side of the link and then the other. Just before the cut was completely through the link the pull of the buoyant mine spread the weakened metal and snapped it free. The mine rose toward the surface, pulling the remaining chain like the tail of a kite. At the surface of the river, it bobbed once or twice and settled, nearly submerged with a couple of prongs above the water.

At eight hundred twenty yards Pete and Robin had cut through and released seven mines, and there were four more to go. NUMSUB followed behind them at a distance of about fifty yards.

218

Now the task became more difficult. They had to change direction by fifty-two degrees and swim at a sharper angle to the current. They had to coordinate their swimming speed and angle with the speed of the current to intercept the next mine. If the current swept them past a mine, it would be impossible to swim upstream and try again.

Pete went first. He moved away with a strong kick. Keeping an eye on the target, he adjusted his strokes to let the current carry him toward the mine. It reminded him of duck hunting, where the hunter had to lead the duck so the shot and the duck met at just the right instant. Now he was the duck. He reached the chain, grasped it and hooked on.

Robin made it to the second mine. She cut it loose as Pete reached the third. One to go. Robin leapfrogged past Pete to reach it. She nearly missed the chain, but grabbed it with one hand and struggled to pull herself up. She attached the safety hook and began to cut through the link.

The cut went smoothly through the first side of the link. She nearly finished her cut through the other side when her torch flamed out. She looked at the pressure gauges. The oxygen gauge read empty. However, the link appeared sufficiently weak that it could be pried open with enough good kicks.

The hard rubber of her swim fin would protect her foot from the sharp edges of the cut. She tried to position herself to get a good angle with her foot, but the safety harness was too short.

She released the safety hook and held on to the chain above the cut to kick it free. The first kick opened the link slightly. While she prepared for the second kick, the current took her safety harness and tangled it in the chain above the cut. She kicked her foot down on the weakened link; it opened and the mine was free. Her tangled harness jerked her into the chain, which broke the oxygen regulator on her scuba tank.

Unable to breathe, she was drawn upward with the mine as it raced for the surface, caught in the current. The mine broke through the surface but stayed mostly submerged, with the chain beneath it trapping Robin underwater. She struggled to keep her tanks from contacting the mine's sensors.

Pete watched the scene unfold before him. When he saw Robin being swept away by the mine, he kicked with all of his strength toward her, using the current to gain speed.

Robin struggled hard against the current and the chain but was beginning to weaken. The lack of oxygen made her want to gasp uncontrollably for air. She fought against the urge and her lungs screamed for relief.

She sensed herself begin to lose consciousness and was about to give up the struggle. Just then, she felt a pair of steel hard arms encircle her and hold her tightly. She felt the hardness of a mouthpiece being forced against her lips. She opened her mouth and bit down on the mouthpiece then blew hard to clear the water out of it. She gasped a rush of fresh oxygen into her starving lungs.

Pete had reached her just in time. He saw her eyes roll back in her head as he pulled his own mouthpiece out of his mouth and pressed it against her lips. She breathed in and her eyes opened and focused on his. A message of trust and relief passed between them. He pulled her tightly against his chest and turned upside down. He placed his feet against the mine to keep it at a distance. While holding her securely with one arm, he reached down and drew his knife out of the sheath on his leg. He sliced through her harness and freed her from the chain. Then he kicked them both away from the mine.

Sharing his oxygen, they waited for NUMSUB to catch up. Then they swam down to reenter the hatch. After the water in the chamber receded, they both slumped onto a bench, exhausted from the exertion.

Tom and Al burst through the inner door. They saw everything through the forward monitor.

"Are you two all right?" cried Tom.

Robin looked at Pete, who caught her eye. She said simply, "We are now."

Chapter 45

Trapped in the Harbor

The NWO radar room buzzed with activity. The electromagnetic pulse from the exploding rocket ten miles away had knocked out most of the radar. The only functional equipment was LOFWAR and the electronic net in the harbor. The excitement drew the radar technician's attention away from his screen.

When he settled back down, he noticed something unusual on his monitor. He studied it for a while, and then called for his superior. A young officer approached.

"What do you have, Corporal?"

"Sir, the harbor net shows some slow-moving objects floating near the surface of the water at the mouth of the river. I know what I think they are, but that would be impossible."

"What do you think they are?"

"Well, I must be crazy, but they appear to be mines."

"Mines?! You're right, that's not possible. They're anchored to the bottom by concrete and heavy chains."

"I know, but it looks like some have broken free. Could the explosion have jarred them loose?"

"I suppose it's possible. Watch them and I'll send out a mine sweeper to investigate." The officer contacted a minesweeper by radio to warn them of possible mines floating free.

The corporal counted four mines. He noticed another emerging from the river. Scratching his chin, he checked his watch, stayed focused on the screen, and waited. Shortly, a sixth mine appeared.

"Lieutenant!"

The lieutenant approached and looked at the screen where the corporal pointed.

"Look, there are now six mines."

"Are they still breaking free?"

"If they were simply breaking free they would appear randomly. I've been timing them, and they appear almost exactly eight minutes apart. Watch, it's been a little over six minutes. I'll bet you next month's pay that another will appear in less than two minutes."

They watched the screen intently. A minute and a half passed, and then as if on cue, another mine appeared and floated into the harbor. Now there were seven.

"Something must be releasing the mines."

The officer rushed to his desk and called security on the telephone. "Have any of the river sentries reported anything unusual in the minefield?"

On the other end of the line, an officer in a crisp black uniform responded to the question.

"They've noticed some of the mines have broken loose. We assumed that they were jarred loose by the explosion."

"Didn't you think to inform someone?"

"Of course, but the confusion from the explosion, communications were down. Until now, the telephones have been inoperative."

"Could there be a submarine in the river?"

"No, that would be impossible. The tide is too low for anything to pass through the minefield. Even the smallest submarine wouldn't make it."

"Tell the sentries to keep a close watch. If they see anything unusual, call me immediately."

He hung up the telephone and returned to the radar screen.

"How many are there now?"

"Eight."

"The sentries have seen no surface activity; I think we are dealing with a submarine. I don't know how he got into the river, but we need to act immediately. I'm sending sub chasers to investigate."

The officer radioed for two small, fast destroyers to head for the mouth of the river. He advised the ship commanders that there may be a hostile submarine emerging shortly. In his haste, he had forgotten to warn them of the loose mines floating in the harbor.

The ships were loaded with ASW (anti-submarine warfare) equipment. Their armament included depth charges, surface-launched torpedoes and two helicopters with dipping sonar as well as torpedoes. Both ships saturated the area with sonar. The helicopters hovered in search of a visible sign of a submarine in the shallow water of the harbor. With NUMSUB's shields engaged, the sonar and visual searches were useless.

After picking up Pete and Robin, NUMSUB left the river and entered the deeper waters of the harbor.

"Are there any ships in the area?" asked Al.

"Three ships on the screen. A minesweeper appears to be searching for the loose mines. The other two are bearing down hard to port. They're leaving sub chaser footprints all over my screen."

"Bring us to periscope depth and let's take a look. Keep a watch out for those mines."

The periscope cameras broke the surface of the water, and three ships appeared on the monitors. The minesweeper worked near the river. The other two ships steamed straight for NUMSUB.

"Looks like we have company. They won't see us with the shields up, but we have to get out of here. What's the status of the gates?"

"Sir, their radios are coming back up after the pulse. The gate controls are malfunctioning. The fleet's been called back to port. They're telling them they can't open the gates. Radar shows twelve surface ships and three submarines waiting outside the harbor. They can't get in and we can't get out."

"It's too dangerous in here; we have to get out of the harbor. Looks like it's time to test one of those torpedoes."

He turned to Tom. "Government engineers, eh? How much are you willing to trust their calculations?"

"At this point, just a little more than I'm willing to trust the NWO."

"Hawk. How far to the gates?"

"Range to the gates is sixteen thousand yards." A little over five miles.

"Let's lock and load." Al picked up the receiver of the intercom and punched in the forward torpedo room. Smitty clicked on the speaker.

"Torpedo room, conn, make torpedo tube one ready. Load an XG-245. Arm at five thousand yards. Prepare to shoot."

Smitty and the other seamen in the torpedo room worked the automatic loaders. A torpedo was unlatched from its rack on the wall and lowered onto a cradle. It was moved into position at the entrance to the torpedo tube. Smitty opened a side door on the warhead and set the arming device to automatically arm the torpedo at five thousand yards from the submarine. He pushed a red button, and the torpedo glided into the tube and the rear door closed behind it.

The other seaman pushed the button on the intercom. "Conn, torpedo room, torpedo tube one ready with an XG-245. Armed at five thousand yards. Prepared to shoot."

"Open outer door." One of the outer torpedo tube doors opened.

"Outer door opened."

"Stand by."

"Standing by."

"The weakest point of the gates will be where they come together. By putting the force of the explosion at that location, the gates should swing out far enough for us to get through," said Tom.

"Match bearing at the junction of the two anti-submarine gates," ordered Al.

"Bearing matched at the junction of the anti-submarine gates."

Al looked at Tom as if to ask if he still wanted to go through with this. Tom looked back and nodded.

Al gave the command. "Match bearing, target. Shoot tube one."

"Match bearing, target. Shoot tube one."

In the control room, Hawk lifted a protective cover on a switch and pushed the switch forward. Immediately, compressed air ejected the torpedo from the forward tube. The torpedo's motor started and sent it toward the closed gates.

"Tube one fired. Unit from tube one running straight and true."

Aboard the lead sub destroyer, a sonarman jumped as he saw something on his screen. "Torpedo!"

The officer on deck quickly turned to the water and began scanning frantically. "Where?!" he shouted. "I don't see it!"

"It's not coming for us, it's heading toward the entrance of the harbor. They can't be shooting at the fleet, the gates are in the way."

"Those idiots!" shouted the officer. "They're shooting at the *gates*. Their torpedo will never damage the gates. Are they crazy? Have you located the sub?"

"No, Sir. I'm unable to locate the sub."

"Identify the exact location where the torpedo first appeared. The sub has to be there."

The sonarman selected the point and plotted the coordinates. He gave them to the officer.

The officer read the coordinates. "Helmsman, here are the coordinates. Set course for two-seven-eight degrees. We will intercept the sub at this exact location." He called for the depth charges to be armed and ready.

The commander of the trailing destroyer stayed back. He watched the lead ship steam toward the location where the torpedo first appeared. He advised his sonarman to watch the torpedo.

Helicopters from both ships were airborne within minutes and hovered over the site where the torpedo originated. They dropped their dipping sonar in the water.

Chapter 46

Escape from the Harbor

In NUMSUB's control room, Hawk announced the approaching destroyer. "He's seen the torpedo. He's heading for its origin. ETA in three minutes."

Al gave the command to move NUMSUB away from the area. "Battle stations. All ahead full. Let's leave them searching empty water."

As a precaution against an errant depth charge or torpedo getting a lucky break, he commanded the crew to make ready for an attack.

"Rig for depth charges." Throughout the sub, the crew stowed all loose items and held onto any available hand hold.

As the first destroyer arrived over the coordinates, NUMSUB silently glided underneath it in the opposite direction. The ship captain gave the order to release the depth charges. "Fire port and starboard catapults one, two, three and four." Immediately, four charges hurled in long arches into the air and landed in the water around the destroyer. They sank slowly toward the site NUMSUB had just left.

The depth charges reached the bottom of the harbor and detonated, sending four giant sprays of water skyward when the explosions reached the surface.

"Any debris?" asked the captain.

"None, Sir. We appear to have missed."

"We will saturate the area with depth charges."

The captain ordered the ship to turn hard to starboard to continue searching for NUMSUB. Directly in the ship's path, unseen by anyone, was a mine from the river. In the middle of the turn it struck the destroyer amidship.

The mine detonated, penetrating the hull of the destroyer immediately below the depth charge depot. Depth charges exploded in a tremendous fireball that broke the destroyer in half, sending pieces of the ship and bodies skyward. It took barely five minutes for the ship to sink, trapping most of the sailors on board below deck. The few that survived were hurled into the water a distance from the sinking ship.

The commander of the second destroyer watched in shock. He asked his sonarman, "What happened? Another torpedo?"

"No torpedo, Sir. I don't know what happened. There are several pieces of debris floating in the water and it appears that he struck one just before the explosion."

"Let's see if there are any survivors," said the commander.

The sonarman's eyes widened. "No!" he shouted. "Sir, stop the ship!"

The Captain gave the order to the engine room, "All stop!"

"Sir, those pieces of debris are mines. They must have come from the river. They surround us. One is a hundred meters to port near the bow and is floating toward us. If it hits the ship it could detonate."

The captain rushed onto the deck with several officers and seamen to search for the mine. Shortly one of the sailors pointed and shouted, "There it is. About seventy-five meters out."

All eyes turned in the direction the sailor pointed. The captain signaled a gunner seated at a machine gun turret above him to fire at the mine. The gunner aimed his sights and let out three short bursts of rapid fire. The mine detonated, sending a spray of water over the deck, drenching the captain and the others.

The captain returned to the bridge and gave instructions. "One man every five meters all around the ship. Watch for more mines."

Entering the bridge, he asked the sonarman, "Where are the other mines?"

The sonarman pointed to four dots on his screen, "Here, here, here and here," he said. "If we remain stopped they will all pass by us in about ten minutes."

"Watch them closely. Let me know immediately when we are out of danger." The captain turned to look toward the entrance to the harbor just as a huge fireball exploded. The flash from the explosion temporarily blinded him.

NUMSUB had moved a safe distance from the destroyers and had settled on the sea floor to wait for the torpedo to strike the gates.

Hawk announced, "Sir, the destroyer dropped four depth charges over the location where we launched the torpedo. All four depth charges detonated harmlessly. When he turned he hit a mine. It exploded and sank him. The other ship is dead in the water. Another mine exploded about fifty yards away. It doesn't seem to have done any damage.. They must have seen it and detonated it with small arms fire. Apparently they're watching for more of the mines."

Tom responded, "How long before the torpedo hits the gates?"

Hawk read the LED clock ticking backwards above his console. "Twenty seconds, Sir."

The torpedo sped its way toward the juncture of the two gates. Unaware of the power about to be unleashed upon them, the fleet waited on the other side. The twelve ships were spread over a distance of five miles from the entrance to the harbor. Six vessels were within three miles and two of those were within five hundred yards. One of the submarines lay stationary just outside the gates; the other two were beneath the furthest ship from the entrance to the harbor.

Hawk watched the track of the torpedo on his monitor. He removed his headset and counted out the last five seconds. "Five . . . , four . . . , three . . . , two . . . , one . . . ."

At that instant the guttural vibrations of a tremendous explosion reverberated through the sub. The small nuclear warhead detonated with the force of a thousand tons of TNT. The heat from the fission reaction instantly vaporized the water. A hole three hundred yards wide from the surface to the sea floor appeared in the water. A small fireball full of steam and debris formed a mushroom cloud over the center of the blast and rose several thousand feet in the air. The force of the explosion picked up the monstrous steel gates and moved them aside like cardboard.

A one hundred foot high tidal wave spread out from the hole in the water in all directions. Within seconds the hole collapsed and the surrounding water crashed in, creating a second, smaller tidal wave.

The wave picked up the closest NWO ships like toy boats and tossed them back toward the rest of the fleet. One ship crashed against a cruiser and they both exploded. One of the heavy gates landed on the nearest submarine and crushed it like an egg.

The wave moved out to sea and entered deeper water, where it rapidly lost energy. The furthest ships rocked wildly as it struck them. Four of the twelve ships sank within minutes. Two others were badly damaged and dead in the water. The remaining six sustained moderate to minimal damage.

NUMSUB rested on the bottom of the harbor in three hundred feet of water as the wave passed overhead. At that depth, the effect of the wave was minimal. However, the blast caused a minor earthquake in the vicinity and the sea floor shook. It sharply jarred the submarine and its occupants. The lights flickered momentarily and went out. Total darkness enveloped the crew and the computers went blank for a brief second. Quickly, the computers sprang back to life and restored power to the rest of the ship.

On the surface of the harbor, the wave struck the docks like a small tsunami and destroyed or heavily damaged most of the piers and the few ships moored against them. The crew on board the stationary sub chaser watched helplessly as the tidal wave roared down upon them. It struck with tremendous force broadside and capsized the ship.

Aboard NUMSUB, Al said, "Give me a damage report."

Hawk checked all monitors and reported, "Damage appears minimal, Sir. Only the operational defense system was damaged and appears to be malfunctioning. It isn't an electronic problem; it appears to be a malfunction of the shield generators."

Al responded with a questioning look on his face, "Give it to me in plain English."

Tom interrupted with a mock Scottish accent, "The shields err down, Cap'n."

"That means we're no longer invisible."

"That's what I'd say it means."

Hawk spoke. "The blast from the torpedo has temporarily knocked out the electronic net. We should have time to run for the gates and get out of the harbor before we're noticed."

"Al, use the hydraulic thrusters. They'll give us the speed we need," said Tom.

"Full speed on thrusters. Let's get out of here."

The front and rear doors of the hydraulic thruster system opened. It took a few minutes for one of the chambers to initially fill with water. When the hydraulic propulsion system was not in use, it was emptied of water to make NUMSUB lighter. Now, as water filled the chamber, part of the water in the ballast tanks had to be expelled to maintain equilibrium and keep NUMSUB from sinking.

One chamber filled and the pistons began their alternating motion. NUMSUB lurched forward and accelerated toward the entrance to the harbor.

"Give me a report on our speed," directed Al.

The helmsman read off the underwater speed indicator as NUMSUB picked up speed. "Twenty knots.......thirty knots.......forty knots."

The sound of water rushing past the hull picked up. A steady and slow *Swish - Swish - Swish* filled the interior of the sub. The sound came from the pistons moving back and forth.

"Forty-seven knots.......fifty-four knots.......fifty-eight knots.......sixty-two knots.......sixty-two knots and holding."

A minor earthquake caused by the explosion struck the base command center. The building shook, objects crashed to the floor, the staff dove under desks and the lights flickered on and off several times.

General Battarian burst through the door of the control room. "What the Hell was that? Another explosion at the launch site?"

"It appears that a low-yield nuclear fission device detonated at the entrance to the harbor, Sir," answered a technician.

"Where did it come from? We had no warning of a missile or bomb attack."

"It didn't come from the air, Sir. Just prior to the explosion, one of our sub destroyers reported they were tracking a torpedo heading for the gates."

"A torpedo? How did a torpedo get into the harbor?"

"We don't know, yet, Sir. Our ships have reported finding nothing in the harbor, and the blast has neutralized LOFWAR. The computers are repairing the damage. It should be restored within a few minutes."

"What's the status of the fleet?"

"Most ships within the harbor have been destroyed or heavily damaged as were six of the fleet outside the harbor. We have six surface ships remaining operational. Two destroyers, a cruiser, two sub destroyers and an aircraft carrier."

"What about our submarines?"

"We've been unable to raise one on the radio. The other two are operational."

"How soon before the electronic net is restored?"

"It's coming on line now, Sir. We should be able to see what's out there within the minute."

Aboard NUMSUB, Al watched the video monitors showing the water in all directions. Faintly at first, then boldly, the red lines of the underwater surveillance net appeared on the screens.

"Surveillance is operational. With our shields down we'll be detected. How soon before we reach the gates?"

"About three minutes, Sir," responded Hawk.

In the installation command center, a sonarman eyed his instruments. He noticed a faint blip on his screen that began to show brighter as the surveillance system powered up.

"Sir, we have the sub."

Chapter 47

Chase

General Battarian rushed to the screen. "Where is it?"

"The sonarman pointed to the rapidly moving blip. "Here. But this doesn't seem possible."

"What doesn't seem possible?"

"His speed, Sir. He's moving toward the gates at 62 knots. No sub we know of can move underwater at that speed."

"Then this is one we don't know of. How much time before he exits the harbor and we lose him on the net?"

"At this speed he will leave the harbor in approximately three minutes."

"Alert the remaining fleet to pick him up. They're in a position to form a blockade to stop him."

He turned to a junior officer who was standing by. "Notify the airfield, scramble anti-submarine aircraft."

In less than a minute two ASW planes loaded with depth charges and air to water torpedoes were airborne and streaking toward the harbor.

NUMSUB cleared the harbor entrance and passed by the badly damaged submarine gates. The remaining ships and submarines in the fleet had picked her up on their sonar and were moving to intercept her.

Hawk gave the alert. "Active sonar. They're saturating the area with soundings. The bay is lit up like Christmas tree. They're showing us where they are as well. I've identified the exact location of all remaining vessels."

Al ordered evasive action as they neared the ships. Hawk examined his screens.

"The six remaining surface vessels are forming a semi-circle. Two Orion class attack submarines are on a course to intercept bearing zero-nine-five and one-one-zero. Range to the nearest ship is 16,000 yards, subs are at 14,000 and 14,500 yards."

"Two Orions? There were three. Where's the third?"

Hawk studied his sonar. After a moment he said, "I found the third Orion."

"Where is it?"

"It was hard to locate from the activity in the water, but it looks like it's under one of the gates. It must have been too close when the XG-245 detonated. They didn't have a chance."

At that moment one of the airplanes dropped a depth charge ahead of the rapidly fleeing NUMSUB. The crew was still at battle stations and rigged for depth charges.

Hawk sounded the alarm calmly, "Depth charge in the water. Bearing one-two-two. We're on a collision course. Contact in twenty seconds." His voice showed only the slightest degree of excitement. Al appreciated the professionalism; there was no value in panic in this situation.

Al gave the command, "Hard to port!"

NUMSUB veered to the left as the depth charge passed through her original heading and exploded less than a hundred yards away. The submarine rocked hard from the shock wave. Lights flickered and sailors caught off guard were banged against walls and bulkheads. The evasive action worked; no serious damage was incurred.

Two miles off the stern, the second aircraft dropped a torpedo into the water that locked onto NUMSUB.

Hawk picked it up immediately on his screen. "Torpedo in the water. Thirty-five hundred yards. Bearing two-niner-five. Speed seventy knots. It's locked on."

The speed of the torpedo and the speed of NUMSUB meant that the torpedo was gaining at eight knots. The computer calculated the time to impact. Hawk announced in his calm monotone voice, "Contact in fifteen minutes five seconds."

Al thought quickly. "Dive to the bottom. Holographics up."

NUMSUB dove steeply to the sea floor and came to a stop behind a coral reef. Rapidly the hull took on the characteristics of the reef. The holographic imager engaged and a replica of NUMSUB appeard to emerge from the camouflaged vessel.

"Image speed fifty knots. Let's let the torpedo catch up a little faster. Take a heading for the lead Orion. Make a collision course."

The image headed directly for the lead submarine. The torpedo passed over the hidden NUMSUB. "Torpedo has locked on the image. It's ignoring us," said Hawk. "Time to impact, six minutes forty-five seconds.

The combined speed of the image and the approaching NWO submarine closed the distance between them at a rate of seventy-five knots.

In the NWO submarine, *Attack Dragon*, the sonarman detected the rapidly approaching image. "Enemy submarine dead ahead five thousand meters, collision course, impact in three minutes."

The sub commander ordered evasive action and *Attack Dragon* veered sharply to the left.

Watching the image on the radar screen, Hawk announced, "The Orion is changing course, taking evasive action hard to port."

TOM HAYNIE

Al ordered, "Bring the image around right. Maintain collision course."

The sailor at the holographic controls steered the image as though she was playing a computer game. The evasive action by the Orion was futile.

On board the cruiser, Captain Ahad Akayev, the fleet vice-commander, watched the underwater action on the ship's sonar monitor. He saw the *Attack Dragon*, NUMSUB and the torpedo all converge in an imminent underwater disaster. "What are those fools doing? They're going to commit suicide!"

Frantically, the *Attack Dragon* tried to avoid a collision with NUMSUB's image. "Hard to starboard!" commanded the captain.

The sonarman continued the alarm. "Impact in one minute."

The *Attack Dragon* was not in a position to launch a slap shot with a torpedo. They were too close and facing the wrong direction. A quick launch would be useless. Facing the inevitable, the captain ordered his sub toward the surface. If they were to be rammed, they should be in a position to allow as many survivors as possible.

Hawk watched intently. "The Orion is trying to surface, impact will occur at a depth of one hundred feet."

"We have to give him credit. It's the only smart thing he can do to save some of his crew," responded Al. "Maintain collision course."

"Impact in thirty seconds."

"At two seconds before impact, kill the image. Pick it up again five seconds later."

At ten seconds Hawk began to countdown, "Ten . . . nine . . . eight . . ."

On the cruiser, all eyes focused on the converging images. Everyone in the radar room stood silently.

Turning wildly to the right and approaching the surface at a forty-degree angle, *Attack Dragon* tried to minimize the damage from a collision with NUMSUB. The helmsman had turned his rudder control to the limit and pulled on it as if to squeeze another inch out of it. The sub's hull squealed and groaned from the pressure on the starboard side of the bow trying to push the water out of the way. The sonar pings bouncing off of the holographic image were deafening. Each ping melted into the next. Then, at two seconds before impact, the image of NUMSUB disappeared from the screen and the loud pings instantly ceased.

Startled eyes looked at the screen where there no longer appeared an oncoming submarine. Did it miss them? Briefly, a wave of relief washed over the control room.

It was short-lived. The pings again grew rapidly in intensity and frequency. Eyes returned to the sonar screen. In place of the large image of the approaching submarine there was a single, smaller image.

In disbelief, the sonarman shouted, "Torpedo!"

The torpedo struck the *Attack Dragon* just below the control room. The explosion ripped through the outer skin, penetrated the ballast tanks and cracked the inner hull from sail to keel. Water roared through the crack as it widened. The impact of the explosion with the pressure of the water and the force of the hard turn pushing against the hull caused the bow and stern to jackknife. The submarine cracked open like the shell of an egg and split apart.

The bow rose rapidly to the surface. The stern sank and struck the sea floor hard, bounced once and rolled over on its side. When the bow broke the surface it seemed to hang suspended for a few brief seconds. It splashed down in a huge spray and temporarily floated while its compartments filled with water. Several of the surviving crew spilled out of the gaping end where the stern used to be. The bodies of the dead and injured began to bob on the surface.

Aboard the cruiser, there was stunned silence. Captain Akayev announced, "I've never seen anything like that before. The enemy submarine sacrificed itself and its entire crew just to destroy one ship. Its commander must have been a madman."

He spoke to the officer of the watch. "Let's pick up any survivors."

He turned to leave the radar room. The sonarman called out, "Sir, take a look!"

The captain stopped and looked at the screen.

"The enemy submarine is still alive and he is heading toward us."

"Tighten the circle!" commanded the captain. He alerted all remaining vessels in the fleet to move closer together and form a ring with ships above and the last submarine below the surface of the water in front of the approaching image of NUMSUB. With the anti-sub planes chasing from behind, the image was surrounded.

Akayev ordered all vessels to fire simultaneously, saturating the water around and over NUMSUB's image with depth charges and torpedoes. The wall of explosives would create an impenetrable barrier through which nothing could escape.

Depth charges were launched in high arches from the ships. Each plane dropped a torpedo and the remaining submarine simultaneously fired two torpedoes from its forward tubes.

Aboard NUMSUB, Al and Tom watched over Hawk's shoulder at the image of four torpedoes and multiple depth charges converging on the holographic image.

Al gave instructions. "At the moment of impact, break the image apart and simulate a surface breach. Sink her and leave her on the bottom."

All explosive devices and the image of NUMSUB converged at a point in the middle of the semi-circle of ships. Simultaneous explosions created a tremendous fountain of water. The pilots banked their airplanes sharply and watched the underwater explosions.

For a moment the only movement was the water settling back into the sea. Then the bow of the image breached the water and slowly slipped beneath the waves.

The sonarman followed NUMSUB to the bottom.

Cheers rang out on each ship.

"We will have to see what we have killed," he stated with obvious pride in his voice. "We will remain here at anchor with two escorts. Have the base send a team of divers. We will see if there is enough to salvage of this mysterious submarine. All other vessels are to return to port."

In NUMSUB, a crewman announced, "Captain, the shields are nearly repaired. They'll be functional in a couple of hours. However, I have some bad news."

"What's the bad news, seaman?"

"The shield generator has been damaged. SUPCOM III can repair it temporarily, but the power demand will burn out the oscillator after a couple of hours. Once it burns out we'll not be able to repair it until we're back at Dogfish Base."

"Understood. We'll wait here until the computer finishes the repairs. Then we'll slip away while the NWO concentrates on the image. We should need only a couple of hours of shields to get to open seas. Once safely at sea, we'll leave them with empty water and lots of questions. For the next few hours we will maintain complete silence. Switch to batteries and reduce unnecessary power consumption."

Activity aboard NUMSUB literally ceased while the crew awaited the opportunity to escape undetected. What little voice communication that must go on was done in whispers. The crew removed their shoes and replaced them with soft leather slippers. All unnecessary movement halted. Some of the crew took the opportunity to catch some much needed sleep. Others were too excited by the situation to think of resting.

Chapter 48

Examining the Wreckage

At Hangzhou Base, four familiar faces assembled in a swift patrol boat and headed toward the site of the recent underwater battle. Gattis, Sadmere, Ling and Hammergren were in their scuba gear seated in the forward section of the boat.

The trip from the docks to the cruiser took about thirty minutes. They passed over the spot where the submarine gates used to be. The water looked no different than it had a couple of days before when the gates were operational. Now, below the surface, the gates were broken and useless. A dead submarine lay beneath one of the steel and concrete behemoths. There was nothing to indicate that over a hundred men were entombed in their broken ship barely seventy meters beneath them.

As the four divers boarded the cruiser, NUMSUB's computer activated the repaired shields and lifted the sub from the sea floor.

Al spoke to SUPCOM III. "Activate hydraulic propulsion and set a course at maximum speed on a heading of zero nine zero."

The cruiser's captain met the divers and briefed them on their mission.

"The enemy submarine split in half and is lying on the bottom. The bow and stern are approximately forty meters apart. You are to go down and determine the most plausible method of salvaging the wreckage. Disturb nothing. Simply observe and return and report your observations. Am I clear?"

"Very clear, Sir," responded Ling. "Gattis and Sadmere will examine the bow, Hammergren and I will take the stern."

They returned to the boat, which took them over the site of the wreckage. Gattis and Sadmere slipped over the right side and began their descent into the water. Ling and Hammergren slid into the water on the left side of the boat. At the beginning of their descent, they saw nothing in the water below. The bay was too deep to see what lay on the bottom. Slowly the four divers made their way toward the wreckage.

Nearing the site, Gattis tapped Sadmere on the shoulder and pointed to the right. There in the distance was the wreckage of the bow. They approached with caution and came no closer than ten meters. Ling and Hammergren had located the stern and conducted a similar examination.

The bow was nose down in the sand. A gaping hole pointed skyward where the stern had been attached. This was indeed a strange looking vessel. They had seen nothing like it before. It was smaller than they expected, and the skin seemed to glow faintly.

Gattis swam above the opening and peered inside. The poor light at the bottom of the bay showed little detail of the interior of the vessel.

The stern was on its starboard side, the propeller bent where it struck the bottom. A stream of bubbles exited from the hull as compartments continued to flood. No one noticed that the bubbles rose only a few meters before disappearing. The site of the wreckage appeared to contain very little of the scattered debris one would expect from so violent a death. A small amount of oil appeared to escape, but it dissipated quickly after leaving the hull. There were no bodies. The broken hull eerily resembled a ghost ship. The scene sent shivers up the spines of the four divers.

By this time, NUMSUB, travelling at over 60 knots, was nearly a hundred miles away from the site of the battle. Al gave the final order to turn off the holographic image. The seaman seated at the electronic panel reached over and flipped off a switch that controlled the image.

The four divers convened in a group between the wrecked bow and stern. They signaled each other that they had completed their observations and were ready to return to the surface.

They turned for one last look at the wreckage. Their eyes grew wide and they nearly choked on the mouthpieces of their scuba gear. They looked rapidly around. The image of the wrecked submarine began to fade from their view until it was completely gone. The sea floor was soon barren of any hint of a submarine or wreckage.

They returned to the location where they had inspected the two halves of the hull. The sand on the sea floor showed no sign of disturbance. It was as if there had never been any wreckage. They searched the area. Could the ocean currents have carried them away from the wrecked submarine? They turned and rose to the surface.

Before the boat arrived to pick them up, they gathered together at the water's surface and removed their facemasks. They looked at each other in stunned silence. No words escaped their mouths.

Finally, Gattis spoke. "What was that? Now who's crazy? We told you before there was something going on and you didn't believe us."

"What do we do now?" asked Sadmere.

"I don't know about the rest of you," spoke Ling, "but I think we had better say we found nothing below. If any of us ever speaks of what we just saw, we'll be labeled lunatics and we'll all be sent to an asylum or the salt mines."

Hammergren responded, "Saw what? I saw nothing below. The captain must have given us the wrong location."

Upon returning to the cruiser, the four divers gave their report. There was no wreckage on the sea floor. There must have been a mistake in the coordinates.

For days, the fleet searched the site of the battle and found no sign of NUMSUB. No one could explain the disappearance of the enemy submarine. Years later there would be legends of a phantom battle that occurred right after the destruction of the HORS II system. The official story by the High Command was that the Naval commander and General Battarian had devised a scheme to blame the AWF for the loss of the satellite system by creating a mock battle involving a highly advanced AWF submarine.

They were charged with the loss of many lives and the destruction of several naval vessels, but they were never tried. To save face, the High Command was unwilling to create the spectacle of a trial. There were too many confusing and conflicting stories from the servicemen at the installation and the crews on board the surviving ships. Too many unanswerable questions.

TOM HAYNIE

Chapter 49

Arrest

Halfway across the Pacific, NUMSUB steamed toward Dogfish Base at sixty knots, three hundred feet below the surface. The hydraulic drive functioned perfectly at full power and was nearly silent. The only noise was the steady *Swish, Swish* as the pistons moved back and forth inside the chambers, forcing seawater in and out of the baffled tubes. Were anyone to be listening, the sound of the propulsion system would be nearly indistinguishable from the wave motion of the sea. Although silence was not the key design criteria for the system, it was an added benefit.

There was no attempt to maintain battle stations or alert status. Aboard the vessel, activity had settled into a routine while the crew anticipated their arrival at Dogfish Base within the next couple of days. The three and a half months of training, culminating in the successful mission, had kept them away from their families and friends through the holidays. Most of the crew was American and Canadian. The Americans had missed Thanksgiving and they all had missed Christmas and the New Year holidays. They were anxious to get home and excited about the prospects of joyous reunions.

Heading east toward China was another submarine. The members of its crew were not so anxious to return. The *Lone Wolf* had learned of the disasters at Hangzhou Base and had heard conflicting stories regarding the cause. There were reports that a computer malfunction caused a catastrophic explosion that destroyed HORS II followed by an explosion of nearly equal power that had destroyed some of the installation's major defenses and a significant part of the fleet stationed there. Many of the crew had friends and family at the base. They were anxious for their safety and concerned that some may have been among the dead and wounded.

The commander of the *Lone Wolf,* Captain Porknoi, and the Intelligence Officer, Sturgaard Ivanovich, sat in the officer's mess discussing what they expected to find upon their return to Hangzhou Base.

"The reports are inconclusive," said Captain Porknoi. "It is too soon to assess the extent of the damage or the cause."

"But, what of the conflicting stories? The destruction of half of the fleet by a nuclear torpedo from a phantom submarine that can disappear without a trace and reappear moments later somewhere else. A conspiracy by Battarian and Abdullah to assassinate General Dillgard and cover it up with the destruction of HORS II. Akayev involved in a bizarre plan to

238

blame the entire crises on the AWF. If you ask me, this whole thing smells of the High Command."

Porknoi caught the insinuation in Ivanovich's voice. This is an intelligence officer, commissioned directly by the High Command to seek out enemies of the NWO. Words such as these from a common military officer would be considered treason. He had known fellow officers who had disappeared without a trace for lesser statements. His contacts on the High Command's adjutant staff would be most anxious to hear about these comments.

During the past four months, Ivanovich had irritated the captain considerably with his frequent dissident remarks. They became more pronounced after he had learned that Hunslinger and O'Donnell had escaped. At that moment, Ivanovich's career became seriously jeopardized. He began to grumble and vent his remarks in the presence of the crew and it was having no small effect. The conscripts were no problem. They generally ignored it when an officer made comments of any kind. Their purpose was to serve the five years of their induction and return to their families and their lowly lives. Matters of politics made no difference to them; they had no say and formed no opinions.

The officers, on the other hand, were prone to be swayed by the words of one with such obvious power. Many were highly educated. They had read of conditions in the free world and sometimes wondered if all of it really was just imperialist propaganda. Were it not for the constant political education to which they were exposed, some might be inclined to question their loyalties.

Ivanovich was a danger. Intelligence officer or not, Porknoi had been secretly recording their conversations. The recordings would support him in the action he was about to take.

He abruptly stood and summoned two armed officers who had been waiting in an adjacent room. Porknoi had been careful to select two of his most trusted staff.

An officer stood on either side of Ivanovich.

Porknoi announced, "Sturgaard Ivanovich, for acts of treason against the NWO and the authority of the High Command, I hereby place you under house arrest. Your seditious remarks have been recorded and will stand as proof of your disloyalty. You will be locked in your quarters until we arrive at Hangzhou Base, at which time you will be remanded to the custody of the base military police until you are tried for your crimes. Gentlemen, escort him to his stateroom and lock him there."

Ivanovich rose in protest. "You have no right to pass judgment on me. I am an officer of the highest authority of the NWO. It is you who commit treason."

"We will leave that for the High Command to determine. Take him to his room. And in case you believe you can try something, your room has been searched and this has been removed." Porknoi held up the automatic pistol found under Sturgaard's pillow.

The two officers escorted Sturgaard to his room. They walked in silence, although they both wondered if they were doing the right thing. Sturgaard entered the room. The door closed behind him with a loud bang and was locked from the outside. He settled down on his bunk and contemplated his fate.

His future appeared hopeless. What of his family? Many times he had considered escaping to the West. At first these thoughts were quickly dismissed. Yet they lingered as time passed. He had heard from other intelligence operatives who had spent time in AWF territory of the kind of lives people lived in the free world. He ached inside for the opportunity to raise his family in such conditions.

He reached down and slipped off his shoe. Just beneath the insole was a two-inch knife blade. He removed it and cut a slit about ten inches long in the mattress he was lying on. He reached inside and pulled out another 9-mm pistol. He had learned long ago the value of a back up. He slipped the weapon in the waistband of his trousers and lay back on the bunk. He needed time to think.

Chapter 50

Encounter

Simultaneously, the sonarmen on board the *Lone Wolf* and NUMSUB picked up signals on their passive sonar. Neither sub had expected to encounter any other traffic in this part of the Pacific, so they were simply monitoring with their towed arrays. Although NUMSUB's hydraulic propulsion system was relatively silent, noises from some of the other systems on board were broadcasting her location.

"I'm picking up sonar activity on a bearing of zero nine five. Range 60,000 yards. Speed thirty-two knots. It's a sub, although I can't tell what class yet, it's too far away," said Hawk. The subs were over thirty miles apart. At that distance it was difficult to pick up a signature.

"Reduce speed two-thirds," commanded Al. "Let's see what we have."

"They must have picked us up because they've slowed as well. Range is 52,000 yards. Now they've stopped. They appear to be listening."

"All stop," commanded Al. "No doubt they heard us and are trying to figure out what we are."

Just before they stopped, the computer read his signature.

"He's an NWO attack sub of the Brezhnev class," said Hawk. "He's about twice the size of NUMSUB and fairly quick and maneuverable for his size. Underwater top speed of forty knots, carries an arsenal of thirty-two torpedoes which he can launch in salvos of six torpedoes each. Not something we'd want to tangle with in an ordinary sub or surface vessel. We could outrun it and likely avoid any torpedoes if we want to."

Tom looked at Al and asked, "What do you think?"

"Have they radioed anyone yet?" Al asked Hawk.

"Not yet, Sir. They know we're here and they're sizing us up. They probably don't know what to radio anyone about yet."

"Since they've spotted us, I don't think we should dazzle them with any of our footwork. We've already raised enough suspicions at the High Command. Another story would simply confirm that we have something they don't know about. Do you agree, Tom?"

"What you're saying is, 'I'd show you what I have, but if I did, I'd have to shoot you.'"

Al and Hawk guffawed.

"Sorry. I couldn't resist. I've used that expression before but this is the first time it's really made sense."

"I agree. Let's wait a while and let them make the first move. Then we'll react."

Aboard the *Lone Wolf*, Captain Porknoi studied the sonar screen. The passive array was quiet. Nothing showed on the screen.

He turned to his first officer. "Mikhail, they've stopped. I suppose they're deciding what to do. Your thoughts?"

"We can't surface and contact the installation right now. That would leave us too vulnerable. Our sonar cannot identify the class of the vessel. Before he stopped, he appeared to be a small craft of unconventional power source. We've detected a small nuclear reactor, but it doesn't appear to be the source of their power. We're not even sure if it's military."

"If it's not military, then it's research. If it's research, it's not one of ours, and our duty is to destroy it."

"True enough, however there is a way we can determine if it's military or not."

"How? Shoot at them and see if they shoot back?" asked Porknoi.

"No, no. We circle around them slowly. If they keep their bow pointed in our direction, we should assume they are military. They will want to keep their torpedo tubes pointed at us."

"Excellent idea. Instruct the engine room to proceed ahead at ten knots. Helmsman, take us to within 5,000 yards, then circle around them slowly."

The *Lone Wolf's* propeller began to turn. The submarine gradually moved toward NUMSUB.

"He's moving," announced Hawk, pressing the headset to his ear. "The screw's turning slowly. He's approaching on a bearing directly for us."

"Keep watching and let me know if he does anything unusual," said Al.

While Hawk watched the approaching sub, Al commanded the crew to prepare for hostilities.

"Battle stations. Rig for torpedoes."

It took approximately two hours to cover forty-seven thousand yards and close to within 5,000 yards of NUMSUB. At 5,000 yards, the helmsman altered the course and *Lone Wolf* began to circle.

The minutes passed by slowly. At ten-minute intervals, Hawk announced the range. Finally at 5,000 yards, there was a change.

"Range, steady at five thousand. He's starting to circle us."

Tom turned to Al. "What do you think they're up to?"

"Our signature didn't tell them anything. They won't have our profile in their data bank, so they haven't any idea who or what we are. They're trying to check us out, maybe hoping we'll move and give them something to identify us by. I think they want to determine if we're a threat. Circling us won't tell them who we are. They're doing it for a reason. I think they want to see what we'll do."

"What do you think they expect us to do?"

"If we were hostile or a threat we'd keep our tubes pointed in their direction. If not, we might simply try to run for it or just sit it out and wait for them to make a move."

"So what do we do? We can outrun them as long as they don't shoot at us, but that would give away some important information they'd take back. We can't activate the shields, so we can't disappear. Using the holographics without the shields would show us splitting in two, and that would really give them something to talk about."

"They may be making that decision for us," interrupted Hawk. "They've moved out to sixty-five hundred yards and turned toward us. They've opened their forward torpedo doors. They appear to be preparing to shoot."

Captain Porknoi and his First Officer waited patiently while the sonarman listened for any activity from the strange submarine.

"Sir, we've nearly circled them completely and they haven't moved. I don't believe they are military."

"That may be precisely what they want us to think," said the First Officer. "I believe they are military and I believe they are Federation."

"What makes you think that, Mikhail?" asked the captain.

"We are unaware of any NWO military or research vessel with a signature like theirs."

"True, but it could be a secret program. The High Command doesn't let all submarine commanders in the fleet know of every new technology while in development."

"I agree, Mustaf. However, they must have identified us from our own signature. Surely they know we are NWO. If they were one of ours, they certainly would have signaled us by now, if for no other reason than to make sure we take no hostile action against them."

"Perhaps, perhaps not. Maybe they are ours and are under orders not to make contact with anyone, friend or foe."

"There is one way to find out."

"And . . .?"

"We turn on them and prepare to fire a torpedo. If they are ours, they will surely break silence and contact us rather than let us destroy them."

"Yes, that's a good idea. We will feign an attack. Helmsman, back off to six thousand meters, turn toward the unknown submarine. Load torpedoes in two forward tubes. Open outer doors and prepare to launch."

Gradually, the *Lone Wolf* came about and faced NUMSUB head on. Torpedoes were loaded and forward doors were opened.

"Hawk, what's happening?" asked Tom.

"Nothing yet, Sir. It's been five minutes and they have only opened the outer doors. I don't think they've decided who we are yet."

"Well, let's force their hand. Let's load torpedoes. Then we'll come about and face them," said Al.

"Torpedo room, conn, make torpedo tubes one and two ready with conventional torpedoes. Arm at two thousand yards. Prepare to shoot."

"Conn, torpedo room, torpedo tubes one and two ready. Armed at two thousand yards. Prepared to shoot."

NUMSUB turned as though on a pivot.

"Open outer doors."

"Outer doors opened," announced the seaman.

"Match bearing at the target," ordered Al.

"Bearing matched at the target."

"Stand by."

"Standing by."

Aboard the *Lone Wolf*. "Captain! The sub has turned toward us. He has torpedo doors and he has opened them. They are definitely military and they are not friendly," announced the sonarman excitedly. Without hesitation, the captain gave the order, "Fire torpedoes!"

Simultaneously, both torpedoes were launched toward NUMSUB. Almost immediately both torpedoes locked on.

"Torpedoes in the water. They shot two, contact in two minutes thirty seconds," said Hawk in his characteristic monotone voice.

"Engines reverse full, put a holograph in our place between us and the torpedoes."

NUMSUB's propeller instantly strained in reverse, pulling NUMSUB backward in the water. At the same time, the holographic image took its place in the path of the torpedoes.

The maneuver by NUMSUB went unnoticed by the *Lone Wolf*.

On the *Lone Wolf*, the sonarman listened to the torpedoes nearing their target.

"Torpedoes on target, impact in sixty seconds."

"Have they returned fire?" asked the captain.

"No, Sir. There has been no response."

"That's strange. They were ready. What are they waiting for?"

Al watched the torpedoes approach the image. "At the moment of impact, we'll shoot both fish and turn off the hologram. The bubbles from the exploding torpedoes will create an ensonified zone and hide us from their sonar. Once our fish have passed through the ensonified zone they will lock onto the target. They should be very surprised."

The *Lone Wolf*'s sonarman continued to countdown to impact, "five… four… three… two… one." The torpedoes detonated in rapid succession against the holographic image.

The sound of the exploding torpedoes rumbled through the *Lone Wolf*.

"Direct hit, Sir. Both torpedoes exploded on target. They have surely been destroyed."

"Very well, we shall surface and determine if there are survivors. We may find …"

"Sir! Torpedoes! Two have locked on to us."

"Torpedoes?! Where did they come from?"

"I don't know, Sir. The submarine was hit. It must have launched a counter attack."

Frantically, the captain gave the order to turn and run. He knew it was futile. There was time neither to take evasive action nor to launch any of their cloaking devices.

Struggling to turn, the *Lone Wolf* presented a broadside to the approaching torpedoes. One struck her beneath the sail and the other near the aft rudder. Her hull cracked open immediately.

Aboard NUMSUB, Hawk announced, "Direct hit with both fish, Sir. The hull is breaking up. He's a goner."

The force of the explosion ripped into the *Lone Wolf* and the hull broke apart. Ivanovich was thrown against the bulkhead in his stateroom. He struck his head and nearly passed out. As the hull twisted and the sub cracked open, the door to his room was ripped from its hinges. Water rushed through the open door, quickly filling the small room. Flailing his arms to try to find air, his hand struck the door of the life vest storage compartment. Almost without thinking, he opened the door and grabbed a life vest.

The break in the hull widened and he was swept out through the gap, holding tightly to the vest. The buoyancy of the vest pulled him rapidly toward the surface while the *Lone Wolf* sank. When the cold seawater reached the hot reactor vessel it exploded, shattering the hull from within.

Ivanovich broke through the surface of the water and gasped for breath. He looked around and saw nothing but empty ocean. There were no other survivors and no evidence of the death of *Lone Wolf* beneath him. Shortly, bits of debris, an oil slick and a few bodies of the *Lone Wolf's* crew began to float to the surface. The scene was eerily silent, with only the sound of the waves lapping against bits of wreckage. He was alone.

Below, in NUMSUB, those in the control room watched the *Lone Wolf* sink. The sub had broken apart into several pieces and the exploding reactor vessel scattered wreckage over a wide area of the sea floor.

Al gave the command to come to periscope depth to see if there were any survivors. He searched the monitors in all directions and saw nothing but floating debris and a few bodies. He was about to give instructions to continue on to base when he saw an arm waving above the surface about two hundred yards to port.

"We have a survivor."

Briefly Tom thought of the highly secret NUMSUB. Could he risk taking aboard a survivor from the NWO? Was the life of one man worth the risk of revealing NUMSUB to the enemy? He was thrown into the often difficult struggle between compassion and duty.

He turned to Al. The expression on Tom's face was not lost on his friend.

Al rested his finger on the monitor switch, ready to turn it off if necessary.

"I know what you're thinking. It's your ship and your mission. Say the word and we turn our backs and leave."

Tom struggled briefly within himself. Compassion prevailed. He almost whispered, "Pick him up."

NUMSUB surfaced and two crewmen scrambled on deck. Al and Tom followed quickly behind.

Ivanovich saw the periscope break the surface of the sea a couple hundred meters away. He had his own struggle within. He had failed in his mission to assassinate O'Donnell and Hunslinger. If he survived he would return to his country in disgrace. He and his family would be banished to a life of hard conditions. However, to die in battle would bring a hero's recognition. His wife would be well taken care of and his children would be given every advantage as the widow and orphans of a valiant officer of the High Command and defender of the homeland.

He quickly made up his mind. He pulled the pistol from the waistband of his pants and held it at eye level. He looked at it for a moment as if contemplating the decision he had just made. Then he dropped it in the water and watched it sink out of sight. He turned toward the periscope and began to wave his arms.

After what seemed like eternity, the submarine surfaced. First the sail appeared, a sail like no other he had ever seen. Then the bow broke through the surface and water washed over hull. He was astonished. The color of the hull appeared to reflect the sky and water at the same time. The surface was nearly translucent. He blinked his eyes. It seemed as though he could almost see through the ship.

Two sailors threw him a line and pulled him from the water. As he rose to his feet, two men, obviously officers from their dress, approached him. One must be the commander of the strange submarine.

Sturgaard stood at rigid attention and stated in near flawless English, "I am Sturgaard Ivanovich, Intelligence Officer of the New World Order's attack submarine *Lone Wolf*. I request political asylum in the Allied West Federation."

Al extended his hand in greeting. "Welcome aboard. I am Captain Al Hunslinger, commander of this vessel, and this is Commander Tom O'Donnell, senior officer on board. Your request for asylum will be transmitted to Montreal and you will receive your answer from there."

Al and Tom exchanged quizzical glances when their new guest turned ashen white and nearly collapsed as his knees began to buckle under him. They each grabbed him by an arm to support him.

"Are you O.K.?" asked Tom. "We'd better have the corpsman take a look at you."

"I'll be all right. We have much to talk about."

Chapter 51

Return Home

Somewhere on the Oregon coast, a lone submarine slipped quietly through an underwater channel into a cavern carved out of the limestone cliffs. The news of the destruction of the space facility at Hangzhou Base preceded her arrival. Al had returned control of the sub to the computer, which skillfully maneuvered her into the berth adjacent to her sister ships.

Captain Fullerton stood on the pier while the crew disembarked the submarine. Near the last to leave the ship were Al and Tom.

"Welcome back, gentlemen," Monica greeted them. "Ever since we received word of the activities at Hangzhou Base, we've been wondering if you had anything to do with it."

Al and Tom exchanged glances. They had a million stories to tell and would have loved to share them. However, the details of NUMSUB's maiden mission must be locked away in their memories until they could report to Montreal. Even then they would be permitted to recount the events of their mission to very few.

Before they responded, they turned and looked back at the sub. A couple of medics were removing the body bag containing the body of Jorge Rojas. In silence, Tom and Al paused while the body was loaded on a stretcher and taken to the base medical facility. Following closely behind, under guard, with a blindfold to assure that there were no secrets revealed, Sturgaard Ivanovich was lead to a waiting elevator. He would wear the blindfold until he was taken from Dogfish Base and was safely on his way to Montreal.

Another familiar figure appeared at the hatch. The large frame of Lieutenant Pete Wilson emerged. He stood and looked around as though savoring the feeling of being home. He turned, leaned toward the hatch and offered his hand to the next person. Lieutenant Robin Buckner grasped his hand and he lifted her with one arm above the deck. For a brief moment they relaxed decorum. She put her arms around his neck as he picked her up and cradled her in his, then turned in a quick pirouette before gently putting her down. They embraced before walking toward the gangplank and onto the dock.

Al and Tom turned to Monica.

"Thanks, Monica. It's good to be back. NUMSUB performed superbly. What action at Hangzhou Base are you talking about?" said Tom.

"We've been in the Straits of Magellan conducting cold water exercises. I'm afraid we've been out of touch for a while."

Monica looked at him, then at Al, then back at Tom. She had been around classified projects enough to know B.S. when she heard it. She also knew when not to pursue a subject.

She smiled broadly at them both and said, "From the news on CNN, there were reports of a huge explosion in the harbor a couple of hours after the space facility blew up. There is speculation of a low-level nuclear device. Some are blaming the AWF, others are pointing the finger at a cover up by the NWO. You don't suppose we're missing any of our XG-245s, do you?"

Al and Tom looked at each other again and broke into smiles. They each stepped to one side of Monica and put an arm on her shoulder. She turned with them and placed her arms around their waists as they headed toward the elevators to the debriefing room.

Tom spoke. "Well, now. I guess that's something we'll have to deal with, won't we? I don't suppose you'd believe us if we said we lost one, would you?"

The look on Monica's face gave him his answer.

On the flight back to Montreal, Tom was lost in thought. In his head, he went over his report for the Central Command. He dozed occasionally, and he thought about Bree. He didn't know if he would ever see her again, but he felt an ache in his chest as he thought about the good times they had together. He dismissed the thoughts and feelings when the plane landed at the airport.

He spent the day giving his report to the Central Command and answering questions. George reviewed the satellite tapes of the launch, the torpedo detonating at the submerged gates and the sea battle that followed. Everything was recorded from the stationary satellite over the installation. At the conclusion of the debriefing, after all had expressed their final congratulations, the meeting broke up.

Tom finished the day in George's office, alone with the Secretary.

"Well, Tom. The congratulations are over. Nothing can ever leave this office. You completed an exemplary mission and the free world will be forever grateful, even though they will never know what you did."

"I know. It's kind of funny. We develop the most sophisticated naval weapon in the history of the world and we can't even let on we have it. The NWO will know that there's something in our arsenal, but they won't be able to figure it out. It will be a long time before they attempt world domination again for fear of reprisal. It kind of reminds me of the cold war of the twentieth century. I guess history will always repeat itself."

"No doubt. That's why we'll always need people like you and Al and the men and women who served with you on the mission."

"There is one question that I've had in the back of my mind."

"What's that?"

"It's about the mole we had in the control center at the launch site. What happened to him? Did he die in the explosion like all the others?"

"That would seem like a blemish on the success of the mission, wouldn't it? No, we got word to her that she might not want to witness the launch. As a result, she called in sick and missed the action. She's perfectly safe and will continue to be a valuable resource behind the scene."

"Called in sick? I guess you don't realize how similar cultures are; seems we always dwell on the differences. By the way, what's happened to Ivanovich?"

"Mr. Ivanovich is cooperating fully with Roy and the FIA. It turns out that he's full of valuable information. It's not often we get to turn a highly placed NWO intelligence officer. Our sources at the NWO report that he has been posthumously decorated as a war hero and his family is being given the royal treatment. We'll extract as much information as we can over the next month or so and then we'll give him a new identity and he'll be relocated. The wheels are already turning to get his family out of Eastern Europe so they can join him. I think things are going to work out quite nicely for him."

"That's good. He seemed like a fairly decent fellow after he got over the shock of meeting Al and me."

"Speaking of Al. Upon your recommendation, the President has approved his commission as the first permanent commander of NUMSUB."

"He'll be very pleased. I was proud to serve with him and he's certainly a credit to the Navy."

"Well, this one is for the history books. What are you going to do now?"

"I'm going to finish my vacation and relax. I'll spend a couple of days here in Montreal, and then I'll take a trip to the Caribbean. I've always wanted to take some time and lay around on a white sand beach with nothing to do or think about."

George extended his hand. "Good luck, my boy. Enjoy your rest. I'm sure we'll have something for you to do when you get back."

They shook hands and Tom exited the Secretary's office.

Later that evening, Tom found himself walking along the boardwalk by the St. Lawrence River. The night was crisp and cold. The smells of the river were familiar. A slight breeze blew a chill across the water and he flipped up the collar of his overcoat to warm his neck. He leaned on the railing and looked over the water. He could see his breath crystallize when he exhaled.

His mind returned to the events of the last few months. He loved his work. But there was something else he loved, too. He had pushed that something aside so many times because he didn't think they could be compatible. But was he right?

His heart ached for Bree. It was always Bree. No matter where he was or what he was doing, she was waiting in the corners of his mind, waiting for a chance to slip into his consciousness. He wanted to call her when he was in Montreal, but he didn't. He knew that if he did they might get back together and then there'd be the pain of separation again.

But, wasn't it worth it? Was it better to have her in his life, sharing a place with his career than not there at all? Yes, he loved his work, but it was empty without her.

The honor of it all. It was honorable to stay apart because they had decided that was the best. *Damn the honor!* He wanted her desperately. Did she want him as much? Maybe he'd never know.

The night was silent. The cold seemed to deaden the noises of the city. Only the gentle lapping of the water against an occasional ice floe floating in the open channel of the river broke the silence. He heard no other sounds while he gazed wistfully at the water.

Then, a creak of a board announced that someone approached. His adrenaline raced. The back of his neck prickled. He peered into the darkness and saw the outline of a figure in the shadows slowly drawing near him. His mind raced through new dangers posed by the NWO keeping him under near constant surveillance. They showed their hand in Idaho. *Will they strike again?*

The figure approached and he made out the shape of a woman in a dark overcoat, her blonde hair cascading over her shoulders. As he looked closer, familiar feelings rushed through his frame.

He spoke softly, risking that it was only wishful thinking, "Bree?"

A voice answered softly, "Tom."

The End

Made in the USA
Lexington, KY
05 January 2011